THE DISINVITED GUEST

Praise for Carol Goodman and Her Previous Novels

"*The Stranger Behind You* is a captivating exploration of sexual harassment, friendship, ambition, and how women join together to overcome trauma. It is as classic as it is timely, as heartbreaking as it is suspenseful. Stunning. I couldn't put it down."

—Danielle Trussoni, *New York Times* bestselling author of *Angelology* and *The Ancestor*

"Carol Goodman's *The Stranger Behind You* is at once a ripped-from-the-headlines thriller, a powerful meditation on the deep bonds and power of female friendship, and a colorful glimpse of New York City old and new. In a twisting, mesmerizing story that is as beautifully written as it is utterly propulsive, Goodman weaves a dream that blends the past and the present, takes us deep into the hearts and souls of her characters, and keeps us breathlessly turning the pages right to the shocking and poignant end. I absolutely loved this layered and moving novel!"

—Lisa Unger, *New York Times* bestselling author of *Confessions on the 7:45*

"[A] superior thriller. . . . The plot takes many terrifying twists and turns en route to the surprising climax. Those with a taste for the gothic will be richly rewarded."

—*Publishers Weekly* (starred review) on *The Stranger Behind You*

"A mesmerizing narrative that culminates in a poignant ending to a brilliant journey. Gothic? Note the phantom lye and bleach stench and wait for it! Make sure fans of Shari Lapena and Alison Gaylin get their hands on this one."

—*Booklist* on *The Stranger Behind You*

THE DISINVITED GUEST

A NOVEL

CAROL GOODMAN

wm

WILLIAM MORROW
An Imprint of HarperCollinsPublishers

Map by Maggie G. Vicknair

P.S.™ is a trademark of HarperCollins Publishers.

HarperCollins books may be purchased for educational, business, or sales promotional use. For information, please email the Special Markets Department at SPsales@harpercollins.com.

FIRST EDITION

Designed by Diahann Sturge
Title page spread image © Isabelle Lafrance/Arcangel
Chapter opener image © Dmitriy Nikiforov/Shutterstock

Library of Congress Cataloging-in-Publication Data has been applied for.

ISBN 978-0-06-302070-2 (paperback)
ISBN 978-0-06-324899-1 (library edition)

22 23 24 25 26 LSC 10 9 8 7 6 5 4 3 2 1

To Stephen T. Dunn
Friend of the Arts
1954–2021

THE DISINVITED GUEST

CHAPTER ONE

"WE'RE HERE."

Reed's voice wakes me from the fitful sleep I'd fallen into somewhere north of Portland, the slap of wipers and sluice of tires accomplishing what bourbon and sleeping pills had failed to do for the past two weeks. I open my eyes to a wall of sodden gray the color of wet cement. I can feel it pressing down my throat—

I cough.

Reed swivels his head toward me, blue eyes feverish in the gloom above his white surgical mask.

"I'm fine." I reach for the water bottle and swig lukewarm water that tastes like copper. "The others—"

"Behind us. Crosby's driving like an old woman, trying to protect his precious Volvo's paint job. Honestly, for a supposed socialist he likes the trappings of the bourgeoisie." He grins, his bones sharpening under sallow skin. With all the stress of the recent news and preparations to come to the island, neither of us has been eating much for the past few weeks.

"They could have gotten lost."

Reed shakes his head. "There's just the one road and it ends here." He points to something outside. A weathered gray sign. *Land's End. Pass at Your Own Risk.*

I shiver. Reed places his hand on my forehead. It feels good to be touched—*when was the last time we touched?*—but I shrug it away. "I'm fine," I say again.

"Check."

I take the thermometer gun out of the cup holder and aim it at my forehead, peering into the fog until an electronic voice pronounces the number 98.6.

"Normal," I say.

Nothing is normal. Nothing has been normal for months. Maybe longer.

I hear tires on gravel behind us. "They're here," Reed says. I want him to touch me again but we promised we wouldn't until we were sure we were both safe, and Reed always keeps his promises. He's gotten us this far, hasn't he?

"Ready?"

I nod. A lie. I hadn't been ready for any of this. Not when the first cases were reported, or my classes at the college went remote, or the restaurants and stores closed. None of us had. Except for Reed. Somehow he had seen it coming and had a plan set in place when most people were still pretending it wasn't real. Now he's opening the car door and stepping out into the fog, moving forward as if the path is clear. I follow him into the mist toward a car that looks unfamiliar.

My heart rate speeds up, and my skin turns clammy. Reed had warned that the locals might not like us coming up here, carrying our contagion from the "big cities." A woman at a rest stop outside of Portland had pressed her unmasked face against the passenger-side window and hissed, "Go back where you came from!" Who knows what crazed vigilantes might be in the grimy car—then I recognize Crosby's beige Volvo beneath the mud splatter and Ada getting out of the car. Her curly red hair looks like it has exploded into a corona around her masked face, like the virus itself has surrounded her with its pestilent nimbus. The spark in her eyes, though, brings me back to the eighteen-year-old who greeted me at the door of our fresh-man dorm with a red Solo cup of watery beer. Now she's holding up a thermometer gun.

"Ninety-eight point six, bitches," she crows. "The only thing nor-mal about me."

"We have to take them together," Reed says.

"Hello to you, too," Crosby says, his loafers sinking into the mud as he gets out of the car. He's wearing a plexiglass face shield designed, it appears, to show off his meticulously trimmed goatee. (*He tends to it like a Zen gardener pruning his prized bonsai,* Ada confided to me once.) "We just thought we'd check before we got out of the car. As a courtesy." He holds up his wrist to display a temperature reading on his Smart Watch. I notice it's the latest model. Reed is right; for a socialist Crosby likes his toys.

"We took ours, too," I say, jumping in before Reed can respond. It isn't strictly true; only I have taken my temperature. "No fevers here. Were Niko and Liz far behind you?" I ask, peering toward the road we drove in on. There's nothing to see, though, as if the fog has already swallowed the world we've come from.

"We waited at the turnoff until we saw them," Crosby says, glanc-ing at Reed as if Reed hadn't done the same for him. *Shit. I shouldn't have fallen asleep.* Reed forgets things when he's focused on a task. "But then we lost them a little ways back. I was too busy trying not to drive into the fucking ocean." He gestures at the water, which I see now is on three sides of us. We're on a muddy spit of land that dribbles out into the ocean as if it just got tired and gave up. Aside from the weathered gray dock with its ominous sign, the only other structure is a long gray shed with a tin roof the exact color of the fog.

"Maybe Niko stopped to take a photograph," Ada says.

"In this pea soup?" Reed asks.

Ada shrugs. "Have you seen Niko's work? Fog is like her *métier.*"

She pronounces the French word with an exaggerated accent, the way she would at school when she was making fun of someone she thought was pretentious.

"Then she's hit the jackpot here," Crosby says, walking toward the pier with his hands in his pockets. "Is it always like this?"

"It's Maine," Reed replies matter-of-factly, going to stand a careful six feet away from him. "My father always said it was good luck to arrive on the island in fog. And for us it is; no one will see us heading out there."

"Is there anyone around to see us?" Crosby asks.

"A few houses—guest cottages in the summer, a couple of lobstermen who live on this road—" He jerks his chin at the shed. "We can store our cars in the boathouse so no one sees them." He looks back toward the road. "I just hope Niko and Liz didn't run into anyone."

"They know not to get out of the car," I say. "They wouldn't take any chances—"

"But if Niko *did* get out of the car to take a picture," Reed says, "and someone *did* approach them—"

"We don't know that's happening," I say, trying to forestall the train of Reed's projections. Once he gets going, predicting each cause and effect, it's hard to derail him. His mind is like a Rube Goldberg machine: once the marble is rolling it's going to trip every hazard and spring every mousetrap. It's what makes him a great city planner, and it's what has gotten us this far today, but I can tell he's about to spin some horror tale in which an angry mob of lobstermen are on their way here with harpoons. "We don't know if she even got out of the car."

"Then where are they?" Reed asks in the calm voice he adopts when he thinks I'm not facing the hard facts. Or, at least, the facts as he sees them.

"There," Crosby says at the same moment we hear the car tires on gravel. But it's *not* Niko and Liz's yellow Mini; it's a rusted orange pickup truck. Just the kind of vehicle angry vigilante lobstermen would drive. My mouth goes dry. *How does Reed do it?* I wonder. *How do all his worst predictions come true?*

But when a big man in a yellow rain slicker, baseball cap, and red bandanna tied over his mouth and nose steps out of the truck, Reed breaks into a grin and heads toward the man as if he's going to wrap him in a bear hug. I've never seen Reed look so happy to see anyone, myself included. He halts a mere three feet away. "Mac, man, you're here!"

Mac tugs the bandanna away from his face, revealing a sunburnt nose, and grins. "Hey, *man,* I'm the one who lives here. Where else would I be? I see you made it."

As if we've arrived for a kegger. Still, I'm relieved. This is Mac, Reed's best friend from high school and the one who's been setting everything up for us on the island.

"Yeah, we did . . . or at least most of us. I'm getting concerned about Liz . . ."

"No worries, I winched her and her girlfriend out of a ditch a couple miles back." He cocks a thumb over his shoulder and the yellow Mini appears as if summoned. It's now a mottled yellow brown, as if someone had stamped a sunflower into the mud. A pestilent color. But then everything looks pestilent these days. When Niko gets out she's covered head to toe in the same muck. Even her black spiky hair, cut so choppily I would think it was a lockdown DIY job, only it's the way Niko's hair always looks, is covered in mud. She's not wearing a mask. I hear Reed swear under his breath.

"The virus isn't transmitted through mud," I say softly.

Niko grins, her teeth eerily white against her mud-streaked face. "I was thinking a good coating of mud might keep the virus out," she says.

"Shut up," Liz says, getting out of the car. *She* is mud-free, immaculate in soft drapey yoga pants, white cotton tunic, and a linen mask fitted to her face in a complicated pattern of origami folds. Her long blond hair gleams as if she's been brushing it all the way up from Boston. It's hard to understand how she could emerge from the same car so spotless. "Niko was trying to push our car out of a ditch. If you idiots hadn't sped away without us"—she glares at her brother, Reed, even though ours hadn't been the car directly ahead of hers—"you'd have seen us and been able to help. Thank God Mac came along." She directs an entirely different sort of look in Mac's direction, and I marvel at the elasticity of a face that can change its expressions so fast. It must be a family trait; Reed has the same ability.

Mac shrugs. "I just took one last beer run, but yeah, it was no problem, Lizzie."

Lizzie? I've never heard anyone call Liz *Lizzie*.

"A beer run?" Crosby repeats. "Aren't you supposed to be self-isolating?"

"Beer doesn't carry the virus," Mac replies. "I picked up a pallet down at Hanny's Market, untouched by human hands since delivery." Mac's voice is calm and matter-of-fact, but he straightens himself up as if to remind us all of how tall he is, which must be around six five. His eyes, shaded by his cap, go a dead flat green, the same color as the water lapping against the wooden pilings. Reed steps between the two men.

"Mac's following the procedure we set in place. New goods from the store stay in the supply shed for fourteen days before being stocked up at the house pantries. Right, Mac?"

Mac visibly relaxes. "Yeah, and I used my gloves while moving and washed my hands afterward. The stuff in the pantries has been there for weeks, clean as a whistle." He looks around as if daring one of us to object. I see that we've formed a circle, with six feet between each couple. Mac's in the middle of it. "Okay, then," he says, "if we're going to do this we'd better get to it. Tide's going out. We got half an hour to pack up or we'll be stuck sitting here with our thumbs in our asses another eight hours."

"We've got to do the tests first," Reed says. He opens the hatchback of our car and withdraws a YETI cooler. Last year we used it for camping out on the Fourth of July. It held hot dogs—Tofutti ones for Liz—potato salad, and beer. Now it holds seven testing kits. Reed holds out one for each of us, maintaining the distance of two outstretched arms even with me.

"You'll need a surface," Mac says. He grabs three weathered crates and lays one out for each couple. Then he gets one for himself.

"Okay," Reed says, opening his kit, "it's pretty simple. Remove the swab and insert it into your right nostril—"

"Why the right?" Ada asks.

"It's just easier—"

"Only if you're right-handed," Niko says, shoving a swab up her left nostril with her left hand . . . and then leaving it there, suspended in the air, like she's a kid sticking straws up her nose to imitate a walrus. Liz laughs. Even from six feet away I can feel Reed stiffen. I know what he's thinking: if the swab falls in the mud the test will be invalidated and we only have seven. They're the new rapid tests that are supposed to be 94 percent accurate. I'm not sure how much he had to pay for them on the black market, but he'd come back the night before we left looking shook and Reed never worries about money. Before he explodes, Niko extracts the moist yellowish swab. "And now?" she asks, guileless.

"You stick it in this vial, cap it, and then swirl it around," Reed says, not rising to the bait. My heart swells with love and pride for him. None of them knows how hard this has been for him, how much he's had to work to keep it together for the rest of us.

We all do as he says, everyone but Crosby taking off their masks. Liz makes a face at the way the swab feels in her nose. Ada makes one at how it looks coming out and says *gross* the way she would in college when she found hair in the shower drains. When we've all sealed our vials, we place them on the crates in front of us.

"What happens now?" Crosby asks.

"It takes ten minutes," Reed replies, setting a timer on his watch. "A positive turns green. A negative just stays the same."

"Shit," Niko says, "my booger looked a little green coming out. I hope you all won't hold that against me."

Before anyone can reply Mac claps his hands together. "Right. I'm not going to stand here contemplating my own snot. I'll start bringing your stuff down to the dock. You folks need to move your cars into the boathouse—" He tosses a ring of keys to Reed. "Let me know if my vial turns green and I'll just take a header into the drink." He grabs three cases of beer from his truck, balances them on his shoulder, and walks out onto the pier, vanishing into the fog.

"What if he *is* positive?" Crosby asks. "He's handled all the supplies for the island."

"He won't be," Reed says, glaring down at our two vials as if daring them to turn green. "He's been careful, and there still aren't many cases up here."

"That's magical thinking," Crosby says. "Have you thought about what we'll do if he's positive? Can you even drive that boat if you have to?"

"Reed and I can both drive the boat," Liz says, "but it won't be necessary. Mac would never endanger our lives."

"Like that's in anyone's control these days," Crosby spits out.

"Look," Ada says, putting her hand on Crosby's arm, "we're going to know in just a few minutes. No use looking into a future we can't see."

As if to demonstrate the opacity of that future, she pulls an old battered purple North Face duffel—the same one she had in college—from the back of their Volvo and carries it up the pier where she, too, vanishes into the churning mist.

"Give me those keys," Liz says, holding her hand out to Reed. "I'll unlock the boathouse and move our car inside."

Reed remains standing guard over the test vials. He's staring down at ours—or is it mine he's staring at? Is he wondering what he'll do if mine is positive? Whether he'd leave me here on the dock?

His timer trills with the opening notes of Beethoven's Fifth. I look down at our tests.

Both are clear.

I look at the rest of the vials. They're all clear.

"Thank God," I say, hoping the test is as accurate as it's supposed to be. Reed wouldn't trust it if it weren't.

He looks at me, a question in his eyes.

"Who were you worried about, Lucy?"

Before I can answer, the pier shakes and we both turn to see what's barreling out of the fog toward us. As a dark hooded shape wielding a crooked staff emerges, I catch my breath. It looks like those cartoons of the Grim Reaper that were so popular ten years ago during the 2020 pandemic. I remember one carrying a carton of toilet paper, another wearing a mask. But it's only Mac, the hood of his slicker up, carrying a loading hook.

"We'd better get going," he says, "before the tide goes out without us."

I let my breath out along with the idea that has seized me: that the death I'd avoided ten years ago has been waiting here for me all along.

CHAPTER TWO

THE BOAT IS SMALLER THAN I THOUGHT IT WOULD BE. I WAS PICTURING some swank cabin cruiser, but I'd forgotten that although Reed is rich, he comes from that kind of old-money Yankee rich family that prides itself on using beat-up old crap instead of ostentatious new. Reed will duct-tape his sneakers before buying new ones, and he's still wearing shirts he wore ten years ago in college.

This boat—dirty, flat-bottomed, about the size of a short school bus—looks like it could use some duct tape. There's a good six inches of water in the bottom sloshing over our suitcases.

"The pump's not working so great," Mac concedes, holding out his hand for me. "I've been too busy to fix it."

I stare at his hand. We stopped shaking hands over six weeks ago, stopped standing closer than six feet one week after that. But Mac just tested negative. There's nothing to worry about. And the boat *is* lurching so much I feel queasy—

Which is one of the symptoms.

No. I tested negative.

I take his hand. It's warm and broad and calloused and it seems to lift me up through the air and into the hull of the boat safely. I don't want to let go. He helps me to a bench at the rear (*the stern?* Reed is always teasing me about my nautical ignorance) and then leaves me there to help Ada across. He deposits her right next to me.

"You've all got to sit in the stern to keep the prow up," he says, going back for Liz.

"Say goodbye to social distancing," Ada says, wriggling her hips against me.

I throw my arms around her and squeeze so hard she yelps. She feels soft and cushiony beneath her down vest, plumper than she was the last time I saw her, probably from being stuck inside comfort-baking and drinking these past weeks. She hugs me back just as hard. "I've missed you," I whisper into her damp curls, inhaling her familiar lemony smell.

"I know! It's been crazy, right?" She pulls away to look at me, holding me at arm's length. "Who would have thought we'd be back in this mess again! That we apparently learned so little from last time. I can't believe how stupid people are!"

I don't tell her that I missed her even before the virus severed our lives. "I'm just so glad that you and Crosby were game for this. I told Reed it was the only way I'd agree to it."

Ada's brown eyes widen and gleam. "Are you kidding? It's literally a lifesaver." She lowers her voice. "If I had to self-isolate with Crosby in that tiny apartment for five more minutes I'd have killed one or both of us." She smirks, and I hug her again.

"I guess there's no need for social distancing anymore," Liz says as she plops down on my other side.

I can't tell if she's being ironic or not; I never can with Liz. She and Reed inherited the same sarcastic bent—along with the Harper blue eyes, patrician bone structure, blond hair, and money—but Reed's got a tell: he always sniffs after irony or falsehood. If Liz has a tell I don't know what it is.

"Well, we all tested negative," Ada says, "and the boat's pretty small."

Liz jerks her chin toward the dock, where Reed is standing next to Mac. "I told Reed to buy a new one last year."

When Liz looks away Ada sucks in her cheeks, looks down her nose, and soundlessly mimics Liz's words. It's all I can do not to giggle. Ada's brand of snark, usually at the expense of someone who'd been mean to one of us, never failed to make me laugh in college. The same holds true all these years later, and I look away from her so I don't crack up, and focus on Reed, who's surveying the distribution of luggage as Niko rearranges boxes and suitcases in the front of the boat. I notice that Reed has adopted the same half-slouch, hands-in-pockets posture as Mac and that he's several inches shorter than Mac. I always think of Reed as tall so it's unsettling to see him looking smaller.

"I didn't realize he and Mac were so close," I say, hoping my voice doesn't betray the twinge of jealousy I feel that I've never met this close friend. Mac's never come down to visit us in Westchester, and Reed's never brought me up to Maine.

"Mac's mother, Hannah, was our housekeeper," Liz says. "We practically all grew up together. And then when things got bad . . ." Her voice trails off and she looks into the fog. ". . . he and his mother took care of things. I don't know what we would have done without them."

"It's really moving how people come together in times like these," Ada says. "The way they help each other out—"

"A woman at Whole Foods nearly tackled me for the last organic peanut butter," Liz cuts in. "People turn into monsters 'in times like these.'"

Ada lifts an eyebrow at me. We're both thinking the same thing: Liz was probably the one doing the tackling.

Any further conversation is forestalled by Mac gunning the engine. Liz scoots over to leave space for Reed next to me, but he remains standing beside Mac at the helm. Crosby sits next to Ada and puts his arm around her. She moves closer to him, and I feel a chill where her warm body had been. Niko stays at the prow, perched on top of a case of condensed milk, her Leica pressed to her face. Cigarette smoke floats back on the air. I see Crosby open his mouth behind his now salt-spackled face shield (he's the only one who's kept his mask on since we did the tests), no doubt to say something about how smoking makes you more vulnerable to the virus, but then shut it.

As we motor away from the dock I glance back for a last view of the mainland but all I can see is the dirty-yellow spume of our wake as it's swallowed up by the fog, all trace of our passage erased. I turn forward but there's nothing to see ahead of us either.

"I guess you have a pretty good compass," Ada says, looking a little queasy. I can't remember if she gets seasick; the only time we were on a boat together was a rowboat in Central Park.

"Nav system's down," Mac says, "but I've been doing this run since I was ten and I've done it twice a day for the last—"

"There's the first buoy," Reed shouts, pointing at a red ball bobbing on the surface of the water. "They mark the route to Fever Island."

Stray wisps of red hair fly around Ada's face like Medusa's snakes. She makes a show of mock shuddering. "I wish it wasn't called that."

"It was a quarantine site in the nineteenth century," Reed says, shifting on his legs to accommodate the swells hitting the boat. The water is getting rougher the farther we go from shore. Bracing myself against the back wall of the boat, I hold on to Reed's voice, the calm measured tone he employs while reciting facts, like a lifeline. "The first hospital was built in 1832 during a cholera epidemic. In 1848 dozens of ships arrived from Ireland fleeing the potato famine and carrying typhus. My five-times-great-grandfather was one of the doctors who treated hundreds of patients, most of whom died."

"Fuck, Reed," Liz says, "no one wants to hear that."

"I think it's interesting," Crosby says. "I wrote my master's thesis on pandemics. Those ships from Ireland were called fever ships."

"Imagine fleeing one disaster only to find yourself in another," Ada says.

"Disaster breeds disaster," Crosby says. "Is that how your family ended up with the island, Reed? Did your great-whatever get it for services rendered?"

Reed shakes his head. "No, but when he was an old man he bought the island because he said he wanted to be buried where, and I quote, his 'soul still dwelt.'"

"And so the rest of the family just decided to have their summer place here?" Crosby asks.

"I think it's kind of sweet," Ada says, "to want to be close to their ancestor's final resting place." I reach across the bench and squeeze her hand. Ada's parents died in South America during the last pandemic, and she's never been able to find out where they were buried. "I bet that felt special, growing up with that history, Reed."

Mac snorts. "We used to find bones out in the woods. They buried the dead in a bog and when a big storm came it swept them out to sea. We'd find 'em in lobster traps and washed up in the harbor. And then, of course, there are the ghosts."

"Shut up, Mac," Reed says. "You'll scare Lucy. She believes in ghosts."

"Metaphorically," I correct him, sorry I ever confessed my thoughts on the subject. "I just feel like the dead are always with us, in our thoughts and our hearts. I love a good ghost story. What's the story for the island?" I look toward Reed but it's Mac who answers.

"There are a lot of them," Mac says, "but they all start with the witch."

"The witch?" Ada and I say together. I see Mac smile, the squint lines around his eyes deepening, obviously enjoying the audience.

"Ay-yup," he says, leaning hard into the Yankee accent for our benefit. "The first settlers here had a hard winter of it. They lost half their supplies and their ship when it foundered on the rocks off the island. Near starved to death, would have if they hadn't traded with the Indians . . . excuse me—" He clears his throat. "Indigenous Americans. As happens when folks are stuck together in bad circumstances, they started blaming one another—the captain who steered the ship into the rocks, the first mate who landed them too far north, the minister who said God would look after them, the servant girl who seemed to stay plump while others starved. The minister's daughter claimed that the servant girl came to her at night and sat on her chest, sucking the life out of her, and that's how she stayed plump while others withered. She was tried and judged a witch, condemned to die, but they didn't want the stain of her blood on their hands. So, they brought her to the far side of the island, buried her alive in the rocks, and left her there to drown when the tide came in."

"That's horrible!" Ada cries, rightfully indignant at the injustice. "Since when is that not murder?"

Mac shrugs, clearly enjoying her outrage. Enjoying, too, I think, the chance to lecture Reed's college friends on a subject he knows more about. "Since when do the haves lack ways to justify their crimes against the have-nots?" he asks. "But she had her revenge. As she died she cursed the island and those who survived to have their souls drawn back to the island at the moment of their deaths and be trapped forever in the rocks, drowning over and over again with every high tide. They say you can see their ghosts in the fog and hear their cries when the tide comes in."

"Well, at least she had her revenge," Ada says, and then, turning to me, adds brightly, "Maybe you could write your next book about her, Lucy."

When she sees the stricken look on my face, she claps her hand over her mouth. She knows how much I hate being asked about my *next book,* the *second book* that never happened. I'd written my first in the two years after college—a book about the way our lives changed when the pandemic hit. It had been successful enough that I'd gotten a job teaching creative writing at a local college and a contract for a second book, but, eight years later, I haven't been able to write it. *I feel,* as I confessed to Ada on a rare weekend we'd spent together last fall, *that I put everything I knew about the world we lost in that book and I haven't really lived since then. How can you write about a life not lived?*

Maybe you write a ghost story?

She squeezes my hand. "I mean," she says, "perhaps if you wrote a historical book you wouldn't have to deal with the pandemic at all."

"You don't want to write about what happened to those fever patients," Mac interjects.

"Didn't it bother your family," Ada asks, looking up at Reed, "living on a cursed island?"

Liz snorts. "Our father considered it a perk. 'Keeps the local riffraff out,' he'd say over G and Ts. No offense, Mac."

"None taken, Lizzie. My uncles all gave the place a wide berth when they were coming into the harbor." He pronounces it *hah-ba*. This time I don't think he's putting on the accent. His dark green eyes, staring ahead into the fog, look hard as malachite. "They said that if you see the Gray Lady standing on the cliff you'd die within the year."

Mac points into the fog with such certainty that I expect to see the specter of the vengeful witch hovering above us. Instead, the island rises out of the fog—a mass of granite fringed with deep-green pine and ringed by enormous boulders that look like the carved idols of Easter Island, standing guard and willing us to go back. Patches of fog cling to the jagged rock, making it easy to imagine a woman standing on the edge looking out to sea, her hair and dress whipped in the wind. Her anger feels palpable in the heavy salt-saturated air, a force emanating from the island itself, as if before she died she poured her rage into the very stone.

"It looks . . ." Ada begins, trying, I imagine, to put a good face on the bleak spot where we have pledged to wait out the storm, but even Ada is having trouble with this one. The best she can come up with is "It looks unwelcoming. At least we'll have it to ourselves."

CHAPTER THREE

AS WE APPROACH THE ISLAND NIKO UNFOLDS FROM HER CROUCH AND, cradling her camera against her chest, leaps onto the dock. Reed tosses her a line, which she deftly figure-eights around an iron cleat.

"I didn't know Niko was so good on boats," I say to Liz.

She rolls her eyes. "Niko is good at everything physical," she says and then blushes, reminding me that for all her defenses and snobbery, Liz has a tender heart. "And she had to learn her way around boats when we came up here last summer."

She gets up then and starts yelling at Niko to be careful with her easel and painting supplies. Ada and Crosby move to the prow and hand up luggage to Reed, while Mac ties off the other end of the boat. As I scramble to get off he holds out his hand and I take it without any hesitation this time. Then I grab suitcases and boxes from Crosby and Ada, careless of who has touched what. Reed is doing the same, although I notice that he's wearing gloves.

"Hey," I say, as we stack the luggage and supplies on the dock. "I didn't know Liz and Niko came up here. Why haven't you ever brought me?"

He looks up at me and swipes the sweat from his face. I wince, thinking of what he could have transferred from those boxes and suitcases to his mouth, nose, and eyes, gloves or no gloves. "What?" he says, furrowing his brow. But he's not confused by my question;

he's thrown by it or he never would have touched his face with possibly contaminated hands. There's no chance to pursue the subject, though, because Mac is yelling out instructions to store the boxes in the supply shed and telling Reed to get "the mule."

Reed turns and vanishes into the fog. I carry a crate marked *Scott Brand Toilet Tissue* to a weathered shed on the edge of the dock, where Mac is explaining the storage system.

"New goods go up against the side opposite to where the last goods were stored." He points to the right side of the shed, where the shelves are full of boxes, and then to the left side, where the shelves are empty. "I let all new goods sit for fourteen days before moving them up to the houses."

Crosby shakes his head at this. "It's not really known how long this virus stays on surfaces."

"That's what Reed and I agreed on," Mac says, shrugging. "Too late to change the protocol now."

As he turns away, I see Crosby look at Ada worriedly. She gives him a tight smile. "The CDC's best estimates suggest three days for plastic, two for cardboard and paper. It should be fine." Seeing me watching she widens her smile. "Look at all this toilet paper! We've been using a bidet at home." She makes a face and for the tenth time today I thank God that Ada is here.

When we're done stacking the new supplies—beer, beans, soup, rubbing alcohol, more toilet paper—onto the shelves, and frozen foods into one of the two freezers, I emerge from the shed sweaty. I don't wipe my face, though, until Ada offers me a sanitized wipe to clean my hands. The others are loading suitcases onto the back of a fat-tired jeep—the mule, I suppose. Mac turns to Crosby.

"Crosby, right? You and Ada are in the Cove House. That's down here. Come with me and we'll get you unloaded. The rest of you can head up to the Main House. I'll drive the mule up after."

Reed nods and slaps the back of the vehicle as if it's a real pack mule. "Come on," he says to me, then turns and starts up a muddy path that's been mown out of tall meadow grasses. I follow with Liz and Niko, too winded by the climb to ask the questions running through my head: *How many times have you two been up here? Has Reed come up without me in the ten years since college? Who else has he brought here?* Instead, I keep my head down to watch my footing in the ankle-deep mud, trying to remember what Reed has said about the island over the years. *My parents have a summer cottage off the coast of Maine . . . kind of remote . . . rustic . . .*

I had pictured a small, quaint cottage with primitive—or no—plumbing. But now when I raise my head a house looms out of the fog that is neither small nor quaint. *Imposing* is the word that comes to mind because it literally seems to *impose* itself on the rocky landscape. It's three stories high, with a stone foundation made of the same granite as the cliff we saw from the boat, cedar shingles faded to the color of fog, and green trim around the rows of windows and peaked eaves. A columned porch runs across the length of the front, culminating in a circular gazebo topped by a tower and a widow's walk. The house looks down at us from its many windows with the same impassive face as the island. *Keep away,* it seems to be saying, *I protect my own.*

"I thought you said it was a cottage," I gasp to Reed when we catch up to him.

Niko snorts. "'Cottage' is what the rich call their honking big summer mansions."

"Let's go to the barn," Liz says, giving Niko a warning look. "We'll come back after we shower or . . ." She pauses, looking at her brother. "Did you want us to quarantine by couple?"

Reed is staring up at the house and doesn't respond at first. I'm about to tell Liz and Niko that yes, that's what we'd talked about doing, but when Reed turns I'm silenced by the look on his face. It's an expression I haven't seen in years.

"What's the point," he says. "We were all over each other in the boat." Then he walks into the house. I stare after him, trying to remember the last time I'd seen that look on Reed's face.

"Wow," Niko says, "was that really Reed Harper or a much chiller simulation?"

"This place always does a number on him," Liz says. Then she lightly punches Niko on the arm. "Come on. Let's get that mud off you." Then to me, "We'll see you after we've cleaned up."

I watch them take a mown path that curves around the house between lilac bushes drooping under the mist, then I climb the steps onto the broad wide-planked porch. A dozen rocking chairs are lined up facing the blank view and a round picnic table fills the circular gazebo. It looks like the porch of a hotel—or a sanitarium. The paint on the chairs is so weathered and speckled with lichen it's hard to tell what color they were originally. Blue-glazed planters sit between the chairs. There's a wreath of dried bayberry leaves on the door, and a floor mat with a faded red lobster and *The Harpers* written below.

The Harpers.

Reed's parents died ten years ago during the first pandemic, right here on the island. I've kept my last name and Reed insists he doesn't want children. Liz had a hysterectomy three years ago when she found out she had the BRCA1 gene. So who, exactly, are *The Harpers?*

I feel a wave of sadness for my own mother, who died three years ago of breast cancer, and then realize what that expression on Reed's face was. Grief. The naked overwhelming grief of knowing you're the end of the line. The last time I saw it was when he came back from the island ten years ago, right after his parents and his girlfriend—his childhood sweetheart, Becky—had died. No wonder he's never brought me here.

And yet, it's not sadness or grief I feel walking through the front doorway of the house; it's nostalgia. It feels like stepping back into a gentler time when people crowded around a table or sprawled on lumpy chintz sofas reading paperback books and playing board games. The long oak table that spans the space between the open kitchen and the living room (the phrase *great room* pops into my head from some old book or decorating vlog) could seat twenty. The kitchen, with its steel French-door refrigerator, industrial-size dishwasher, cobalt-blue KitchenAid appliances arrayed across the granite counter, looks like it could feed an army. I'm tempted to open the cabinets to inspect the vaunted stores that Mac, at Reed's behest, has laid in for us but even if I washed my hands I'd feel too tainted to step foot on the bleached-oak floors and touch the whitewashed cabinets.

Instead, after toeing off my boots and leaving them in the boot tray, I pad on stocking feet over the rag rugs, like islands themselves between the faded easy chairs and sofas, peering into the framed photographs on every surface. There are old ones in silver frames of sepia-tinted ancestors in formal poses, many of them with Reed's light, wide-spaced eyes and square jaw, and newer, wooden frames holding color pictures of lobster bakes and boating parties. There's one of a young Reed, blonder and tanner, his arm casually draped over some girl's shoulder. I wonder if it's Becky, the girlfriend who died. I've never seen a clear photograph of her, just the out-of-focus one he kept in his college dorm room, so I'm not sure, but who else could it be? Most of the people peering out of the silver and wood frames are probably dead, of course, but drifting past their faces, my reflection smeary in dusty glass, I feel like I am the ghost intruding on their innocent lives.

I come to an eight-by-ten framed sepia-toned photograph hanging on the wall beside the fireplace of a dozen or so people standing in front of a large house—this house, I realize. From the old-fashioned nuns' habits and the men's sideburns and bushy mustaches I guess that the photograph is from when the house was a quarantine hospital—and yet they stand so close to each other! I suppose it was before they really understood germ theory. Peering closer through the film of dust I can feel the tension in their rigid bodies and still faces—except for one dark-haired woman, the only one not wearing a nun's habit, who's standing a little to the side of the group beside a tall man. Her face is a soft blur of white and dark eyes beneath thick curls piled high on her head, but the camera has caught a faint smile on her face, as if the man beside her had just said something funny. As I look at him I hear the rushing in my ears that sometimes precedes a panic attack. The man could be Reed's twin.

I step back from the picture and realize the rushing sound is coming from over my head. A shower running.

The thought of a hot shower after the past twelve hours of traveling nearly unbuckles my knees with relief. I leave the great room with its innocent ghosts and follow the sound up the stairs, down a long corridor filled with more framed photographs, to a bedroom with a candlewick bedspread and sheets printed with blueberries. A breeze blows through an open window, stirring lace curtains and carrying with it the smell of pine and salt without a whiff of disinfectant or bleach. I close my eyes and breathe it in—and see the face of the dark-haired woman in the old photograph. What teasing flatteries had Reed's handsome ancestor whispered in her ear to bring that smile to her face?

I hear a step behind me and turn, eager, as if the doctor himself will be there to repeat what he just said—

But there's no humor in Reed's grave, pale eyes. Damp from his shower, he dispenses instructions for disposing of my tainted clothing and how to work the shower knobs. He still has that look of grief in his eyes, as if I am, indeed, a ghost and he is already mourning me.

CHAPTER FOUR

WHEN I HAVE SCOURED EVERY INCH OF MY POOR TIRED FLESH I CHANGE into the clean clothes Reed has left for me. Wanting to be extra sure we didn't carry the virus with us, we all agreed we'd put the clothes we packed aside for a few days. Reed had asked Mac to wash some clothes that had been left in the house. They look, I think as I put on worn canvas trousers, a striped sailor's shirt, and a faded Choate sweatshirt, as if they're from decades rather than years ago. When I come into the great room it looks like we all might be from another era in our L.L.Bean castoffs and outdated collegiate wear from back when campuses were places where we lived. Certainly, these people barely resemble the careworn stragglers who came over here in the boat.

Crosby, in a loose faded oxford button-down and khaki shorts, shaggy blond hair damp from the shower, is standing at the kitchen counter meticulously measuring shots of whiskey into a silver cocktail shaker. Ada is behind him opening cabinets with little yelps of glee at each discovery. Peanut butter! Tuna fish! Flour! Niko is kneeling in front of the fireplace arranging logs, a fine coating of ash replacing the mud she'd worn earlier.

She's like Pig-Pen from those old Charlie Brown comics, I'd once heard Liz say fondly, *dirt just finds her.*

Mac is on the couch, his long legs stretched out in front of him, drinking beer from a bottle, and Liz is sitting cross-legged in front of a stack of board games and jigsaw puzzles, her long blond hair falling like a curtain over her face.

"Do you remember when we played Risk for three days straight during that big nor'easter?" she says to Mac.

"You mean when we realized Reed's penchant for world domination?" Mac replies, taking a long pull of his beer. "I've never been so bored in my life."

"I vote for Scrabble!" Ada yells from the kitchen. "Oh. My. God. We have cocktail franks! I am making pigs in blankets to have with cocktails."

I move toward the kitchen to help Ada—and then notice that the only one not here is Reed.

"Where's Reed?" I ask.

"He went down to the dock to make sure everything is secure," Mac says, "because—"

"That's Reed," Liz finishes for him, twisting her hair into a knot, then letting it go. "Our father was the same way. 'Measure twice, cut once,'" she intones in a lockjaw baritone wholly unlike her usual voice. "'An ounce of prevention is worth a pound of—'"

"Stop," Niko says, lighting a match. "Let's not channel your anal-retentive forebears. Bad enough we've got them glaring down at us from every surface in the room. Speaking of which, could we put some of the 'family' away?"

"I like them," Ada says, coming into the great room with a tray of frosty drinks in martini glasses and a plate of saltines with Cheez Whiz and olives. She's scraped her unruly red hair into a high ponytail. With the boatneck sweater and red capris she's wearing she looks like a hostess from a 1950s television show. "They make me feel like I'm part of a big family." I try to return her grin but I'm worried about Reed. Checking things twice is not a good sign for him. If I'd been here I would have had him practice the strategy his therapist suggested of visualizing completing the task the first time instead of allowing the endless loop of double-checking that always leaves him more unsure than when he began. But short of following him out into the dark, which will only undermine his confidence more, there's nothing I can do. I pick up one of the drinks from Ada's tray and take a sip.

Strong. Citrusy. Sweet. The first sip feels like an ice cube applied to my frontal lobe. I take another.

"Here's Reed," Ada cries. "We should toast."

She goes to the door with a drink in each hand. "Ex-Pats," she says, holding out a trembling glass that glows virulent green in the porch light. "Remember you taught us how to make them in college? I thought it was appropriate for our current status since we've left our old lives behind."

Reed regards the glass. He doesn't usually drink, and he's been adamant these past weeks that we need to keep up our immunity. But as he takes the glass he says, "Good choice. Plenty of vitamin C." Then he looks at the rest of us. "Here's to our brave new world. May it fare better than the old one."

THE FOOD IS certainly better in this world than the one we left in the suburbs and cities where the supermarket shelves had been cleared weeks ago. Mac has provided fresh halibut, clam chowder from clams he gathered himself, corn on the cob, coleslaw, and potato salad from the local farmers market, and oven-hot dinner rolls from the well-stocked freezer. There's cold white wine to follow the Ex-Pats. Blueberry pie for dessert. We eat at the big table, passing dishes and butter and lemon wedges and refilling each other's wineglasses. At first it feels strange to be sitting so close to each other, but the liquor and wine help to ease the unfamiliarity and soon it's as if the last two months of cowering in our homes had never happened.

After dinner we repair to the great room for *coffee and snifters of brandy,* as Crosby ironically puts it, as if we are characters in an Agatha Christie novel. Ada wanders over to the old photograph of the hospital staff. "Man," she says, "how did these nuns work in those habits and keep them clean during a typhus epidemic?" She turns to Mac, who's by the fireplace rearranging the logs. "What were you saying before about the fever victims? Is it another ghost story?" Her eyes are gleaming as she sits down between me and Crosby on the couch and pulls a blanket over our feet. I remember that she loved ghost stories and horror movies in college.

Mac's eyes slide over to Reed as if to see if he'll object to the story but Reed, who's stretched out in a Morris chair, keeps staring into the fire.

"Well," Mac says, leaning forward, his windburned face ruddy in the firelight, "you could say so. Enough died of the fever to populate this whole island with ghosts. But they didn't just die of the fever. The hospital boat wrecked in a storm and all of them—patients, nurses, nuns, some of the sailors from the fever ships, *and* Reed's doctor-ancestor—were stranded out here. They were all so crazed with hunger by the time the rescue boat came that they tried swimming out to it. The good doctor, Nathaniel Reed Harper, was able to get aboard but the oarsmen were worried the rest would swamp the boat so they rowed away, supposedly"—Mac glanced at Reed—"over Nathaniel Reed's protests."

"My brave namesake," Reed says, waving his brandy snifter in a toast.

"Oh shit," Niko says, "tell me he didn't ditch those old nuns and sick people. Didn't he come back for them?"

"He kept a journal," Reed says, "but it ends before he leaves the island. According to family history, he was taken ill after his dunking in the ocean and wasn't able to send a rescue boat right away, and the locals on the mainland were too afraid to attempt another rescue."

"What were they afraid of?" Ada asks.

"I suppose having their boats swamped by half-starved fever patients," Reed says.

"There were also rumors of something the boatmen saw that scared them," Mac says.

Reed shrugs. "Rumors or not, the stormy season began and by the time Nathaniel returned to the island everyone was gone—nuns, patients, sailors—even the Irish girl whom he'd apparently been sweet on. They were all gone. He believed they might have been rescued by a passing ship but whether he ever found out for sure"—Reed shrugs and drains his glass—"no one knows."

"Do you still have the journal?" Ada asks. "Maybe Lucy could use it for her book."

"No. I don't. It went missing that last summer we were here." Reed gets up to poke the fire, and Mac takes up the story.

"Some say that the ghost on the cliff is the Irish girl Nathaniel Harper abandoned, and that you can hear her wailing in the wind, the Harpers' own personal banshee."

"I thought it was the witch who was buried alive," Niko says.

Mac shrugs. "Witch, vengeful Irish banshee, take your pick. My great-aunt told a story that the witch had possessed one of the Irish immigrants."

"Wow," Niko says. "This island has some bad mojo. Remind me why we came, Liz?"

"Because you couldn't be trusted to quarantine," Liz says, "and I didn't want to spend the next year, or who knows how long, keeping you from getting us both killed."

"Oh yeah," Niko says, grinning. "Liz has been a nervous wreck since the first cases. Me . . . well, I stuck out the last one in the East Village—"

"That's where you got your start, isn't it?" Crosby asks. "Those pictures you took—empty streets and crying doctors, piled up bodies, people who were homeless sleeping on the subways, that one you took of a rat eating another rat—"

"Dude," Mac says, "you took the cannibal rat picture?"

Niko grins. "Yeah, on the fucking A train—"

"You kept riding the subway?" Crosby asks. "During a pandemic?"

"Hell, they were never cleaner," Niko says, eyes lighting up, a wicked grin on her lean face that makes her look wolfish. "And relatively free of assholes. They'd all decamped to their summer homes—" She catches a look from Liz and ducks her head, running a hand over her spiky hair, looking like a kid caught swearing. "But yeah, I didn't need to stick around to take those pictures this time. It would have been redundant. I've been wanting to do a study of the island since we were here last year, but you guys"—she looks at Crosby and Ada—"aren't you medical professionals? Shouldn't you be on the front lines saving lives? Especially you, Crosby. You're in admin. Are you going to run your hospital *remotely*?"

Crosby's jaw clenches and a vein on his forehead pulses. Ada grips his hand, whether to comfort him or hold him back, I'm not sure. The truth is I've wondered myself why she and Crosby agreed to come. Especially Ada. Her family valued social service; both her parents were doctors who'd died serving for Doctors Without Borders during the last pandemic. Ada, who had planned to be an actress before, had volunteered at a hospital and registered in a nursing training program. She had been working ever since as an emergency room nurse in the same inner-city hospital where she'd met Crosby the year after college. I'd expected her to tell me that her place was on the front lines when I asked her to come with us to the island but instead she had said yes.

"We're older now," I say, trying to catch Ada's eye to let her know it's all right, she doesn't have to answer Niko's question. "I suspect

none of us is as reckless as we were last time—at least I hope not."
I nudge Ada with my foot under the blanket. "Remember how we
holed up in our dorm with a carton of ramen noodles and a case of
White Claws? We thought we'd be fine—"

"Instead, you got sick and ruined your lungs," Reed says, spoiling
my trip down memory lane. "Which is why we're here"—he glares
at Niko—"in case you're wondering. Lucy came away from the last
pandemic with lesions in her lungs and respiratory issues. She can't
afford to get this new one—"

"And besides," I say, eager to direct the conversation away from
my poor, weak lungs, "I don't have to teach for the summer—even
remotely—and Reed's on leave from his job so why not spend the
summer with friends and family on a beautiful island, fully stocked
with delicious food thanks to Reed's foresight and Mac's hard work.
We've got enough food to last for six months even without supply runs,
and we're together. We don't have to worry about getting stranded like
those fever patients—" I point toward the photograph. Was the dark-
haired girl the one Nathaniel Reed Harper was sweet on? Had he really abandoned her? Did he ever find her? Or did she die here waiting
for him? I shake off the questions and smile at Reed—"because we
have the internet—"

"No cell service, though," Crosby says, tapping his Smart Watch.

"—and an emergency radio," I continue, even though I, too, had
been surprised to discover there was no cell signal. "I, for one, am
grateful for all that. Niko will take beautiful photographs, Liz will
paint her gorgeous landscapes—"

"And Lucy's going to finally write her long-awaited second novel,
right, Lucy?"

Ada looks at me, her eyes vast and gleaming. I'm taken back to our
dorm room, the two of us sitting up on our single beds, talking late
into the night about our hopes and dreams for the future. I was going

to be a writer and she was going to be an actress. We were going to backpack through Europe after college and then share an apartment in New York City. We'd waitress and bartend to pay the rent and stick by each other until we both made it. Then the pandemic hit.

I'd gotten to write my novel, but it didn't give me the life I thought it would. Ada had given up on her dream of acting entirely—first because the theaters were closed, and then even when they reopened, she said she had realized how *frivolous* a profession it was. Maybe it was because her parents had died fighting the virus in South America and she thought she had to follow their example. I wish that the island could offer a second chance to Ada as well as to me.

"I'm afraid the acting opportunities won't be great here on the island," she says, as if reading my mind, as she so often did in college, "but I plan to revive the short-order cooking skills that paid my way through college and nursing school. And if anyone breaks a bone or gets a bad case of poison ivy, I'll be glad to help out. Thanks to Crosby's emergency access to the hospital dispensary, we're fully stocked with medical supplies. I've brought enough drugs for every eventuality."

"We're lucky to have a trained nurse," Reed says. I flash him a grateful smile for coming to Ada's rescue, especially since he'd been reluctant at first to invite her to come, but only because he didn't get along with Crosby. "Whatever your reasons for coming—"

"Ada's pregnant," Crosby blurts out. "That's why we're here. The prognosis for pregnant women and their unborn children infected with the virus is bleak. We agreed we should give our unborn child his best shot."

"You're pregnant?" I repeat, unable to disguise the shock in my voice. Before I can follow up with *How come you didn't tell me?* Reed nearly shouts "Pregnant? How long—"

"Three months," Crosby says, laying his hand protectively over Ada's belly and stroking it with the same fondness as he had his goatee a moment ago.

Ada turns to me with a wobbly smile. "I was going to tell you, but then with the pandemic—"

"You could have mentioned it to *me*," Reed snaps. I stare at him. His face has gone white and the vein at the base of his throat is throbbing the way it does when he is upset. He stands up, looks once around the room, and walks out, letting the screen door slap behind him.

"He's just upset because this wasn't part of the plan," I say, getting up to follow him. Ada grabs my hand. "You know how he likes to plan everything," I tell her. "This has just thrown him for a loop."

Me too! I want to scream. *Why didn't you tell me?*

"Well, this wasn't exactly planned," Crosby says with a sheepish grin. I feel Ada's fingers turn cold on my arm and fall limply to her lap—her full, rounded lap. To my horror, I feel a tear streak down my face.

"I'll go talk to him," I say. "I'll—" I turn and head outside. Reed is on the porch, facing away from me, staring out at the water, which is visible now under a clearing sky and a full moon.

"Hey," I say, laying my hand on his arm. It feels as taut as the line Niko tied to the dock earlier. "It will be all right. She's only three months along. We'll all probably be back home before the baby's due—"

"Is that what you think?" he says, turning to me. "That this will be over in six months? Do you think I went to all this trouble for a summer vacation?" he asks sardonically. "We don't know how bad things will get on the mainland or how long we might have to stay here."

Perhaps it's the backdrop of fitful clouds and moonlight on a choppy sea that makes me feel as if he's standing on the prow of a pitching ship as he sails away, leaving me behind as Nathaniel Harper left his Irish sweetheart. But Reed hasn't abandoned me. He's brought me—and all of us—to this safe harbor.

"However long we have to stay we'll be all right," I tell him. "And if we're still here when Ada's close to her due date we'll figure something out even if it means she has to leave." I only add the last because I am the one who begged Reed to invite Ada.

His face darkens, but it's only the shadow of a cloud moving across it. When it passes he nods. "Okay, as long as we're agreed on that. I'm going down to the dock, to check that the boat's secure . . . the wind is picking up . . ."

I could remind him that he checked earlier, but I don't. I let him go so that I can stand out here in the moonlight, breathing in the fresh air, alone.

Only I'm not alone.

"Everything okay?"

It's Mac, standing in the shadow of the tower at the end of the porch. How long has he been out here? How much did he hear?

"Fine," I say briskly. "Reed just doesn't like surprises and he started planning this two months ago, when the virus appeared at the beginning of April." It's on the tip of my tongue to add that all his gruesome ghost stories aren't helping, but he speaks first.

"I think Reed's been planning this for ten years," Mac says. "Since the last time. I think he always knew it would happen again."

"No one could have known this would happen—" I begin.

"Reed knew," Mac replies. "That husband of yours knows everything."

I shiver.

"You'd better get inside," he says. "Wind's picking up."

"In a minute," I say. "I'm going to wait for Reed."

Mac nods and ambles off the porch and into the woods, toward the cabin where he'll be staying, I suppose. As I watch him leave, I think about what Mac said. I had no idea Reed had been thinking about coming to the island all these years. It makes me wonder what else I don't know about my husband.

CHAPTER FIVE

WHEN REED DOESN'T RETURN, I GO UPSTAIRS, PLANNING TO WAIT UP for him, but my eyes shut before my head touches the pillow.

I go right back to the car in my nightmares, stuck in the dirty bilgewater wake of bigger vehicles, the wipers a maddening metronome, the windows sealed by fog opaque as wax, cutting off light and air—

I can't breathe. There's a weight on my chest as heavy as the granite boulder that trapped the dying witch. I turn to Reed for help. But it isn't Reed in the driver's seat; it's Ada. She looks at me, her eyes as wet and dark as the water pressing on the window behind her.

I wanted to tell you, she says, her voice muted as if coming from underwater—

We *are* underwater. We're driving beneath the sea. That's what she wanted to tell me: we had to travel underwater to get to the island. Over her shoulder, someone taps on the window and a face appears. It's the Irish girl from the photograph, only her face is smeared and bloated, as if she'd drowned, her tapping fingernails green with algae.

It's not fair, I say to Ada. *We didn't abandon her.*

Didn't you? Ada asks, as the window begins to crack under the banshee's green nails. *Just like you abandoned me?*

I wake gasping for air, slick with sweat, the banshee's tapping echoing in my ears. It takes only a moment to realize the sound is coming from the shade pull batting against the window ledge in a crisp, salty breeze. Bright morning sunlight, fractured by the pattern of the lace curtains, lies on the floor like broken glass. I practice the breathing techniques the respiratory therapist had taught me after I was sick. *Breathe in for a count of seven, hold for four, out for—*

Where is Reed? Didn't he come to bed last night?

I sit up and run my hand over the undisturbed surface of the candlewick bedspread on the other side of the bed. It tells me nothing. Reed sleeps so still he barely rumples the sheets, and he always smooths his side of the bed when he gets up, as if erasing all trace of his presence. More informative is the note on the night table.

Didn't want to wake you. Breakfast downstairs xoxo R.

It's weighted down by a jam jar full of lilacs still wet with dew.

Like the offerings he'd bring me in college—wildflowers and birds' nests—and leave on our ground-floor windowsill *like some demented wood sprite,* Ada would joke.

My breathing eases, coaxed by lilac and the aromas of coffee and baking from downstairs. I pull on the canvas pants, sailor's shirt, and Choate sweatshirt I'd worn last night. When I look in the window my reflection startles me. My dark hair floats wild and thick, my face white and blurry, like the banshee in my dream. But it's just that the glass is covered with a film of salt air and my hair, uncut since the lockdown began, has expanded in the humidity. I finger comb it into a braid and splash cold water on my face, then head downstairs. Voices rise up through the old house like bubbles rising to the surface of the sea, but the kitchen and great room are empty as if those voices belong to the ghosts of Harpers past.

But then I realize that they're coming from the porch. I push open the screen door, its hinges sighing. Everything looks scrubbed clean:

the indigo sea, the feathery pines, the round picnic table covered with blue-and-white china plates of eggs and bacon, mugs of coffee, and a basket heaped with blueberry muffins. Even the people—Reed seated at the table, sipping from a mug that says *The Captain;* Liz cross-legged on a yoga mat; Mac leaning against the porch railing; and Ada buttering a muffin—look strangely shiny, all the tension from last night gone as if it has been scrubbed away by the crisp, Maine air and replaced by a radiant aura. As if we've been dead for decades and our souls have been drawn back to the island.

Ada smiles and rattles the muffin basket at me, exclaiming, "Comfort baking!" and I feel a tether pull me back to the living.

"Great," Niko says, unspooling herself from a rocking chair. "This was the thing that drove me crazy last time: people taking up silly hobbies like gardening and jigsaw puzzles and that silly kids' video game—"

"I *loved* that game!" Ada cries.

"We've got lots of jigsaw puzzles," Liz announces from the depths of a Down Dog. "Remember when Mom accused Dad of hiding pieces, Reed?"

"And it turned out Roxy was eating them," Mac chimed in.

"Roxy?" I ask, accepting a steaming cup of coffee from Ada and sitting down.

"Our yellow Lab," Liz says, executing a flawless Cobra. "I wish we had brought a dog."

"They can carry the virus," Crosby says. He's on one of the rocking chairs on the far side of the porch, a copy of *Moby-Dick* splayed across his knee.

"I'm afraid I didn't bring enough books," I say, taking a muffin from the basket. "But we can still download things, right? We have Wi-Fi."

"High-speed 12G," Mac says, glancing at Reed. "Just like the man ordered. Password: 'Fever Island.'"

"About that," Reed says. "I think we'd better go over some ground rules before anyone goes online."

Liz groans—or maybe she's just doing some kind of fire breath.

"What, no porn?" Niko asks.

Ada giggles. "Do you remember when people started posting Animal Crossing porn?"

"What I was thinking," Reed says, clearing his throat, "were some rules about social media posts and location services."

"I have to post my work," Niko says. "It's how I make my living, and unlike some of you I *do* still have to make a living."

"And I have to videoconference with the hospital," Crosby adds, tapping his useless Smart Watch. "I couldn't find a Wi-Fi signal at our house."

"There isn't one down at the Cove House," Reed says. "Just here at the Main House." Turning to Liz he adds, "You might get a signal at the barn."

"I got one this morning and did a Zoom Pilates class."

"I thought we were all going to have Wi-Fi connection," Crosby says, agitated. Ada gets up and starts clearing dishes.

"We do," Reed answers, "it just doesn't reach to the Cove. You're welcome to come up here and use the internet anytime. There's the den and great room on this floor and my father's study and three spare bedrooms upstairs. My father's old study is soundproof, and his law library provides the ultimate in credibility bookshelf. *Everyone's* welcome to use the whole house." He spreads his arms wide, an eager expression on his face. What people don't realize about Reed is that despite his awkwardness—maybe *because* of his awkwardness—he wants to solve all the world's problems and make everybody happy. "The only thing I ask is that you don't post anything that gives away our location. No idyllic shots of the island or still lifes of our full pantries or social media bragging about living off the grid on Fever Island."

"Do you think," Niko asks, "that pirates will be jealous of our bounty and launch a raiding party?"

"Of course not," I answer for Reed. "Things aren't *that* bad. But it pays to be careful. People do get jealous. Remember how divisive and chaotic things got last time—"

"This isn't last time," Reed retorts, as if I were contradicting him instead of trying to back him up. "Things are going to get far worse, and when they do this island is going to look very inviting to a whole lot of people."

"In that case," Crosby says, "it might take more than abstaining from social media posts to keep out the invading hordes."

Mac shifts from his perch on the railing and Reed looks at him.

"Oh please," Liz moans, "don't tell me you guys have *gunned up*."

"Guns?" Ada repeats, looking up from the plates she's been stacking. She rests one hand on her belly as if protecting her unborn child. "Are there guns on the island?"

Mac starts to smirk but then tries to mask it. "Everyone up here has a gun. You don't want to be the fellow without one."

"Don't worry," Reed says. "It's just my father's old hunting rifle, and it's locked up in a gun closet. So yes, to answer your question, Crosby, we're prepared but we'd like to avoid having to defend ourselves. So, no social media posts with pictures of the island, and please disable all location-finding apps on your devices. And don't sound too *smug* about our situation."

"That's good advice in general," Ada says with a forced smile at Crosby. "I hate smugness. Why don't we find a place inside to set up for your conference, honey? That's really nice of Reed to offer his father's study."

Crosby follows Ada into the house, grumbling about credibility bookcases. Liz rolls up her yoga mat and announces she's going back to the barn to paint and suggests to Niko she might want to set up her darkroom. I'm hoping I'll get a chance to talk to Reed alone, but Mac says something about wanting him to look at the boat engine, and after Reed plants a hurried kiss on the top of my head, they walk toward the dock, their voices gradually fading into the ambient birdsong and soughing of pine trees.

I gather up the rest of the dishes and go back inside, pausing on the threshold to listen for Crosby and Ada, but the house is silent save for the tick of an old clock and the shushing of wind stirring the curtains. It's a quality of quiet I've rarely heard but instinctively know is the kind bought with money. It feels like a balm, like lotion soothed into hands cracked from repeated scrubbing and alcohol wipes. As I wash the dishes, I try to remember the last time I felt this kind of peace. It's not just that Reed and I have been stuck inside our house for two months, but that there's always been one anxiety or another scratching at us. Since the lockdown began, there's been a cacophony of conflicting reports on television and the internet, which has felt like a constant grating chatter in my head, not to mention the endless videoconferences with panicked colleagues and my distraught students.

It's like they've never experienced a pandemic before, Zach, my office-mate and fellow creative writing teacher, texted me during one of our virtual faculty meetings. *What a bunch of basket cases.*

Who are you calling a basket case? I'd texted back.

He'd sent me a GIF of Nicholas Cage in *The Wicker Man* that had made me laugh so hard I had to fake a lost signal to get out of the meeting. It hadn't helped with my jittery nerves, though. But here on this beautiful island, in this solid old house, with only the sound of the birds and wind sifting through the pines—

There's something else. A *thwump, thwump, thwump* that I thought was the sound of my own heart but realize now is coming from outside the house.

I dry my hands and step out onto the porch to see if the sound is coming from the dock—some piece of equipment Mac and Reed are tinkering with—but there's no one on the dock. No sign of Reed or Mac and the sound is coming from behind the house.

Thwump, thwump, thwump.

It sounds like the windshield wipers in my dream. Like the pump in the hospital that saved my life when my lungs filled with fluid.

I follow the sound around to the side of the house, bending under the lilac bushes, which are still heavy with last night's rain, damp grass tickling my ankles, and come out in a little clearing. To my left there's an open shed where a lawn mower is parked. To the right is the barn, but the noise isn't coming from there; it's coming from the dark woods on the other side of the clearing where something red hangs from a branch.

Drawn to it like a hummingbird to a red flower, I find myself crossing the clearing, my thin-soled canvas shoes sinking into the damp soil, the mown grass whisking against my bare ankles. I think about ticks and insect repellent, but I keep going, an opening between the trees beckoning.

It must be a path. Reed said there was a five-mile trail that circled the island. We could take hikes, he'd promised me, through mossy woods to secluded coves full of seals. There is moss, I see, as I get closer to the opening, deep emerald moss starred with tiny white flowers like something out of a fairy tale. A velvet carpet. And the thing hanging from the tree is a red buoy. I recall that Reed said the trails were marked by buoys.

You can't get lost.

When I step between the trees the temperature drops five degrees and the silence deepens as if sound is muffled by the moss that covers everything, not just the ground but the roots of the trees and humps of granite that break through the earth like dolphins breaching the surface of the sea. The only sound is that steady *thwump, thwump, thwump*. I can feel it in the soles of my feet, vibrating in the earth. It feels like the beating heart of the island.

The path curves right and then I see it, rising above the trees like a freak spore sprouted from the moss, a white stalk crowned by spinning blades.

Of course. It's the wind turbine that powers the island: the electricity, the lights, the internet, and the pump that draws up water from the well. *True off-the-grid self-sufficiency,* Reed had boasted.

What if the wind doesn't blow? I had asked.

On an island in the Atlantic? he had replied. *Hardly ever happens. And we do have a backup generator.*

So, it must happen sometimes.

Right now, its steady revolution looks like that of an engine of a spaceship that's about to lift off, its *thwump, thwump, thwump* pounding a tattoo on my heart. I should feel relieved that there's an explanation for the sound, but I don't. It feels like it's beating its way through my skin, into my bloodstream, like it's inside my body, running through my veins—

Like the virus felt when I got sick last time—a flame sizzling beneath my skin.

I feel that prickle now on the back of my neck, as if something is watching me. Something that makes a dry *clacking* sound. I turn and the green haze of the forest spins with me, like algae smeared over water, broken by the black ribs of tree trunks. Something is stirring within the green, moving behind trunk and branch—or *made* of trunk and branch, as if the trees themselves have come to life and are following me, swallowing up the path. When the forest stills, two eyes stare back at me from the gloom, pinning my heart to my ribs.

My heart had stopped in the hospital, Reed told me afterward, for three minutes and thirty seconds. Not long enough to cause damage, he reassured me, but I have always felt that a hole opened up inside me in those three minutes and thirty seconds that is still there, a yawning abyss waiting to swallow me.

Like the hollow pits staring back at me from inside a narrow skull. A deer skull, I tell myself, stepping closer, its antlers bound in twine and hung from a tree with bones and shells like some gruesome wind chime. There's a design carved into its forehead, some kind of intertwined knot. When I touch it the skull and bones and shells clack together. That was the sound I'd heard. And all I'd seen were the trees blurring together as I moved, creating the flickering illusion of a horned man striding through the forest.

CHAPTER SIX

AT OUR COCKTAIL HOUR I PRODUCE THE DEER SKULL.

"That's one of the stag markers we made," Liz exclaims excitedly. "I didn't know there were any left."

"You made that?" Ada asks, looking suspiciously from the cheese sticks she's just brought out onto the porch. She's spent the afternoon baking in the Main House because the oven down at the Cove was off by five degrees. Her cheeks are pink and her red hair, twisted into a knot, is dusted with flour as if she herself were a sugar-coated strawberry and cream pastry. I remember how in college she would come back from her job at the cafeteria smelling like grease and french fries.

"Not crafty enough for you?" Niko asks, pulling a beer from the ice-filled tub Mac and Crosby have set up on the porch. She raps one of the bones hanging from the skull and it sets the whole thing clacking. "I think it's pretty cool. Did you carve the doohickey on its forehead? Can we hang it in the barn?"

"It wasn't a craft project," Liz says, rolling her eyes with fond exasperation. "It was a game we played for years called Stags and Hags."

"Yeah," Mac says, tapping the mobile with his beer bottle as if toasting the skull, "we played it every summer. Reed made it up."

"It was Becky," Reed says, looking up from the book he's been reading all afternoon on the porch—something about boat engines—and giving me a guilty look as he mentions his ex-girlfriend's name. "It was the summer after she came back from Ireland. That 'doohickey' carved on its forehead is a Celtic knot, a symbol for life or death or infinity . . . it seemed like it could mean just about anything. The hags were witches—"

"And we were the stags." Mac grins. The sunburnt strip over his nose reddens. "Becky had a kinky side. Remember how she and Liz drove your cousin Tobin into the bog and he went crying to your parents and they made us promise to stop?"

"Tobin was a wuss," Liz says, sipping her wine and twirling a lock of hair with her long fingers. "It wasn't like we were going to leave him to drown there."

"How was the game played?" I ask. What I really want to ask is what was Becky like. Reed will never talk about her. Even bringing her up the way he has must be the influence of the island.

"It was really just an elaborate game of tag," Reed says, accepting an Ex-Pat from Ada. Once again she's whipped up cocktails even though she's not drinking them. "There were two teams—stags and hags. If you tagged someone from the other team, they had to stay in jail. This thing"—he jabs his finger at the skull but doesn't touch it—"was a marker for the stag jail."

"We had to move it from Dead Man's Cove because the Boston cousins kept getting marooned on the rocks at high tide," Liz says, rolling her eyes. "The hags' jail was out at the Witch Stone."

"Dead Man's Cove?" Crosby echoes. "The Witch Stone? Jeez. Did you all grow up in a Hardy Boys book? We played a game like that in Queens, but we called it cops and robbers, and our jail was a bus stop."

"It sounds like ring-a-levio," I say, hanging the skull mobile on a hook by the door. It doesn't seem so frightening now that I know what it's for. "My grandmother told me that kids played it in Brooklyn. The game could go on for hours."

"Ours went on for days," Reed says fondly. "Weeks, even. There was a map—wait . . ." He gets up from his rocking chair and disappears into the house.

"Now you've set him off," Liz says. "He was a bit . . . *intense* about that game."

"And you weren't?" Mac asks. "Didn't you make the map?"

"Well," Liz admits, "I do love a map. And that last summer we needed something to occupy our minds."

"So, Becky was here with you that last summer?" I ask, daring to say her name now that Reed is out of earshot.

Mac and Liz glance at each other, and Liz says, "She wasn't supposed to be, because of the quarantine, but—" The squeak of the screen door cuts her off as Reed comes back brandishing a scroll of paper like a battle flag.

"Here it is! I found it in the map drawer. 'The Fever Island Campaign Between Stags and Hags.'" There's a hectic flush in his cheeks and a gleam in his eyes, which I haven't seen in a long time. Not since college, when he'd come bursting into our dorm room with some discovery—a way to break into the library tower or a magic lantern he'd found in the drama department closet. I remember thinking then how he seemed like a boy in a children's adventure book, and I realize now that this is where he'd picked up that spirit. Here on Fever Island with Becky, the girlfriend who died. It's the first time since we arrived that something about the island seems to make him happy, maybe because it's a reminder of his childhood here before the pandemic. Maybe because it reminds him of Becky.

Reed spreads the map out on the picnic table, shoving aside the place settings Ada and I had carefully put out earlier. I glance over and see her mouth set in that forced smile she used to adopt at frat parties and boring lectures. I try to catch her eye to commiserate but she's gotten up to look over Reed's shoulder at the map.

"Oh, it looks just like the Hundred Aker Wood map from Winnie the Pooh," she says wistfully.

"I don't recall Pooh having a Boneyard or a Dead Pool," Crosby says, stabbing his finger at the landmarks on the map. The Dead Pool, situated in the middle of the island, has a skull at its center.

"We wanted it to sound scary," Liz says, smoothing the furled edges flat. The entire island is represented as a green amoeba floating in a dark blue sea. There's an elaborate compass rose in the right-hand corner, a Celtic knot incorporated into the design. In the bottom center I make out the dock and the path up to the Main House rendered in childlike but effective simplicity. I make out the path I took into the woods and the crossroads marked by a stag's skull. A path goes south around the island to a small cove marked "Sea Witch Cove" and then to a lighthouse on the southeast edge of the island. The whole eastern side of the island, facing the Atlantic, is drawn as a boulder-scape with a tall standing stone labeled "The Witch Stone." From there, the path circles around the north side of the island, past a graveyard called "The Boneyard," and then splits, the main trail continuing to the crossroads and the branch going past a craggy cliff called "Gray Lady Cliff." A figure of a woman, her face hidden in her hands, is drawn on the cliff. Below, the path winds back to the dock, passing Dead Man's Cove.

"Why is it called Dead Man's Cove?" I ask.

"Because the currents bring all sorts of stuff into the cove. My dad called the logs that floated in tidewalkers. And these fishing floats"—he touches one of the glass orbs that hang, suspended in fishing nets, from the porch rafters—"washed ashore into Dead Man's Cove along with all sorts of flotsam and jetsam."

"I can never remember which is flotsam and which is jetsam," Ada says.

"Flotsam is what falls in the water by accident," Reed explains, "while jetsam is debris thrown overboard deliberately."

"Why would anyone throw stuff overboard deliberately?" Crosby asks.

"To lighten their load, I suppose," Ada says.

"Dead bodies float into the cove whether they drowned by accident or not," Mac says. "Remember when that rich stockbroker from Boston drowned himself in Bar Harbor and his body floated into the cove three weeks later—"

Reed gives Mac a warning look.

"Why is our house labeled 'The Fever House'?" I ask, to change the subject.

Liz raises her eyebrow at *our* as if she would like to dispute my possession of her childhood home, but Reed doesn't notice. He still seems upset at the mention of the body. "It was the hospital where the fever patients were kept," he says.

"Actually, they kept the fever patients in the barn, but we called the Main House the Fever House because the object was to stay out of it," Liz says. "Mom and Dad were fighting a lot that summer and then when they got sick . . ." Her voice trails off, and I imagine she's remembering her parents' death. Did they quarantine themselves in this house? I wonder. Reed has always refused to talk about the details of what happened the summer of the quarantine. But I guess this must be what happened from what Liz says next.

"Remember we all slept out in the barn?" She taps the picture of the barn, which has a clearing in front of it marked by a scarecrow.

"'The Tibster'?" Ada asks, reading the name scrawled over the scarecrow's head.

"A pun on our father's nickname, Tibs," Reed says, "short for Tiberius. Our mother, when she'd had too much to drink—"

"Which was every night," Liz interjects.

"—called him Mr. Tibster. There *was* a scarecrow in the clearing, though. Mac's mother, Hannah, planted a garden there that summer. We should do that, too. Early June's not too late to start a garden up here."

"Already got the seeds, bro," Mac says, laying an arm across Reed's shoulders, which are, I only notice now, scrunched up to his ears. Was he thinking about his father? I wonder as he lowers them under Mac's touch. He looks more relaxed as his finger traces the path that I took today to a spot marked "The Crossroads."

"The path splits here—right to follow the southern side of the island until you get to the lighthouse."

"We have a lighthouse?" Ada asks excitedly.

Reed gives her one of his repressive looks. "A retired nonworking lighthouse. Not much more than a ruin. The lighthouse keeper's cottage is what Liz has labeled 'Sea Witch Cottage.'"

"Also pretty much a ruin," Liz says. "Niko took some great photographs there last summer."

Niko taps the map, looking neither pleased nor embarrassed by Liz's praise. "They came out . . . *odd*. This whole terrain"—she runs her finger along the eastern shore of the island, drawn as a jumble of boulders and standing stones facing the sea, including one labeled "The Witch Stone"—"is like the moon. Huge boulders in different colors, worn and carved by the sea into freaky shapes. When you scramble over them you can get lost, especially when the fog comes in. I found myself in this spooky cemetery—"

"The Boneyard," Mac says, pointing to a spot on the north side of the island. "That's where they buried the fever victims. And here"—he taps a serpentine line—"is the path up to Gray Lady Cliff, and below it is Dead Man's Cove."

"The whole place sounds like an accident waiting to happen,"

Crosby says, tugging his goatee. "Maybe we should just stay on this end of the island. If anyone gets hurt and has to go to the hospital, we'd all be exposed to the virus."

"No way, man," Niko says. "I came here to take pictures."

"And I want to walk," I say. "The paths are marked with those buoys, right?"

"Yeah," Mac says, tracing the dotted lines that loop around the island. "I walked all the trails and replaced any buoys that had fallen. If you follow them and stay off the cliff and out of Dead Man's Cove at high tide you should all be fine. And besides, we've got a nurse." He grins at Ada.

"That's right," Ada says, clinking her seltzer can against his beer bottle. "Can we get copies of these maps? I'd like to have one when I go exploring."

"I brought a scanner to scan my pencil sketches into my computer," Liz says, "so I'll make copies." She starts to roll the map up but Crosby, still sulking at Mac's response to his concerns, jabs his finger into its center. "What's the Dead Pool?"

"It's a deep pool at the center of the island. There's an old story that it's bottomless and that if you drown there your body will never be found. You should all stay away from it—it's surrounded by bog."

"Shit, man," Crosby says, "glad you've brought us to a safe place."

"And on that note," Ada adds, handing her husband a beer, "dinner is served."

ADA MANAGES TO keep Crosby and Reed from crossing horns at dinner by a relentless parade of dishes she has prepared. Even I, who helped her with some of it, am amazed by the plenitude. There's corn bread *and* biscuits; potato salad, macaroni salad, *and* coleslaw; three types of grilled meat; homemade baked beans—vegan and with bacon—and two different kinds of green salad.

"We'll have to be more careful about our food usage," Reed says, looking nervously at the array of food.

"Oh?" Ada asks, raising her eyebrows. "I didn't think there was any need as long as Mac was making regular supply runs. I guess I cook when I'm stressed. I can't indulge in my creative outlet like the rest of you . . . speaking of which, have you decided what you plan to write your book about, Lucy?"

"Maybe I'll write a book about seven castaways stranded on a desert island," I say impetuously.

"Oooh, and they die one by one, mysteriously, like in that Agatha Christie book?" Ada asks.

I'm sure Ada just means to be encouraging but the idea of killing off the occupants of our island—even fictitiously—seems too close for comfort. It clearly does to Reed, too, who has gone pale at Ada's remark.

"Actually," I say, to stop Ada from enumerating the ways we could all die on the island, "I *have* been thinking about that story Mac told, the one about the fever ships that came from Ireland."

"That's a better idea," Ada says, flashing me a smile. "Didn't you say your ancestor kept a journal, Reed? Wouldn't that be good for Lucy's research?"

Reed looks at her blankly, as if he'd forgotten what he'd said, and then replies, "I said I thought that book got lost."

"Really?" Ada says, clucking her tongue. "What a shame. Are you sure—"

Reed gets up abruptly. "I can't be expected to keep track of *everything* around here. Speaking of which, I have to go check on the pump. I noticed the water pressure was low . . ."

Crosby stares after him. Mac and Liz exchange a look and then Liz turns to me. "Is Reed okay? Is he taking his medication?"

"What medication?" Crosby asks.

Ada punches him in the arm. "Jeez, Cros, that's rude to ask." And then to me, "It's just a little OCD, right, Lu? It started in college and got worse in the pandemic."

"He's fine," I say, hoping Reed doesn't find out we were all talking about him like this. He would hate it.

The silence that follows breaks up the dinner table. Ada begins clearing plates, helped by Mac; Crosby makes an excuse to go back to the Cove House; Niko ambles off the porch to light a cigarette. Only Liz remains on the porch, sipping what must be her fourth or fifth glass of wine.

"You want to be careful sending Reed down that road," Liz says.

"Down what road?"

"The one that leads into the past. That summer when we were quarantined here last time didn't end well. I don't think Reed's ever gotten over it."

"I asked Reed if coming here would stir up painful memories of his parents' death and he said he could handle it."

Liz stares at me as if I'm an idiot and then finally says, "It's not our parents' death he can't handle, although God knows those were awful enough. It's Becky's."

"Oh," I say, feeling even more stupid. Becky, Reed's childhood sweetheart, whose specter hovered over Reed even before she died. "I knew she died that summer, but . . . Reed's never spoken about how it happened. It must have been a shock . . . such a young, healthy person dying of the virus."

Liz's eyes widen. She no longer is looking at me as if I'm stupid; she's looking at me as if I'm crazy. "Becky didn't die of the virus, Lucy," she says slowly. "She died in the bog. At least, that's what we assumed. We found a piece of her shirt on a branch in the bog, right above the Dead Pool. She must have drowned there. Her body was never found."

CHAPTER SEVEN

I KNEW REED HAD A GIRLFRIEND WHEN I MET HIM, AT A KEGGER AT SOME
frat house freshman year. Everyone knew. He was that quiet guy,
the *genius,* who was going to cure cancer or win a Pulitzer or invent
the first sentient AI, whose zeal and focus were enabled by having a
girlfriend back home. She was the ballast that kept his fast, delicate
craft on an even keel.

The boating metaphors came easily; in his sockless mocs and tattered yacht club T-shirts he looked as if he'd just anchored off our
landlocked Connecticut campus and rowed ashore. *Ugh,* Ada had
pronounced at that inaugural kegger, *could anyone be whiter or more
privileged?* That Ada was white didn't make her any less judgmen-
tal; she came from New York City, and her parents were the kind of
left-wing progressives who traveled around living in yurts and worked
for not-for-profits and composted. She was a scholarship student, she
informed me our first day. I was, too; but Ada mentioned it more as
if it were a badge of merit. When she told people her parents were
doctors, she always made sure to add, *But not the kind who make a
lot of money.* When she said she was from the city she always speci-
fied that she'd grown up in a rent-controlled apartment on the Upper
West Side. When we wound up in the same Philosophy 101 class she
rolled her eyes at the pretentiousness of Reed's remarks on Plato and
Descartes. But when he started hanging around—showing up in the

dorm lounge for late-night movies, surprising us with doughnuts from the Mexican bakery in town—she hypothesized that he liked me.

He has a girlfriend back home.

To which she snorted. *The famous Becky? Do you notice he never talks about her? I think she's made-up. Why else doesn't she ever visit?*

But Becky was real. An indistinct picture of her—wispy white-blond hair blowing across tan skin, a hand, bare save for a thin black string encircling her wrist, lifted to ward off the camera—was tucked into the frame of his dorm room mirror. Reed wore an identical bracelet, which held a brass disk inscribed with a Celtic design. When I asked him about it once he said *a friend* had brought it back from Ireland for him to ward off bad luck.

Becky was a Medieval Studies major, according to someone who had gone to Choate with Reed. *No,* someone else whose family summered near Becky's family's summer cottage reported, *she was in that really competitive combined BS/MD program in Boston.* Or, she was spending a year at Trinity College in Dublin, writing her senior thesis about Irish folklore. She was so busy doing fabulous things she never had time to visit.

Because of Becky I assumed that Reed and I would remain platonic friends. And we did. He never kissed me, except on the cheek, or held my hand, except when he was helping me across a stream on one of our hikes, or touched me anywhere else except for when he cupped my foot to give me a boost over a wall or circled my waist when we sat on the edge of the library roof but only because I was afraid of falling.

He's always touching you, Ada said. *You notice he never touches me.*

That's because he's afraid you'd bite his hand off.

And yet, because Reed wasn't my boyfriend and Ada was my best friend, the three of us spent almost all our time together exploring the campus as if it were our private playground, from sneaking under the stage trapdoor (*The space under the stage was called "hell"*

at the Globe, Reed informed us) to climbing up to the catwalks of
Main Hall (*buildering,* Reed referred to scaling the old buildings).
Although it was true Reed never touched Ada the way he touched me
I sometimes thought they were better suited to each other. They had
the same adventurous spirit, often daring each other to climb higher
and take bigger risks. When I told her so, she dismissed the idea that
Reed might like her. I wondered, though, if she was afraid of admitting she liked him because then she'd have to admit he was picking
his childhood girlfriend over her. Ada, I learned early on, hated not
being picked first. She would pretend not to like something rather
than be seen failing to get it.

It was Ada who suggested one winter night after the first snow-
storm that we climb up to the catwalks of Main Hall, which were
strictly off-limits because a girl had plunged to her death from them
in the seventies. We had to squeeze through an iron security gate
and jimmy a lock to get out onto them. As soon as we were out there
I saw why they were off-limits. The narrow wrought-iron walkways
were rusted and full of holes, the intricate vine-patterned railings dissolved into thin air in places. Even without the thin coating of snow
the footing was treacherous.

This is so cool! Reed had declared and Ada had smiled her secret
smile, pleased that she had been the one to suggest it.

Look! she had cried. *There are stairs to the tower. We'll be able to
see for miles from there.*

I wasn't sure what the point was of getting to see miles of Connecticut farmland and woods, but Reed was already climbing up the
spindly ladder behind her. I trailed behind, baby-stepping over the
grating and watching out for holes, while on top of the tower Ada
yodeled at the moon. When he reached the tower roof, Reed turned
around and saw that I was frozen at the top of the ladder where a
broken rung had left a gap of several feet.

It's okay, Lu, he said, *you just have to let go.*

But I might fall, I barked back. *This is so dangerous. How can I let go?*

I mean, he replied, reaching his hand down for mine, *you have to let go of your fear. I've got you.*

And he did. He took my hand in his and I no longer felt afraid. I climbed up the rest of the way, his grip propelling me over the gap and onto the tower. The moon was just rising over the mountains in the east, turning the snow-tipped pines into a magical wonderland. It was like falling into Narnia. When Ada turned to me she smiled her secret smile.

See, Lu, she said, *this is what you get when you conquer your fear.*

I think she meant the view, but what I cared about was being part of this threesome, which felt as sturdy as a tripod.

The summer before senior year Ada and I shared a house on Martha's Vineyard with some girls I'd gone to camp with. We waitressed at night in a seafood restaurant and spent the days lying on the beach or by a pond where dragonflies flitted through the tall grass. Reed came down to visit us twice, and we talked about all of us sharing an apartment in New York City after graduation. He was applying to an urban planning program at Columbia. Ada was applying to Juilliard's acting program against her parents' protests that she go to medical school, or at least do something "socially meaningful" like the Peace Corps. I'd conceded to my mother's anxieties for my future by getting a teacher's certification but my intent was to spend a year waitressing in the city while writing a novel, which I had already begun imagining as a bildungsroman about three college friends.

We had it all planned.

And then midway through our last semester our college shut down because of the pandemic. Reed's parents decided to "shelter" at their summer place in Maine. *Which won't last long,* he told us when he came to say goodbye, *my parents have never stayed in the same house for longer than a month. As soon as the cracks begin to show I'll head back here.*

Everyone thought the quarantine would be over quickly. The virus didn't even seem as harmful as a particularly virulent flu. Ada's parents said there were half a dozen viruses they saw every day that were far worse. Ada could stay in their Upper West Side apartment, but if she wasn't going to use it, could they offer it to some doctor friends who were coming to the city to volunteer at the local hospital?

Oh no, I don't mind, Ada mocked to me, *give my childhood room to some nasty germ-laden interns. I've got a perfectly good dorm room here.*

The college was allowing foreign students—or students who did not feel safe in their home environments—to stay on campus. When I called home, my mother actually suggested I might want to stay on campus through the spring and summer semesters. She worked as a psychological social worker at an assisted living facility and was worried that she might bring the virus home to me. *Stay with your friends,* she told me.

I didn't tell her Reed had gone to Maine. I still thought he would come back. He was certainly jealous when we FaceTimed and he saw we basically had the campus to ourselves. *Think of all the buildering you can do!* he exclaimed.

Of course, we were *supposed* to be doing our classes remotely but the teachers, confused and stunned themselves, didn't seem to expect very much of us. Ada and I picnicked on rooftops, sending Reed the videos to make him envious. He sent us back videos of seals frolicking on rocks and giant piles of steamed lobster claws.

I may go insane from all the comfort-baking and jigsaw puzzles, he texted.

Where was Becky? I wondered. Surely his parents wouldn't let in anyone outside the family. Unless she was considered part of the family already. She was probably, I realized, just the kind of girl that

Reed's parents would want him to end up with, someone of his own social class whose family knew his family and all the strange customs and manners of the wealthy.

As spring turned into summer (we were allowed to stay on campus even after we graduated, as long as we obeyed pandemic protocols), Ada seemed restless, constantly scrolling through her Instagram and Snapchat and TikTok accounts, monitoring how everyone else was spending their lockdown. *Alexa Harris's family have bought a compound in the Catskills and are raising llamas,* she reported one day. Alexa was one of the three girls who had a suite on our hall freshman year. They were all from Long Island and had practically the same name—Alexa, Lexie, and Alexandra—so Ada dubbed them the Lexas from Levittown and mercilessly mocked their accents, clothing, and oblivious entitlement. She didn't seem to think that since *I* was from Long Island I might be offended.

Ugh, Ada reported from her scrolling another day, *the remaining two Lexas have rented a house in town and gotten into baking sourdough bread and macrobiotics. They sound like they're enjoying their pandemic.*

When she announced one night in late May that the Lexas were having a party in their house I thought she was going to launch into a rant against hedonism and carelessness but instead she said, *Let's go.*

But it's against the rules, I said, remembering the agreement we had signed to stay in the dorms over the summer. *We could get kicked out of the dorm.*

We'll just go to tell them they shouldn't be having a party, Ada replied, changing into a slinky shirt and applying lipstick even though no one would see it under a mask.

As we approached their off-campus house we could see their porch was festooned with fairy lights and paper lanterns. Most of the dozen or so people there were wearing masks, and it definitely didn't look like a wild party. In fact, the mood was subdued. Lexie was sitting on a glider, tears soaking her mask, Alexandra and Alexa (apparently taking a hiatus from the llama farm) on either side of her.

Did someone die? I blurted out.

Three pairs of outraged mascara-ringed eyes glared up at me.

Duh, Alexa said, *Lexie's nana. What are you doing here if you didn't know that?*

Oh, I said, turning to find Ada. Had she known? *I'm so sorry, I didn't realize—*

We were just coming back from the liquor store, Ada said, producing a bottle of tequila. *We're so sorry to hear about your grandmother, Lexie, that sucks. Let's have a toast to her.*

Ada found a stack of red Solo cups and unscrewed the bottle. She poured shots and passed them around until everyone had one. *Here's to Lexie's grandma,* Ada said, holding up her cup and downing her shot. Everyone followed suit.

I didn't even get to say goodbye, Lexie murmured.

That's rough, Ada said, refilling her cup.

We all drank another shot to Lexie's grandmother and then one to the end of this "horrendous virus." Masks slipped off and the mood shifted. Someone put on the sound system and turned up the volume. Ada bumped her hip against mine and started dancing. Soon everyone was dancing. Students from neighboring houses drifted onto the lawn and up onto the porch and into the house. Dimly I realized this wasn't a smart idea, but it felt good to be with people again. At some point Ada materialized and tugged me out of the house. She gave me a mask to put on—I'd somehow lost mine—and we stumbled back to the dorm. The last thing I remembered was Ada scrolling through her phone, smiling. At least, I thought, we were in the pictures that would make *other* people jealous.

The pictures were all over social media by the next morning. By noon there was an all-campus email from the dean of students stating that students in violation of pandemic protocols would be identified and punished.

Shit, were we in the pictures? I asked. I'd scrolled through without seeing either of us, but I hadn't looked at all of them. *Do you think we'll be expelled?*

Ada smiled. *I was careful not to take any of you. Besides, it wasn't our party. If anyone gets expelled it should be the Lexas.*

Wait, I began, my head pounding from all the tequila I'd drunk, *you took the pictures? Did you post them?*

Ada shrugged. *Hey, if you're going to throw a party during a pandemic, then you have to deal with the consequences.*

But they were only trying to make poor Lexie feel better about her grandmother dying . . .

Poor Lexie? she repeated acidly. *Are you taking her side against mine?*

I'm not taking sides, I'd said, my head beginning to spin. *It's just . . . I mean, you brought the tequila—*

Are you saying it was my fault? Ada asked, the edge in her voice so sharp I could feel it piercing my brain.

No, I mean . . . I was trying to remember why Ada had that bottle of tequila. Had she been trying to get the Lexas into trouble?

Because if that's what you think, you're just like them. She got up and started stuffing clothes in her purple North Face duffel bag. *A spoiled rich kid from Long Island.*

I'm not a spoiled rich kid— I began.

I mean people like the Lexas and . . . and like Reed, she added, suddenly furious. *Reed with his rich-boy's privilege acting like he's so principled, saving himself for his saintly girlfriend while slumming with trash.*

You think I'm trash?

She had looked startled. And then she said, *I think you treat your-self like trash.*

Says the person unloading their trash on me, I'd replied.

I thought she'd laugh. That's what she did when Reed called her on her bullshit, but instead she turned bright pink and said, *Well, I won't bother you with my shit anymore.* She stuffed her clothes into her duffel bag and took her half of our stash of granola bars and Vi-taminwater, scrupulously leaving my share.

You can take your share of the toilet paper, too, I said, still hoping she'd see the humor in the situation and change her mind. Was she really going for good? *Where* was she going?

Aren't there, like, people living in your apartment? I asked finally, scared that she was putting herself at risk because of a stupid fight.

I'll sleep on the couch, she said. *You're welcome to come if you want.*

Although cases had been going down in the city, it still seemed like a scary place to go, especially with hospital workers staying in Ada's apartment. *Don't you think that sounds risky?* I asked.

She shrugged. *Life is risky, Lu. I'm tired of hiding from it.*

Then she left.

I thought she would come back. That she'd get to the Trailways station (*were the buses even running?*) and realize how foolish she was being. When she didn't come back by dinnertime, I realized she must really have gone.

The next day I got an email from the dean asking me to attend a Zoom session on following COVID protocol. I dutifully signed in and listened to an hour-long presentation on safety precautions that left me with a splitting headache. At the end of it all of us on the call were warned that one more infraction would result in being asked to leave the campus.

I texted Ada to tell her that no one was being punished so she could come back, but she didn't answer. I spent the next two days scrolling through all my social media feeds to see if she'd posted anything anywhere, but she hadn't. On the third night after she left I woke struggling to catch my breath, as if I had inhaled poison. The weight on my chest felt as if I were drowning. I lurched to my feet, trying to reach the surface of the water that was pressing down on my chest, squeezing my lungs . . . and found myself on the floor.

I dragged myself to the mini-fridge, drank a cold Vitaminwater, then to the hall bathroom and threw up. I felt like every bone in my body had been broken, like I'd been trampled by a stampede of jackbooted soldiers, like my lungs had been filled with toxins, like—

I had the virus.

My skin prickled with fear at the realization but also with a queer sense of relief. Here, at last, was what we'd all been running from. I didn't have to run anymore. Mixed into the stew of terror and relief was the craven thought that Ada would feel sorry when she realized she'd left me here sick. I wouldn't call my mother, I decided, feeling valiant at my own maturity and self-sacrifice, because she might come up and expose herself to the virus. I was young, after all, not like the old people who died of the virus. As long as I took plenty of Tylenol and Advil and kept drinking Vitaminwater, I figured I would be all right.

And I was for the first week. I even thought I was getting better . . . and then sometime during the second week I suddenly got worse. I had trouble breathing. I realized I should call someone, but somehow I'd let my phone go dead and I couldn't find the charger. I stumbled out into the hall and knocked on a few doors, but no one answered. The dorm seemed to be empty. It gave me the creeps . . . and chills. I went back to bed and shivered under the covers.

I lost track of time after that (later I figured out I'd been sick for two weeks), and when Reed's face hovered over me I thought he was nothing more than a projection with a clever screen backdrop of my dorm ceiling behind him. Then that backdrop was replaced by one of a hospital, masked faces floating over me like balloons that popped, opening up into a longer, deeper pit of darkness.

The Dead Pool.

The three minutes and thirty seconds that my heart had stopped.

I thought we'd lost you was the first thing Reed said to me when I opened my eyes.

We?

As in the royal, he said, *I thought I'd lost you.* Then he had bent over and kissed my forehead. He didn't leave my side until I was let out of the hospital.

When I was released, he took me back to my dorm. Ada's bed had been stripped bare and all her things were gone. I let out a cry, sure that this meant she was dead, but Reed said that she had texted him to say that she was in the city, living at her parents' apartment, volunteering at the hospital. Reed stayed with me, sleeping on Ada's bed; and then when I was better, he crawled into my bed and we made love for the first time.

Afterward I thought, disloyally, that maybe it was a good thing that Ada had left. Maybe it had been Ada—not Becky—who had kept Reed and me apart all those years. But I had to be sure—I had to stop living in fear—so in the morning I asked Reed about Becky, and he told me that she had died on the island. He had looked away, grief-stricken and ashamed. Ashamed, I thought, because he'd slept with me so soon after his girlfriend had died. I didn't ask him for details. I assumed she had died of the virus.

Only now I know that she died in the Dead Pool, which means, I suppose, that she's still here.

CHAPTER EIGHT

AFTER EVERYONE LEAVES, I GO OUT ONTO THE PORCH TO WAIT, AGAIN, for Reed. I can't let another night go by without talking to him. I've already let too much time go by, years of silence that have amassed a crushing weight. I should have made him talk about his parents and Becky right away, but he said he wanted to put "all that" behind us and start anew. It's what we all wanted after the virus finally receded—like a tide going out, leaving strange detritus in the mud—and we emerged blinking into the light, at first cautiously, still wearing our masks and practicing social distancing but soon recklessly, as if we needed to make up for lost time.

The truth is, I admit to myself now, sitting in the dark, I was content to leave his parents and Becky behind. Content, even, to let Ada leave for her nursing training program without saying goodbye. Content to move to the house Reed bought for us in the suburbs and write my novel, in which I tried to capture, like a fly in amber, the world that was already gone. Content to create the world we had lost and retreat into silence about what had happened.

But silence isn't empty, I think now as I parse the quiet of the night on an island three miles out to sea. There's the sift of wind in the pines, the lap of surf down at the shore, the call of an owl somewhere close by, and, under it all, the persistent *thwump, thwump, thwump* of the wind turbine that keeps the lights on and the water pumping up from the stone heart of the island—from the subterranean caverns where Becky's bones have been slowly leaching into the water all these years. *She* is the heart of the island, the silent invisible presence that has haunted my marriage since its beginning.

Looking down toward the water I see a white shape emerge on the rocks between the dock and the Cove House. For a moment I think it is Becky's ghost, rising from the water to finally come and claim her rightful place. I get up and start walking toward the shore, my heart beating in sync with the blades of the windmill. What do I have to say to Becky's ghost? How do I make my claim on Reed's heart in this place already claimed by her?

When I reach the shore, I see that the white shape is Reed's pale blue oxford shirt. He's sitting on a rock in the shadow of the cliff, knees drawn up to his chest, gazing at the waves. He turns at the sound of my feet on the pebbled shore and his face is so white and drawn that he might well be a ghost.

"We need to talk," I say, climbing the rock to sit beside him. I see that below us is a small cove carved out of the coast, rimmed by wild roses that sweeten the night air. "I didn't know Becky died . . . *here.*" What I really mean to say is that I didn't know she's *still here.* "I mean, I thought she died of the virus."

"I never said that," he says, looking back to sea.

"You never said anything," I counter. "You never talk about her—or that time—at all."

"I thought you wanted it that way," he says, turning toward me. He looks hurt, as if I've accused him of lying. "I thought you were jealous."

"Of course I was jealous!" I cry out, my voice too loud in this quiet, secluded cove. It's just the kind of place, I think, where Reed might have met Becky. "She was your perfect childhood sweetheart. She came from the same world as you. Who could compete with *that,* especially once she died and she could never disappoint . . ."

My voice cracks on the last word. Reed edges closer to me and reaches for my hand. His fingers are cold and the cuff of his shirt is damp. Has he been swimming? The water must be freezing. "Is that what you're afraid of?" he asks. "That you disappoint me?"

"Don't I? I'm not brilliant like Becky was or beautiful or brave. You only stuck with me because I was sick and you'd lost her."

He pulls me closer and lays his head on my shoulder. His hair is wet. "You're all of those things—brilliant, beautiful, *and* brave. You saved me when I was broken—when I came back from here that summer. I, I'm still broken—"

I run my hands through his wet hair and wrap my arms around him. He's trembling all over, as if he has a fever, but his skin is as cold as the granite rock beneath us. I remember that when he found me in the dorm his hands felt so cool against my forehead that I thought he'd come straight out of the ocean, that he'd swum all the way from his island in Maine to find me. Now as he kisses me—*I can't remember the last time we kissed like this*—I taste salt and seaweed. He pulls me down into the cove and presses me into the sand. When he takes his shirt off, sand and wild rose petals sift over my skin. I hold on to him, eyes shut, like a mollusk clinging to its shell as we rock to the beat of the surf licking up closer and closer to us, cold seawater grazing my scalp, the incoming tide giving urgency to our lovemaking.

Or maybe it's just that it's been so long since we made love. We both come quickly, our cries muffled by the slap of the waves, our bodies spent on the sand like the bodies of the drowned. If we stayed here our bodies would be washed out to sea and our bones would sink down through rock and sand until we became part of the island.

When I open my eyes, I notice how the cove is tucked beneath the cliff, and I recognize it from the map—Dead Man's Cove, the place where the dead return.

IN THE MORNING Reed is gone again but there's another note folded on the nightstand. When I open it up, sand and white petals fall out, scenting the room with the ocean and wild roses and memories of last night.

> *Leaving you alone to read and write,* it reads, *my brilliant, beautiful, brave wife. Feel free to use my father's old study at the end of the hall.* —R.

We've healed ourselves, I tell myself, although it feels more like we've broken something—a glaze of ice that has frozen us in place. Now we'll be able to grow closer to each other.

I get up and dress without showering, not yet wanting to rinse away the salt traces of last night, and go downstairs. Ada is in the kitchen sliding a tray of muffins out of the oven.

"Good morning," I say, reaching for a mug. "More baking? We won't fit into any of our clothes if you keep this up."

"I'm sorry," she says.

"I was kidding!" I say, pouring coffee into my mug and sitting down on the stool beside her. "It's sweet you're feeding us. It's like you're practicing being maternal."

She makes a face at me. "Ugh. I certainly didn't learn any of that from my mother. But that's not what I was apologizing for. I'm really sorry I didn't tell you I'm pregnant. That wasn't fair to drop on you now, in the middle of a crisis, with everybody there. I wanted to tell you alone in case . . . well . . ." She falters and looks embarrassed. "I know you and Reed have had some . . . *issues* on the subject."

Now it's my turn to feel uncomfortable. Last fall, Ada and I got together for a rare gals' weekend. It was hard for her to get out to the suburbs with her night shifts in a big-city hospital, and my teaching schedule, but we'd managed to carve out a weekend when Reed was away for a conference and she could come up to the house. I'd excit-edly laid in supplies of food and liquor and queued up the movies and television shows we'd loved to watch in college. I made an ap-pointment for us at a nearby spa for massages and pedicures. From the start, though, it had been tense, Ada making comments about how much everything cost and whether the spa employees were paid enough and had good working conditions and how "fancy" the town was. I realized that beneath it all was anxiety about money. Crosby made a decent salary, but living in the city was expensive and they were both still paying off student loans. Still, it was a little hard to take. When she made a crack about our future children going to all-white schools, I replied that it wouldn't be an issue because Reed didn't want kids. Then I burst into tears.

She'd felt terrible, of course, and over several rounds of Ex-Pats I'd spilled out all my frustrations and resentments at Reed's unilat-eral refusal to even consider having children.

He says it's because he doesn't think the world is a fit place for chil-dren, I'd said angrily.

Ugh, she'd said in disgust, *ever the high-minded idealist. Reed's problem is he always wants to look like the good guy. He can't stand being the bad guy.*

I know it's something to do with his father being an asshole, I'd re-plied, a little surprised at Ada's resentful tone, *but it's like he doesn't love me enough to think it would be different with us."* And then, because I was drunk and it was such a relief to unburden myself to a real friend, I told her everything. I admitted to her that I'd scrapped two books in the last three years and hadn't been able to write at all for a year. That I was afraid I'd been a disappointment to Reed because I wasn't accomplished like Becky had been. *Sometimes I feel like the life he's leading with me is a pale second to the one he would have had with Becky.*

Ada had looked genuinely stricken by the remark. *I guess,* she'd said, *none of us are leading the lives we'd thought we would.*

I'd felt terrible then, remembering that Ada had lost her parents in the pandemic, and we'd hugged and cried and made up. When she left, we both said we'd do a better job staying in touch and *do this again soon.* I promised that I'd come into the city when Reed had a conference in March and we could spend time together. But instead of bringing us closer, it felt like our gals' weekend had driven us further apart, highlighting the differences in our circumstances. Then in March there were rumors about the new virus, and I stayed home instead of going with Reed to Manhattan. When I texted Ada to tell her I wouldn't be coming she texted back a disappointed-face emoji and a heart and said *no worries,* but I could tell she was disappointed in me.

When Reed started talking about coming to the island, I saw how those *differences in our circumstances* would once again drive a wedge between us—unless we invited her and Crosby to come with us. I saw it as a second chance for our friendship. Now, though, I see that all this time she must have been wondering how I was going to feel about her pregnancy when she knew that the question of having children was such a sore point between Reed and me.

"I understand," I say now, laying my hand over hers, "why you must have felt uncomfortable telling me, but it's all right. Things are much better between us."

"Oh?" Ada says, upending the tray of muffins and dumping them into a basket. "I thought you had a fight last night."

"It wasn't really a fight," I say, "and anyhow, I went down to the cove and we talked . . . and . . ." I feel heat rising in my face and Ada's eyes widen. I shrug. "Well, we *made up.* This whole thing has been really stressful for Reed, setting up all the details to come here and then reigniting the memories of that summer . . ." My voice trails off as I think about Becky, but I'm not going to betray Reed again by confiding my doubts in him to Ada. "But I think it's going to be all right now. We're all here together, safe, and we've got time to do all the things we missed out on last time. You get to have a restful and safe pregnancy and bake all you want, and I'm going to finally write my second book. Look, Reed left this note this morning telling me to use his father's study . . ."

As I unfold the note a few grains of sand and wild rose petals drift to the counter. Ada sweeps them away with a swift chopping motion of her hand.

"Oh," I say, feeling as if I've put my foot in it again. "Is Crosby using the study for his videoconferencing?"

"No," Ada says, still sweeping invisible grains of sand off the counter, "he said it looked like the backdrop for an injury-attorney's commercial, so I helped him move his stuff from there to the screened-in porch at the back of the house—what Liz calls 'the TV room.'" She looks up, and I'm relieved to see her smile. I smile back, sharing the feeling that we are cohorts again. "The study will be perfect for you to write this historical novel you were talking about. Maybe you'll even find that journal—"

"Reed said it was lost."

"Maybe," Ada says, lowering her voice, "Reed was just nervous about you reading it. He knows how imaginative you are. Remember how freaked out you got after that séance we did in college?"

"Yeah," I say, feeling a chill at the memory. "Reed is very protective of me. He's always telling me not to let my imagination carry me away—"

"What Reed doesn't appreciate," Ada says, squeezing my hand, "is that it's your imagination that makes you such a great writer."

Even more than Reed's encouragement, Ada's faith in me lights a spark in my chest that spreads outward. Tears prick my eyes. I throw my arms around her and hug her tightly, burrowing my nose in the nape of her neck, which smells salty and sweet from all her baking. When I let her go she wipes her eyes. She's as moved by the moment as I am.

"Here," she says, thrusting a warm muffin at me as if it's a hand grenade. "Take this and get to work. No more lollygagging."

It's what we used to say in college when it was time to buckle down to our studies. I laugh, take the muffin and coffee, promise to come back later to help with dinner, and head upstairs before she can see me cry. I stop at our bedroom to pick up my laptop, then continue down the hall, past the framed pictures of the dead Harpers. At the end of the hall is the door to the tower room above the gazebo. The door is shut; a hand-tooled and -painted sign hanging from a nail reads *Lasciate ogne speranza voi ch'entrate.* Reed showed Ada and me a picture of the sign sophomore year and said it was a joke Father's Day present. His father had reacted by correcting their Italian spelling and making him and Liz spend the summer reading Dante in Italian.

I'd always suspected that Reed exaggerated his father's authoritarian manner, but as I turn the brass doorknob and the door opens, releasing an aroma of cherry tobacco and old books, it occurs to me that maybe he was actually downplaying it all these years, that the jokes—the Mr. Tibster scarecrow and Dantesque warnings—were propitiations made to an angry god. That his father ruled this family like a tyrannical sea captain—an Ahab to their *Pequod*—from his tower.

The tower room is certainly crafted like a ship's cabin, paneled in polished teak, fitted with shelves lined with gilt-edged leather-bound books, and trimmed with brass lamps and brackets. The windows look out onto sea and sky so that it feels like being aboard a ship.

I can see why it must have been intimidating to enter for a child. It feels like whoever commands this room is master not just of this house and island but of the sea and sky. A brass telescope stands by one of the windows, aimed at the reach between the island and the mainland, where a few lobster trawlers and sailboats dot the water. Large nautical maps hang behind the desk, a captain's clock keeps time on the wall. The room exudes authority.

I run my finger along the books' spines, searching for one that looks like a journal. My finger stops on a row of a dozen books without titles on their spines. I tilt the last one in the row off the shelf and see that the oxblood leather front is stamped and embossed with the initials *NRH*. I open the book and find, disappointingly, that the pages are blank. The next book I take out is blank, too, as is the next. Working right to left, I find eleven blank books until I come to the last—or first, I suppose, if this is supposed to be a set. This one feels different in my hand, more worn, the gold leaf flaking, the edges of the binding foxed, the pages swollen as if bursting to get out of their confinement. It even feels warm, as if recently handled, but that's probably my imagination. When I flip through the pages I see that they're full of handwriting.

I sink down into the chair behind the desk, its upholstery creaking and releasing a scent of tanned leather, a musky smell that, combined with the pipe tobacco, feels masculine. For a moment I have a sense of foreboding. Reed said the journal was lost, but here it is. Why would he have said that unless he didn't want me to read it? It's true that I really had freaked out in college after that séance, but I'm older now, and it's time Reed knows that. I lay the journal on the leather blotter—these Harper men liked their leather—and open to the first page. The flyleaf contains an inscription in large blocky print.

May 4, 1848

To my son, on the occasion of his graduation from Harvard
Medical School. May you have many worthy deeds to record in
these dozen books.

Yr Loving Father

What a lot to lay on a kid—worthy deeds, indeed! The eleven
blank books stare down reproachfully. Why had Nathaniel Reed
Harper filled only one?

I flip to the next pages, which are covered in a thin spidery
cursive. The ink is so faded I can barely make out the words. I turn
on the brass desk lamp and train its head to shine directly on the
page. The elegant, slanting handwriting looks like decorative filigree,
as abstract and meaningless as the elaborate borders in medieval
manuscripts. I remember one of our older professors sighing when a
student told her she couldn't read cursive. *It's the end of civilization
as we know it,* the professor had pronounced melodramatically, little
knowing how much our civilization was about to change.

Later Reed, who took all his notes by hand and kept a journal,
had made fun of the student. *It's just letters strung together with loops
and curlicues. What's hard about reading that?* Ada had grabbed his
journal and pronounced it "indecipherable," but I had studied his
handwritten notes until I could read them easily. This couldn't be
much harder.

I stare at the rise and dip of each letter until I feel a little seasick,
as if I really am in a ship riding the swells. It takes only a few minutes to get my sea legs and then the words appear, like flotsam from
a shipwreck rising to the surface.

CHAPTER NINE

June 10, 1848

I arrived today at Fever Island, which the locals say is cursed. They say a witch was buried alive here and with her dying breath called down the devil to condemn her torturers to eternal damnation. They say you can see the spirits of the damned in the fog that always seems to hover here. Dr. Fleming, who always exhorted our class at Harvard to free ourselves of superstition, gave a perfectly scientific explanation to the stories as we were rowed out to sea through a thick fog.

"It's this pestilent miasma that surrounds it," he said, coughing into a calico handkerchief. "Most insalubrious. No wonder the locals avoid it." At which remark our oarsman, a rough fellow in a dirty oilcloth, snorted and said something indecipherable in the local patois. Fleming went on as if the rower had not spoken. "But it was all the Board of Health could get for the quarantine."

"Do you think there will be many aboard who are sick?" I asked, endeavoring to retrieve my notebook—the first in the series given to me by my father as a graduation present—and pen to take down the figures. Our passage was too rough, our oarsman seeming to steer directly into the crest of each wave, though, so I consigned this little book to the pocket of my mackintosh and took out my father's other graduation present—a brass spyglass which he'd inscribed with my initials. It was equally useless, as there was nothing to see but fog.

"They are likely to be all sick of the ship fever," Fleming told me. Typhus, that is. As most of the boats coming out of Ireland were "full of it" owing to the unhealthy air on the crossing and the dreadful conditions in their homeland. He rattled off some figures involving the number of ships that had arrived last year at Grosse Ile, the quarantine station 30 miles downriver from Quebec, and here at the Quarantine Island at the mouth of the St. Lawrence in Passamaquoddy Bay, how many passengers who had died at sea, how many sick upon landing, how many who died subsequently. I could barely take in the multitudes or believe so many had died. I had heard some news of it in Boston last year, read a letter in the *Boston Bee* decrying our ill-directed national sympathies for the vicious offscouring of Ireland, and seen our upstairs maid Colleen crying over some relative's demise, but I'd had no idea the devastation had been so widespread. Now Fleming was blithely making predictions for how many might die this summer. "Our job," he concluded, "is to make sure they don't spread the contagion to our shores."

"Surely our job should also include healing the infected and relieving the suffering of the dying," I said, hastily appending a "sir." It did nothing to mitigate the offense of seeming to question his authority.

"When you've walked through as many plague holes as I have, boy, I'll thank you for your advice." Then he tossed a printed neckerchief of cheap cambric to me and suggested I tie it over my nose and mouth to avoid the contagious miasmata hovering over the sick.

I think he meant to muzzle me more than protect my health. I have found that these older doctors are resentful of new theories. Just this year, one of my classmates brought up the theories coming out of Europe questioning the validity of miasma theory. "Such theories," Fleming had quipped, "prove their adherents wrong by propagating a great deal of foul air."

The class had erupted in laughter, the interrogator had turned an alarming shade of red, and later had failed the class. I had kept my silence and been rewarded with an apprenticeship with the great man himself, little guessing that it would begin not in Boston's Back Bay, but on a remote island off the northern coast of Maine where Fleming had been called in by the local Board of Health to supervise the quarantining of ships arriving from Ireland.

"I hope to publish a paper about the experience," Fleming had remarked when he visited my parents' house in Portland. "If you play your cards right, boy, you'll get your name on it as well."

Which meant, I well knew, that I would most likely be writing the paper. Still, it was an opportunity, as my father pointed out, and, he had added, he had been thinking of purchasing property in the area for a summer house. Nor would it hurt, my mother had added, to be on good terms with the Flemings, who, she recalled, had a very marriageable daughter.

Overlooking my father's real estate schemes and my mother's marital machinations, I did think it could be the making of my career and would keep me in the cooler climes of northern Maine for the summer months. Nor was I inclined to dispute Fleming's miasma theories as we approached the vessel through thick fog that became increasingly so foul my eyes stung with it and I had to use the neckerchief to wipe them. When I opened my eyes, I saw with horror that the source of the odor was a body floating on the waves. I stood to point to it, upsetting our fragile bark and bringing forth a stream of curses from our oarsman.

"We must recover him!" I cried.

In reply the oarsman struck the body with his oar and lifted it into the air, a dripping mass—

Of soiled cloth. My drowned man was only cloth. Many scraps now floated past us, accompanied by soiled straw, broken planking, rusted cups, and cook pots. "Has the ship been wrecked?" I asked.

"Nay," Fleming answered, "her captain has no doubt ordered her hold emptied and washed to trick us into believing his ship clean and his passengers healthy. Do not be fooled by such false pretenses."

The ship then emerged from the fog, looking very much as if it were an apparition. I thought of the stories of ghost ships that haunt these islands, but shook off such morbid thoughts as we were hailed by a very lively sailor in a striped cap and red muttonchops. We came aside and tied on where a rope ladder had been let down for us. At which point our oarsman declared his disinclination to come aboard.

"I'll not board a death ship," he said darkly, the most clearly he had spoken throughout the voyage. "I'll take my pay now and be heading back to port."

An argument ensued between Fleming and the oarsman about the terms of service, but upon receiving reassurances from the ship's captain that we could use his lifeboat and crew for our conveyance to the island, we settled with our Charon. I gave Fleming a boost up to the ladder and then prepared to follow, but the ill-mannered tar grabbed my arm roughly and pressed his mouth to my ear.

"Do not tarry on that island, sir. 'Tis haunted by a witch and the ghosts of those she damned."

"Every island on this coast has some tale of that kind," I retorted, fishing out a coin to settle the man's true aim. "Every place has seen its share of death."

"Aye, but they say the witch's ghost lures boats to founder on the island's rocks. A ship went aground there and the survivors fed on each other's flesh until none were left. They say the ghosts are still hungry and that they feed on the living and that even the survivors will find their souls drawn back to the island at the hour of their death."

I tried not to smile at the old man's dramatics. "I'm afraid the inhabitants of the *Stella Maris* will provide poor nourishment for those hungry ghosts," I said, handing the man a coin. "They're no doubt half-starved already."

As I began climbing, I heard the old man mutter below me. "No better roost for the damned than amongst the starving and the desperate."

On deck I indeed found an abundance of the starving and the desperate—and the dead. The captain had arrayed the passengers on deck for our inspection, including three dead bodies stitched up in canvas shrouds. The living were as white as the sun-bleached canvas and looked as if they had already given up the ghost, leaving scarecrows made of sticks and straw. Indeed, as they stood at inspection one fell to the deck, collapsing in a puddle of clothing less animate than the soiled refuse we'd observed floating in the surf.

"'Tis the scurvy," the captain assured us as I knelt to attend the fallen passenger. "We ran out of limes halfway through the journey."

Indeed, the boy, who looked to be eleven or twelve, showed all the signs of scurvy—bleeding gums, bulging eyes, scaly skin— but he was also severely malnourished and wasted.

"Did you run out of food as well," I asked the portly captain, observing that he did not show any signs of deprivation, "or did you just keep it all to yourself?"

The captain bristled at my insult and began defending his treatment of his passengers' rations of oatmeal and biscuit. "They were half-starved when they came aboard," he said. "I'm a seaman not a nursemaid."

One of the passengers knelt beside me and whispered, "We've had no rations for a fortnight, nor barely a drop of water."

I immediately took my canteen from my satchel and poured water into the boy's mouth and then moistened a bit of the bread I'd brought for my supper and touched it to his lips. At the sound of water and smell of bread the row of passengers all turned their heads as one toward me, their eyes wide and empty with hunger. The sight recalled the oarsman's stories of the cannibal ghosts and my hand shook. The helpful passenger steadied it with a surprisingly firm grip. I noticed that he was a hale-looking fellow of thirty or so, that he seemed less wasted than the others, and that his clothes were of a better quality. There was a quick spark of intelligence in his eyes that the others lacked, and the boy was looking to him as though for guidance.

"Surely the terms of passage must have stipulated that there be enough food and water for each passenger," I said, recalling something I had read about a Passenger Act passed to ensure better treatment for emigrants.

"Yes," the man replied, "as I well know since I arranged

the passage myself. I was estate agent for Lord Dunleavy, whose tenants these people were. I was entrusted to make the arrangements to offer passage to any of those who wished to emigrate and I can assure you I wouldn't have sent these poor souls on this death ship had I known how poorly used we would be. I have tried my best to alleviate their sufferings with what provisions I brought."

"I will write to the shipping board to complain," I assured the man, seeing at once that he had assumed a leadership role and it would be useful to enlist his help with the other passengers. "In the meantime, I applaud your humanity and charity." I extended my hand. "I am Dr. Nathaniel Harper."

"Dunstan McCree at your service, sir. Do you know if we are to be detained here or allowed to continue into the port of St. Andrews?"

"That will depend on the state of the rest of your passengers—and the determination of Dr. Fleming. Has there been illness?"

He nodded. "I cannot say there hasn't, Dr. Harper, grievous illness made worse by our close conditions and lack of clean water. As you will soon see for yourself."

He motioned to where Fleming was preparing to go down into the hold, waving me to join him. I rose and did so, Dunstan McCree following close behind me with a noticeable limp. As the captain opened the hatch, which had been barred from the outside, a pestilent gas issued forth, so thick and odious it felt alive, as if it had volition and sought to climb down our throats and into our lungs. Like the oarsman's apocryphal cannibals, it seemed to want to devour us.

Holding the cambric neckerchief over my face I followed the captain and Dr. Fleming down the steps into the hold. It took a moment for my eyes to adjust to the dark and then I wished they hadn't. Thirty or forty poor souls lay shivering and clutching a few rags to their emaciated bodies. They were nearly naked and, though they looked as if they'd been bathed, reeked of disease and death.

"Don't they have clothes or blankets?" I asked, but then I realized that we had seen their clothes and bedding in the water, discarded for appearance's sake with no regard for the comfort of the suffering.

As we walked amongst them some called for water. I had left my canteen above with the estate agent, nor did it matter much as it would not have been enough to go around. "We must get the sick to the hospital where they can be tended," I said, once again forgetting how little Fleming liked to be given advice by his inferiors. For once, though, he seemed not to take offense.

"We must bring all the passengers and the crew to the island for quarantine," he said, his voice muffled behind the handkerchief he had tied over his mouth and nose. "Until we know if they carry the fever they cannot be let go to the mainland."

At this the captain took exception, insisting that he be left at least a few men to maintain the ship should there be rough weather overnight. I climbed back on deck and told the crew to ready the lifeboats to take the sick to the island. They responded more briskly than I'd hoped, perhaps because they were in a hurry to be rid of the diseased belowdecks and be on their way, little knowing they would be detained as well and perhaps end up on the island if they showed signs of typhus.

Dunstan McCree began helping at one of the boats. I thought it best to alert him to the state of affairs so I might enlist him in breaking the news to the crew and "well" passengers, not that they looked in any shape to cause trouble in their weakened state. Still, as my father always says, never underestimate the ferocity of the desperate. As I approached there was a cry from one of the sailors and I feared that the news that they would all be quarantined had spread amongst the crew. What would we do if they resisted Fleming's decree? I wished I had brought my pistol.

As I came closer, though, I saw that the exclamation was due to something the sailors had found in the lifeboat. They were all peering into the hull, along with McCree, who had turned even paler than he had a moment before. When I came up beside him I saw why.

Lying in the curve of the lifeboat was a creature only glimpsed in books or nightmares. Its flesh was fish-belly white, shimmering with a crust of salt, and clung to the ribs of the vessel like a mollusk tethered to its shell. Seaweed and shells wreathed its form so densely I could not make out whether its lower body was split into two limbs or, as I think we all were wondering, culminated in a fish's tail. Let me be plain. In that instant I believed, as I think all the men beside me did, that we were looking at a mermaid.

"No wonder the ship ran afoul of bad luck with that unnatural creature aboard us," one of the sailors said, spitting on the deck. They all crossed themselves except McCree, who looked as if he had been enspelled by the creature as Odysseus's crew were bewitched by the sirens. "Is she . . . alive?" he asked in a faltering voice.

I had hardly thought to imagine it possible, or to think of the creature as a "she," but recalling then my role as a man of science I reached into the vessel and lay my fingers on the carotid artery to check for a pulse. The creature's eyes flashed open.

Aquamarine glittered between seaweed-dark lashes. I imagined her veins must run with seawater—

She stirred, two legs emerging from the nest of seaweed, and the spell was broken. She was a woman, alive—although barely, as indicated by the faintness of her pulse—naked and half-starved.

"Give me some water!" I demanded.

The creature—the woman—continued to stare up at me as a sailor brought me my canteen. I poured a few drops between her cracked, salt-crusted lips.

"We've found one of your passengers in a lifeboat," I said to the captain, who'd come up from the hold with Fleming. "She's half-starved and dehydrated but not feverish."

The captain shook his head. "We had no passenger who looked like her," he said. "She must be a stowaway."

"I believe I recognize the poor creature," McCree said. "Some connections of hers were tenants on Lord Dunleavy's estate. The girl was sent away to the workhouse for some indiscretion—" He looked away, embarrassed, I supposed, to divulge the girl's history amongst such rough men. "She must have run away and stolen aboard while the ship was in port. But how did she survive for five weeks at sea without food?"

"She must have brought food and water," Fleming said, "but then run out. She's so wasted away I doubt she'll live."

"I'll see to her," Dunstan McCree offered, "to ease her passing."

"I think we might give her a chance to see if she lives first," I said.

"Whatever course you take," Fleming said, "the girl must be removed. We need this boat."

"It will be easier," McCree suggested, "if we lower the boat with her in it. Let me go down with her; I don't weigh much."

Since this seemed sensible, for both the girl and McCree, whose limp might make it difficult to climb the rope ladder, the man climbed aboard and the sailors lifted the boat and lowered it over the side. I watched their progress until Dr. Fleming commanded me to organize the passengers into the boat on the other side of the vessel.

"We'll bring the fever patients in the first boat and then the rest of the crew and the patients without fever in the second. I've allowed the captain to keep a few men behind to man the ship but have given strict orders that they not sail until I give the order to release them."

I could see that Dr. Fleming had been rattled by his tussle with the captain and was anxious to assert his authority. I quickly began shepherding the passengers onto the lifeboats—many tugging at my sleeve, begging for water, asking if this was Quebec or would these little boats be taking us there, when I heard a cry from the other side and a loud splash. Running to the railing I observed that the boat was empty and Dunstan McCree was clinging to its side. The mermaid girl was nowhere to be seen.

Without thinking, I dove into the water. The cold slammed the breath out of me. When I opened my eyes, I was in a world of darkness—death, I thought, this is what death will feel like— but then I saw a glimmer of light and something white. It was the girl drifting downward in her wreath of seaweed. I dove for her and grasped her round the waist. Her eyes opened and stared into mine and for a moment I was so transfixed that I believe I forgot we were underwater and we both began to sink.

But then I came to myself and stroked upward. When we broke the surface we both gasped at the same time, eager for the air. A sailor helped us into the lifeboat, where Dunstan McCree was already aboard, huddling and shivering, looking so miserable

I left off asking him what had happened for now. We needed to get the poor girl somewhere warm lest she take a chill in her weakened state. I ordered the sailor to row for the island directly without waiting for the other passengers. "You can come back for them," I told him. "We must get her to shelter."

I must have conveyed my desperation because he obeyed me. He rowed for the island, which soon appeared through the mist. The girl shivered in my arms and clung to me. I admit that I, too, felt cold at the sight of the place—the massive granite boulders staring out to sea like the faces of pagan gods, the way the fog ringed the shore as if guarding it from invaders. It felt as if we were arriving on the shores of the Underworld. Even the nuns waiting for us on the shore looked like ancient priestesses of the dead in their gray robes.

At least they were most efficient priestesses. They bundled the mermaid-girl, as I'd begun to think of her, off to the infirmary and tried to do the same with me even as I explained that I was a doctor. They looked skeptical until Dr. Fleming arrived with the second boat and ordered me to stop "mooning about the woman" and get to work.

The rest of the day was taken up in sorting the patients into those with fever and those who were merely starving to death. The former were relegated to a long barn-like building behind the hospital, while the latter were placed in wards in the main hospital. I made sure the mermaid was placed in the hospital as she showed no signs of fever.

I had no opportunity of looking in on her, though, as I was kept constantly on my feet, carrying patients from the dock to the wards. Acting as a pack mule was not what I had imagined doing with my medical training, but I found I enjoyed the physical exertion and it gained me, I think, some grudging

respect from the nuns, who never seemed to tire or show any fear
of handling the fever patients. They belonged, I learned, to a
Canadian order called "the Gray Nuns" and dedicated their lives
to serving the sick and the poor.

We worked well into the night by the light of lanterns and
tallow candles. In the end there were thirty-two patients in the
fever ward, and twenty-three in the hospital. The crew members
who had not remained on board the *Stella Maris* chose to camp
out in the woods so they might hunt for fresh meat in the
morning. Dr. Fleming engaged one of the sailors to ferry him
back to St. Andrews so he could make his report to the Board of
Health and to arrange for supplies. He offered to take me back
with him, but I declined, saying I wanted to familiarize myself
with the patients and the routines of the hospital.

I watched his boat vanish into the fog and then turned to
leave the dock. There, hovering in the shadows of the pines, as if
he'd been waiting for me, was Dunstan McCree. "Dr. Harper," he
hailed me. "I wanted to make sure you had not taken a chill from
your dunk in the water today. I would never forgive myself if I
was the cause of you taking ill."

"Doesn't your Catholic faith offer a path to forgiveness?"
I asked, only trying to jolly the man out of his gloom, but he
looked as if I had insulted him.

"God may forgive our sins," he replied dourly, "but that does
not mean a man shouldn't hold himself accountable for his
mistakes. As I told you, I knew Liadan—"

"Liadan?" I repeated.

"That is the girl's name—a pagan name and one with an
unfortunate story attached that may have set the poor girl
on the wrong path to begin with. I didn't want to say in front
of the others, but I recall now that there was some story of

loose behavior connected to her. I should have anticipated her desperation and restrained her from leaping over the side."

"She leapt over?" I asked, incredulous. "But she could barely move. And why would she do such a thing after clinging to life for the whole journey?"

"Perhaps the sins of her past life weigh heavily upon her. I'm only glad that you were able to rescue her; you saved not only her mortal body but her immortal soul. Imagine if she had died a suicide in such a place." He let his eyes drift over the rugged coastline and those implacable stone faces staring out to sea. "There is a taint of evil here."

I was surprised to hear a seemingly intelligent man indulge in superstition, but I have often heard that the Irish are a superstitious lot. "The only evil," I told him, "is the treatment of your fellow passengers. When we leave here I hope you'll accompany me to the shipping authorities to lodge a complaint. Such unscrupulous men will not go unpunished in this country."

"Of course," he conceded, bowing his head. "No one is more fervid to see justice done than I, Dr. Harper."

I excused myself then to make my way uphill to the hospital. I was troubled by what McCree had insinuated about the girl . . . Liadan. I repeated the name to myself as I walked up the hill. It was a strange name, but one that seemed to suit her.

I climbed the stairs to the hospital and entered the long ward where, at the very end, I found her beside a window, eyes closed, long black hair lying on either side of her face, skin as white as the bedclothes. I sat down in a chair beside her and took out this notebook, which I'd brought to take notes of the medical procedures I observed and, as my father suggested on the flyleaf, fill with "worthy deeds," and began this account. I have written late into the night, this one day seeming fuller than all the years before it.

I thought about what the oarsman said about the souls of the survivors being drawn back to the island to be devoured by those they had consumed and about what Dunstan McCree had said about the island being evil. When I closed my eyes, I was underwater with Liadan, her arms around me, her flesh pressed to my flesh, her eyes locked on mine . . .

Had I imagined that for a moment I had felt her pulling us both down to the bottom of the sea?

Had I imagined that for a moment I had done nothing to stop her?

CHAPTER TEN

WHEN I RAISE MY HEAD FROM THE JOURNAL I HALF EXPECT TO SEE THE girl Liadan lying before me, so thoroughly have I lost myself in Nathaniel Harper's world. Before I lose that sense of being transported, I open up my notebook and begin to write—notes at first, lists of characters and questions, stray phrases from the journal—and then, at some point I find myself writing bits of dialogue in the characters' voices and even a whole passage in Liadan's voice—a voice that Nathaniel hasn't even heard yet.

The next time I look up, I see by the length of the shadows crossing the floor and the flush of pink in the clouds drifting past the tower windows that it is almost evening. Voices and the clink of glasses rise from the porch; it must be cocktail hour. I flip through the pages of my notebook and see that I've filled more than a dozen of them. The present world feels as distant as it had when I awoke in the hospital all those years ago, as though I'm stuck with Nathaniel Harper at Liadan's bedside.

I open my laptop, sign on to the Wi-Fi, and pull up a browser. The news service set as my homepage blares reports of rising case numbers, death tolls, food shortages, political unrest, and riots. I remind myself that it was the same last time, but Reed is right: this looks like it's going to be worse than last time. I open the web browser and type in a search term unlikely to generate more bad news.

Liadan.

My search takes me first to a baby name site that tells me Liadan translates from the Gaelic as "gray lady." Could that be the origin of the story Mac told about the Gray Lady who appears on the cliff and foreshadows death? Or perhaps that story comes from the Gray Nuns in their long gray habits who tended to the sick during the quarantine. The baby name site also tells me that Liadan was a ninth-century poetess who became a nun, but then missed her lover Cuirithir so much she died of grief. That must be the "unfortunate story" Dunstan McCree referred to. What had happened to Liadan, I wonder, that made her so desperate to stow away on a ship and spend five weeks hidden inside a lifeboat without food or water? And why, after surviving that, would she try to end her own life?

I reread the last two lines of Nathaniel's entry.

Had I imagined that for a moment I had felt her pulling us both down to the bottom of the sea?

Had I imagined that for a moment I had done nothing to stop her?

I shiver, picturing the doctor and the mermaid entwined beneath the sea, encircled by seaweed and long black hair. Then I picture the banshee of my nightmare, her sharp green nails tapping at the car window—

A sharp knock startles me. I look toward the window, afraid I'll see that bloated face floating outside the tower, but there are only innocent pink clouds in the evening sky. The sound comes from the door, which creaks open a few inches to allow Reed to poke his head in.

"I just wanted to see if you were okay . . ." His eyes scan the desk and catch on the leather journal.

"Yeah, I'm great. I've been reading Nathaniel Harper's journal and I kind of got lost in it."

He stares at the book blankly as if *he* were the one who has gotten lost. "Where did you get that?"

"It was right here," I say, pointing to the bookshelf. Then I remember how upset he'd been at the idea of me reading the journal. "You don't have to worry. I'm not going to freak out the way I did in college after that séance. That was a long time ago. I have a feeling that this is what's going to help me write my next book. I'll be really careful with it. I know it's a valuable family heirloom."

"I don't care about that," he says, his face reddening as he picks up the book. He hates any suggestion that he cares about his family pedigree. "I thought it had gotten lost—" Sand sifts out of the pages and a few rose petals like the ones that had been in his note this morning. "I'm just not sure you should read it . . . I remember that some of it is disturbing."

"I can handle it," I tell him. "And I think this is *it*. I've got an idea, and I've already started taking notes—" The red in his face deepens and I realize that he's remembering all the times I've said that over the past decade: *Now I've got an idea I can write about. This time it's for real*. "Really," I assure him. "I'll be fine. In fact, I'm just going to make a few more notes. Why don't you go on down? It sounds like everyone's on the porch having drinks."

He nods again and moves toward the door.

"Reed?" I call him back.

He turns and I hold out my hand. "Can I have the journal back?"

He hesitates. "I just don't understand why you'd want to read about people dying almost two hundred years ago. Haven't we had enough of that in our lifetime?"

It's what a lot of people said last time—*Why dwell on a bad time? It's time to move on*—but some of us, I suspect, have a harder time than others moving on.

"Maybe it will help me understand what happened to us all," I say, reaching for the book. "And that understanding will lead to healing."

He lets me take it without further argument, but I can see in his eyes that he doesn't think much of my chances to achieve either understanding or healing.

THE PARTY HAS moved indoors by the time I arrive downstairs. "Mosquitoes," Ada says, handing me a frosty glass. "We're going to make citronella candles tomorrow."

"And then we're going to crochet our own mosquito nets," Niko adds with a dramatic eye roll. She's smiling, though, and looks happy, a sprinkle of unlikely freckles across her face and flashes of red in her spiky dark hair. Everyone looks happy and rosy at the table; even dour Crosby looks less worried as he takes a long pull on his beer. Maybe it's the alcohol, or the peace of the island, or the delicious food that Ada has prepared. We pass plates and tuck in, everyone sharing their adventures from the day as we eat.

"Seriously, though," Niko says, when the mosquitoes come up again toward the end of dinner. "Did anyone bring real bug spray? Liz brought all this natural crap that basically attracted the fuckers to me today."

"I stocked up on the industrial-strength kind that gives you cancer and destroys the environment," Mac says. "You need it if you're going to hike in these woods."

"Great," Niko replies, grinning. "It's okay out on the rocks in the breeze but once you're in the woods the bastards eat you alive. Especially in the bog."

"You were in the bog?" Reed asks, looking worried.

"I got some great shots of dead trees. They look like hands reaching up out of the muck."

"You have to be careful," Reed says. "There are sinkholes—"

"No kidding," Niko says, still grinning. "I made one wrong step and got stuck up to my kneecaps."

"I want to get out for a walk tomorrow!" Ada cries, as if getting caught in muck and being eaten alive by insects sounds like terrific fun.

"If you lost your footing and fell—" Crosby begins.

"I'll stay on the buoy paths," she says. "Liz made copies of the Hundred Akers map."

"I'll go with you for a walk tomorrow," I say, and then add in a whisper, "So Crosby doesn't worry."

She rolls her eyes. "Don't you want to write, though? You must have gotten really in the zone. I haven't seen you down here all day."

"Crap! I told you I'd help cook tonight, didn't I? I'm so sorry—"

"No worries," she says. "I'm just glad the writing was going well."

"*Did* you get a lot of writing done?" Liz asks.

"Some," I say, trying not to sound overly confident. "Mostly I took notes. I started reading Nathaniel Harper's journal. I found it in the study"—I look toward Reed but he is carefully removing bones from his halibut—"and it's fascinating. Do you know that the great room was a ward? They kept the patients who didn't have fever here to separate them from the typhus cases in the barn. Reed's ancestor Nathaniel sounds like a very sincere and brave man. When one of the passengers fell into the water he dived in to save her."

I tell them the story, describing how Liadan looked like a mermaid, but leaving out Dunstan McCree's insinuations about her character and that Nathaniel almost let himself drown with her, finishing instead with Nathaniel keeping vigil at Liadan's bed.

"So, it's a love story," Ada says.

"A weird kind of love story," Niko says, "if Nathaniel really abandoned her."

"Ada's got a weird idea of what constitutes a love story," Crosby says. "*Wuthering Heights* is her favorite romance."

"I do love Cathy and Heathcliff," Ada says.

I remember Ada reading the book late at night and saying *I want to be like Cathy, so in love with Heathcliff she is Heathcliff.* Watching Crosby stroke his goatee I wonder if that's how she feels about him, but I can't quite imagine it. I'd been surprised when Ada first introduced me to Crosby a year after college when we could finally all see each other again. He didn't really seem like her type—more like the pretentious hipsters she'd mocked in college—but then, the pandemic had thrown together a lot of unlikely couples forced into sheltering together. When she married him—just a month after Reed and I got married—I even wondered if she hadn't rushed into marriage because so many of our classmates were getting married, but I dismissed the thought as ungenerous. Who ever really saw inside another person's relationship, anyway?

"We don't know for sure that Nathaniel abandoned Liadan," I say now. "I'll just have to see if I can figure it out from his journal."

"Or you can change the ending to suit yourself," Ada says, giving me a sympathetic smile. "After all, you're writing fiction."

I INSIST ON doing the dishes to make up for not helping with cooking. Crosby offers to give me a hand, and Liz suggests we draw up a chore schedule. While I scrub crusty pots and pans—Ada seems to have used every single one in the kitchen—and Crosby dries, Liz designs a color-coded chart on a blackboard. We have a brief spat on gender stereotyping when it turns out only Ada and I want to cook and clean, while Reed, Mac, and Crosby all want to do "maintenance duty."

"Mac and I are the only ones who know how to work the machinery that runs the island," Reed says.

"That's a problem right there," Crosby says. "What if something happened to you two? We should all know how that stuff works."

"Sure," Mac says, "we'll conduct weekly tutorials and you're welcome to tag along, man, but there's really no substitute for a lifetime's worth of experience. So, keep that in mind"—he waves his beer bottle (his sixth or seventh for the night, I reckon)—"if any of you college grads are thinking of knocking me off."

"That's Lucy's department," Ada says, winking at me. "She's going to kill us all off in her book."

"I guess that means you won't want me cooking," I say with a wink, although that's not the kind of book I'm planning to write at all. "I don't mind doing cleanup."

"And Niko and I are going to put in a garden at the barn," Liz says, ignoring the joke.

"So that just leaves Crosby," Ada says.

"Garbage detail, man," Mac says, pulling a bulging bag out of the trash can. "Allow me to show you to the garbage shed. Once a week we gotta haul it to the dump on the mainland."

"There's one more thing," Reed says as everyone begins to leave.

"Not another social media rule," Niko groans, then, with wide, innocent eyes, says, "I swear I didn't mean to post that 'Greetings from Fever Island' pic."

Reed goes on as if she hadn't spoken. "It's about the water. So far we're in good shape. We've had a wet spring and the well levels look good. But if we have a dry spell we'll have to conserve, so we might as well start getting used to a few basic practices: One, don't run the water while doing dishes; two, take military-style showers—"

"What the—" Crosby begins.

"That means get wet, turn the shower off while you soap up, then rinse; and three, don't flush—"

"'If it's yellow, let it mellow,'" Niko recites gleefully, "'if it's brown, send it down.'"

There's a chorus of good-natured moans as everyone leaves. Ada hugs me and promises we'll take a walk together tomorrow. Crosby, carrying the heavy bag of garbage, follows Mac to the garbage shed and Reed goes along to check on the pump, which is apparently in the same shed. I stay downstairs straightening up the great room. I don't really mind being in charge of cleanup, I think, as I plump pillows and wipe glass rings off the tables, it makes me feel more as if this is really my home. Even the photographs of Harper ancestors no longer seem so intimidating. I pause in front of the group photograph from 1848 and peer at the face of the young doctor, Nathaniel Reed Harper. He looks so young, just out of medical school, a naive innocent with good intentions but no experience of the real world. He certainly had no preparation for dealing with a typhus epidemic. In this photograph he looks confident, happy, even. What went wrong? What could possibly have made him abandon his patients, including Liadan, on the island? There must be some explanation.

I switch my gaze to the young woman by his side, noticing the abundant hair piled atop her head, the sharpness of her eyes beneath thick lashes, and the amused set of her lips. This must be Liadan. The other women are dressed in the long gray robes and black wimples of the Gray Nuns. I guess that the thin black-coated man standing stiffly a few feet away from the rest of the group must be Dunstan McCree, the estate agent. The rest are rough-looking men in sailor's shirts and canvas jackets. Where did they come from? I wonder. Looking back at the dark-haired girl I feel strongly that she is Liadan, that she got well—after all, she didn't have typhus, only the side effects of starvation—and volunteered to help at the hospital.

The truth lies in Nathaniel Harper's journal, which I have in the pocket of my sweatshirt for safekeeping. For now, though, I'm content to gaze at the face in the photograph and imagine her waking up to find the handsome doctor sitting by her bed, just as I awoke in my dorm room to find Reed come back for me. Who wouldn't fall in love with the man who pulled them out of that darkness?

I shiver and chafe my arms to ward off the chill. The cold is coming from an open window at the far end of the room, and I go over to close it. The curtains billow toward me, like the sails of a ship filling up, and enfold me, heavy canvas brushing against my face—

Like the canvas shrouds for the dead laid out on the deck of the *Stella Maris*.

I tug the curtains shut and hear something tear. A corner has gotten stuck on a piece of broken molding. I kneel to release it and notice that there's a pattern in the wood, sinuous curves that interlock in the same pattern as the one carved into the stag head, and the same design on the bracelet Reed used to wear. A Celtic knot. Someone carved it here—Reed, maybe, or Liz. Or Becky.

Then I realize where I am: the far corner of the great room beneath a window facing the lilac bushes. This must be where Liadan's bed was. I look closer at the ancient Celtic symbol and notice that there are words carved into the wood beneath it. Most of them are in a language I don't know, but two names are clear. I recognize them from the story I read on the internet—*Liadan and Cuirithir*.

CHAPTER ELEVEN

BEFORE I GO TO SLEEP I FIND A TRANSLATION APP ONLINE AND TYPE IN the words scratched on the wall. They are, as I guessed, Gaelic and they translate to:

I am Liadan
who loved Cuirithir.
It is true as they say.

A little research reveals that the lines come from a poem that tells the story of Liadan, the ninth-century poetess who falls in love with a poet named Cuirithir, but rejects his offer of marriage and becomes a nun. Later she regrets her choice and goes to see Cuirithir, but he has become a priest by then and, to avoid temptation, takes off in a boat before she arrives.

Did Liadan scratch the words on the wall, I wonder, because she had fallen in love with Nathaniel Harper, who then abandoned her and sailed away from the island? I write some notes in my notebook, imagining how Liadan's story will fill out Nathaniel's and wondering how much Nathaniel will learn about her and how much I will have to make up. I can barely wait to read the next part of the journal.

When Reed gets up in the morning, I go downstairs with him to get coffee and a muffin, telling Ada that I'll come back later to clean up the breakfast dishes and take a walk with her. When I open the door to the study the curtains suck in and out with a quick gasp, as if the room is as excited to see me as I am to be there. I sit down at the desk, lay the journal down on the blotter, and open it up.

June 21, 1848

I am afraid I have already disappointed my father's expectation that I will fill these pages with the daily record of my "many worthy deeds." Most nights I simply collapse on my cot in the tower room, where I sleep so I can easily be summoned if I am needed. The fever ward grows daily, while the "hunger ward," as Mother Brigitte calls our patients who are merely suffering from starvation—diminishes. A few of our hunger ward patients have recovered, but most succumbed to the fever within a day or two of disembarking. The sailors who were stranded when the captain and the rest of the crew of the *Stella Maris* sailed off the next morning despite Dr. Fleming's orders have set up camp in the woods to avoid contagion. Fleming has wired on to Quebec to notify the authorities of the unlawful departure of the *Stella Maris* but, he confided to me, the station at Grosse Ile was no doubt too overwhelmed to attend to one runaway ship. The sailors who did not succumb to the fever have seemingly taken their desertion in stride and have built a camp of sorts on an inlet on the northeast side of the island where there is an abundance of sea fowl to shoot and fish to net. Dunstan McCree, who was also left behind by the *Stella Maris,* goes daily to collect the bounty of their hunt and bring it back to the hospital. As I supposed, he has much influence with the passengers who were tenants of the estate he managed and holds himself responsible for their welfare.

"It's unusual," Mother Brigitte confided in me the other day. "I heard tales from the Irish emigrants I tended last year in

Montreal of the most heinous treatment of the Irish tenants by their landlords and their agents. Rather than help the souls who depended on them when the failure of the potato crop made the peasantry destitute, the landlords made quick work to divest themselves of those poor souls by sending them on ships abroad."

"Surely they only meant to help by offering them a better life in a new country," I replied. "What else could they have done?"

Mother Brigitte looked askance at me. "Fed them," she replied.

Dr. Fleming, who happened to be nearby eavesdropping on our conversation, interjected, "My dear woman, you don't know what you're talking about. Any relief program would have caused irreparable harm to the natural order of free trade and caused the poor to become more dependent on aid that could not be sustained. It is better to leave such matters alone—and for you to leave them to those who know how to handle them."

Mother Brigitte's lips thinned, but she did not speak until Dr. Fleming had gone, when she muttered to me, "The good doctor is apparently a believer in Monsieur Legendre's philosophy of laissez-faire, which has about as much substance to it as the miasmata he is so fond of."

I had to refrain from laughing. Mother Brigitte, who tended the sick during the cholera epidemic of 1832, is remarkably forward-thinking in her ideas about preventing the spread of sickness—more so than Dr. Fleming, I must say. She has set up a washing station in the clearing between the hospital and the fever ward where water from the well is heated and all of us—nuns and doctors alike—are expected to wash our hands each time we pass from one ward to the other. At the end of the day, we shed our clothes in changing rooms that have been hastily assembled from stripped saplings and canvas curtains.

Our clothes are boiled while we scrub our persons. The sisters all wait until I am done each evening, affording me a modicum of privacy. At least I thought so until I realized that the canvas screens behind which I bathed offered no protection from the loft of the fever ward where the nuns sleep. I discovered this one night as I sat here in my tower room and heard two sisters discussing the merits of my physiognomy. I was shocked to learn that nuns could be so immodest in their talk, but then I have found out that many have only recently entered the order and that all of them are used to going out into the world and caring for the most destitute and desperate—experiences that leave them with little time or patience for obfuscation or reticence. (Their verdict, by the way, was that I could do with some fattening up.)

I won't fatten here, I'm afraid. Even if there were time to finish our scant meals of porridge, watery broth, and biscuit, I can barely take a mouthful without feeling I am taking it from the mouths of those more in need than I.

Liadan, for instance.

Liadan is one of the few who have remained in the hunger ward. She has not succumbed to the fever, perhaps because she was isolated in the lifeboat and not down below in the hold. Still her recovery is slow. For the first day she would not take anything but water.

"Her throat muscles have grown unused to swallowing food," Mother Brigitte observed.

What I observed, though, was that she seemed nervous around nuns, perhaps because they ran the workhouse where she had been remanded, and the men from the estate, perhaps because she feared they knew her ignominious history. Since I was neither in clerical garb, nor represented any unpleasant past associations, I took it upon myself to bring her meals and urge her to take a few more spoonfuls of broth or porridge. It has been restful, too, to sit at the end of the hunger ward by the window with the scent of lilac and wild roses sweetening the air and chasing away the foul odors of the fever.

Do I sound like a romantic?

If so, I'm not the only one here who regards Liadan as an object of romantic interest. The Irish passengers, the remaining crew of the *Stella Maris*, even the Gray Nuns, are all drawn into the mystery of how she survived the crossing on a bed of seaweed without food or water. The Gray Nuns have begun to speak of her as a miracle. I see them shyly creeping to her bedside when she's asleep to steal a look at her and touch the hem of her nightgown. Sometimes they leave a posy of lilacs or a stub of candle lit in a saucer. Some of the passengers leave offerings too—sprinklings of salt, shells gathered from the shore, seagrasses tied in curious knots.

"Pagan superstition," Dr. Fleming mutters when he comes across the simple gifts.

But still the patients and the nuns continue to come and leave their offerings. One young nun in particular sits by her bed often, always leaving some token behind. When I asked Mother Brigitte about her she told me that the girl, Mairi, was a novice who had herself come on one of the ships from Ireland last year. "Perhaps," Mother Brigitte hypothesized, "she recognizes Liadan from the estate where her people were tenants."

When I asked Mairi if this were true, she told me that she had never seen Liadan before. She said, though, that she believed she was a selkie—a kind of fairy that can shed its skin and walk on land as a woman—who had been sent as a comfort for the loss of Mairi's family, who had died at sea.

"Did they die on the crossing?" I asked, afraid that the poor girl had been addled by her loss.

"So to speak, sir, although they had not gotten very far. They were on a ship that left before me. There wasn't enough money to pay for the passage for all of us so I decided to wait for the next ship and give my spot to my little brother, who was too young to be separated from our parents. Their ship had barely left port before it sank to the bottom, drowning all aboard it. It was a terrible thing to see, sir, and worse when we learned that the agent who had procured the passage knew the ship was old and unsound. They're terrible men, the landlords and their agents. I have felt since that it was me who was supposed to drown in my brother's place, and I believe Liadan has been sent to carry me tidings from my family below the sea."

Little Mairi may have to wait a long time for any such tidings, as Liadan lies still and silent as a stone. She has yet to speak. I wonder if she can.

Today, Dr. Fleming said she is a distraction. He said he's seen freakish fancies such as these take hold of quarantine stations. "Superstitions spread as promiscuously as the pox," he opined tonight at an assembly of the staff. "We must stamp it out to preserve decorum. It's high time the lass be sent on to St. Andrews, and hence to Quebec, along with all the other recovered patients, where the Canadian government has made provisions for the emigrants."

"The government is sending the emigrants on steamers whether they have fever or not," Mother Brigitte said. "Most are dead before they arrive and all that awaits the survivors is the poorhouse or starvation on the streets. A young woman like Liadan won't last a week."

"Surely she could remain here a little longer," I argued.

Dr. Fleming said that I had allowed my emotions to compromise my professional objectivity. "They will leave in the morning," he concluded. "I will personally accompany her to St. Andrews."

I came up here to my tower room, unable to trust myself not to express my anger to Dr. Fleming. I felt as if I were burning with anger. In fact, I felt overheated, as if the argument had lit a fever in me. I will wait until the morning when I am calmer and make one more attempt to dissuade him from his course. Mother Brigitte remarked as I was leaving that it is the summer solstice, the shortest night of the year. I am determined to sit vigil and wait for the light and then try to change Dr. Fleming's mind.

July 20, 1848

A month has passed since my last entry, but much has happened during that time to cause my delay in writing. I had intended to stay awake the night of the summer solstice so that I could approach Dr. Fleming at first light, but I must have fallen asleep on my watch. I woke to a smell of something burning. I was afraid that the house had caught fire from all those candles the nuns are always leaving about, but when I went to the window I saw that there was a fire in the clearing between the hospital and the fever ward. I conjectured that perhaps one of the nuns had left a candle burning on a ledge of the bathing huts. It was a dry night and windy. I was afraid that if the sparks blew toward the house or the fever ward the buildings could catch; if they blew toward the woods the whole island could burn.

I ran downstairs, through the back door, and out into the clearing where a great bonfire had been built. Sparks flew up into the night sky, dazzling my eyes, which already stung from the smoke. Through the haze I made out figures moving in and out of the flames and for a horrible moment I thought it was the fever patients—that the fever had at last burned so fiercely that they had burst into a spontaneous combustion of flesh and spirit. Feeling the heat on my face, I felt like I, too, would soon combust.

Then I saw that the figures were dancing around the fire, holding candles and weaving around each other so that it looked as if they were dancing with the fire itself. I recognized some of the women I had tended in the fever ward, and I realized that these were the Irish patients practicing some sort of pagan ritual. Fleming had been right, I had to concede; fever patients were susceptible to dangerous fancies. And yet I also couldn't help feeling that he had fanned the flames by banishing Liadan. I saw, though, that it had to be stopped. I was afraid that in their frenzy the women would burn down the whole island.

I stepped back, meaning to go to the well for a bucket of water to douse the flames, and bumped into one of the onlookers. To my surprise I saw that it was Dunstan McCree.

"Why are you doing nothing to stop this?" I asked.

He smiled at me, his face glowing in the firelight with a fervor that made me think he might have succumbed to the fever. "I might as well try to stop the sun and the moon from turning in their orbits. The people have burned fires on the night of the summer solstice since before the birth of our Savior."

"But surely you don't condone such pagan practices?"

"Sometimes it's easier to bend than to break," he replied, "as our early church fathers found when they celebrated St. John's Eve on or near the solstice to commemorate the birth of St. John the Baptist, who was a burning and shining light and the torchbearer for the way of Christ."

He nodded toward the fire, where the women were adding
sticks to the pyre and then drawing them out, holding them up
alit, and waving them in the air so that they drew arcs of fire like
shooting stars. Together they seemed to braid a plait of fire that
circled the bonfire as if to seal in the fire. Then the women began
to sing a high keening song in a language I did not know but that
raised the hair on the back of my neck. Some of the women, I
noticed, were of the Gray Nuns—I saw young Mairi amongst
them—and Mother Brigitte herself stood on the periphery with
a grim but resigned expression.

"If we cannot stop it then we must keep watch to make sure
the fire does not spread," I said.

"That is part of the tradition as well," he replied, "to stand
vigil over the bone fire."

He moved away then to mingle with the women. He weaved in
and out, in his peculiar halting gait, so that he seemed to be part
of their dance. As I followed his progress I felt as if I, too, were
being braided into the pattern of the women's steps. I believe I
had begun to sway to the rhythm of the strange song when my
trance was broken by a loud shout.

Dr. Fleming ran into the clearing, dressed only in his
nightshirt, his face bright red in the firelight, screaming, "Put it
out, you fools, put it out!" When he saw me he yelled, "What are
you doing standing there, boy? Fetch water from the well to put
out this infernal blaze!"

I bestirred myself to go to the well, but a scream from one of
the women stopped me. To my horror, I saw that it was Mairi.
Dr. Fleming must have reached for her arm to wrest away her
torch but the cuff of his nightshirt had caught on fire. He was
waving his arm around, fanning the flames, which raced up his
sleeve to engulf his chest. I ran toward him, meaning to knock

him to the ground, but the dancers were in my way. I dodged and
wove between them as Fleming, too, thrashed around the circle,
the women screaming and darting away from him. At last, it was
Mother Brigitte who doused the doctor with a bucket of water
and muffled the last of the flames in her own robes.

She and I—with two of the Gray Nuns—carried him into the
hunger ward, Mother Brigitte barking orders for salve and linens
and shears. We lay him out on a cot, restraining him with some
difficulty as Mother Brigitte cut away the charred cloth of his
nightshirt.

Or was it skin? I wondered, beginning to feel myself growing
faint.

A cool hand placed a dollop of sweet-smelling salve in my
hand and showed me how to apply it to the burned flesh. Mother
Brigitte called for laudanum, directing one of the sisters to drip
it into Fleming's mouth. At least, I thought, the fire had not
reached his face, although it was red and inflamed and his eyes
rolled in their sockets like marbles. One nun wiped his brow with
a damp cloth while the other smoothed the sweet-smelling salve
across his burnt flesh—

For a moment I felt myself rise up out of my body and drift to
the ceiling, as weightless as the embers that had flown above the
bonfire. From my new vantage point I could see the Gray Nuns
surrounding Fleming's body. They looked like a flock of gray
mourning doves pecking at his raw flesh—

Then I was lying on the floor, all light extinguished.

When I opened my eyes, I was in a cot in the fever ward and
Liadan sat in a chair beside me. We had changed places. My
throat felt scorched; my flesh, seared. In my delirium I thought
that I was the one who had caught on fire, but of course I know
now that I had caught the fever. Liadan tended me through the

delusions of fever. Sometimes I thought I was dead, sometimes I thought I was lying in a boat, rocked by the surf. Sometimes the air turned green around me and I believed I was at the bottom of the sea. I drowned over and over again and was tumbled in the surf like a wave-tossed stone. I felt as if my flesh had been flayed and my bones picked clean by the seagulls and bleached white in the sun. Always there was Liadan's face above me, waiting patiently for me to finish my transformation into whatever new shape the fever had in store for me, whether it be stone, bird, or bone.

Then one day I opened my eyes, and Mother Brigitte's face was above me.

"There you are," she said, as if I had made a long journey across the sea. "Are you strong enough to walk? There's something I want you to see."

I would have said no, I wasn't strong enough, but there was no saying no to Mother Brigitte. She helped me up and gave me a robe to wear and a stick to lean on. I felt about a hundred years old and also like a helpless infant. As we walked through the fever ward I saw patients I didn't recognize.

"There was another ship," she told me. "Worse than the first, but by the grace of God we've been able to save many."

"Dr. Fleming?" I asked.

She shook her head. "He lingered a few days and then died of his burns. We kept him as comfortable as possible."

"How have you managed?" I asked as she led me out to the clearing. I stopped at the sight of the clearing. A garden had been planted where the fire had been. Tomato plants stood three feet high, squash and cucumbers sprawled across the burnt earth. How long had I been sick?

"Without a doctor?" she finished for me. "Well enough,

Dr. Harper, but we'll be glad of your help now that you are better. We especially need your assistance in some matters concerning the Board of Health." She took me inside the house to the hunger ward. I was relieved to see that only half the beds were full. The room was clean and well aired with only the faintest breath of disease beneath the scent of lavender and rosemary. Several Gray Nuns moved from cot to cot, consulting placards tied to each bedstead and checking for signs of fever. One of the women came toward us. She was in gray but her head was uncovered, dark hair piled on top—

"Liadan." I whispered her name under my breath.

"Yes, Liadan has been a great help," Mother Brigitte said. "She had some experience assisting the nurses at the workhouse she was in and shows great promise of becoming a fine nurse herself. I wanted you to see how fortunate it was that she was not sent away."

"Yes," I agreed, "fortunate for me, certainly. She nursed me back to health."

"You'll undo all I've done," Liadan said as she reached us, "if you take things too fast. I think I should escort my patient back to his bed."

I allowed her to steer me out of the hunger ward and through the clearing, but she was stopped by one of the nuns who had a question about a patient. As I stood waiting I admired the garden, the lushness of the plants growing so quickly on burnt soil. I poked my walking stick into the rich, dark soil—and unearthed bits of charred wood. Remains of the bonfire—

I remembered that Dunstan McCree had called it something else as I unearthed a piece of wood that was white and splintery—

Not wood. It was bone. That's what McCree had called it—a bone fire.

CHAPTER TWELVE

WHEN I RAISE MY HEAD FROM NATHANIEL HARPER'S JOURNAL I CAN AL-most smell the smoke. I've been transported back to that summer solstice night in 1848 when the Irish passengers and Gray Nuns danced together around the bonfire.

The bone fire.

I open my laptop and look up *bonfire* and find that the word does, indeed, come from "bone fire" and goes back to ancient rituals of sacrifice. I shudder at the idea—and notice that the smell of smoke has grown sharper. I stand and walk to the window on the south-east side of the tower, following in Nathaniel Harper's footsteps the night he awoke to the smell of burning. When I look outside, I do see a fire in the clearing but no robed women dancers, only Liz and Niko standing around it, drinking beer. What, I wonder, are they burning?

Tucking the journal in my sweatshirt pocket I go downstairs and out the back door to find out. The fire, I see as I approach the clearing, is nowhere near as big as the bonfire Nathaniel Harper described, but I can still feel the heat of it fanning against my face as I get closer. How horrible it must have been for Dr. Fleming, I think, to feel the flames engulf his body.

Niko turns as I approach and salutes me with her beer bottle. "The writer emerges."

"What are you burning?" I ask.

"Dead things," Niko replies.

Liz slaps her arm. "Brush we cleared," Liz says. "And some junk that was cluttering up the barn."

"*And* dead things," Niko adds, holding up a scorched antler.

"Did you find any other bones?"

Liz and Niko exchange a look, then Liz says to me, "We haven't done much digging yet, but . . . how do you know about the bones?"

"Nathaniel Harper writes in his journal that the Irish fever patients and the nuns made a bonfire and that there were bones in it. *Did* you find any other bones?"

"Some deer skulls," Liz says. "We believe some rabbit and fox bones, too, although it's hard to know for sure. We found more that summer when Mac and his mother dug up the clearing to make a garden. We figured they were leftovers from a couple centuries' worth of venison and rabbit barbecues on the island. The skulls were cool so we kept them and used them for the Stags and Hags game. Like I told you."

"Did they have that knot design carved in them when you found them?" I ask.

Liz frowns and shakes her head. "Becky came up with that. She was into all that Celtic stuff that summer after spending the year in Ireland. And then Reed gave her that journal you're reading, and she said the Irish immigrants who came here were performing some kind of rites. There are carvings like that all over the island . . . I can show you," Liz offers.

"Now?" I ask.

"Why not?" She turns to Niko. "Can you look after the fire and try not to burn down the barn while we're gone?"

"Absolutely," Niko says, grinning. "I've got important shit in the barn. What about the house? Can I burn down the house?"

Liz rolls her eyes and starts walking toward the woods. Behind us I hear the fire crackle. I turn and see Niko adding armfuls of brush to it, her face orange and gleeful in the firelight. What would happen, I wonder, if there was a fire on the island? What would we do? When I step through the trees, though, my feet sink into the moss and the air settles on me like a wet blanket. Surely a place this wet couldn't burn.

It takes a moment for my eyes to adjust to the dim, shadowy woods and to make out Liz, camouflaged in earth tones ten feet down the path. I walk toward her, trying to avoid the wetter patches on the path, my canvas sneakers sinking through the moss into the mud below. I would have changed into hiking boots if I'd known I was going into the woods.

Liz waits until I reach her. She points to the buoy hanging over her head.

"Do you see the mark on it?"

I look up, shading my eyes from the sunlight piercing down through the pine trees, and make out the faded design—the same knot that was on the stag's skull and scratched onto the wall.

"Becky went over the whole island marking every buoy," Liz says. "It was part of the game—at least *at first* it was a game. She said the marks on the stones were spells, wards against the devil—or some shit like that—and she was reinforcing them. I don't know"—Liz waves her hand in front of her face to clear the gnats that cluster around us as soon as we stop—"sometimes I thought she just liked marking shit, that it was her way of making the island *hers*. She marked things that she thought belonged to her."

"You make her sound kind of possessive," I say, thinking that *crazy* might be more apt.

Liz stares at me for a moment and then smiles at me pityingly. "That would be a very reductive way of looking at Becky. The thing about Becky was that you wanted to be possessed by her. She made everything she touched more alive, including this island. Come on—" She turns to continue and I consider stopping her to say I'm not wearing the right shoes to slog through the woods but she's already too far ahead of me. Besides, I've wanted someone to tell me more about Becky. Who knows when Liz will feel like sharing information if I don't take advantage of this moment?

When I catch up to her, she's talking as if she'd assumed I'd been right behind her all along.

". . . was upset when my father said she couldn't come to the island. She was holed up at her parents' house on the mainland all alone because her parents got stuck in Florida when the lockdown began. My mother would have let her stay with us; my mother *loved* Becky . . . oh, sorry, you probably don't want to hear that, but yeah, Mom had gone to school with Becky's aunt and she thought Becky was perfect for Reed. She wanted to invite Becky to stay, but my father, who actually really disliked Becky's father because of some ancient disagreement over docking rights on the mainland, wouldn't have it. We all thought it was ridiculous that my father was so hardcore about the quarantine, especially by the summer when cases were dropping. Remember how we all thought it was gone by then?"

I nod, although the truth is that my memories of that summer are scattershot. After waking up in the hospital I seemed to have lost pieces of time from before I was sick, as if the darkness from my illness had bled around the edges, encroaching on the past. Or the virus had eaten part of my brain. Sometimes I'm afraid that it will keep eating into my memories until nothing is left. Liz doesn't need my agreement, though; she keeps walking and talking faster than I can catch up.

"My father used the quarantine as an excuse to cancel the parties he hated anyway and retreat deeper into the misanthropic bastard he'd always been bent on becoming. It was all about control for him, getting to call the shots, making Reed and me come back—"

"He made Reed come back?" I ask, wondering if this was a bit I'd forgotten or if Reed had never told me.

"Well . . ." She breaks a pine branch off and begins to strip it of its needles. The trees grow closer on either side of the path, hemming us in, so we have to walk single file. The air is still and heavy, the humidity settling over us like a wet blanket and eliminating the chill of the shadows. Liz lets the branches she pushes snap back so I have to hold up my arms to keep from being smacked in the face. "He had that plan to move to New York City with you and Ada, right? Weren't you all going to live in some dumpy fifth-floor walk-up and live out your boho dreams?"

This stings more than the slap of pine branches but I only reply, "That was the plan."

"Yeah, well, Tibs hated it. 'Harper men live in Boston, son,'" she says; her impersonation of her father makes my scalp itch. Or maybe it's the airless heat that is beginning to make me sweat. "Not New York City. I honestly think my father saw the pandemic as a chance to redirect Reed into law or medicine—the only acceptable professions for a Harper—and to change my sexual orientation, which he saw as a *phase*."

"You'd come out to your parents?"

She snorts. "I came out when I was sixteen because my mother tried to make me do the whole debutante thing. I said only if my date could be Shoshanna Greenleaf." She pauses and turns to me, a soft smile on her face. "Don't tell Niko I mentioned Shoshanna. She gets jealous even though Shoshanna is married—to a *man*—has three kids, and lives in Brookline. But yeah . . ." The smile vanishes and in the green pine-filtered light her face looks suddenly pale and drawn.

"Daddy said all the girls went through those silly crushes and I'd think better of leading that *lifestyle* if I wanted to see anything from my trust before I turned thirty."

"Really?" I ask, appalled. "He threatened to cut off your money because you're gay?"

She laughs at the look of horror on my face. "You have no idea what a monster—"

A sharp sound cuts her off, and she reels around to scan the woods. I do, too. But there's nothing but pine trees, their straight trunks arrayed like a standing army, as far as the eye can see. That word *monster* seems to echo in the silence.

"Must have been a deer," Liz says, turning to continue on the path, which doesn't look much like a path anymore, only a narrow track through increasingly dense woods. Liz is clearly, justifiably, upset at the recounting of her father's bullying, but hopefully she's been paying attention to where we're going. We seem to be heading into the heart of the island with its treacherous bogs and sinkholes. The ground has become wetter and spongier, my feet sinking deeper with each step, the mud seeping through my thin canvas shoes—

Then I spy one of the red buoys and a clearing in the trees and smell salt air. We come out onto a rocky cove, which I assume from Liz's map is Sea Witch Cove. I stand gulping mouthfuls of fresh air as the breeze evaporates the sweat off my brow and throat. My lungs feel as if they are filled with bog water.

Liz wipes her face with a bandanna and twists her long hair off her neck. I don't think I've ever seen Liz sweat—it only makes her look dewy—but I wonder if it's the humid woods or talking about her horrible father that's heated her up. "Come on, we have some bouldering ahead of us."

With my canvas shoes, I don't feel prepared to scramble over the enormous boulders that lie tumbled across the coastline like die cast

by a race of giants. But at first, it's not too hard. Liz knows where the
hand- and footholds are and most of the surfaces are smooth—and
beautiful. Each granite rock face has its own topography of speckled
colors—green, pink, white, and yellow—like Easter eggs. I'm transfixed by the colors and patterns and remember that Niko had said
the landscape out here was like the moon. It certainly does feel oth-
erworldly. Inside the cool deep pockets of the boulders you can't see
anything but curved stone walls. On the surface the sun warms the
rock, and there are shallow depressions holding seawater and small
tentacled sea creatures. Lobster shells and dried seaweed litter the
surfaces like detritus from some wild party.

"Seals," Liz says, pointing out to the water where black humpy
shapes dot the rocks off the shore. We've come around the south side
of the island and are now facing east, the Atlantic Ocean stretching
to the horizon. The wind here is steady and fierce. I can see why
Niko said that mosquitoes weren't a problem; nothing can withstand
this scouring wind. It feels as if it wants to wipe Liz and me off the
rock face. Even the stones here look as if they've been shaped by the
gale. The tall ones have been sculpted into windblown figures facing
east, out to sea, as if they are waiting for a ship to take them away.
The only sign of man out here are the ruins of the old lighthouse and
keeper's cottage.

"Is that the Sea Witch Cottage?" I ask, recalling the quaint picture on the map.

Liz barely glances at it. "Yes, but that's not what I want to show
you." She heads out across the boulders, nimbly leaping from one to
another, toward the shoreline. The waves crash over the slick rocks,
rushing in between them and spurting up geysers. I'm drenched by
the time I reach Liz, my hands scraped and bloody. She's standing
by a group of three tall stones that look like the megaliths of prehistoric Britain.

"Wow," I say, "it looks like something out of Stonehenge. Did someone put them here?"

Liz shakes her head. "No one knows. They were here when the first settlers came. This was where they buried the witch—" She points to a deep, narrow chasm between the stones. I inch forward to look down but she grabs my arm to hold me back. "Careful. The rock's slippery here because of the spring." I look up to see a thin trickle of water forming a path across the rock face, dropping into the chasm. Beneath the roar of the wind and the crash of the waves I can just make out the sound of something dripping far below and a low moan as if someone is trapped deep in the rock.

"What is that sound?" I ask. "It sounds like someone—"

"Weeping?" Liz asks. "It's just the wind blowing through underground caverns but the legend is that it's the witch cursing the island. They lowered her in here, headfirst, until she was hanging upside down, wedged into the rock. The water from the spring would have dripped into her mouth, keeping her alive so she would suffer longer."

"That's . . . *horrible*," I say, imagining the press of stone against my chest and the relentless drip.

"Yeah, well, *Puritans*. That's the stock I come from."

I wrench my eyes away from the dark gash in the rocks and look up at one of the standing stones. There's something carved on it, a faint pattern that looks like it's been all but worn away by centuries of wind and rain. At first I think it's another Celtic knot, but then I see that it's more like a flower inside a circle.

"It's a daisy wheel," Liz says, moving around the chasm so that she can lay her hand on the stone and trace the pattern. "It's a medieval apotropaic symbol; that means—"

"To ward off evil," I say, recalling a folklore class I took in college. "Like the evil eye. But a daisy?"

"It's a continuous pattern," she says, tracing the lines around and around. "The idea is that if a demon flies into it they get stuck following the pattern."

"Like a dream catcher," I say, remembering that Ada had hung one up in our dorm room during the pandemic, *to keep the virus out*, she had joked.

"Yeah, same idea. Becky said the Celtic knot worked the same way and that's why the Irish fever patients marked the island with it." She points to the other two rocks, and I see that there are Celtic knots carved into each one. "Becky thought the Irish passengers made those because they believed the devil was loose on the island."

"So, they thought the knots would keep him away?"

"Or to call him. Becky thought the Irish fever victims had begun to worship the devil and perform sacrifices to him."

Becky thought, Becky thought. I'm beginning to think that Reed wasn't the only one in love with Becky. Then I remember Nathaniel Harper's description of the bonfire, the nuns and Irish passengers dancing around the fire, Dr. Fleming's horrible death, the bones in the firepit. "Where did Becky get that idea?" I ask.

"From Nathaniel Harper's journal. That's why I wanted you to see this—to warn you off reading that journal. It drove Becky mad. She got the idea that we had to perform a sacrifice to 'appease the plague gods.' I think—" Liz swipes the back of her hand across her face. "It sounds crazy, but I think she may have sacrificed herself in the bog."

CHAPTER THIRTEEN

"THAT'S . . ."

"Crazy, like I said."

"I was going to say *horrible,* but yeah, crazy, too. How could she believe such a thing?"

Liz shakes her head. "I don't know. We were all going a little nuts here, confined to the island, my parents drinking and bickering, Becky stuck in her family's summer place because my father was being such an asshole about the quarantine. She would sneak out here with Mac when he did the supply runs for his mother and then she started camping out in the lighthouse cottage. I think being out here all alone started getting to her. She said she heard voices and saw strange lights in the woods. Toward the end she said she saw a horned man."

"A horned man?" I say, recalling the figure I'd imagined the first day in the woods.

"The Horned One, she called it. The devil. She thought the witch had summoned him and that the fever patients performed rites to appease him. At first I thought it was all part of the Stags and Hags game and Becky was just trying to make it interesting." She pauses, examining me. "I think she was afraid she was losing her hold on Reed."

"Because of me?" I ask.

"Who else?" she asks back. "He was planning on moving to New York with you and Ada, right? She had to make the game more interesting so the 'stags' weren't just boys wearing antlers—they were pagan gods—and the hag was the Irish witch, that woman in the journal—"

"Liadan," I say, feeling possessive of her as I say her name. "She was just a poor Irish girl who stowed away on the ship."

"Becky thought Liadan had been possessed by the witch of the island and that she was making sacrifices to the devil to cure the fever victims of typhus. We even held a séance to summon her to help us."

"Wow," I say, thinking about the séance from college, "that sounds—"

"Stupid?" Liz suggests. "Mac got really mad after the séance. He said we were all losing it, but honestly, I think it spooked him. He vanished for a couple of weeks and things did get freaky, as if the séance really had unleashed . . . *something*. Becky said she saw . . . things . . . the horned figure in the woods and the devil's footprints." She stares out to sea, loose strands of hair whipping around her face, leaning into the wind. "That's when my mother got sick and my dad blamed Hannah because she had been doing the supply run while Mac was gone."

"But Becky was going back and forth, too," I say.

"Yeah, but Becky said it couldn't be her because she was 'protected.'" Liz holds up both her arms, wrists out. The gesture, framed by the standing stones behind her, looks like one an ancient priestess might make performing a ritual. But then I see what she's showing me. On the underside of each wrist is a pale blue design, a coil of snaking lines identical to the mark on the stag's skull. "She made all of us do these homemade tattoos because she thought they would keep the devil—and the virus—out. None of us ever got sick, but I think Reed always wondered if Becky brought the virus to the island and that's how our parents got sick."

"Reed doesn't have one—" I begin, but then I recall that when he came back from the island that summer he had bandages on his wrists. When I asked him about them later he told me he scraped himself hauling in a boat line during a storm.

"Reed cut them out after Becky died," she said.

I wince. "Reed never talks about what happened that summer *at all*."

"Because he blames himself for our parents getting sick."

"That's awful," I say, and then after a moment's hesitation, "There's one thing I've never understood: Why didn't your parents go to the hospital when they got sick? You had the boat—or you could have called the coast guard."

Liz gives me a pitying smile. "I know Reed's made a big deal of assuring you that the mainland's only a half hour boat ride away and that we could go back anytime we want, but it's not that simple. Sure, when my parents got sick we could have gotten them to the hospital *at first*. But my father didn't want to go then. He said he didn't trust how the doctors were treating the virus and they were just as likely to kill them as to heal them. And then there was a storm—a real nor'easter that raged for six days straight. We couldn't get to the mainland. By the time the storm was over, my parents—and Becky—were dead."

I start to say *I didn't know* but it's already been made abundantly clear how little I knew, how much Reed has failed to tell me about the past, and also about what our real situation is here on the island. Staring off to sea I realize for the first time how trapped we could be here, as cut off from the world as the Irish passengers who were stranded here almost two hundred years ago.

"So," Liz says after a moment, "I just thought you should know what reading Nathaniel Harper's journal has led to before. If I were you, I'd chuck it in the sea and take up knitting instead. Just saying."

My hand reaches reflexively for the journal in my pocket. Does she know I have it on me? Does she mean for me to throw it in the ocean *now*? Is that why she's brought me here, to have me offer my own sacrifice to the devil? The chasm in front of the stones yawns as if awaiting my decision. I can feel the dark hungry pull of it, but Liz doesn't wait for me to respond.

"Shit," she says, pointing toward the sky, "speaking of storms. There's one heading our way. We'd better get going."

On the horizon is a single dark cloud with slanted lines streaking down into the water, but it looks very far away.

"You go on ahead," I say, wanting some time alone to process everything Liz just told me. "I'll be along in a few minutes."

She gives me a worried look.

"Really," I assure her, "I just want a few minutes . . . to sketch these rocks. Research for my book."

"Okay," she says, clearly anxious to be gone, "but don't stay too long."

"I won't," I say. "And thank you for telling me about what happened. It can't be easy to talk about."

"Yeah, well, I thought you had a right to know." She glances at the sky. "Don't wait too long. Weather changes quickly on the island."

I tell her I'll be right behind her. When she leaves I sit down on the rock and take out Nathaniel Harper's journal. It's warm from resting against my hip, an ember ready to ignite. I understand why Liz is trying to warn me off reading it because it had driven Becky crazy.

But I'm not Becky. I've spent the last ten years painfully aware that I'm Reed's second choice. I've long suspected that our marriage was built on Becky's death, and now I know it's true; her bones are buried in our foundation. But, if I'm to believe everything I've just learned, it seems Becky wasn't perfect. Far from it. She had gone crazy that summer and caused the deaths of Reed's parents and then drowned herself in the bog.

I look down at the book in my hands. She went crazy reading *this* book. Maybe I *should* toss it into the chasm, let it wash out to sea. But I already know I won't do that. It's not just that the journal is the key to writing the book I haven't been able to write all these years; it's that I'm hooked. I have to know what happened to Nathaniel and Liadan. I have to keep reading—

Being careful not to let it lead me into the pit.

WHEN I GET up I see that the storm cloud is surprisingly close. The air is colder and charged with electricity. I scramble over the boulders, which takes longer without Liz as a guide, and reach the shelter of the woods just as the storm hits. The heavy pine canopy keeps out the worst of the rain, but the air is heavy and wet and filled with small biting insects. I walk fast, keeping my eyes peeled for the red buoys, but I also have to keep an eye on the ground to avoid the wetter spots. The moss seems to have swollen in the rain, expanding like a sponge. The roots knuckling out of the green cover look like bones breaking through rotting skin.

They buried the dead in the bogs, Mac had said, *we used to find them everywhere.*

I could be walking on the bodies of the dead, I think, just as my right foot sinks ankle-deep into the mud.

Crap.

I try to pull it out but it feels as if the mud has a hold of my ankle—

As if a hand has encircled it and is pulling me down.

"Stop it!" I say aloud, meaning *Stop thinking like that,* but it comes out sounding scared and weak, as if I'm pleading with the mud—*the bodies beneath the mud*—to let me go.

The mud doesn't care. Crosby was right when he warned Ada not to walk out here alone. Reed had said we'd be okay if we stuck to the buoy path, but clearly I'm not all right. Have I somehow gone off the path? When I try to shift my weight for leverage my left foot sinks to the middle of my calf. I let out a cry that startles something in the woods. Looking up I glimpse a dark shape flitting just out of my peripheral vision—a horned figure like the creature Becky said she saw—but I can't track it because I'm stuck—

Stuck in the bog where Becky died. Where her body still lies, preserved and stained peat-colored like those prehistoric bog people they dig up in Europe. I can see her, opening her eyes and reaching for me—

A hand touches the back of my arm and I scream, flailing and thrashing myself deeper into the mud.

"Stop it!" a voice says, a delayed echo of my earlier plea. Only it's not my voice; it's Ada's. She's crouched in the roots of a pine tree holding her hand out to me. "You're making it worse. Take my hand and let me pull you out."

I grab her hand, and she pulls until I'm able to extract one foot and, bracing it against a root, the other. I emerge, muddy to the knees and missing one shoe, weeping with relief. I collapse against her and we sit huddled in the roots. "How did you find me?" I wail.

"I saw Liz come back and she said she left you on the rocks so I came to look for you. We were supposed to take a walk together, remember?"

"I'm so sorry! Liz said she had something to show me, but she really just wanted to scare me off reading Nathaniel Harper's journal— shit!" I pat my pockets for the journal, afraid that it might have fallen out while I was thrashing in the mud—

Afraid that Becky had reached into my pocket to take it back.

—but it's still there.

"What a bitch," Ada says, linking her arm through mine and propelling us back onto the path. With one shoe on and one off my gait is unsteady. It feels like college, when we'd stumble drunkenly back to the dorm from a party, rehashing the sketchy behavior of our classmates.

"She says Becky was reading it that summer, and it made her go crazy," I say as we make our halting way through the rain-drenched woods. "She got this idea that the Irish fever patients had gone pagan and started performing human sacrifices and that Liadan was possessed by the witch of the island and that she'd summoned the devil. She and Reed and Liz and Mac even did a séance."

Ada snorts. "Becky sounds like quite the drama queen."

I'm grateful for the support. It was girlfriend code, Ada always maintained, to put down "the competition," but out here in the woods where Becky died it also makes me feel uneasy. "Yeah, maybe, but the journal is seriously weird. I can see how it might have gotten under Becky's skin." I shudder, picturing what that *skin* might look like after all these years in the bog. "I know I feel like it's getting under mine."

Ada gives me a worried look. "Apparently so much so that you walked off the path into the bog. Like you were trying to sacrifice yourself the way Becky did."

"Did I walk off the path?" I ask, looking around us. "I thought I was following the buoys."

"You must have missed one and followed a deer track into the bog. Jeez, Lucy, if I hadn't come along and heard you thrashing about you could have been buried alive—like that witch—and Becky. Promise me you'll be more careful—and if you start getting any crazy ideas about human sacrifice—"

"I'll come to you first," I say, squeezing her hand.

"I was going to suggest we consider Liz as a candidate; she's riding my last nerve."

We laugh as I stumble against her. "Here," she says, handing me the nylon drawstring bag she has over her shoulder. "I was going to use this for collecting plants, but you should put your other shoe in it so you're not lopsided."

I put the shoe in the bag and sling it over my shoulder. We go faster, my bare feet squelching in the mud. At least it's stopped raining. When we get back to the clearing all that's left of Liz and Niko's bonfire is a steaming pile of black sludge. No skulls. No bones.

"You go up and shower," Ada tells me. "I'm going to make cocktails and hors d'oeuvres."

"Thanks, Ada. I'd hug you but I'd get mud all over you."

"Yeah, you stink, too, by the way. God knows what's in that mud."

Decomposing bodies, I think, padding up the stairs. I can smell it on me, the smell of death, which I remember from the hospital, always lurking just beneath the thin layer of antiseptic. Once you've smelled it, I think, as I make my way carefully across my bedroom and peel off my muddy clothes in the bathroom, it's always there—in the meat about to go bad, in the flowers wilting in the vase, in the ground beneath your feet. You never forget that it's there waiting for you.

That's why I'm not going to go crazy the way Becky did, I think, as I take out Nathaniel Harper's journal and place it in the towel closet for safekeeping while I shower. *I've been inoculated against death. I've already been there and back.*

I scrub the mud off, the water running peat-dark down the drain, where it will seep back into the bones of the island. Let the dead stay with the dead.

I dress in a pair of white jeans, a silky Indian kurta, and pretty jeweled sandals—clothes I'd bought for a trip to Greece we'd planned for this summer that might never happen now. Before I go downstairs, I notice the drawstring bag Ada lent me. I smile, thinking how lucky I am that I have my best friend here, that we have this chance to be together.

But then maybe the virus owes me that from last time.

CHAPTER FOURTEEN

AS WE SETTLE INTO THE ISLAND OVER THE NEXT FEW WEEKS, WE ALL
fall into our separate chores and hobbies. Ada cooks and I clean
up. Mac and Reed go off after breakfast each morning to check on
the machinery that keeps the island running: the pump that draws
water up from the well, the wind turbine that produces electricity,
the backup generator in case the wind ever stops, the boat that is our
only access to the mainland. Crosby tries to tag along with them at
first but is so clearly unwanted that eventually he volunteers to help
Niko and Liz with the garden instead.

When we are done with our chores, we each retreat into our separate projects. Sometimes I think that what the last pandemic taught
us best was how to be alone. Even if we thought we couldn't wait to
run back to bars and crowded beaches and noisy restaurants, by the
time we were allowed to do those things it never felt entirely safe to
be in a crowd.

At least, it never did for me.

Far safer to slip behind our screens and craft our separate shel-
ters. And so it's not too difficult now to slip into those patterns: for
Niko to slink behind her camera lens, Liz to set up an easel between
herself and a field of wildflowers, Crosby to pontificate to an invisible audience on his computer screen, Reed to find one more bit of
machinery to check on, and Ada to bury her nose in a cookbook or

What to Expect When You're Expecting, an ancient copy of which she unearthed from a basket in the TV room. Only Mac appears to have no hobbies besides his chores, but he has a seemingly endless supply of chilled beer bottles to hide behind.

I have Nathaniel Harper's journal to get lost inside. I decide to keep it to myself until I've finished reading it and started writing my own book. I'll show Reed that I am made of solider stuff than Becky. Maybe I'm not as brilliant or mercurial as she was made out to be, but at least I won't endanger us and then sacrifice myself to the bog.

After the drama of the solstice bonfire and the horrific tragedy of Dr. Fleming's death, the next entries seem deliberately unemotional and controlled. Perhaps after his long illness Nathaniel was trying to find normalcy wherever he could, just as we all cling to our chores and projects, habits and rituals. For Nathaniel it was the daily rounds of checking on his patients—noting fevers and rashes, pulse rates and skin color—observing the sanitary protocols set in place by Mother Brigitte, and reams of paperwork.

I sometimes think, he wrote, *that Mother Brigitte had me nursed back to health so that I could take over the chore of filling out forms for the Board of Health and writing letters to the municipal authorities pleading for money and supplies.*

Those pleas often fell on deaf ears. There were chronic shortages of blankets and bed linens, morphine and copper salts, flour and salt pork—and vegetables, which is why the nuns had planted the garden in the ashes of the bonfire.

Not, Nathaniel wrote, *as I had imagined in the delirium of my convalescence, to cover up the charred remains of pagan sacrifices. The bones were only evidence of the success of Dunstan McCree and the men he had gathered to him—recovered patients and sailors from the* Stella Maris—*to supplement our meager supply of meat by hunting. The island is well stocked with wild game: deer, rabbits, grouse, and, of course, an abundance of fish. Seal, too, but the Irish refuse to eat seal, which they maintain might be selkies, while the sailors refuse to eat seagulls because they are believed to hold the souls of drowned sailors.*

Superstitions spread as promiscuously as the pox, Dr. Fleming said shortly before he became a victim to those superstitions.

I notice that the men who have banded together as hunters under McCree's management do not attend the services held nightly by Mother Brigitte. Instead, they make bonfires down in the cove below the cliff and sing their own songs of devotion—keening sea chanties and Irish folk songs that echo mournfully against the rock cliff and drift up to the house along with the smell of roasting meat. At night I see ghostly shapes flitting down to the cove and I fear that some of the young girls, recovered from one fever, have succumbed to another. An answering refrain of the sisters chanting their rosaries comes from the barn behind the house, where Mother Brigitte has set up her house of worship.

We haven't had to ration our provisions yet, thanks to Mac's weekly supply runs, but we do stop having such lavish meals. Instead of prayers and sea chanties we have puzzles and games and cocktails. Liz sets up a card table in the corner—the same corner where Liadan's bed was—and starts a jigsaw puzzle that we all take a turn at throughout the day. It becomes part of the daily ritual to stop at the card table and pick up a jigsaw piece and try to find a place for it. Liz and Crosby are best at it, Liz at corners, Crosby at borders. Niko is always trying to force a piece where it doesn't belong, while Reed can pick up any random piece, look at its plain cardboard back, and find its correct place instantly, but then he quickly grows bored and moves on.

"He always wanted us to do the whole puzzle upside down," Liz teased, "without looking at the picture."

When we finish a puzzle, Niko enjoys breaking the pieces apart and sweeping them back into their box. That's her favorite part of every game: tipping the tiles on the Scrabble board into their velvet sack, tossing Monopoly money into the air, toppling Jenga towers, burning Pictionary sketches.

"You're a sore loser," Ada told her at the end of a contentious Monopoly game in which Niko had consistently landed on Reed's properties until she accused him of being a capitalist overlord and threw a plastic hotel into the fire.

"I just don't buy into the capitalist rules of the game," she countered. "Buy up all the real estate so you can fleece the little people. Is it any wonder that the landed rich are the ones who are good at that?"

It was true that Reed was good at games that required acquisition: Risk, Monopoly, Catan. Crosby played the best words in Scrabble, but Ada knew how to get the most points out of them. I was lucky if I could find anything to put down on my turn. Mac watched from behind his beer bottle, smirking at us college grads who couldn't fix a running toilet but knew how to spell *hegemony*. When Ada accused him of "having no craft" he took out a length of rope from his backpack and demonstrated a dozen complicated knots in five minutes— half hitches, figure eights, and something called a Palomar—his fingers moving so fast they blurred in the air like dragonfly wings.

"Why do you even *have* a rope in your backpack?" Ada asked, taking her hand off her belly, where she so often rested it, to finger the nylon line. "Are you planning to tie one of us up?"

"More like I'll have to haul one of your sorry asses out of the bog," Mac replied.

"It reminds me of something I read today," Crosby said. "'All men live enveloped in whale lines. All are born with halters round their necks.'"

"Nice," Mac said.

"It's from *Moby-Dick*," Crosby said prissily.

"Yeah, I've heard of it," Mac said. "Book about a big fish, right?"

"What it reminds *me* of," Ada said, no doubt to head off a spat between Mac and Crosby, "is making friendship bracelets that summer on the Vineyard . . . hey . . ." Which sent Ada searching the house for cords and strings and beads. Soon all our wrists were encircled by macramé and seashells, even Niko's; she turned out to know all the most complicated patterns.

It felt, I thought as June turned into July, reassuring to fall into roles. Ada, her contours softened by voluminous sweats, the mother; Reed, the cool and distant patriarch; Liz, the bossy older sister; Niko, the brat; Crosby, the snarky middle brother; Mac, the cool older brother . . . and me? Often I felt as if I were watching from the sidelines—the writer observing. But even as the observer I had a sense of *belonging*, stronger than I'd had since college.

Nathaniel was also the observer, watching and making his careful notes, not just on his patients' symptoms and their dwindling supplies, but on the workings of the people on the island: the hunters saved the best cuts of meat for Dunstan McCree; the Gray Nuns were no longer careful to tuck their hair inside their veils; Mother Brigitte watched McCree but never spoke to him; the patients Liadan nursed healed more quickly and were more likely to survive; some of the nuns crept down to the cove at night to join the hunters. Nathaniel overheard the novice Mairi humming a sea chanty.

I noticed that whenever Liz asked Ada if something was gluten-free Ada's left eyebrow would twitch; that whenever Crosby made a pronouncement (*The virus could have been stopped if the government had allocated enough funds; Ignorance is the real virus*) Mac would look toward Reed and smirk. I noted that Niko shirked her chores in the garden and disappeared into the woods every day. I saw Ada filling the gluten-free-flour container with regular flour.

were tensions. There always were when people
.... That's why Ada and I had fought last time.

....nd rivalries, Nathaniel wrote in his journal, _sprout up
....shrooms after the rain. And there's been plenty of rain. Even
amongst the nuns there are tensions—one who is accused of eating more
than her share of porridge, another who is said to always shirk her turn at
latrine cleaning. Squabbles break out over missing items—bars of soap,
biscuits, pots of salve._

We have our missing items, too. At first it's just a few puzzle pieces
that leave a hole in the finished puzzle, which enrages Liz.

"Didn't you say your dog ate them last time?" Ada remarks.

"But I just opened this one," Liz insists.

Then Scrabble tiles: all the _s_'s and three of the _e_'s.

"I counted the tiles when we started," Liz hisses.

"I guess you counted wrong," Ada says sweetly.

The next day all the baking powder is gone. "I had three cans,"
Ada says.

"I guess you counted wrong," Liz replies.

Liz's Madder Violet disappears from her paint set the next day.
When she accuses Ada of stealing it Mac meows and whispers _cat
fight._ The next day two six-packs of Mac's beer are missing from the
storage shed. Mac shrugs it off, but Reed gets furious.

"These are our supplies, people, they're the only thing between
us and disaster."

"I thought we had plenty of everything," Niko says. "And Mac can
always make another supply run if we run out of something."

"And what happens if the supply chains go down out there?" Reed
says, pointing west. "Or the weather turns and we can't take the boat
to the mainland? We need to start rationing. We're low on beans and
soap, and someone is using up all the matches," he finishes with a
pointed look at Niko.

"Hey, don't look at me just because I smoke. Mac smokes, too, and Ada's the one who's been making candles."

This prompts Reed to lock up all the medical supplies and pharmaceuticals in a safe upstairs and then to make an inventory chart on which everyone has to write what they take out of the supply shed and initial it.

"*Yavolt*," Niko mutters under her breath.

The next day all the matches are gone and replaced by Monopoly hotels. They are signed out on the chart by Mr. Monopoly.

Like us, the inhabitants of the island in 1848 also noticed missing items. Nathaniel reported that Mother Brigitte found her supply of ink depleted.

"It cannot be one of the patients who took it," she complained to me. "Most of them, poor souls, are illiterate." I saw her looking at my ink-stained hands and I offered to give her some from my supply—part of my graduation gift from my father—and she looked ashamed to have suspected me.

"I'll make some from the berries in the wood," she said.

Liadan offered to gather the berries for her. I think she wanted an excuse to get away from the hospital and the fever ward. Mother Brigitte was worried, though, that it wasn't safe for her to go alone into the woods. I wasn't sure what she thought the danger was—bogs, bears, or the hunters—but I offered to go with her. I told Mother Brigitte that I wanted to do a botanical survey of the island, and she gave me an amused smile and asked me to be on the lookout for rose hips and willow bark for tea.

Liadan and I set out the next day at dawn—the best time, she told me, to collect herbs. As we walked through the woods, with her stooping to collect berries, mushrooms, grasses, and bark, I asked how she had learned about plants. She told me that before they came to live on Lord Dunleavy's estate her father was a fisherman and her family lived in a stone cottage on the southern coast of Ireland and so she knew something about the plants that grew near the sea. When we reached a little cove, she showed me the seaweed that the Irish farmers used to fertilize their potato crops. It reminded me of how we found her in the lifeboat.

"Did you gather seaweed to keep yourself warm for the crossing?" I asked.

She didn't answer at first and I thought I had offended her. We had never spoken about how she came to stow away on the *Stella Maris,* and I had never alluded to what Dunstan McCree had told me about her history. I found it hard to credit that she had done anything to be sent to a workhouse, so purely fresh and new did she seem, as if she had been birthed on that bed of seaweed like Botticelli's Venus on the half shell.

Or perhaps that was how I preferred to think of her.

After a few moments she began to speak.

"That would have been a good idea to prepare for the journey, but I had no such thought." She looked up at me, her sea-green eyes glinting in the sunlight like a secret cove. "Did you know I was in a workhouse?"

I nodded, my face hot in the sun. "Dunstan McCree said something—"

"Ah, McCree. He was the agent at the estate my family moved to after my father died. My mother and sisters moved in with my aunt's family. I went to work in the landlord's house as a laundry maid. A clumsy one, I'm afraid. I burnt one of the napkins while ironing it, and I hid it because I was ashamed. I was accused of stealing the napkin and sent to the workhouse."

"For a napkin?" I cried, thinking this was not the story that Dunstan McCree had hinted at. "That's outrageous. That's—"

"The way the world works, Dr. Harper. The workhouse was not the worst place to be when the famine came. At least there was food—at first. But when the potatoes failed a second year, the landlords could not afford to keep their tenants on the land so they let us out. I walked back to where my aunt's house had been, but it was gone."

"Gone?"

"Yes, the landlord had it razed to the ground so his tenants wouldn't be tempted to return to it. There was nothing but a pile of rubble where the house had stood. I took one of the stones . . ." She laughed. "As if it might lead me to my mother and sisters." She stopped and I saw tears glinting in her eyes. "I went to the landlord's house to ask what had become of my family but the housekeeper slammed the door in my face. One of the maids took pity on me, though, and followed me out to the lane. She told me that all the tenants had been sent for emigration to Canada. She thought my mother and sisters had set sail from New Ross. She gave me a piece of bread and made me promise to look for her brother, who had been sent out as well.

"I walked to New Ross and checked in every shipping office for the lists of emigrants, searching for my mother's name—" She broke off and swayed on her feet. I reached out to steady her. Her flesh was cold and the hand that was holding the stone was clenched into a fist. "I found no trace of them but I smelled the sea and it made me homesick for the seaside cottage and my mother. Then I saw that one of the ships was called the *Stella Maris*, Star of the Sea, which is what the fishermen in our village called the Virgin Mary. I thought—" She pursed her lips. "I don't know what I thought, only that I wanted to be held and carried away at the same time. I waited until night and climbed aboard and hid in the hull of one of the small boats on deck. I used to go out fishing with my da and lie in the hull looking up at the sky, rocked in the arms of the sea. That's all I wanted. I didn't think of bringing food or water and no doubt I would have died, but two days out to sea there was a storm and a wave crashed over the deck, washing seaweed into my boat. There were shells and little fish, too, so I ate the fish and sucked the shells dry. When it rained the water collected in the canvas and dripped down for me to drink. I collected some in the shells to last me through the rainless days. It felt as if the sea had decided I would live."

"Everyone thinks you're a miracle," I said, not adding that, watching her dark hair moving in the breeze like seaweed swaying beneath the water and her eyes glinting green as the sea, I did too.

"Only because they need one," she said. "Come, I want to show you something."

Instead of going back into the woods she kicked off her shoes and scrambled barefoot up one of the boulders, nimble as a mountain goat. She laughed at my clumsy attempts to follow her and suggested I take off my shoes as well. I could picture her as a little girl darting in and out of the waves. She really did seem to be a creature of the sea, like one of the seals that barked at us as we approached the lighthouse keeper's cottage.

The lighthouse had been abandoned some years ago when the keeper died of the cholera and the island garnered a reputation that made it difficult to employ another. Mother Brigitte told me she suspected that smugglers used the cottage, and she warned her flock to stay away from it. As Liadan opened the door I saw that she had not been obeyed. Bare of furniture, the cottage was nonetheless inhabited. A statue of a woman stood in a stone niche above the fireplace. At first I thought it was the Virgin Mary—or some Catholic saint—but as I came closer and made out the statue in the flickering light of the candles that had been set around it I saw that the woman was naked and that the lower part of her body was imprinted with marks meant to indicate scales. Her long hair was intertwined with seaweed and shells. A design was inscribed on her forehead. It looked like one of the intricate knots the sailors make to while away their time at sea. The same symbol had been painted on rocks placed around her feet.

Painted with ink.

"I think I know what's become of Mother Brigitte's ink," I said.

"I feared as much," she said. "I've been finding stones painted so for weeks now."

"Do you know who made this?"

She shook her head. "I imagine one of the sailors carved her. Quite a few of them are skilled at carving. I've heard them telling a story about a witch who was buried alive on the island."

"I've heard that story, too, but it's just a local myth. These islands are full of stories like that."

She looked at me for a moment, her steady eyes holding me the way my mother's would when she knew I had committed some sin and she was waiting for me to confess. What sin was Liadan waiting for me to confess? When I said nothing she looked away, disappointed.

"Don't underestimate the power of stories, Dr. Harper. Sometimes it's all we poor folk have to pass our truth along."

"Do you believe, then, that a witch called the devil and cursed this island?"

"I'm not sure it's cursed," she said, "but it has been marked. I can feel it in the way the land has been carved by sea and wind." She laid her hand on my chest. Her touch was light, but it seemed to sear through my shirt and skin, down to my bone, as if she were marking me. "The island ties a knot in your heart that binds you to it."

She looked back at the statue. "As for who set her up here and who brings her offerings, I don't know." She placed the stone she had carried from her ruined home at the feet of the idol. Amongst the stones and shells were also twists of grass made into crosses and crude dolls. When I held up one of the crosses, Liadan said, "That's St. Brigid's Cross. We used to make them on St. Brigid's Day and hang them over the door."

"So, this is a Catholic observance?" I asked, looking skeptically at the naked figure and the straw crosses and dolls, some of which were adorned with flowers and bits of seaweed tucked into their skirts.

"This is what people do when they're desperate and have nothing left to lose," she replied. "They begin making their own idols and gods."

She turned to go, her hair brushing my shoulder as she walked past me, stirring a scent of seaweed and wild roses. I turned back to look at the statue—and recognized her. Perhaps the sculptor had meant to evoke the buried witch but he had given her Liadan's likeness. It was Liadan as I'd first seen her, wreathed in seaweed and bearing the marks of the sea on her flesh. She was the island's idol and its god.

CHAPTER FIFTEEN

WHEN I TURNED THE PAGE A BIT OF DRIED SEAGRASS FELL OUT ALONG with a scrap of paper on which was written a line in purple ink: *Found in Sea Witch Cottage. Liadan was possessed by the island witch and she's still here.*

The seagrass is woven into a crosshatch design that I determine from a quick internet search is the St. Brigid's Cross Liadan described. The handwriting on the note is distinctly modern. In fact, I'm pretty sure it was written with a gel pen. I recognize its style from notes Reed had tacked up in his dorm room. Becky. Here with this journal before me, as she was before me with Reed.

I close the book, no longer feeling like it is mine, but leave the note out on the blotter.

She's still here.

Was this part of the Stags & Hags game, to pretend that Liadan had been possessed by the island witch and was still haunting the island? Or was Becky right? Did a presence such as Liadan, so powerful that the Irish passengers and sailors and nuns alike worshipped her, *linger*? When I told Reed that I only believed in ghosts *metaphorically,* I hadn't been completely honest. That might have been how I thought before I got sick, but after my heart stopped for three minutes and thirty seconds, I found myself wondering what other ways there were to *come back.* Zach, my friend at the college, maintained that we were a haunted generation—not just by the people who died in the pandemic, but by all the plans and dreams derailed by it. I'd laughed it off and told him only a creative writing teacher would come up with that metaphor. But what if those of us who survived really *were* haunted by those who didn't?

I shake the thought away and get up. For the first time I leave the journal on the blotter instead of tucking it into my pocket. Maybe I am spending too much time with it. Maybe I'm spending too much time alone. I listen to the house for a moment. I've gotten used to its creaks and sighs as the wind rattles its centuries-old joists and floorboards, shingles and window frames. Reed was right: the wind blows all the time on the island.

Where is Reed? Pump priming? Radiator flushing? Gear oiling? He spends his days meticulously checking and rechecking all the systems that make the island work and taking stock of our supplies, falls into bed at night exhausted, and is gone before I wake up in the morning. After that first night in the cove, I had hoped we would get closer, but in the three weeks we've been here we've only made love twice since then and never with that passion.

Because he's so busy keeping the island machinery oiled and humming? Or because I've locked myself away in this study with Nathaniel Harper's journal?

I open the study door and hear a timer beep downstairs in the kitchen; Ada must be baking. A rocking chair creaks on the porch; Crosby still reading *Moby-Dick*. I walk down the hall, feeling curiously light without the weight of Nathaniel Harper's diary in my pocket. My deerskin moccasins—an ancient pair of Minnetonkas I'd found in a closet to replace my lost sneakers—glide silently over the carpet. I pause at the open door to our bedroom and peer in, feeling as if I'm spying on invisible occupants. The lace curtains stir in the breeze, casting patterns over the room that remind me of the magic lantern shows that Reed used to put on—silhouette puppet shows that told fairy tales or stories about our adventures buildering on the campus. I feel, standing on the threshold, as I often did after I came back from the hospital—as if I'm looking at my own life from the outside. Walking down the stairs I feel as if the others have long vanished and I am the ghost haunting the house, tethered to this spot by some crime I can't even recall.

The kitchen and great room are empty. Where is Ada? There's an old Fannie Farmer cookbook on the counter, its egg- and butter-stained pages rustling in the breeze from the open door. When I step outside I see that the rockers are empty, moving on their own. Ice is melting in a glass on the railing beside Crosby's splayed copy of *Moby-Dick*.

Where is everybody?

Maybe they're all working on some joint project together and they didn't want to bother me. I recall that Ada had said something at breakfast about taking an inventory of supplies and Crosby had asked if that was where she was always disappearing to. What did he mean? I'd assumed that when Ada wasn't in the kitchen, she was down at the Cove House. Where else would she go?

I start walking down to the supply shed on the dock. The quiet reminds me of when campus emptied out all those years ago. *Like in a zombie movie,* Ada had said, lurching at me while chanting *They're coming to get you, Barbara. They're coming for you, Barbara.* I'd laughed and batted her away, but her rendition of the line and her dead eyes and limp body were so spot-on that I had zombie nightmares for a week.

She really would have made a great actress.

Maybe this is all a practical joke and when I get to the supply shed they'll all jump out and yell *Surprise!*

But when I get there I see it's locked and bolted on the outside.

I remember Mac locking the door on our first day here, but I don't recall the heavy padlock. Was this one of the projects Reed had been working on? Was he that worried about someone stealing from the supply shed? And was it outside marauders he was worried about, or one of us? Those missing bars of soap and boxes of matches he'd mentioned the other night at dinner—he must have decided that the inventory checklist wasn't enough.

I look down at the dock and notice that the boat is gone.

Scanning the horizon, I search for Reed out fishing with Mac, but there are no boats.

Isn't it a little strange that there aren't *any* boats? Shouldn't there be fishermen and lobster boats and pleasure sailors? Had the virus gotten so bad that people weren't taking boats out? When *was* the last time I'd checked the news?

Uneasy, I turn toward the Cove House, where Ada and Crosby are staying. Since Ada spent so much time in the Main House, I'd only been in it once. It's a low wooden and stone structure built right on the water. I approach it cautiously, not wanting to interrupt a moment of stolen intimacy—maybe everyone *else* was stealing away to have sex in the afternoons—but the house is so quiet and so abandoned-looking it's clear no one is there. I knock anyway and stick my head in the door and call out, my voice echoing in the empty rooms. Except for a towel drying on the porch railing and an empty mug in the dish drainer the place looks uninhabited.

Maybe they've all left without you.

The thought seems to come from outside myself, as if someone had whispered it in my ear.

"Don't be stupid," I say out loud. "It's a big island. They could be anywhere."

Only it isn't a very big island and no one seems to be anywhere. I walk back up to the house, through the empty great room, past the happy faces in the photographs, and out the back door to the clearing. A spade is leaning on one of the fence posts and the scarecrow Niko had made out of tattered L.L.Bean cast-offs flutters in the wind. Clothes flap on the clothesline that Liz strung up a few weeks ago, the breeze filling empty sleeves and pant legs with a semblance of life. When I walk into the barn a mourning dove startles and swoops up to the loft.

"Liz?" I call. "Niko? Anyone home?"

The mourning dove coos back its lonesome cry. *No one home, no one home, you're all alone.*

I check the well house and the generator shed. They both have acquired padlocks, too. Does Reed think someone is stealing water and electricity? Has he stopped taking his OCD medication? I'd asked him before we left if he had enough and he said he had a year's worth of his prescription, but I knew that his psychiatrist often had to adjust his dosage. Should I talk to Ada about it? She is a nurse, after all, and had done some psychiatric training, but Reed might see it as a betrayal.

But what if he is getting worse? A year ago he had an episode while he was under deadline to complete a city planning project. The stress had gotten so bad he'd stopped sleeping—

Is he sleeping? Lately he's been coming to bed after I fall asleep and leaving before I wake up.

—and had begun to think that his coworkers were trying to sabotage his project by stealing his blueprints. He'd even accused his assistant of hiding his pencils and erasers—

Just as now he thinks someone is taking soap and matches.

—and eventually he'd had to take a leave from work and needed to be hospitalized. What would we do if that happened now?

What if something has already happened? Did Reed have an episode and the others took him to the hospital on the mainland?

No, I tell myself firmly, *they wouldn't do that without telling me first. Reed and Mac have just taken the boat . . .* somewhere. And the others . . . maybe they are in the woods. Maybe they are all out hiking.

The gap between the trees yawns like an open mouth, like it has already swallowed everyone else on the island. Part of me wants to run back to the house and lock myself in the tower study, but another part of me feels drawn into that empty black space. I head in, moccasins squelching in the mud, and listen for voices as I go. Straining through the green haze of trees and ferns for sight of the next buoy, I wonder what it would feel like to be the only one left on the island.

I wave away the thought as I bat at a cloud of gnats circling my head. The air is close and heavy under the trees, my skin prickling with moisture and dread. When I come out onto the rocky shore of Sea Witch Cove the sudden blast of cold air turns my sweat icy. I scan the water for the boat—and see a rain cloud far out to sea. I consider turning back but then I notice something painted on one of the boulders.

Was that there before?

I walk across the pebbled beach to get a closer look at the mark. It's a spiral knot painted in purple—the color of Becky's gel pen.

Or the berry ink that Liadan made.

I shiver in the wind that's coming off the ocean and touch my finger to the marking. It's dry, but that doesn't tell me how long it's been here. Or who made it. Hadn't Liz said that her Madder Violet paint was missing? But why would someone steal her paint to make this design? More likely it's Liz herself, who warned me about reading the journal, painting the markings to make me paranoid. Could she also have orchestrated this disappearance of everyone to show me how deeply I've been sucked in?

I climb the boulder, expecting Liz to pop out from behind one of the rocks and shout *Boo!* Instead, I find another knot three boulders away. And when I get there, another one a few more boulders down. A blazed path leading . . . where else but to the abandoned light-house keeper's cottage.

The Sea Witch Cottage.

"Okay, I get it," I shout into the stiff-chill wind blowing in from the sea. This is an object lesson in how distracted I've become. I should be paying more attention—to Reed's obsessive checking and rechecking, Ada and Liz's squabbling, Mac's lurking, Crosby's neediness, and Ada's afternoon disappearances. They'll all be waiting for me inside the cottage . . .

But when I walk through the open doorway into the roofless space it's clear that no one is in the cottage but *her*—the sea witch herself, wreathed in seaweed, her salt tears glimmering in flickering candlelight. She is as alone on the island as I am.

CHAPTER SIXTEEN

SOMETHING SNAPS BEHIND ME. AS I TURN, I PICTURE LIADAN AND NA-
thaniel Harper looking straight through me to the statue. Instead,
it's Niko, camera affixed to her face like a cyborg mask.

"Don't move," she commands. "The way you're standing in front of
her looks like you're praying."

"Did you set this up?" I ask.

Niko lowers the camera and looks past me to the statue. The
look on her face makes me think that *she's* the one who's praying. "I
thought you did. You're the one who's writing a book about the history of the island."

"I've never been here before," I point out, "but you have. You said
you took pictures of this cottage last year. Was this statue here then?"

"No," Niko says, holding the camera back up to her eye and moving closer to the statue, "I've never seen her before."

I'm startled by how quickly Niko, who is the least sentimental
person I know, regards the statue as a person, not as an object. But
then, maybe to Niko people and objects are the same: surfaces that
reflect or absorb light. The way she moves around the statue, lens
clicking, reminds me of a fashion shoot. I don't blame her for her fas-
cination. Although crudely carved out of some kind of ivory or bone
and worn smooth, the face of the woman—goddess? sea creature?—
glows with an inner serenity and power. Her ivory body, draped in

seaweed, is lithe and graceful. Beginning at her waist are tiny half-moon indentations like fish scales. Her seaweed cloak wraps around her lower body, making it impossible to see if there are legs or a tail beneath it. She seems to be balanced on a wave.

Rocked in the arms of the sea.

Shells and round stones are arranged around her, as well as fresh flowers and lit candle stubs. She looks exactly like the statue described in Nathaniel's journal, but these flowers are fresh.

"Someone's been here recently," I say. "Did you see anyone? Everybody's gone from the house."

"I've been in the rocks all day shooting tide pools and granite surfaces. Liz said she was going to sketch some grasses on the north side of the island. I saw the boat an hour ago over by the lighthouse."

"You did?" I say, seizing on that detail. "Was Reed on it?"

Niko turns and trains her camera lens on me. "I couldn't see." *Click.* "Is anything wrong with Reed?" *Click.*

"Why do you ask that?" I demand, holding my hand up to shield my face from the insistent click of the camera shutter. "Have you noticed anything? Has Liz said anything?"

She lowers the camera and gazes straight at me. It's unnerving to have those piercing eyes trained on me. "Mostly she just complains about what a pain in the ass he is. Do you know he tried to tell her we couldn't come?"

"No," I say, "that's not right. He told me right away he was asking Liz."

"*Asking?* Like the island isn't half hers?"

"Oh—I know Reed considers the island as belonging to them both. I just meant that he was the one who asked Mac to get things ready"—*and the one who paid for the supplies*—"and who had the idea to come. That's what I meant by him asking Liz to join us."

"Yeah, but he didn't want me," Niko says, lifting the camera back up to her face and turning back to the statue. "Reed thought I was too big a risk. That I wouldn't quarantine seriously enough before coming here."

"Oh," I say again, remembering how he'd expressed that concern to me, "you shouldn't take that personally. Reed's just really super meticulous. He didn't even want to ask Ada!"

"Really?" Niko lowers her camera and looks at me with such naked pleasure I'm instantly sorry I said anything.

"Only because she and Crosby work in a hospital," I say. "It's just that he's worried about my health. I still have respiratory issues."

"Oh yeah," she says, "you were sick last time. Bad break. Me, I went all over the city and never got it. Liz says I'm indestructible. Were you very sick?"

"Yeah, I was," I say. "And very stupid. I thought I could ride it out myself, but by the second week I couldn't get out of bed. If Reed hadn't shown up when he did, I think I would have died."

"Huh," Niko says. "So I guess it was lucky the Harpers died when they did."

"What do you mean?" I ask, appalled.

Niko shrugs. "If they hadn't died then Reed wouldn't have left the island and reached you in time to get you to the hospital. Liz says it's the one unselfish thing her bastard of a father ever did—dying in time so Reed could save you."

IT BEGINS TO rain as we leave the cottage. Niko slides her camera inside a waterproof case, which she tucks under her jacket. "We'd better make a run for it," she says and proceeds to scramble over the slick rocks. I follow, but her heavy boots have more traction than my moccasins, and I can't keep up with her. When I slip, though, I'm surprised to find her right there to catch me. She holds on to my hand to help me over the rocks, her grip strong and warm. When we get to the cove we find that the tide has come in and erased the sliver of beach. We stare at the water for a moment and then Niko turns to me, grins, and shouts, "Geronimo!" as she leaps into the water, one hand holding up her camera, the other dragging me with her.

The water's only up to our knees but it's freezing and takes my breath away. Niko doesn't give me a chance to rest, though. She pulls me through the water and into the woods. Only then does she release my hand but she lets out a whoop that stirs something in my blood and spurs me into a run right behind her. We splash through puddles and leap across roots and fallen logs. My soaked moccasins weld to my feet like a second skin. Like hooves. I feel like a deer sprinting through the woods—

Fleeing the hunter.

The crack of a breaking branch draws my eyes into the woods, into the streaming green haze broken by branch and trunk flying by so fast they merge into an antlered man—

Running beside us.

An illusion, I tell myself, *a magic lantern show.*

Still, I run faster despite the burn in my damaged lungs, passing Niko, who hoots with wild delight at my speed and doubles her own. We race each other—and the antlered hunter in the woods—into the clearing, where we find him waiting for us, grown giant, barring our way. I slide to a halt in the mud and land on my knees below him—

The Horned One. The devil.

"It's just Mr. Tibster," Niko says, grabbing my hand and pulling me to my feet.

She's right, of course. It's just the scarecrow in his L.L.Bean cast-offs, only someone has added a rack of antlers to his straw-stuffed head.

Niko and I continue on toward the house and burst onto the porch, soaked and laughing, spraying mud onto the cocktail party. Their surprised faces—Ada in a caftan holding out a tray of cocktail franks,

Crosby gripping *Moby-Dick* like a shield, Reed and Liz scooching their rockers backward, Mac raising his beer out of the line of splatter—sends Niko into a fresh peal of laughter that I find contagious. Mostly I'm happy to see them all here, not gone off the island, not dead, especially Reed, the same as ever in worn khakis and loose button-down shirt.

"Where were you?" he asks, scanning my mud-soaked clothes.

"Where . . . were . . . *you*?" I counter, gasping between words. My lungs feel like they're going to explode. "Every . . . one . . . was . . . *gone*."

"So, you and Niko launched a search party through the bog?" Ada asks, handing me a beach towel. She's glancing between me and Niko, her face pinched and concerned.

"I ran into Niko at the Sea Witch Cottage," I say, collapsing into a rocker. My lungs feel like they're on fire. "Which has a statue in it now. Who put that up?"

"What statue?" Ada asks.

I look toward Liz, who's wiping mud from Niko's face while trying to dodge her attempts to embrace her in a muddy hug. "The sea witch," I say. "I think it's the same statue one of the sailors carved of Liadan in 1848. I read about it today in Nathaniel Harper's journal—" I look up to find Reed staring at me and realize I've broken my rule about not mentioning the journal. I realize something else. "There were lit candles so someone must have put it up recently. Niko took pictures," I add, as if that will divert the blame from me.

"Yeah, I came in and found Lucy there with the statue," she says. "I got some great shots."

"So," Reed says, leaning forward, "you read about this statue in the journal and then you went and found it in the lighthouse keeper's cottage?"

"Yes," I say, wondering why the way he's put it makes it sound suspicious. Then I remember what Niko said about seeing the boat at the lighthouse. "You and Mac were out there today, right? Niko said she saw your boat." I look from Reed to Mac, who's sitting a little separate from the group, his feet up on the railing, beer in hand.

"We went fishing," Reed says. "The cove near the lighthouse is a good spot."

"So, you didn't go to the cottage?" I ask.

"Why would we go there?" Reed counters.

Because you used to meet Becky there, I think, but instead I look back at Liz. "You told me about the cottage. Did you find the old statue and put it up?"

"Why would I do that? I haven't seen that statue since the summer of 2020. I thought . . ." She looks past me to her brother. "I thought it ended up in the bog along with—"

Reed gets up so fast the runners of his rocking chair scrape paint off the porch floorboards. "Shouldn't that fish be done?" he asks, giving Ada an accusatory look. "It would be a shame to let it burn after Mac and I spent all afternoon catching it." Then he looks at me. "Maybe you'd better go clean up."

He walks inside before I can answer, leaving me staring at his chair, which is still rocking as if it holds the ghost of his anger.

BY THE TIME I get downstairs from showering, dinner is in full swing. "We didn't want to let the fish get cold," Ada murmurs apologetically as I sit down next to her at the end of the table. Reed is at the head, flanked by Mac and Liz. "But I saved you one." She slides me a covered plate. I notice that an uncomfortable silence has descended on the group, which suggests to me that they must have been talking about me and my obsession with Nathaniel Harper's journal before I

came down. I don't plan to say anything about the statue or the journal, but Ada, no doubt trying to be supportive, says, "I think it's great
you're working on your book, Lucy. What else have you learned?"

"Well," I say reluctantly, glancing at Reed. "I found out how Liadan survived the crossing."

"Really?" Crosby asks. "How?"

I have no choice but to tell the story of how Liadan survived on
fish and mollusks swept into her boat and how she collected rainwa-
ter in shells to drink.

"That sounds highly unlikely," Crosby says. "More probably she
traded sexual favors for food from the sailors, which would explain
why one of them carved a statue of her."

"It's not like that," I object. "The statue isn't . . . *sexy*."

"I guess that depends on whether you're into tentacle porn or
not," Niko says. "Here, you can look at the photos I posted on my
website—don't worry, Reed, I don't say where they're taken—so you
all can judge for yourself."

She passes her tablet around the table, first to Liz, who tilts her
head and says, "I like tentacle porn as much as the next girl but this
doesn't do anything for me," and then to Reed, who looks at it as if
it were a piece of poisonous blowfish, to Mac, who leers and says,
"Not bad," and Crosby, who uses his napkin to pick up the tablet and
hold it at arm's length. It feels as if Liadan herself is being passed
around, as splayed and eviscerated as the fish on our plates. Only
Ada touches the screen tenderly.

"I think she's beautiful," Ada says.

I crane forward to look at the picture. Niko has caught the candlelight moving over the ivory surface like a caress, as if the light is
in love with her and has brought her back to life. Ada must feel it,
too. She runs her finger over the line of the statue's hip—and swipes

to a previous picture. It's me standing in front of the statue, looking as entranced as an acolyte.

"I'm sure you're going to write something amazing about her, Lu. Her story is like our story, right? She came here seeking safety—"

"She was a stowaway," Reed says. "She didn't belong here."

Everyone is shocked for a moment. Then Liz says, "Wow, you sound just like Dad. Next you'll be railing against immigrants and liberals."

All the color washes out of Reed's face. It's the meanest thing Liz could have said to him. "Well, if we had closed the border after last time we wouldn't be here now."

"Actually," Crosby says, "that's far from clear—"

"I think our government made it in a lab," Niko says, to which Reed snorts and mutters something about "crackpot conspiracy theorists," and Liz calls him a fascist.

"People!" Ada cries, patting the air with her hands as if tamping down a rising miasma. "This is ridiculous. Let's remember we're all lucky to be here—"

"Yeah," Niko says, "especially you, Ada, considering Reed didn't want you to come in the first place."

"That's not—" I begin, but the red flush of shame that rises on Reed's face makes it pointless to deny the truth. "It was just because you work in the E.R.," I tell Ada, laying my hand on her arm. Her muscles are tight as a steel cable. She flinches and turns on me, her face white with fury, her fingers drawn back like claws. For a moment I think she's going to tear my eyes out but then she forces a smile on her face, which is almost worse.

"It's all right," she says. "That makes perfect sense. I would have done the same." Then she turns back to Reed. "I'm sure you were only doing what you thought best to protect what you love best. And the most important thing is that you changed your mind and we're all here together now." She looks back at me. The same smile is pasted on her face but it looks as if it has been seared into her flesh. "Why don't you clear up, Lucy," she says through tight lips, "and I'll bring the pie and coffee into the great room."

CHAPTER SEVENTEEN

"DO YOU THINK SHE'S POISONED THE PIE?" NIKO MOCK-WHISPERS AS she sits down next to me on the couch. She's abandoned her usual perch by the fireplace either because we bonded on our run through the rain today or she feels guilty for giving away what I told her before.

No, I think, noting her mischievous smile, *Niko never feels guilty about anything.* She loves stirring up drama. I'd like to yell at her for giving away my confidence but Ada is being so determinedly cheery that it would only draw attention to the slight.

"What should we play tonight?" Ada chirps. "Monopoly? Risk?"

"Risk makes me feel sad that I may never see those countries again," Liz says, settling on the other side of Niko. I see Ada measuring the available space on the couch and choosing the Morris chair where Reed usually sits.

"You mean our cruise to Kamchatka is off?" Niko asks.

"People traveled too much in the anteviral," Crosby says, perching on the Morris chair hassock.

"Didn't you two go to Iceland last winter?" Reed asks.

"That was a conference on world health," Crosby replies. "I mean idle tourism—"

"So that's a hard no on Risk." Ada cuts off what's sure to be a screed against tourism and jet fuel usage and pops off her chair to sit cross-legged in front of the games cabinet. She starts pulling out the games we've already played—Monopoly, Catan, Scrabble, Life—holding up each box and shaking it like a kid trying to guess the contents of their Christmas presents. "Too morbid?" she asks, holding up a box labeled *Pandemic*.

I recognize her forced cheer from college gatherings at which she felt she'd been slighted—the sorority rush where she learned she hadn't been accepted, the dorm party where she overheard one of the girls from the triple down the hall call her a skank because of how many boys she'd dated, the kegger where some frat boy called her an SJW. *We could just leave,* I suggested once, but she'd curled her lip and said that would be *letting the bastards grind her down.* I'd like to talk to her alone to explain that it was only Reed's OCD and hypochondria that had made him hesitate to invite her and Crosby to the island, but I know I'll never get her out of here. She wants to distract everyone with a game but she's gotten to the bottom of the cupboard without finding anything to her liking.

"Oh wow!" she cries, pulling out the last box. "I can't believe you have one of these!"

I lean forward to see what she's holding. The box is old and battered, the edges rubbed down to gray cardboard, the faux-wood-grain laminate peeling off in strips that look like someone clawed them away, making it hard to read the name of the game. When she opens the box, though, and I see the double arch of letters above a row of numbers I recognize what it is.

"Is that a Ouija board?" Niko asks. "I haven't seen one of those since middle school sleepovers."

"Put that crap away."

I startle at Mac's voice. He'd been out on the deck having a cigarette and I hadn't heard him come in.

"Don't tell me you're afraid of a little board game?" Ada asks, pouting. "You're the one always telling ghost stories."

"Telling ghost stories is one thing," he says, "*calling* ghosts is another."

"Mac's right," Reed says. "Put it away."

Ada looks up at Reed, her pout curdling into a close-lipped smile. "I thought you didn't believe in ghosts."

"I don't"—his eyes flick toward me—"so it's stupid sitting around a table pretending to talk to them."

"So, you've played this before?" Niko asks. "I didn't figure you for the kind of guy who went to sleepovers."

"We played it once in college," I say, "and I got kind of freaked out. That's why Reed doesn't want to play. He's worried it will scare me." I'm remembering, too, what Liz said about the séance they held here on the island and how it had spooked Mac so badly he had left.

"Oh yeah," Ada says. "I forgot. One of the Lexas from Levittown had a board and invited us over for a séance. We 'contacted'"—she makes air quotes with her fingers—"a girl from the class of 1963 who died."

"That was just those idiot girls from *Lawng Giland* messing with us," Reed says, exaggerating the local accent.

"Yeah, I'm pretty sure Lexie was deliberately moving the planchette to spell out the ghost's name," Ada says, taking out the heart-shaped wooden block. She turns it over to spin one of the wheels on its underside. "Who else would come up with such a lame name? What was it again?"

"Désirée," I say.

Liz snorts. "Like out of some bayou bodice-ripper."

"It was stupid," I agree, tucking my hands into my sweatshirt pockets. "I don't mind if we play. Really. At least it will be something new." I only say it because I can tell it's what Ada wants to do—and to prove to Reed that I'm not overimaginative and fragile. Maybe I also want to prove to myself that I only believe in ghosts *metaphorically*.

"Yeah, let's do it," Niko says, grabbing Liz's hand. "I want to see who bolts from the table first."

Liz looks up at Reed. "It's only a game—" she begins.

"Stop calling it that," Mac says. "It's not just a fucking *game*."

"It says so right here," Ada says sweetly, holding up the box lid and pointing to the writing in the corner. "'Board Game for two or more players, ages eight and up.' Ooooh, scary!"

"You guys have fun, then," Mac says. "I'm going to go down to check the gennie." He looks toward Reed and I expect that Reed will object to the séance or go with Mac, given what happened the last time a séance was held on the island, but he shakes his head grimly.

"I'm going to keep an eye on things here," he says.

"Your funeral, man," Mac says, taking another beer from the cooler then letting the screen door slam behind him.

"Wow," Niko says, grinning, "who would have thought that big, brawny Mac would be the first to chicken out. Any other pussies here?"

"I'm going to bed," Crosby says, "I've got an early videoconference in the morning." He looks at Ada. "Unless you want me to wait up to walk you back to our house."

"I'll be fine," she says. "I ain't scared of no stinking ghosts."

WE SET UP the board on the card table in the corner, first dismantling a half-finished puzzle of the *Mona Lisa*. There are only four chairs around the table and I expect that Reed will use this as an excuse to sit it out, but he goes and gets a chair from the dining room. I follow him.

"Hey," I say softly, "you don't have to do this. I just wanted to make Ada happy after she found out about you not wanting her to come."

He looks toward the great room where Ada is turning off lights and lighting a candle. "Good luck with that," he says bitterly. "I'm not sure anything will ever be enough to make her happy."

Before I can respond he carries the chair back to the table.

"There really shouldn't be more than four people touching the planchette," Ada says. "But you can write down the responses, Reed."

Reed looks like he wants to object but he goes and gets a bridge scorepad from a drawer in a side table and sits between me and Ada. Niko sits across from Ada, and Liz takes a seat under the window next to Niko.

"Okay," Ada says, placing the planchette in the middle of the board, its pointed end resting at the center of the arc of letters, "rest your fingertips lightly on the planchette and close your eyes. Clear your mind of all distracting thoughts—"

"I've never really understood how to do that," Niko says.

"Because you've got a monkey brain," Liz says fondly.

"Just be quiet," Ada says, "and relax."

I look out at the lilac bushes, now past their bloom. The air coming in through the window smells like salt and pine and it makes the candle beside Ada's elbow waver. Where we're seated, I recall, is where Liadan's bed was in the hospital. I close my eyes and hear the rustle of leaves, the lap of water down at the dock, and the distant beat of the wind turbine, which I hardly ever notice anymore. It's slower than usual, as if the heartbeat of the island is letting Ada's soothing voice lull it to sleep. In the silence I picture the island—the amoeba-shaped blob of it from Liz's hand-drawn map—from the dock to Dead Man's Cove to Gray Lady Cliff to the Witch Stone and the lighthouse and Sea Witch Cottage, all of it surrounded by the ocean.

Rocked in the arms of the sea.

As Liadan was held in her father's boat.

"Is anyone there?" Ada asks. "Is there a spirit who wants to speak to us?"

The planchette trembles beneath my fingertips—or maybe my hands are shaking from the tension of holding my breath. *Don't forget to breathe,* my respiratory therapist would tell me in the months following my illness. *It's not that I forget,* I once tried to explain, *it's that I'm afraid I won't be able to draw in the next breath.* What I couldn't tell her was that I was afraid of being back in that moment in the hospital when my heart stopped beating—a place as dark as the bottom of the sea. Just thinking about it now makes me imagine Liadan's face beneath the water looking into Nathaniel Harper's eyes, neither one of them moving to the surface.

The planchette jerks under my fingertips. I open my eyes and let out my breath at the same time and meet Ada's eyes across the table.

"Hey, it moved," Niko says.

I look down at the board. The planchette is pointing to the right corner—to the place on the board where YES is printed.

"Is someone there?" Ada asks.

The planchette jerks on the *YES.*

"Ask it something that's not a yes or no question," Liz suggests.

"Who are you?" Ada asks.

The planchette trembles for a moment as if whoever is directing it—one of us? I wonder, scanning the faces at the table for a smirk or guilty look, but even Niko's face is for once free of her habitual sarcasm—isn't sure how to answer. Or maybe, I think as the trembling travels up my arms, it's the thing on the other side that is uncertain. I recognize that uncertainty.

"Do you remember who you are?" I ask.

The planchette flies across the board to the left corner and judders on the *NO,* stabbing at the word three times. *NO NO NO.*

"So . . . what?" Niko asks with a forced casualness that doesn't quite hide the tremor in her voice. "We have an amnesiac ghost?"

"Maybe death makes you forget who you are," I say, remembering that when I woke up in the hospital after my heart stopped there'd been a horrible moment when I couldn't remember my name. I feel Reed press his leg against mine as if he's remembering it, too. The planchette drifts slowly down to the letters and lands on *D*, then slides haltingly to *E, A,* and *D* again. There's no question mark on the board but I can feel the plaintive query in the trembling wood— and the fear.

"Way to make our ghost feel bad, Lucy," Niko says.

"What do you remember?" Ada asks.

After a long pause the planchette moves to *C*, then *O, L, D.* It hangs for a moment on the *D* and then moves to *W, A, T, E, R.*

"Cold water," Ada repeats. "Did you write that down, Reed?" I turn to Reed and see he's staring at the board, pencil frozen above his pad.

"It's a pretty good bet that any ghost here on the island would have died by drowning," he says.

The planchette jerks to the *NO* in the left corner and then dips back to the letters. It moves so fast I can't separate out the words but Ada shouts out the letters, her voice half submerged beneath the roaring in my ears, as if I'm the one who's underwater, while Reed jots them down. When the planchette finally stops we all stare at it. The wood is warm to the touch and I smell something burning, as if the friction of the planchette moving over the board has ignited a fire—

I picture Dr. Fleming bursting into flames and pull my hands away.

"Well," Niko says, her voice high and nervous. "What does it say?"

I turn to Reed. His face is white in the candlelight. He looks up at me and I see the same look of fear on his face I'd seen when I woke up in the hospital.

I thought I'd lost you, he'd cried out then.

What, I wonder, is he afraid he's lost now?

"Yes, Reed," Ada says, "tell us what it says."

His throat constricts as he swallows. "It says: *Not drowned not drowned blood in the water murderer—*" Reed's voice cracks. "*—murderer murderer you you you.*"

CHAPTER EIGHTEEN

"I SUPPOSE YOU THINK THAT'S FUNNY," REED SAYS, RISING TO HIS FEET and looking accusingly at Ada.

"I don't know what you're talking about," Ada says.

"Making it move to spell out that message because you're mad that I didn't want you to come."

Ada furrows her brow. "First of all, I'm not mad. I completely understand your concerns." She turns to me. "In fact, I voiced the same ones to Lucy when she called to invite us, didn't I, Lucy?"

I nod. What she had said was *Isn't Reed worried that I'll bring the virus from the hospital?* And I had told her—

"And Lucy told me that you trusted me to take all the necessary precautions." Ada smiles at me as if proud that she has recalled my exact words. "And we did. So why would I be mad at you, Reed? And even if I were mad at you, *why* would I manufacture a message from the beyond, and *why* would you think that message was for you?" She looks around the table. "The ghost didn't say who it was calling a murderer."

"Yeah, Reed," Niko says, "it sounds like you've got a guilty conscience."

"Shut up." Reed spits the words at Niko.

"Don't you dare tell my girlfriend to shut up," Liz spits back at her brother. You're acting—"

"Like Dad?" Reed asks. "Is that your response to everything when anyone disagrees with you? That they're the intolerant one and you're the victim? If anyone should feel guilty about what happened, it should be you. You're the one who was on Dad all summer, stirring up trouble—"

"Fuck you, Reed. You're the one who was breaking the quarantine by screwing your girlfriend. You gave Mom and Dad the virus and let poor Hannah take the blame. You're the murderer—"

Reed raises his arm as if to slap Liz but I grab it to stop him and he jerks away so hard that I stumble backward, colliding with the table and knocking in one of the flimsy metal folding legs. The table crashes to the floor, sending board, planchette, scorepad, and candle flying. Hot wax spills across my bare feet. Niko nimbly slides out of the way and goes to Liz, putting her arm around her. Ada switches on a standing lamp.

"Let's get out of here," Liz says.

"I think that's a good idea," Reed says. Then he looks at me. "I'm going—"

"To check on something?" I ask, too upset to keep the bitterness out of my voice. "I know. But what's the point, Reed? Everything's already broken."

His face contorts into an expression I've never seen on him before. I don't know if he wants to cry or hit me. He does neither; he leaves. I kneel on the floor to straighten up the mess. Ada kneels beside me and takes the folded Ouija board out of my trembling hands.

"I'm so sorry, Lu. I didn't mean for any of that to happen. I swear I didn't make it say those things."

"I didn't think you did," I say, picking up the scorepad with Reed's neat block print spelling out *MURDERER* over and over again. Red wax from the candle has splattered across it like blood.

"I think it was Liz," she whispers. "Did you see how mad at Reed she is? I guess because of the will."

"What do you mean?" I ask, lowering my voice. "What do you know about the will?"

Ada sits back on her heels looking puzzled and hurt. "Lucy," she says gently. "Don't you remember? You told me about it that weekend I came to your house. You said Liz was angry because their father left the controlling interest in the island and all the family property to Reed. Didn't you say he left Liz's money in a trust with Reed as the executor?"

Had I told her that? I knew about the trust. Reed paid out any money Liz asked for and it meant Reed had to do all the work of managing the money. I knew it bothered Liz and that she'd be mad if she knew I'd told anyone, but Ada and I *had* drunk a lot of Ex-Pats that weekend and spilled our secrets. I might have said something—

"Please don't tell her I told you that," I say. Then, "Do you really think she blames Reed for their parents' deaths?" I look around but we're alone in the great room, crouched beneath the window. *"Because of Becky?"* I whisper.

Ada looks thoughtful for a moment, looking out the window as if the rustling lilac bushes and the distant susurration of the tide hold the secret of what happened on the island ten years ago. "I think," she says, "that Reed has been acting weird since we got here and if he did blame himself for bringing the virus on the island that would explain a lot. I mean"—she looks back at me, her eyes wide—"that would be awful, right? If his parents got sick because he was sneaking off with Becky and—" She claps her hand over her mouth.

"What?" I say, wondering what could be worse.

"Didn't his parents blame Mac's mother for bringing the virus?"

"Yes," I say, feeling ill. "Hannah was doing the supply runs because

Mac was gone so they thought she was the only one who could have brought the virus. They fired her. Reed said she was heartbroken. She never really recovered. She started drinking heavily and died a few years later from cirrhosis of the liver."

"Oh wow," Ada says. "So, if Reed had confessed that he was seeing Becky and that she might have been the one with the virus, then maybe they wouldn't have fired Hannah."

"That's . . . *horrible,*" I say. "But Mac . . ." The bushes outside the window stir for a moment and I stop, listening.

"I hope Mac doesn't blame Reed," Ada says. "After all, we depend on him." She gets up and holds out her hand—to give me a hand up, I think, but then I see that she's waiting for me to hand her the planchette. I hesitate. I don't want to touch it again. Even if it was Liz who was moving it, it still feels . . . *bad.* It's squatting on the floor like a toad, its pointy end nosed into the corner. I grit my teeth and pick it up as I might pick up a dead rat and notice something scratched onto the wooden molding.

"What is it?" Ada asks, taking the planchette from me and laying it on top of the game box.

"Nothing," I reply, getting to my feet. "You go on. I'm going to clean up." I try for a laugh. "I realized while I was down there that I've fallen behind on my sweeping."

Ada joins my laughter, doing a better job of it. "That's all we are to them—cook and housekeeper—and we see how well the Harpers treated their last cook and housekeeper." She hugs me tightly. "You and me, babe, we peasants gotta stick together."

I hug her back and walk her to the front door. Then I go to the broom closet and take out the broom and dustpan. When we first arrived, I asked Reed where the broom closet was and he didn't know. Nor did Liz. I found it eventually, tucked in an angle of the staircase, cleverly camouflaged into the wallpaper and wainscoting,

as if someone had decided it should be concealed. Like a priest's
hole in an English castle. I stand for a moment in its narrow doorway, inhaling the scent of lemon oil and cedar chips. Hanging from
a hook is a faded flowered apron, which I imagine belonged to Hannah. I've never worn it, but now I run my hands over it, thinking
about the woman who cleaned this house for twenty years and then
was banished—yet another restless spirit haunting the island.

I pull out the broom and sweep the kitchen and the great room.
When I reach the corner, I kneel under the window and look again
at the words scratched on the wall. The last lines of the poem about
Liadan and Cuirithir have been added, this time in English.

A roaring flame
Dissolved this heart of mine.

I stand up—and catch the whiff of smoke as I had during the séance. I empty the dustpan into the trash, put the broom and dustpan
back in the closet, and then let myself out the back door.

The clearing is lit by a full moon, the antlered scarecrow casting a
gruesome shadow over the staked squash and tomato plants.

Mr. Tibster.

Had Liz put the antlers on the scarecrow to complete the effigy
of her dead father?

I sniff the air again for the smell of smoke, a vestige of that long-
ago bonfire—

A roaring flame
Dissolved this heart of mine.

—and smell only pine trees. I walk around the side of the house
until I come to the window open to the great room. The lamp I've left
on spills a circle of light over the game box—*For ages 8 and up!*—and
empty chairs, but I can picture us sitting there, the planchette sliding under our hands. Moved by one of us? By Liz, to get back at her
brother for controlling her money? By Niko, to spread chaos? By Ada,

to punish Reed for not wanting her here? But why would Ada think to call Reed a murderer when she didn't know that he blamed himself for his parents' death? Only Liz knew that—and Niko, whom Liz tells everything to, Niko, who loves to stir up trouble and light fires—

I sniff the air—

A roaring flame

Dissolved this heart of mine.

—and catch a dying trace of sulfur and smoke. Kneeling down I run my hands over the ground until I find what I'm looking for—a cigarette butt and safety match, both still warm.

I SIT IN the great room drinking coffee to keep myself awake while I wait for Reed to return. I hear voices coming up from the dock, Mac's laconic "Later, man," and then Reed's quick footsteps on the porch and the squeal of the screen door. I've left the light off, and he startles when I say his name.

"Jesus, Lucy, you scared me. Why are you sitting in the dark?"

"It helps me think," I say, although really, it's because I didn't want him to sneak in a different way if he knew I was waiting up for him. "Can you sit down a minute? I want to talk to you."

He's silhouetted against the stove light in the kitchen, the only light I've left on, so I can't see his expression but I can see his shoulders hunch. "I'm really tired, Lu—"

"Please," I say in the gentlest voice I've got, "we can't keep going on like this, you running off to check everything over and over again, keeping secrets—"

"I have to keep watch," he says defensively. "If something breaks we'll be stranded here. We could run out of food and water. We might not be able to make it back to the mainland. It's *my* responsibility."

"It's because you blame yourself for what happened last time that you feel so responsible, isn't it?"

"It wasn't my fault," he says, still defensive but also defeated, shoulders slumped, like a child who's tired himself out repeating his defense.

"Of course it wasn't," I say, holding my hand out to him. He comes and sits down beside me on the couch. He smells like beer and cigarettes—from Mac's secondhand smoke or because he's started smoking? "Is that why you've been so tense here? Because you've been thinking about how your parents died and whether it was because of Becky?" I say her name with forced casualness, as if we talk about his dead girlfriend every day.

"It wasn't Becky," he says. "She was careful and by the end she was staying on the island in the lighthouse keeper's cottage."

"So, it couldn't have been her who got your parents sick. Why does Liz think it was?"

"Because she needs someone to be angry at. My father, the homophobic bastard, really was awful to her, but I *defended* her. And I sure as hell didn't want to be the executor of her trust. If I could dissolve it I would, but old Tibs, lawyer that he was, wrapped it in barbwire codicils that I can't even understand, far less untangle. I give her whatever money she asks for even when it's for ridiculous things. Honestly, she's better off that the principal is with me. She probably would have wasted the whole lot years ago."

"I know you do a really good job managing the money," I say, "and clearly there's no reason to blame yourself for what happened to your parents. I mean, even if it was Becky who brought the virus to the island, it's not like she did it deliberately."

"It wasn't Becky," he says firmly, "but Liz thinks that if I'd told my parents that Becky was on the island they wouldn't have blamed Hannah and fired her."

"Does Mac think that?" I ask, remembering the discarded cigarette outside the window.

"Mac blamed Becky for everything," he says. "He thought she brought something evil to the island by holding that séance. That's why he left and went to stay at his uncle's house on the mainland. But I think he blamed himself, too, for leaving his mother here to take the blame for bringing the virus. He told me she was never the same after that summer. I tried to help, though. After my parents died, I sent Hannah a check every month."

"Oh," I say, "that was really generous." I move closer and put my arm around him. "You're a generous person, Reed, inviting all these people to stay here, even Ada, whom I know you've had issues with."

"I don't have issues with Ada," he says, "she's the one who has issues with me with all her left-wing, progressive, eat-the-rich bullshit."

"Is that why you thought she was moving the planchette tonight?"

He looks embarrassed. "I shouldn't have accused her of that. It's just, well, remember in college when we held the séance with the Lexas from Levittown?"

"Yeah," I say. "When one of them made up the Désirée story to freak me out."

"Yeah, well, it wasn't one of them. A few days after I remembered that we'd read that Kate Chopin short story in English 101 together—do you remember it?"

"The one about the racist husband who blames his wife for producing a mixed-race baby? Didn't Ada write her term paper on it?"

"Uh-huh. Do you remember the title?"

I search my brain but apparently the title of that story has fallen through one of the holes eaten through by the virus. I shake my head.

"It was called 'Désirée's Baby.'"

"Oh!" I say, startled. "But that doesn't mean . . . one of those girls could have read it, too."

"Sure, but I asked Ada about it, making a joke of it, and she admitted she'd been moving the planchette and she made up the whole Désirée story."

"She did? But . . ." According to the Ouija board, "Désirée" was an unhappy, lonely freshman who got stuck in the tunnels beneath the campus during winter break and starved to death. For weeks afterward I would wake up to the sound of our radiator pipes knocking, sure that it was Désirée trying to get out of the tunnels. "I didn't sleep for weeks."

"She didn't mean to scare you; she was pissed off at one of those girls. Lexie, I think."

The one who called her a skank.

"That makes sense, I guess, but still, that doesn't mean she was doing it tonight. Why would she? I really don't think she's mad you had concerns about inviting her. It's more likely it was Liz or . . ."

"Or who?"

"Niko," I say quickly, "she's got agile fingers."

"Maybe," he says, looking at me suspiciously, as if he knew what I'd been about to say. "Still, you might want to be a little careful with Ada. She really is a good actress."

"I'll be careful," I say, "if you promise to stop blaming yourself for what happened last time and stop running off all the time." I tousle his hair and he dips his head.

"I'm not running anywhere now," he says hoarsely, kissing me.

I return his kiss eagerly but when he pushes me down on the couch, I slip out from under him and hold out my hand to lead him upstairs—away from the room where the planchette sits on top of the Ouija box like a toad, like the unsaid thing I'd been about to say:

If it wasn't Liz or Ada or Niko moving the planchette, maybe it was Liadan.

CHAPTER NINETEEN

WHEN I WAKE UP THE NEXT MORNING I FEEL RIGHT AWAY THAT SOME-thing is different. A fitful breeze tugs at the lace curtains, doors slam, the smell of burning hangs in the air. As if we'd summoned an angry ghost with the Ouija board.

Or we've all been cooped up together too long.

Downstairs I find Liz cooking breakfast in the kitchen. "I can't keep eating blueberry pancakes and bacon every day," she says. "We'll all end up fat and diabetic by the end of this." She's already burned one tofu scramble and is starting on another one. There's a bowl of muesli soaked in oat milk sitting on the table. "We need more oat milk," she adds, slamming a cabinet. "Niko, make a list."

"Sure, babe," Niko says from the porch. Liz continues to shout all the things she wants out the window. I go out onto the porch and find Niko sitting on the railing, her camera aimed at something down by the water, not writing down anything.

"I don't know why we all have to eat breakfast together," Niko mutters under her breath when I come up next to her. "I'd be happy with black coffee and cold pizza. It's what I lived on through the twenties."

"You are not going to live on junk while my brother dines in the big house like a king," Liz calls out from inside.

I pick up the binoculars, which someone has left hanging from the railing, and train them in the direction Niko is pointing her camera.

I'm expecting an exotic waterbird or a grazing deer but instead I see Ada and Reed standing on the rock jetty beside Dead Man's Cove. Ada is leaning toward him, her hands balled into fists, and Reed has his arms crossed over his chest, head bowed, as if protecting himself.

"What do you think they're arguing about?" Niko asks. "The fact Reed didn't want her to come to the island? Or her summoning an evil spirit in last night's séance?"

"Oh," I say, trying to keep my voice light, "in college they argued about everything. They once had a three-week feud over whether Bergman was a better director than Fellini." I see Reed pick his head up and look at Ada and I'm startled by how angry his face looks. What can Ada have said to him? I remember she had a knack for making the most cutting remarks. He takes a step toward Ada and for a horrible moment I think he's going to push her off the rock, but instead he walks past her, lifting his head to look up at the house. I quickly put down the binoculars and step back from the railing.

"You and Niko are welcome to stay in the Main House," I shout through the screen door. "There's plenty of room."

"That's so gracious of you, Lucy," Liz shouts back. "Thank you for inviting me to stay at my own ancestral home."

Ignoring Liz's sarcasm, I shade my eyes and look down toward the cove. Reed is heading back up. I wave and go down to meet him halfway, eager to find out what he and Ada were fighting about.

"What was that about?" I ask, when I reach him. "Ada looked really mad."

He shrugs. "You know Ada and her ever-ready ire. She's upset I didn't want her to come at first but I explained my reasoning and apologized."

"Oh," I say, thinking that Ada hadn't *looked* like she'd been listening to an apology. But Reed is right about her ever-ready ire. She often takes offense at the smallest things and pregnancy seems to have made her even more touchy. "I'm glad you apologized. I'm afraid you might have one more to make to Liz before she burns down the house." I loop my arm in his and draw him up the mown path.

"It wouldn't be the first time she's tried," Reed says. "You know, after the séance she built a bonfire in the clearing that spread to the house."

"On purpose?" I ask, shocked. But we've reached the house now and Liz is standing in the doorway calling us in for breakfast. He doesn't have time to answer—or maybe he doesn't want to tell me. Is this why he was hesitant to ask Liz to come? He'd claimed it was Niko whose behavior he was worried about, but maybe it had been Liz all along.

The house smells as if someone *has* tried to burn it down. When Crosby bursts into the great room disheveled and wild-eyed, I expect him to yell *Fire!* Instead, he rakes his hand through his hair and pro-claims, "The internet's not working."

"No?" Reed inquires. "Did you try restarting the modem?"

"Yes, I tried restarting that fucking piece of trash." Crosby bites off each word. "But it's still not working."

"Hm," Reed says, sitting down at the table and pouring himself a cup of coffee. "I'll have a look at it after breakfast."

"I have a videoconference *now*," Crosby says.

A muscle along Reed's jaw twitches. "I'm sure they'll manage through one meeting without you. You have, like, six a day. What could have happened since last night's meeting that's so urgent this morning?"

Crosby's head snaps back as if Reed had struck him. "Are you seri-ous? Have you forgotten that there's a global pandemic raging? Are you aware that cases and death rates have been escalating sharply since we got here? My hospital is facing shortages of PPE, ventila-tors, antibiotics—"

"If it's that bad," Reed says, his voice cold and controlled, which is the way it gets when he's really angry, "maybe you should be there."

"Are you . . . are you . . ." Crosby splutters, "kicking us out? My wife and unborn child?"

"Ada's welcome to stay," Reed says, as Ada herself walks in the door. "And you are, too, but I never promised you 24/7 connectivity. If you can't do your job here, man, you can go back and leave Ada here. That is, if the point all along was to keep her safe."

Crosby's mouth drops open and then his lips twist into a mean smile. "You'd like that, wouldn't you? So you can go back to your cozy college ménage à trois."

I can't help myself from laughing. It's the kind of thing that Lexie of the Lexas from Levittown used to say, her pet theory being that we were all sleeping with each other. Unfortunately, my laugh is the last straw for Crosby.

"We're going," he says to Ada. "Pack your bags."

"And how do you expect to go?" Reed asks. "Are you calling an Uber?"

"Actually," Liz says, "I've already asked Mac to do a supply run for me later today. He's got some work to do on the boat but then he plans to leave on the late afternoon tide at four. I'm sure he won't mind taking you two along." She smiles sweetly at Ada, but it's Crosby who answers her.

"Great. We'll be ready on the dock at four."

"DON'T WORRY," ADA tells me after Crosby goes back to the Cove House, "he doesn't mean it. I'll talk to him."

When she follows him, I turn on Reed. "You didn't have to suggest they leave."

"I suggested *he* leave, not Ada. He was being an asshole—"

"Takes one to know one," Liz says.

"You didn't need to point out that Mac was making a supply run," Reed says.

"I need more oat milk," Liz says innocently.

They continue bickering as I head upstairs to the study. There's plenty of time and I'll be able to watch out the window to see when the boat is getting ready to launch. Hopefully without Ada on it. As for Crosby—maybe it would be better if he left, I think a little meanly. He *has* been making things difficult, and he brings out the worst in Reed.

When I enter the study a breeze riffles through the pages of the journal, which is lying on the desk where I left it. I don't recall leaving it open, though. Had the wind been strong enough to peel back the leather cover? I picture ghostly fingers plucking at the journal— Liadan's ghostly fingers.

Hers was the face I saw when the planchette moved last night. Hers the voice I imagined crying out *murderer murderer murderer.* Was *she* murdered? I wonder.

I flip through the pages to find where I left Nathaniel standing in front of the statue in the sea witch's cottage, mesmerized as he recognized Liadan's face. So mesmerized that he didn't write for the next fortnight. The next entry is dated two weeks later, and his handwriting has changed—the letters lean far to the right as if they're rushing to get to the end—or as if they have been blown over in a stiff gale.

We have been inundated with the sick and dying. Three boats, one after another, have arrived bearing hundreds of passengers stricken with the fever. *The Black Fever,* Liadan calls it. We've had to open the hospital for the fever patients and still there aren't enough beds. I enlisted some of the men to help build a crude shelter down in the cove to house patients as we take them off the lifeboats. The only mercy is that many of them die before we can even move them up to the fever ward. Then there is the question of what to do with their bodies. McCree has organized a grave-digging team to bury the bodies on the north side of the island, far enough from our well so as not to contaminate our water supply. I pity the men who carry the bodies through the boggy woods and across the stony coast. In truth, I pity us all. Three of the Gray Nuns have died of the fever and several more are sick with it. Instead of bringing them to the hospital they are kept in the sleeping loft above the fever ward, where their sisters can tend to them.

It is heartening to see their devotion to one another. Day and night, Mairi can be seen going back and forth to the well to fetch fresh water for her sisters. She seems to never sleep, and I worry that she is working herself to the bone to exculpate the guilt that still lingers from watching her family drown on that ill-fated ship. I stopped the other day to speak with her and endeavor to soothe her conscience.

"You must not work so hard," I said as gently as I could. "Your mother and brother would not want you to pay for their deaths with your own."

She looked at me queerly and replied, "It's not my life that will pay for theirs; it's his."

"His?" I asked. She leaned closer and whispered in my ear. "He is here, Dr. Harper. The devil is here on this island."

I reared back to stare at her and saw the glint of madness in her eyes. I would have tried to reason with her but just then some of McCree's men came out of the woods and Mairi, seeing them, hurried away. I'm not sure what I would have said to the poor addled girl. It is not just the fever that I fear we will fall to if the ships keep coming; I fear we will all succumb to madness.

My heart sank as another ship flying a black flag appeared on the horizon yesterday morning. I hurried down to the dock and found Dunstan McCree and his gang of hunters in a heated dispute. When I asked what the trouble was McCree told me that the men were against taking in the passengers from the new ship.

"We have not enough to feed ourselves," a burly fellow, whom I recognized as a sailor from the *Stella Maris,* complained.

"We have no choice," I pointed out. "We are commissioned by the Board of Health to act as a quarantine station."

"Let them go on to Quebec," said an Irishman who had come on a later ship.

"The Quebec station on Grosse Ile is also overwhelmed," I explained. "I've received letters to that effect. We are charged with aiding these poor souls—"

"Let them go to the bottom of the sea," a rowdy member of the hunt expostulated. This one, I noticed, had a crude tattoo on his forehead, the same knot design I'd seen painted on the rocks. It looked as if it had been inflicted on his flesh recently and was in danger of infection. Looking around me I saw that many of the men sported the same symbol on their flesh and all of them had the look of madness in their eyes. What strange worship united them? Typhus was not the only fever raging on the island.

"Can you not control your men, Mr. McCree?" I demanded in a low voice.

He looked at me and said, "Sometimes it's easier to bend than to break." As he had at the bonfire. I stared at him and then I noticed that at the base of his throat he wore the same knot symbol as the others, only it was paler, as if it was an older mark. What dangerous beliefs had he been seeding in these men?

"I will take a boat to the ship and we will return to the island with the sick," I said.

"As you wish," McCree replied. He nodded at two men and told them to ready the small boat. I heard him whispering some words in Gaelic to the man with the raw mark upon his forehead. As they rowed me out to the ship I interrogated my oarsmen about the marks they wore on their skin. Were they traditional for sailors? But all they would say was that they bedeviled the fever and kept "bad'uns" from getting in. When I asked what bad'uns they meant, they grew silent and one muttered that it "didna do to name 'em aloud," so we rowed the rest of the way in silence.

The ship was even worse than the last one, a pestilent hole, the dead wrapped in canvas and stacked like firewood, the living lying in their own filth. When I asked the men to help me load the worst patients for the first crossing they looked at each other and then one said there was a storm coming and they wouldn't be able to do the crossing a second time. He jerked his chin toward the horizon where there was indeed a dark cloud tethered to the sea by slanting lines of rain. It was a long way off but I'd learned that the weather changed quickly on the island.

"Hurry then," I told them, "to get these patients across, and we'll come back for the rest tomorrow."

The two men, to do them credit, moved quickly, nor did they seem at all worried about catching the fever, so certain were they that the marks they wore would protect them. I was thinking about talking to Liadan about the design, and perhaps not paying close enough attention to the weather. It was only when we were aboard the now overburdened boat that I saw how dark the sky had become. There was nothing for it, though, but to make for the island through the chop and slap of the waves as fast as we could. Our frail craft was tossed and rocked like a child's paper boat upon the surf, the moans of the sick merging with the shrieks of the wind. I found myself thinking that it would be better for the poor souls to go to the bottom of the sea as the sailor had wished them. Then as we neared the shore, an enormous wave rose up and crashed down upon us, swamping the boat and dashing us all into the water. The next few moments were all darkness and I believe might have been my final ones, but a rough hand yanked me to the surface and dragged me through the churning sea. I was thrown onto the rocks like a dead fish, my mouth and nose streaming salt water, and when I opened my eyes, Liadan's face was above mine.

"That's twice you've dared the deep to take you. The third time she may have her way with you."

I started to laugh but spit up seawater instead, which was just as well as I soon learned that all the sick passengers aboard the boat had been lost to the sea and it would have looked unseemly to be laughing.

"It's a mercy upon them," I heard Dunstan McCree say.

As Liadan led me back to the hospital I couldn't help thinking that he had gotten his wish. And then this morning when we learned that the ship had foundered on the rocks and all the souls aboard had been lost, I began to wonder if the stories were right, that the island had been cursed by the witch who was buried alive here, and that if we ever managed to leave, our souls would be tethered to this damned place even after death.

CHAPTER TWENTY

AFTER READING THE JOURNAL I BECOME SO IMMERSED IN MY WRITING that I don't notice the room has turned dark, the air heavy with salt water, and the windows opaque with sea spray. I am on a boat rocking in a storm. When I stand, I even feel the floor beneath me pitch.

It's only that I've been sitting too long in one place and my legs are cramped. The captain's clock on the wall reads almost four. At least I won't have missed Ada and Crosby leaving. I look out the rain-spattered window and can make out several figures on the dock standing around the boat in bright rain slickers. I run downstairs, through the empty great room, and out onto the porch. The rain wafts against my face like a wet curtain—

Like the canvas shrouds that wrapped the bodies on the fever ship.

I grab a raincoat off the back of one of the rockers and hurry down to the dock. My heart sinks when I see the suitcases piled there, including Ada's faded purple North Face duffel. As I step onto the floating dock Ada turns to me. For a second I'm startled by how big she's gotten, but then I realize it's just that she's wearing a life jacket beneath her rain slicker.

"Oh, thank God," she says, "I didn't want to disturb your writing but I was afraid I wouldn't get to say goodbye."

"Are you really going?" I wail. "In this?" The waves are slapping against the dock and the wind is blowing so hard my words feel as if they're being snatched out of my mouth.

"He won't budge," she says, looking at Crosby over her shoulder where he's standing between Mac and Reed a couple of yards away. "Even when Reed came down to apologize."

"Reed apologized?" I ask, knowing how hard it must have been to do.

"Yes, and he offered to drive to Bangor to buy a new modem."

Knowing how much the possible exposure of a trip to a big box store in Bangor—were they even open these days?—would worry Reed, my heart swells for him. "But where will you go? Back to New York?"

She shakes her head and makes a face. "Crosby's parents' house in New Jersey."

I know how much she dislikes her in-laws. "Maybe he'll change his mind," I say, "or . . . I mean . . . could *you* just stay?"

She looks at me and holds my gaze for a moment. "Would you stay if Reed were leaving?" she asks finally.

The question surprises me. I could say it's not the same thing—Reed wouldn't be leaving his own island, after all—but I know that's not the real question. I remember one of the questions we'd debate late at night in our dorm room—along with *If you could time-travel and change one thing, what would it be? What would we be willing to give up for each other? If I needed a kidney, would you give me yours? Would you carry a baby for me? Would you cover up a murder?*—

Would you leave your husband for me?

Hell, yeah, she would say to the last, *sisters over misters every time.*

Although she never said so, I knew that when I chose Reed over her—even though she was the one who had left me in the dorm—she thought I had broken that code.

Crosby calls her to hurry up, but she stays, brown eyes locked on mine as if her life depended on my answer. If I say that I would leave Reed for her sake, will she stay now?

Would I?

But I can't say it—even if it were true—it would be too much of a betrayal of Reed. "No, I guess not."

She doesn't, as I feared, look hurt or surprised. She looks as if I've confirmed something she already knew. Which hurts more. I want to take it back, tell her I was lying, that I'd choose her, but she's already turned and is walking toward Crosby. She picks up her purple duffel bag, swings it to Mac in the boat, and then gets in without looking back. Reed says something to Mac and then walks back toward me. I can see by his face that he's troubled. Before he even reaches me he's telling me that he tried to talk them out of going.

"I know," I tell him, putting my arm around him. "Ada told me you apologized to Crosby. Thank you. I know that must have been hard seeing as he's been kind of an ass. I appreciate your trying for Ada's sake."

"I did it for *your* sake," he says. "I know how much she means to you." He says it almost bitterly, and I wonder if he knows what Ada asked me and if he suspects that I almost told her I'd choose her over him. Has he always wondered if I'd have chosen her over him if she hadn't left first?

"Not as much as you mean to me," I say, laying my head on his shoulder. I feel a release of tension in him—almost a shudder—as we turn to watch Mac steer the motorboat out of the harbor. It rides even lower in the water than when we came over. "I thought you and Mac have been working on the boat," I say.

"We have," he says, "it may be taking on water because of the surf. I told them it wasn't safe to go in this weather."

The little boat does seem to be struggling through the surf and it hasn't even cleared the cove yet. I think of Nathaniel Harper's description of returning to the island in the boat overburdened with fever patients and how they were swamped by one giant wave. Everything is suddenly quiet, even the wind, as if the moment has frozen in time—

If you could time-travel and change one thing, what would it be?

Would I have followed Ada to the bus station and made her come back even if it meant I wouldn't have been alone when Reed returned?

"It's dead," I hear Reed say.

"What?" I ask, my voice loud in the unnatural hush.

"The engine. It's dead and he's not able to steer the boat without it."

That's why it's so quiet, I realize, the boat engine has died. The wind is, of course, still blowing, driving the boat sideways so that the waves are crashing over the side. I can see Crosby standing in the prow, bailing water, as Mac struggles with the motor. Ada is getting to her feet, teetering awkwardly. *Pregnancy messes with your balance,* she'd said just the other day. I want to shout at her to sit down but even though they're only twenty or thirty yards out she'd never hear me over this wind. How could I have ever thought it was quiet? The wind is howling like a banshee—like the sea witch come to snatch her victims. I can see a wave gathering itself from the deep like a hand coming up to grab the boat—

Rocked in the arms of the sea.

—and then it comes down over the boat like a stage curtain at the end of a play. Surely that's all this is. The wave will wash over them and then the boat will emerge and Mac will get the engine running and Ada will wave—

But the boat is gone. Erased from the surface of the sea. As if it never existed.

I turn to Reed but he's no longer next to me, he's running to the end of the dock, stripping off shirt and jeans and shoes, and diving into the water before I can even scream his name. I stumble after him, the dock pitching under my feet the way I imagined the study floor was moving half an hour ago. It's as if I've conjured up this horror from reading Nathaniel Harper's journal.

I see the white of Reed's arm breaking the surface as he swims toward where the boat was, and then I see the boat, or at least the bottom of it—bobbing between swells. There should be three heads buoyed up by their life jackets—

Were they wearing life jackets?

Ada had been, I recall; Mac definitely hadn't been. Crosby? I couldn't remember. I see, though, one head bobbing up near the overturned boat and then a second. One of those has to be Ada, I tell myself. I'm straining to see better, wishing I had binoculars, when something slams into me, nearly sending me into the water. It's Niko, wet hair matted over her face, shucking her boots off as she hops to the end of the dock.

"Don't you dare go out there!" yells Liz, close behind with a pair of binoculars in her hand.

Ignoring her, Niko peels her jeans off and executes a neat racing dive into the water.

"Idiot!" Liz cries, coming to stand beside me at the edge of the dock, binoculars glued to the surface of the water. Niko emerges a good ten feet out and strokes seaward. I snatch the binoculars out of Liz's hands and train them on the capsized boat. I see three heads on the surface. One, holding onto the edge of the boat, is definitely Ada. Reed is next to her, treading water, shouting something at her. The other head disappears before I can identify who it is.

"What happened?" Liz asks. "We saw the boat capsize from the house."

"It looked like it was taking on water then the engine stopped and a big wave came—" The sequence of mishaps doesn't seem like enough to account for the present disaster. Surely it goes back further. Liz apparently thinks so, too.

"I told him to buy a new boat," she cries. Her face is wet but I can't tell if that's from the rain or tears. "But no, he always has to be so frigging frugal, just like our father . . ." Her voice warbles and I put my arm around her while still looking through the binoculars.

"I can see Reed," I tell her. "And Niko. They look like they're taking turns diving. For Crosby, I think." I see Mac surface, shaking his head like a wet dog. "I don't think Crosby was wearing a life jacket."

"Idiot men," Liz says, although I don't recall her wearing one on the trip over. *Thank God Ada had one,* I think, but she could still drown.

"Why aren't they swimming to shore?" I ask.

Liz takes the binoculars back from me and raises them to her face. "Your friend is refusing," she says. "Doesn't want to leave hubby, I suppose, but she's putting everyone else at risk by staying."

"Would you leave if it were Niko missing?" I ask. As soon as the words are out of my mouth I hear an echo of the question Ada posed to me earlier. Is this what we've come to, I wonder, having to choose one loved one over another?

"Niko must have talked sense into her," Liz says instead of answering my question. "They're swimming back together."

"What about Reed and Mac?" I ask, trying to get the binoculars away from her.

She evades me and keeps them fixed to the scene unfolding on the water. "They're still taking turns diving. If Crosby has been under all this time he's gone."

It's a harsh assessment but I find myself agreeing. I want Reed back. I want to take back that Faustian bargain I'd been willing to make half an hour ago—Ada for Reed—even as I help Ada out of the water onto the dock and wrap my arms around her, trying to chafe warmth into her trembling limbs. Even as I tell her it's okay, Reed will find Crosby, I want to shout at her that she should have made Reed come back with her. He would have listened to her if she told him she knew Crosby was gone. But she's already anticipated my accusation.

"I told . . . them . . . to come back . . ." she gasps, ". . . but . . . Reed . . ."

She doesn't have to finish. Reed feels responsible. He'd invited Crosby and Ada to come to the island in the first place. Crosby had left because they argued. Liz had told him he should buy a new boat. I know Reed well enough to know that he will trace the domino chain of cause and effect back to the original sin of his failing. He's out there now tracking those gears and levers down to the bottom of the sea.

"They're heading back," Liz announces.

"Is Crosby with them?" Ada asks.

Liz looks at Ada. "I'm sorry, honey," she says in an unusually warm voice for her, "he isn't. Maybe . . . maybe he was able to swim to shore . . ."

"Crosby can't swim," Ada whispers.

Liz looks away, and I hug Ada. There's nothing more to say although what I'd like to ask is, *If Crosby can't swim, why the hell didn't he wear a life jacket?*

CHAPTER TWENTY-ONE

IT'S RAINING SO HARD THAT BY THE TIME WE GET UP TO THE HOUSE WE are all soaked to the skin—those of us who have been in the sea and those of us who haven't.

Not as soaked to the skin as Crosby, I think horribly.

There are no lights on, and it's cold in the great room.

"Wind must have taken down the power line from the wind turbine," Reed says, getting ready to go out again.

"It can wait till tomorrow," I bark, suppressing the observation that the *wind* shouldn't be able to disable the *wind* turbine. "You need to get out of those wet clothes."

He looks like he's going to argue but he must see that I already have my hands full with Ada, whose teeth are chattering so hard I'm afraid she's going to bite her tongue. I bring her up to one of the guest rooms, sit her on the side of the bed, and peel off her life jacket—

Why wasn't Crosby wearing one?

She bats my hand away when I get to her shirt. "I can do that. You need to get out of your wet clothes, too."

I toss her towels and a robe from the bathroom and go to my bedroom. Reed is sitting on the side of our bed, still in his wet clothes.

"What are you doing?" I cry. "You'll get sick."

He lifts his hand to his shirt but it's shaking so hard he can't undo the buttons. Chastising myself for scolding him, I unbutton his shirt and peel it off, releasing an odor of seaweed and brine. His skin is so cold and white it feels as if I am undressing a drowned person.

"Crosby . . ." he says.

"It's not your fault," I say automatically. "He should have worn a life jacket, especially since he couldn't swim."

He grabs my wrist, his fingers a manacle of icy steel. "The life jackets were gone," he whispers, as if afraid someone will overhear us. "All but one of them were missing when we got down to the boat. Crosby insisted that Ada take that one."

"Oh," I say, "that's—" I'm going to say *awful* but he finishes more aptly.

"Suspicious?" he suggests. "The boat was taking on water as if a hole had been punched in the hull. Crosby was the only one who couldn't swim. It's like someone sabotaged the boat so he would drown."

"But who would do that? Who would want Crosby dead?"

A hoarse strangled bark escapes his mouth. For a moment I'm afraid he's drowning. I saw something on a television show once about a child rescued from the sea only to drown hours later from seawater in his lungs—secondary drowning, it was called—but then I realize, with no relief, that he's laughing. "Don't you see? *I'm* the one who would want Crosby dead. Someone has made it look like I've killed him."

WHEN WE GET downstairs, we find that Mac has made a huge fire in the fireplace and Liz is handing around hot spiked drinks. Ada is wrapped in blankets on the couch and Niko, engulfed in a pink Bar Harbor sweatshirt, is perched on the hearth, nearly *in* the fire, as if she can't get warm. Crosby's absence is palpable in the room. I glance uneasily into the shadows gathered around our fire-lit circle imagining him crouching in the corner where we called to the dead last night.

"Shouldn't we . . ." Ada croaks, her voice so raw she has to swallow and begin again. "Shouldn't we notify someone? The police? Or the coast guard?"

"I'll get the radio," Reed says, clearly relieved to have something to do. "It's in the TV room."

He leaves without taking a flashlight or candle, swallowed up by the dark. It's unnerving to think how far and deep that dark extends here on this island in the sea, our little circle of firelight the only spark for miles, as if we are the first settlers on the edge of the wilderness.

"I know Reed's probably blaming himself," Ada says softly in her husky, raw voice, "but it was just an accident."

"Someone took the life jackets from the boat," Mac says, poking the fire. "And tinkered with the engine."

"When did you see them last?" Liz asks.

"I checked them before last week's supply run," Mac says.

"They could have been stolen when you tied up to the dock on the mainland," Liz says, "and that engine's been on its last legs for years. Reed should have—"

"Bought a new boat." Reed's voice comes out of the dark and then his corporal form follows, holding up the VHF radio. "I know. But I *did* buy a new radio, only the batteries are gone."

"There must be extra batteries," Niko says, unfolding herself from the hearth. Liz is ahead of her, rattling through kitchen drawers with a flashlight. "They're not where they should be," she announces.

"So," Mac says, wiping soot off his hands, "someone stole the batteries *and* the life jackets *and* messed with the boat engine *and* punched a hole in the hull. Someone who wants us all to be trapped here."

"Well, it sure as hell wasn't me," Niko says. "I've about had it with this place. I've got all the pictures I need."

"Wait," Ada says plaintively, her voice hoarse from crying, "we're trapped? There must be some way to contact the mainland for help."

Mac snorts. "We can send up smoke signals. Spell out *S.O.S.* in the sand."

"There's a dinghy in the lighthouse," Reed says, "from when it was a coast guard station."

"That thing's old, man," Mac says, "and we'd have to row three miles."

"We can mend any holes," he says, "and you and I have rowed further."

A look passes between them that makes me wonder what secret history they're recalling. Whatever it is either convinces Mac or at least makes him want to avoid talking about it. "Yeah, sure, we'll go out tomorrow morning when the storm has passed and check it out. The other boat might wash up, too. Lots of shit gets washed up in Dead Man's Cove."

He looks guiltily at Ada, which only underlines what we're all thinking—that Crosby's body might be among the dead things that return to the island.

NO ONE HAS much appetite for dinner, but I heat up canned soup and make grilled cheese sandwiches to have something to do. The rain brings a premature nightfall and we're all exhausted from the adrenaline rush of the shipwreck. When I notice Ada fighting back yawns between tears I suggest she go up to bed here at the Main House.

"I really am an orphan of the storm," she sobs. "Maybe we should all stay in the Main House tonight because, you know . . ."

"One of us is a murderer?" Liz asks, rolling her eyes. "Are we going to go full Agatha Christie now? No, thank you. Niko and I will stay in the barn, which has a padlock in case anyone's wondering."

"I'm going to bunk out here," Mac says, stretching out on the couch. "Not really in the mood to bushwhack through the woods in this."

"There are plenty of rooms," Reed says.

"Nah, I'm good, man," he says.

"It makes me feel a little funny," Ada whispers as we make our journey up the dark stairs, "to have him sleeping down there."

"Why?" I ask, pausing outside the door to one of the guest rooms. The flashlight is shining upward on her face, reminding me of nights in our dorm room when I'd look over to see her face lit up by the light of her phone as she scrolled through Instagram and Twitter.

She shrugs. "I don't know. He was acting strange on the boat. He made Crosby sit on the prow to keep the boat balanced, so of course when the wave hit he went right over . . ." Her voice catches. "Of course, Mac couldn't have known we'd be hit by a big wave."

"Unless he knew that the engine would fail—or he purposefully stalled it," I whisper, looking over my shoulder into the shadows. "But why would Mac want Crosby dead?"

She shakes her head, scattering tears. "I, I don't know . . . he never seemed to like him . . . I know Crosby could be a bit . . . bossy, but he never hurt anyone." Her tears are falling freely now.

"Of course he didn't," I say, hugging her tightly. "I can't believe anyone would deliberately hurt him. And why would Mac sabotage the boat? He's as stranded here as the rest of us."

"Is he?" Ada asks, stepping out of my embrace to look me in the eye. "How do we know he doesn't have another boat stashed somewhere? And another radio? Have you ever been in that cabin of his?"

"No," I admit. She has a point, but I can also hear the edge of hysteria creeping into her voice, the way she'd get during finals week when she'd go without sleep and live on caffeine and sugar. "But I don't see why Mac would want to hurt any of us."

"Haven't you noticed how much he resents all of us 'college grads,' as he calls us?"

"That's just a defense mechanism," I say. "After all, one of those college grads is Reed, his best friend. Why would he want to hurt Reed?"

"I don't know . . ." Ada says, looking nervously into the shadows. "Reed could have kept his mother from getting fired by admitting that Becky was on the island. If Mac overheard that last night, it might have set him off. What if killing Crosby is his way of setting Reed up so Reed is punished for someone else's death?"

I could tell her about the cigarette butt and match I found outside the window but that will only feed into her hysteria. "Reed says Mac knew about Becky being on the island and that he didn't hold any of that against him," I say instead, trying to sound like I believe it. "Besides, do you really think Mac is *smart* enough to come up with a plan like that?"

It's a mean thing to say but it has the desired effect of making Ada smile. Ragging on our classmates was always a sure way of cheering her up in college. "I guess not," she admits. "He'd probably just hit Reed over the head with a six-pack if he wanted to punish him."

"Definitely," I say, giving her a last hug. I wait to hear the click of her door locking behind her. The image of Mac hitting someone over the head accompanies me down the darkened hall to my bedroom. I can't lock my door behind me because Reed is still downstairs. With Mac. Mac, who could hit Reed over the head with any number of implements—the fire poker he was handling earlier comes readily to mind—and then come upstairs to finish off me and Ada. He's acted resentful of all of us "college grads" since we got here. And why not? He's the one who put in all the work to make this place ready for us, who puts himself at risk every week for supply runs so we can have our oat milk and organic peanut butter. Reed is the only one he can stand, and then he found out last night that Reed could have prevented Hannah from getting fired if he'd confessed to his parents that Becky was on the island.

I sit down on the edge of the bed and stare at the rain lashing against the windowpane. I can picture Mac standing outside the window last night. But why? He'd seemed genuinely scared of us using the Ouija board, afraid we'd summon up one of the many vengeful spirits of the island. So why lurk outside the window? What was he waiting to hear—and what had he thought when he heard Ada calling out the letters that spelled *murderer*? Who did he think the ghost was? And who the murderer?

I don't change out of my heavy sweatpants and sweatshirt for bed. I don't think I'll be able to sleep but I huddle under the blankets for warmth and eventually the adrenaline crash after the horrors of the day and the sound of the rain and wind lead me into a fitful slumber full of nightmare visions. I am in the car in the rest stop and a woman is pressing her unmasked face to the window yelling at me to *go back*. Then the car is under the sea and it's the sea witch's face at the window, her sharp nails tapping at the glass. Then it's Crosby's face, his mouth open in a horrible silent scream, his face already bloated, his eyes glazed and vacant, fingers pressed against the glass—except there's something wrong with his fingers. Each tip is distended, swollen—an octopus's sucker that has latched onto the window glass, splintering it into a million pieces—

I startle awake to the sound of breaking glass and lurch up in bed, groping for the flashlight on the night table. When I turn it on I see that horrible bloated face and hungry suckers in the window—

My own reflection turned fright mask by the angle of the flashlight. The glass is intact, though. I must have dreamed the sound of breaking glass. Or it came from downstairs where Reed must still be—with Mac.

I sit on the edge of the bed listening. It's hard to hear anything over the rain and wind. I creep to the door and open it cautiously, strafing the hallway with my flashlight. The startled faces of Reed's ancestors glare back at me from the photographs on the wall, their expressions suggesting that I am the interloper here. *Go back to your room,* they say, *and lock your door.* I am tempted to do exactly that but then I hear another crash from downstairs, and I think of Reed. He may need me.

As I creep down the stairs the flashlight makes me feel like a target so I switch it off. My bare feet are silent on the worn wood, but also frozen. The house is freezing. It's hard to believe it could get this cold in July but then Reed had warned me that an island in the Atlantic this far north could turn frigid even in summer. I can barely feel my feet by the time I reach the great room—and then the rest of me freezes.

The room is cast in the red glow of the dying embers of the fire. The light turns the glass shards scattered across the floor into a hundred bloody daggers, the largest of which is caught in Reed's up-turned palm. He's kneeling below the window in the corner and Mac is looming over him, his face a mask of rage, a fire poker held aloft in his hand.

"Stop!" I cry, rushing forward. Mac and Reed turn toward me, frozen in a tableau that shifts before my eyes, the glass shard in Reed's hand becoming a dagger, the look of rage in Mac's face turning into fear. They're both looking at me as if I am the threat here.

CHAPTER TWENTY-TWO

"DON'T MOVE," REED BARKS.

I think he's ordering me back because of the broken glass scattered on the floor, but then Mac says, "It's gone."

It?

"Are you sure?" Reed asks, rising to look out the window. "Should we go after it?"

"I'll go," Mac says. "You stay here with Lucy." He walks toward me, boots crunching on glass, fire poker swinging by his side. It would be the work of a moment to strike me with it. I try not to flinch, but as he passes by me our eyes lock and he's the one who flinches, as if he knows that I'm afraid of him and it confirms all his worst suspicions about me.

"Don't worry," he says, "I'll take care of it."

Like I take care of everything, he might as well add.

When he's gone I turn to Reed, who's still standing at the window looking out. "What's *it*?" I ask. "What did you see out there?"

"I don't know," he says. "I didn't really see anything but a blur, but Mac said it was someone in a hood . . . you're barefoot." I look down at the floor and see that wherever I move there's more glass. In an instant he strides across the glass and picks me up. I'm so startled I yelp. The only time he ever picked me up was when he found me sick in my dorm room. It makes me feel a swell of love for him. He lowers me onto the couch, sinks down beside me, and wraps his arms around me.

"I should never have brought you here," he says.

"I always thought you avoided bringing me here in the past because the island was a place you had shared with Becky."

He holds me at arm's length to stare at me. "What are you talking about? I never brought you here because I thought the place was cursed and I didn't want it to take the one person I love away—" He swipes at his eyes and I see tears glinting in the firelight.

"I love you, too," I say, burrowing into his chest. "I was so scared when I came in and saw Mac holding that poker. I thought—"

"Mac saw something at the window. It broke the glass and Mac scared it away with the poker. I only caught a glimpse . . . Mac said it was someone wearing a gray cloak."

The Gray Lady.

"Are you sure you didn't imagine it?" I ask. What I mean is, *Are you sure Mac didn't make it up and break the window himself?* I look over at the coffee table and notice all the empty beer bottles and the half-empty bottle of Jack Daniel's. "You and Mac were drinking, and it's been a long, horrible day."

"There was someone there," he insists, looking toward the window. "It broke the window and it . . . it *screamed*." His face is ashen. "Mac said it looked like a skull instead of a face beneath the hood. A deer skull."

"Like the ones hanging in the barn," I say, thinking of Liz's resentment and anger toward Reed. "Could it be Liz?" I suggest softly. "She seemed really angry with you last night. I know brothers and sisters play tricks on each other and she was really into that game you used to play."

"It wasn't like that," he says. "You don't understand."

"How *can* I understand if you never talk about it?" I say, more sharply than I'd intended.

"Becky was the one who was into the game," he says bitterly. "Liz only went along because she had a crush on Becky."

"Oh," I say, recalling how Liz talked about Becky. "That must have been awkward. Did Becky . . . ?"

"Reciprocate her feelings?" He shrugs. "Becky liked being adored and she was happy to use your adoration to get what she wanted. That summer she wanted to be here on the island with us and not alone in her parents' empty house on the mainland. She needed Liz to go along with that so she came up with ever more elaborate games to play and stories to tell to entertain Liz."

"Just Liz?" I ask.

He blushes. "It all seemed a little childish to me by then, and I didn't really want to be here." He looks up at me. "I wanted to be with you, and I think Becky sensed that she had lost me. It made her all the more desperate to make the game exciting. She came up with using the Ouija board to summon Liadan. She thought Liadan had been possessed by the buried witch and that she had to be propitiated."

"How?" I ask, feeling both a queer sense of relief that Reed had grown tired of Becky that summer, that he wanted me all along, and a queasy sense of dread at hearing what he might say next.

"By making a sacrifice," he says. "She thought we had to make a sacrifice to Liadan to free us from the Harper Curse."

"That's crazy," I say.

"Yeah, but you had to be here to understand. My dad was going out of his mind. It was like being in a house with a madman. Sometimes Hannah had to lock him in the study to keep him from going on a rampage. It *felt* like we were cursed. I thought maybe if we went along with the game and lit candles and poured libations and recited some shit in Gaelic it would be . . . cleansing somehow, and then at the end of the summer I could tell Becky that I was moving on and it would be okay, like we'd had this last summer together and had closure."

He looks up at me and smiles ruefully. "Yeah, I was an idiot. When I finally did tell her, she didn't even act mad, she just said I was *mistaken*. I didn't know what I was saying because I was under the Harper Curse. Then she said—" He swallows. "She said she didn't intend to be abandoned the way Liadan had been."

I feel a chill go through me and I look up toward the window, as if checking to make sure that the cloaked figure of the Gray Lady—Liadan, the sea witch—hasn't come to exact her revenge for her abandonment. "That's crazy," I say for the second time, only now what I mean is *Becky was crazy*.

"Yes," he agrees, "it was. But what was I supposed to do? I couldn't leave. Mac had gone to his uncle's house on the mainland, so I had to keep everything here working all by myself. And I couldn't banish Becky from the island in the middle of a pandemic. I thought if I just went along with her that it would work itself out, that she'd get tired of the game. But then she decided we needed to make a bigger sacrifice."

"*Bigger?*"

His face looks haunted in the firelight. "A human sacrifice. She said we should sacrifice my father. Of course, I thought she was joking. Or being—I don't know—*symbolic*? She and Liz made a Mr. Tibster scarecrow and added stag horns so it would be like some medieval pagan rite. They lit a fire in the clearing. I thought they just meant to burn my father in effigy but then the fire spread."

"You said that was an accident."

He pauses to collect himself. Telling me all this after years of silence is taking a toll on him. "I think Becky talked Liz into spreading the fire to the house while my father was passed out drunk. Liz was supposed to get my mother and Hannah out. But my father, drunk as he was, woke up first and blundered outside. Everyone else got out but Hannah's apron caught fire. I had to push her to the ground to smother the flames. I can still smell the smoke and singed flesh."

I can smell it, too. "Reed," I say, "do you smell smoke now?"

His head jerks up and he sniffs the air. There is an unmistakable tinge of smoke in the air coming through the broken window.

"Stay here," he says, getting up and grabbing my flashlight.

I have no intention of staying behind but first I have to find a pair of shoes in the boot tray, and I have to navigate over the broken glass in the dark because Reed took the flashlight. As I shove my bare feet into someone's rubber clogs a hysterical litany is running through my brain demanding, *What's happening What's happening What's happening*.

"What's happening?"

Has my fear become a disembodied spirit? Is that what happens to us on this island—our worst fears become manifest? Then a flashlight turns on and Ada, huddled in a hooded sweatshirt, takes shape out of the dark.

"We smelled smoke," I say. "Reed's gone to check it out."

"Why is there glass all over?" she asks, sweeping the floor with her flashlight beam. She sounds groggy and I wonder if she took something to help her sleep. But would she, when she's pregnant?

"Something—someone broke the window," I tell her. "I'll explain later. Do you know where the fire extinguisher is?"

She nods and turns from me, taking the light with her. I follow helplessly, frustrated at her slow fumbling pace. I remind myself that she's been woken in the middle of the night after losing her husband. She finds the extinguisher and I grab it, then head out the back door, the beam of Ada's flashlight showing the way. But we don't need it. The clearing is ablaze with light. At first I think it's just the scarecrow and the garden but then I see that the loft windows in the barn are glowing red. Reed is pounding on the heavy sliding doors—which Liz bragged about being padlocked—shouting Liz's name in between throwing his body at the hard wood. He's going to break his shoulder if he keeps it up.

I scan the façade of the barn. There are no windows at ground level, but flames are now leaping out of the loft windows.

A figure comes running out of the woods—Mac holding aloft an ax. He rushes straight for Reed and I have the horrible thought that he's going to cleave him in two in revenge for his mother's death, but instead he swings the ax at the barn door. Splinters and sparks fly everywhere. Mac swings again—and again, pulling chunks of wood out with the flat of the ax head. Lit up by the fire he looks like some mad deity—Thor or Vulcan—or Jack Torrance from *The Shining*. As soon as he's cleared a few feet of space Reed pushes past him and claws his way through the gap.

"Wait!" I shout, stumbling forward with the extinguisher.

Reed is already through but Mac takes the extinguisher from my hands and turns to me, his face black with soot. "Stay back," he barks, "get the hose if you want to help, but stay far back." Then he's gone. Smoke wafts out of the hole in his place as if he's been vaporized. I can feel the heat on my face and see flames along the walls and the stairs leading up to the loft. I want to follow and make Reed come back but Ada is tugging at my sleeve, making me back up.

"Here's the hose," she says. "I'll go back to the house for buckets if you promise not to go in."

I grab the hose and tug it toward the black hole that's swallowed my husband. I should have realized he would run in and stopped him. Let Mac go instead—

Mac, who rushed out of the house chasing a phantom just moments before the barn caught on fire and then conveniently appeared with an ax. And who is now in that burning building with that ax and my husband. He could do anything to Reed in there.

"Are they still inside?" Ada has come back with two buckets.

"Yes," I say, aiming the hose and squeezing the lever. The water barely reaches the door, and the pressure seems to be waning. "Is there any way to increase the pressure from the well house? Or to find a longer hose?"

"There's no electricity to power the pump; this is just what's left in the reservoir. Fill the buckets and we'll throw it at the fire. We can keep the fire from spreading any further."

"At least the ground is wet from the rain—" I begin. The rain has stopped but I remember hearing it when I fell asleep, and the garden and woods are still sodden and dripping. "How could this have started in the middle of a rainstorm?"

"Lightning?" Ada suggests. "Or . . . Niko does smoke and then there are all the chemicals she uses in her darkroom—"

Her voice is cut off by shouts coming from inside the barn. I lower the hose and Mac appears, a hunched, hulking shape silhouetted against the orange glow of flames. He's carrying Liz, who's kicking and screaming like she's being forcibly evicted from her home. Mac drops her next to me and barks at her, "Stay here if you want me to get your boneheaded girlfriend out."

Then he's back through the door and Liz is trying to follow him. I grab her arm. "What does he mean about Niko?" I demand. "And where's Reed?"

"Niko ran down to the darkroom to save her negatives and Reed went after her. But I'm the only one who knows how to reason with her—"

I slap her, shocking both of us. When I find my voice it's surprisingly level. "If you go in there you'll only give Reed one more person he has to save."

Liz looks like she's getting ready to hit me back but then Mac is pushing Niko, who's clutching her camera bag to her chest, out the hole in the door. He turns to go back in before I can make him tell me where Reed is. The answer comes soon enough. Mac returns carrying Reed over his shoulder. I can't see his face but I can see that his body is limp. I rush forward but Mac barrels past me until he's ten feet away from the burning barn and then lays Reed down in the grass. Reed's face is blackened with soot, his eyes closed. When I fall to my knees by his side, I smell singed flesh and smoke. His clothes must have caught on fire and he passed out from the shock of the pain. Mac pummels Reed's chest and leans down to breathe air into his mouth. He repeats those steps again and again while I helplessly grasp Reed's burnt hand until I feel it twitch in my grasp. Mac turns Reed's head to the side, and he coughs and retches into the grass, black foamy bile that looks like he swallowed bog water, like he's drowned on dry land.

CHAPTER TWENTY-THREE

MAC, ADA, AND I CARRY REED INTO THE HOUSE WHILE LIZ HELPS NIKO IN.
We lay Reed down on the couch, and Ada goes to get antibiotic
cream and painkillers from the safe upstairs.

"Run cool water over his hands while I'm gone," she shouts over
her shoulder. "Cool, not ice cold."

I hurry to the sink but nothing comes out. "We've gone through
what was in the reservoir," Mac says, hauling ice trays out of the
freezer and emptying the melted ice into a shallow basin. "Check
the cooler outside on the porch. It might have melted ice water in
it, too."

I go out onto the porch, where I'm startled to see that the sky is
lightening in the east, and drag in the big YETI cooler where Mac
keeps his beers each night during our cocktail hour. I hear bottles
sloshing around as I drag it over to the couch where Mac is pouring
water over Reed's burnt hands.

"Stick your hands in there," he tells Reed. Then he looks up at
Niko, who's sitting cross-legged on the floor, sorting through prints
and negatives she rescued from the fire. "You too, dude, if you ever
want to use those hands to hold a camera again."

Niko looks up, her face a strange Noh mask of impassivity. It's
because her eyebrows have burned off, I realize. She must be in
shock, I think, or she'd be screaming in pain.

"I'll handle these," Liz says, gently taking the photos and negatives out of her hands. "Oh," she says, holding up one of her own water-color studies of flowers. "You idiot," she says, wiping soot across her face with her shirtsleeve. "Go take care of your hands. I'm not going to spoon-feed you for the rest of your life."

Niko silently scooches herself across the floor to the other side of the cooler and plunges her hands in, wincing at the contact of cool water on her burns. She looks up at Reed across the cooler. "Thank you for coming for me, man," she croaks, her voice a rasp, saw on sandpaper, "but you really didn't have to. I knew exactly how long I had before it all blew."

Reed laughs, which turns into a hacking cough.

"Could you tell where the fire started?" I ask, thinking of what Ada said about flammable chemicals and Niko's cigarettes.

"The worst was in Liz's studio," Niko says, looking over her shoulder at Liz. "That's why I couldn't get your paintings out, babe, only the ones I'd hung up on my side."

"Some of the solvents I use are flammable," Liz says, "but I always seal them carefully and leave rags drying outside."

"None of the chemicals I use are flammable," Niko says, "but I could smell turpentine downstairs and all my blank paper was soaked in it."

"I don't even use turpentine," Liz says, wrinkling her nose, "but there could have been some old cans in the supply shed."

"Someone deliberately set this fire," Mac says.

"But who?" Ada asks, coming back into the room with her medical kit. She sits down next to Reed and asks me to get her a clean dish towel and plastic cling wrap.

"Well, it wasn't me or Niko since we were the most at risk," Liz says.

"You've come out okay, Liz," Ada says, "and Niko's hands will be all right."

"Do you think I'd put my girlfriend's life in danger?" Liz snaps. "And burn up all the work I've done this summer?"

"It may not be one of us," Mac says. "Reed and I saw someone at the window just before the fire."

"The Gray Lady," Reed croaks, flailing one of his burnt hands toward the window in the corner. "She was looking in. Mac went after her."

Ada corrals his hand back into her lap, where she has spread out the clean dish towel and tube of antibiotic salve. "Is that what you were doing, Mac?" she asks coyly, spreading salve on Reed's poor damaged hands. "When the fire started? Chasing ghosts?"

"I was chasing *someone*," Mac says, "who I lost in the woods. When I saw the fire I went to the generator shed to get an ax to break down the door. What were you doing, Ada?"

"I was fast asleep," she says, an edge creeping into her voice. "I'd taken a sleeping pill because, you know, my husband had just *died* on your boat."

"Ada came downstairs when you were gone," I tell Mac. "Look, if we start accusing each other we'll go crazy. That—*thing*—you saw at the window could have been a person in a cloak. There could be someone else on the island."

"It's Becky," Liz says.

Reed flinches but Mac looks curious. "You mean, like the ghost of Becky?"

"No, I mean maybe Becky's not dead."

"We found a piece of her shirt caught on the thornbushes above the Dead Pool," Reed croaks. "We never saw her again. Her parents hired detectives."

"So, *they* didn't believe she was dead?" I ask, surprised at this never-before-mentioned detail.

Reed shrugs. "They were angry and felt guilty that they had all but abandoned her that summer so they threw money at the problem."

"I always thought it was because her brothers, *Sterling and Aubrey*"—Mac pronounces their names as if they taste bad in his mouth—"were trying to cover their asses in case Becky showed up years later demanding her share of the inheritance."

"Why would she have pretended to be dead?" I ask.

"To punish us," Reed answers without hesitation.

"But how would she have been able to do anything if she was declared dead? What would she have lived on?" I ask.

"People manage," Ada says. "They get off-the-books service jobs, change their names, steal identities. There were a lot of dead people back then and chaos and confusion in the hospitals where people were dying."

"So . . . what?" Reed asks his sister. "You think Becky's been alive all these years and she's picked now to come back and mess with us?"

"Maybe she's been here all along," Liz says. "Living off the grid on the island."

"It would explain all the things that have gone missing," Ada says.

"She'd come for me first," Reed says. "She wouldn't bother with killing Crosby and lighting the barn on fire. I'm the one who betrayed her. She'd kill me first."

Although he had just told me about her possessiveness and jealousy, I'm still startled to hear Reed state with such conviction that his childhood sweetheart, the girl I've always been jealous of and believed was the love of his life, would want to *kill* him. I'm not sure if I should feel grateful that he's not still carrying a torch for her or horrified at how resigned he sounds that he would be her target.

"Maybe," Liz says, chewing on her lip. I notice she doesn't contest Reed's assessment of Becky's appetite for vengeance or that Reed might deserve it. "Or maybe she wants you to suffer first. She wants you to see everyone else die and everything you've made here fall apart before she comes for you."

He stares at Liz but doesn't contradict her. He can't; she's pinpointed exactly how to make Reed suffer. Maybe he's also a little alarmed, as I am, that Liz has apparently given some thought to how best to get to her brother.

"This is crazy," Mac says. "I'd know if she was here."

"You think it's less crazy to believe there's a ghost?" Ada asks.

"We need to search the island," Reed says, looking at Mac. "Starting with the lighthouse to see if anyone has broken into it and if the boat there is seaworthy."

Mac holds Reed's gaze and something passes between them, some secret message I can't decipher.

"You're not going anywhere," Ada says, rattling a bottle of pills at Reed. "You're in shock now but once that wears off you're in for a world of pain. Plus, that smoke you inhaled is taxing your whole respiratory system." She takes out a pill. He opens his mouth to object and she pops it right in, then holds a glass of water to his lips to wash it down. I can tell he must be feeling the pain already by how little he resists.

"You too," Ada says, extending the bottle to Niko, whose hands have been bandaged by Liz. Liz intercepts the bottle, takes out one pill, and hands the bottle back to Ada.

"So," Ada says, "who's going—and who's going to stay behind?"

WE DECIDE TO split up in threes. Reed and Niko clearly have to stay. Liz wants to, but Ada argues that it makes more sense for her to stay and monitor "her patients." "Besides," she says, resting her hand over her stomach, "I should probably be taking it easy. I've had some cramps."

After it's decided, Liz takes Ada aside for a whispered consultation. While they're talking I watch Niko humming as she sorts through photos and negatives with her bandaged hands. She's either still in shock or the pill has kicked in very quickly.

"I'm glad you were able to save these," I tell her, looking down at a black-and-white series of trees. There's something . . . *mysterious* in them."

Niko nods. "Yes, there's definitely *something* in them."

I leave her rearranging her pictures and go upstairs to check on Reed. Mac and Ada helped him up to our bedroom and put him into our bed. His bandaged hands lie on top of the white candlewick bedspread like puffy white caterpillar cocoons. He's staring out the window but when I come in his eyes swivel toward me like marbles rolling across his pale face. His hands lift and lower as if rising on a wave. I can feel all the jittery tension roiling below the surface.

"You need to check on the lighthouse," he says. "See if the boat's sound enough to use—and see if there are flares—"

"We'll do all that," I say, sitting on the side of the bed and laying my hand on his chest to still him. I can feel his heart racing under my hand.

"I don't like you going without me," he says.

"I'll be with Mac and Liz," I remind him. "They know the island best. We'll find a boat and get help from the mainland."

"Be careful not to go into the bog. It's treacherous, Lucy. Seriously. One wrong step and you can go under so fast there's no saving you, no coming back—"

"We'll be safe," I say, leaning forward so my face is close to his. His pupils are so dilated from the pain medication that there's no blue left in his irises. "Is that what happened to Becky?" I ask. "Did you see her go into the Dead Pool? Is that why you don't believe she could be alive?"

He shakes his head. "If Becky were alive she would have killed me long ago."

I startle back at the vehemence of his voice, tears stinging my eyes at his own self-reproach. "No one's going to hurt you," I promise. "We'll be back soon with help."

He lifts a bandaged hand and paws at me as I get up to leave. "If anything were to happen to you I couldn't go on. You're the only reason I had to keep living after everything that happened last time. You've been the only reason all these years."

I'm too stunned to know what to say, then Ada comes in to plump his pillows and refill his water glass and I watch his eyes flutter closed.

"Don't worry," she says. "I'll take good care of him. You just make sure you're careful. Stay on the buoy path."

I leave quickly. Before going down the stairs I stop in the study and grab Nathaniel's journal. After everything that has happened it feels safer to have it with me. Mac and Liz are waiting in the great room, day packs on their backs, in hiking boots and baseball caps, Liz in a neon-orange vest, Mac in a long-sleeved red-plaid flannel shirt, as if they're both afraid of being shot accidentally by a hunter.

"Can we take the mule?" I ask.

Mac and Liz look at me as if I'm crazy.

"It wouldn't make it six feet in the interior before its weight sunk it into the bog. I'm afraid we have to hoof it," Mac explains.

I sigh and sit down at the boot bench to put on my hiking boots while Liz says goodbye to Niko, who's spread her photos and negatives all across the great room.

"Be good, babe, I'll be back soon."

Niko barely lifts her eyes from the photos and Liz pushes out the door, letting the screen door slam behind her.

"Let's go," Mac says, following her. "We need to hurry if we want to get the boat and take it to the mainland before dark."

It seems an alarmist statement—we've got all day—but considering the unexpected and alarming things that have happened so far on the island, Mac is probably right to hurry.

CHAPTER TWENTY-FOUR

WE PASS BY THE SMOLDERING REMAINS OF THE BARN IN SILENCE, AS IF paying our respects to the dead. When we get to the tree where I'd found the stag head Liz keeps going straight.

"Hey," Mac calls, "the coast trail is safer. A lot of trees came down in the storm last night."

"I thought you wanted to hurry," Liz says. "The interior path is faster. Didn't you say you blazed it before we got here?"

"Yeah, but those buoys could have come down, too."

"Not if you tied them right," she says, thumbs hooked in her pack straps as she turns to glare at Mac. "Did you tie them right?"

"I know how to tie a knot, Lizzie."

Liz turns on her heel and plunges into the woods.

Mac shakes his head and looks at me. "You go next," he tells me. "I'll bring up the rear."

I do as he says even though I don't like having him behind me. I can't help thinking about Ada's suspicion that Mac could have killed Crosby, that Mac is taking his revenge for the Harpers ruining his mother's life, and that it was Mac who went running out into the woods last night just before the fire started. Mac was the only one who even saw the cloaked figure. He could hit me over the head without Liz even hearing, especially since Liz is so far ahead—so far ahead that if not for the buoys I might lose my way. I speed up and get closer to her but then I get slapped by the branches she pushes back and lets go without a thought to who's behind her.

The trail is overgrown and clogged by fallen limbs, the detritus of last night's storm. It's difficult to pick out the path through all the wreckage, but each time I feel worried that we've wandered off it I look ahead and spot a red buoy. Mac certainly tied them on tightly. I can't imagine how else we'd find our way. As we go deeper inland the trees grow closer together as if they have gathered here, at the center of the island, to plot and whisper about the humans encroaching on their shores. When I lose sight of Liz it's easy to believe she has been swallowed up by the vegetation. I hurry to catch up with her and shout for her to wait for me.

She slows, but only because a fallen tree is in her way. "I don't want to leave Niko alone any longer than I have to," she says.

"You can't be worried that Reed will hurt her. He can barely move. And Ada would have no reason—"

"It's not that," she says, impatiently swatting a fallen branch away. "I'm worried about her taking that codeine. She . . . she's had a problem with it in the past."

"With drug use?" I ask, feigning ignorance. Reed told me once that Liz had spent a fortune on rehab for Niko. It was one of the reasons he didn't want to invite her to the island. I'd scolded him for holding that against her, for not allowing for the possibility of a person changing.

"Yeah," Liz says. "She started using drugs during the first pandemic. She likes to make out that the lockdown didn't affect her, that she was the fearless one, but the isolation took a toll on her mental health and then she fell climbing over a fence and messed up her back. She was prescribed Vicodin for the pain and got addicted. She kicked it, but a few years ago she hurt her back again. At first, she wouldn't take anything. I thought she was just acting tough, the way she wouldn't leave the city or take precautions. I *begged* her to take the Vicodin. I didn't know she'd had a habit before, that she was afraid of using. It was my fault she got hooked again."

"But then you helped her fight it," I say, disarmed by the anguish in Liz's voice. "Don't worry. Ada won't give her too much—"

Liz rounds on me. "You don't know how she gets when she's using. She'll want more, she'll be willing to do anything . . ."

"Is that what you were talking to Ada about?"

She nods. "I warned her to lock up the pills but . . . I'm not sure she took me seriously." Her face, white and damp against the tangle of green around us, looks more vulnerable than I've ever seen it before. A tear streaks down her cheek—or maybe it's sweat. Now that we've stopped I'm aware of how hot it is, how airless with the trees and brush pressing in on us from all sides, far from the freshening breeze of the ocean. We must be near the center of the island.

"She's an E.R. nurse," I say, trying to reassure Liz—and myself. I don't like the idea of a drug-crazed Niko loose in the house with Reed. "She knows about addiction. She'll be careful."

"I hope so," Liz says. "For her sake."

Leave it to Liz to spend the ounce of pity I felt for her so quickly. She turns to keep walking but then we both hear something moving through the brush—something *large*. I spin around and the woods blur—branch and trunk kaleidoscoping into a horned figure. I catch a flash of red flannel and picture the scarecrow—Mr. Tibster— charging through the woods.

It's Mac who crashes out of the underbrush, twigs in his hair, a wild look in his eyes.

"What the fuck," Liz says. "What are you doing off the path?"

"I thought I saw—" He looks around. "Something's wrong. The path isn't right."

"What are you talking about?" Liz asks impatiently. "You blazed it yourself. There's the next buoy." She points through a haze of green to a red buoy hanging from a high branch.

Mac shakes his head. "It doesn't feel right," he repeats. "I've taken this trail a hundred times—"

"Me too," Liz says. "It only feels different because the storm took down a lot of trees. Come on. We're wasting time."

She turns and charges on ahead, swatting branches away impatiently. Impatient, I imagine, with her own fears and weaknesses as much as with the fallen wreckage of the storm. I follow her, Mac close on my heels. I can feel the breath of the whole forest at my back, the dank heavy weight of the pine boughs sagging from the recent rainfall; the fetid muck of the bog beneath my feet, oozing upward through my laces and socks; the humid, pollen-filled air pressing down into my lungs. It feels as if, as we approach its center, the island is collapsing in on itself, like a Venus flytrap snapping shut its jaws to consume us. I'm only able to stay upright by keeping my eyes on the orange blaze of Liz's vest—

Then she's gone. Erased into the green with a slick *whoosh* and a startled cry that could be the call of a bird, followed by a gargled scream.

"Liz!" I call, rushing forward.

Mac grabs my arm and pulls me back. "Wait! Let me go first. Stay behind me."

He squeezes by me on the trail—only it's hardly a trail anymore, more like a narrow funnel—and eases forward with agonizing slowness, calling Liz's name. As he goes, he slides his pack off one shoulder and digs inside, pulling out a nylon rope.

Then he vanishes.

"Mac!" I scream, sure he, too, has been swallowed up.

I nearly trip over him. He's lying flat on the ground, peering into a crater that's opened up in the earth below us like a giant mouth. He gestures for me to get down and I do so readily, determined to dig my fingernails into the soil to keep from sliding into the abyss. Only there's nothing to hang on to. The ground is spongy, more moss than soil, more water than moss. I inch forward just enough to look over the edge of the crater into dark water. It's a pool about thirty feet across, its shores rimmed with fat black cattails and thick-leaved skunk cabbage, its surface studded with water lilies and dragonflies and one bobbing head: Liz, treading water, her lips level with the surface. She's trying to grab on to the cattails along the shore to pull herself up but they come off in her hands.

"Lizzie," Mac shouts, "take hold of the rope."

He's tied the end of the rope into a noose, which he spins once, like a lasso, and then lofts down into the pool where it lands inches from Liz's head. She splutters and splashes toward it, pushing it away instead of getting ahold of it. Her head goes under for one horrible moment and then pops up, mouth open, gasping for air, her face tea stained.

"Lizzie," Mac says, his voice low and gentle, "be still. I'm going to toss the rope over your head."

I can see Liz's frantic eyes skittering upward, trying to lock on to Mac's voice, but craning her neck back only seems to upset her balance and make her sink again beneath the surface. This time she stays below longer and goes deeper, only the tips of her fingers piercing the viscous black surface. As if something below is pulling her down.

"You have to help her," I scream at Mac. "She's drowning."

"I'm trying," he bites off between clenched lips. "If I go in there you won't be able to pull either of us out."

I start to object—surely there must be another way—but then Liz's head appears and Mac launches the lasso again and it falls over her head. She thrashes her arms and manages to link one arm through the loop and grasp the rope with both hands, which makes her sink.

Mac gives the rope a small tug and Liz surfaces, much quicker now, her hands gripped around the rope.

"Get behind me," Mac barks, "and take the rope. See if you can find a sturdy tree to tie it to."

I crawl backward with the rope in my hands and scan the tree line for a sturdy trunk. The red buoy catches my eye. I wrap the end of the rope around the trunk of the tree from which it hangs and secure the rope with a clove hitch, the only knot I recall from Mac's tutorials. Then I cautiously inch my way back to Mac—

Who's now much closer to the edge. His feet are braced against a root at the rim of the crater and he's hauling in the rope, hand over hand, every muscle in his arms, back, and legs taut as steel. I peer over the edge to see that Liz is halfway up the slope, her feet braced against the wall of the pit like a rock climber's.

"Get back," Mac mutters to me. "The edge is collapsing."

I can see he's right. Mud is crumbling under his feet, falling in clods into the water, the ground sliding into the hungry maw of the pit, like plankton sifting through a whale's teeth.

Into the belly of the beast.

That's not all that's falling apart. Following the line from Liz to Mac's hand I can see that the rope is unraveling, thread by thread.

"Mac!" I cry, pointing to the weak spot in the rope.

"Shit."

It's only six inches from his hand. He just has to reach past it. He lunges for it at the same moment that the rope snaps. The release sends him flying backward, crashing into me, sinking us both into the mud. Beneath our thud I hear a cry and a loud splash. Mac is off me in an instant, elbow-crawling through the mud to the edge of the pool. I am close behind him but when I look over the edge there's nothing to see. The surface of the Dead Pool is as still and tranquil as a closed mouth.

CHAPTER TWENTY-FIVE

"WE HAVE TO GO IN AFTER HER!" I CRY.

"She's gone," Mac says gravely, holding me back. "If you go in after her you won't come back."

"How can we not try to help her?" I shout. "This is Reed's sister—"

"Do you think Reed would want you to die with her? Do you think he needs to lose someone else in this stinking hellhole?"

I see with alarm that he's crying, tears streaking through the mud on his face. "I'm sorry," I say. "I know you cared about Liz."

He swipes angrily at his face. "We didn't always get along, but she was like a sister to me. If I thought I could save her I'd go in there. I tried with Becky and almost died myself."

"With Becky? What do you mean? I thought you weren't on the island when she died."

"I came back to the island just before the nor'easter hit. The motorboat was broken—Reed thought Becky might have sabotaged it—so Reed picked me up in the rowboat and we rowed across. His parents were sick, Liz had lit a fire, and Becky had gone off somewhere ranting about horned devils. Reed begged me to go with him to find Becky and bring her back to the mainland. I couldn't tell if he was afraid *for* her or *of* her. We were on this path when we saw her running—or at least I thought it was her. Reed took off after her but then she doubled back so I followed her. She turned when she heard me . . . her face . . ."

Mac scrubs his hand over his own face as if trying to erase the memory. "I'll never forget how *terrified* she looked, as if she'd just seen the devil himself. Then she vanished. Like the earth swallowed her. I went in after her but she was just . . . *gone,* like she sank straight to the bottom of the island. I could feel myself being pulled down, like by a riptide, like there's a whirlpool at the bottom of the island that wants to suck you down—" His voice is shaking, his face stark white under the mud. I've never seen him look so afraid. I don't think I've ever seen *anyone* look so afraid.

"I'd be dead if Reed hadn't dropped a buoy for me to grab and hauled me out of there."

I picture Reed telling me about Becky's death, how scared he had looked, but I also remember what he had left out. "Why didn't Reed say he saw Becky go into the Dead Pool? Why didn't he tell his parents and Liz and . . ." *Me?*

"Because he didn't see her go in; I did."

"Yes, but—"

"He thought that I would be blamed," Mac says. "At least, that's what he told me. That he'd probably be okay—the police wouldn't arrest him—but a kid like me, the *housekeeper's* son, would be suspected. He said it was better that no one knew I was on the island. So we kept it to ourselves."

What a terrible secret to share, I think, and one that explains Mac's devotion to Reed. But then Mac adds, "I've always wondered if he didn't think I pushed her into the pit."

"Oh!" I say, horrified. "If he thought that he wouldn't—"

"Protect the friend who murdered his girlfriend?" He shrugs. "Reed's very loyal." He wipes his bandanna across his face, scrubbing it of mud and tears and the last bit of sentiment. His face has become hard and practical. "Anyway, that's how I know Becky's not the one doing this—unless it's her ghost—and I don't believe a ghost sawed through this rope." He holds up the rope and runs his cal-loused thumb over the frayed end. Then he looks up at the tree we're under. "Or moved those buoys. See that knot? It's a square knot. I'd never use one to tie the buoys; I used a figure-eight loop."

"You mean someone deliberately led us to the Dead Pool so one of us would fall in? But who—?"

"I don't know," he says. "Clearly not Liz." He casts a sad look to-ward the pool. "And I don't think Reed has any reason to want any of us dead. I've been thinking it could be your friend Ada."

"Ada! But why?"

"To get you out of the way. Haven't you ever wondered if she's jeal-ous that you married Reed—the rich golden boy?"

"No! She's always disapproved of Reed and in college all she ever did was tell me that she thought Reed liked me."

"Maybe she was just trying to figure out if you liked him back," he says, looking distinctly uncomfortable. "Not that I know how girls work, but I do remember Reed saying once when you guys were in college that he had a feeling Ada had a thing for him."

I shake my head. "No, that must be wrong. Besides, she has Crosby—"

"*Had* Crosby. She could have sabotaged the boat as well. If she wanted him dead it would be a convenient way to kill him."

"But why?" I cry again.

Mac shrugs. "Having never been married myself I can't say I un-derstand married people, but I have observed they're often unhappy with each other."

"Oh," I say, my pity of a moment ago turning to anger at his supe-rior tone, "I suppose you think Reed and I are miserable together."

He shakes his head. "No, actually, I think you make him happy—or at least as happy as he ever lets himself be."

I surprise myself by laughing. "Great, *thanks*, I guess."

"No, really," he says, looking embarrassed. "I mean it. You know how hard he is on himself. I think it comes from having an asshole for a father. But I know he really wanted you. He told me that summer that he wanted to break up with Becky to be with you. I remember he said, 'With Lucy, what you see is what you get. No deception, no airs. It makes me feel like I can be myself.'"

I feel my eyes sting. I've always wanted to know that Reed *chose* me. I can't help but think, though, of how little he's been able to be himself around me all these years, how much he's had to hide from me. None of which do I feel like sharing with Mac. "It's not Ada," I say firmly. "She loved Crosby. They were perfect for each other." I see the skeptical look on his face. "Yes, I know Crosby could be a little self-important and priggish but he was well-intentioned and really believed in doing the right thing. That was important to Ada. She's always been an idealist. She holds people—including herself—to a high standard."

"And when they don't live up to those standards?" he asks.

I remember the look of disappointment on her face when she asked me on the dock if I'd leave Reed to stay with her.

"She leaves," I say, getting to my feet. "She just . . . leaves. She'd have no reason for doing anything else. Certainly not *killing* someone."

He nods, still crouched on the ground. "I suppose you think it's me."

We're alone in the woods, inches from the precipice of a bottomless pit where Liz has just died and Becky died ten years ago. Has Mac told me the truth about her death? Was there a reason why Reed suspected he had pushed Becky in? My skin prickles with the awareness of danger. Should I run? But how far would I get in these woods? "I think if you wanted to kill me you could have done it already. What about you? Do you think it's me?"

He shakes his head. "I think it's this fucking island. *Something* is here—the ghost of that buried witch or the devil she called up or the Irish girl she possessed. Something . . . *evil*. Something Becky saw before she died that scared her so much she ran into the Dead Pool. Something that chased her through the woods and sucked her to the bottom. Something that will kill us if we don't get off this island." He stands up, looming over me. "Come on, we have to get to the lighthouse and get the boat before dark."

"You think we should still go?" I ask, looking over my shoulder at the black pit. "After . . . shouldn't we go back and tell Niko and Reed what happened to Liz?"

"How will that help if we still don't have a way to get off the island?"

He's right. Part of me is relieved. I can't bear the thought of breaking the news of Liz's death to Reed and Niko. Then I think of something else. "How are we going to find our way out of here if we can't follow the buoys?"

"I don't need the buoys," he says, heading through a gap in the trees. "I know this island like the back of my hand."

As I follow him I can't help but wonder why, if he knows the island so well, he was so easily tricked by the false buoy trail that led Liz to die . . . and whether he did push Becky into the Dead Pool.

MAC IS A politer trail guide than Liz was. He holds branches back until I pass, points out boggy spots to avoid, and gives me a hand when climbing over downed trees. Moving through the dense woods feels as if we are dancing with the trees and they are leading us on a merry circle around and around the island. How can anyone tell, I wonder, one pine—or rock or fern—from another?

Maybe that's why someone has marked them. At first I take the faint scratches for knots in the wood but then realize they are Celtic knots carved so long ago that the bark has all but absorbed the pattern into itself. Is this the trail Mac is following? Before I can ask, we emerge onto the rocky shore, open to the blue blaze of sea and sky and the freshening salt air, within sight of the lighthouse. Mac picks up his pace, leaving me to scramble my own way across the rocks. I have the distinct impression that he wants to get there before me. Is there something he doesn't want me to see? I recall the look that passed between him and Reed before we left and Niko mentioning that she'd seen the boat moored near the lighthouse. Reed had said they'd been fishing in the protected cove, but this stretch of rocky shore looks far wilder, and the surf rougher, than on the other side of the island.

I hurry to catch up with Mac at the lighthouse door, where he's delayed opening the lock. I'm surprised that it *is* locked. "Have you been using this as storage?" I ask. "Isn't there enough storage near the house?"

Mac doesn't answer. He opens the door and steps in, the solid bulk of him blocking my view. I hear a sharp intake of breath.

"What?" I demand, pushing at his back. "What is it?"

He steps in, giving me room to squeeze by him. The only light in the room is a large glowing circle in the center of the room coming from far over our heads. It's so bright that the outer perimeter of the room is completely dark. But Mac must be able to make out something because he passes through the circle of light muttering curses. I look up, drawn to see where the light is coming from.

It's like being inside a nautilus shell. A cast iron staircase spirals up and up to a glass orb that stares back unblinkingly. I feel pinned by that relentless gaze, prey frozen by the eye of the predator. Even when I look away my vision is dazzled. I grope my way across the room and find a locker to sit down on. Mac is rummaging through another metal locker, cursing.

"The flares are gone and so is the emergency radio."

Emergency radio? As my eyes adjust to the light I take in the perimeter of the room. An overturned rowboat takes up half of it. The hull has been caved in, raw wooden splinters scattered across the stone floor.

"I take it the damage to the boat is new," I say.

He looks up from the locker toward the boat, reaches over, and runs his hand over the gash. "Yeah, she was seaworthy two days ago when we were here last." He gets up and checks another locker. "The ax they used is gone, too."

"Why were you keeping all this stuff here?" I ask.

"Reed thought it was a good idea to have an extra storage area in case the ones near the house were raided."

That sounds like something Reed would think of, but there's something wrong with it. "Why didn't either of you say anything about it?"

"Reed thought—we both agreed—we should keep it to ourselves just in case somebody decided to tweet about it or post it on their . . . I don't know . . . *Instagram*."

"No one's used Twitter or Instagram since the early twenties," I say.

Mac gives me a withering glare. "Yeah, well, I never really got into all that."

"Right," I say, staring up at the piercing orb above us. It feels like we're being watched. "At any rate your plan seems not to have worked. Someone found out about your secret stash and your secret boat. Someone who had a key. Who else had one?"

"Just me and Reed," he says, taking the keys out of his pocket. I think he's just displaying them to me but he picks out the smallest key on the ring and opens a tall thin metal locker. This is the only locker, I think, that's actually locked. I'm curious to see what's inside but when he swings open the door it's empty.

"What was in it?" I ask.

"The guns," he answers.

CHAPTER TWENTY-SIX

"REED SAID THERE WAS ONLY THE ONE RIFLE AT THE HOUSE," I SAY, FOL-lowing Mac out of the lighthouse.

"That's all we kept at the house," he says, scanning the shore. "We stored these here to make sure no one else would get them."

"But why? And just how many guns are we talking about?"

"Four or five," he says.

"Four or five?"

"Reed asked me last year to stock up."

"Last year? But that was before the new virus."

"I told you that Reed's been preparing for this for years. He never stopped thinking it would happen again."

I open my mouth to object but then I think of all the conferences Reed has gone to over the years on pandemic preparedness and disaster planning. "Why didn't he tell me?"

He sighs. "He didn't want to worry you. And he knew you'd be upset by having guns around since you didn't grow up in the country so you—"

"Wait a second," I say, holding up my hand. "Please don't mansplain guns to me. Or expect me to believe you put in an armory because you were afraid of . . . what? . . . feral hogs or . . ." I splutter. "Sea monsters!"

His lip twitches but he stifles the smile and says calmly, "We were afraid of looters from the mainland. In case you haven't noticed, we're isolated out here."

"No shit, Sherlock. We're stuck on this rock with someone who's now armed to the teeth."

"We're not *stuck*," he says, his eyes on the horizon where dark clouds are massing. "There's another boat."

"Oh? And where have you got this one stashed?"

"At my cabin—if no one's gotten to it. I'm going to go check—" He looks at the horizon where a rain cloud has appeared. "You can come if you like or go back to the Main House on your own. You'll probably make it before it rains, and if you follow the shoreline, you'll find it no matter what's been done to the buoys."

As I think about going back alone to Reed and Niko—to whom I'll have to explain where Liz is—I'm startled by a low moan. It sounds like a woman weeping and it seems to be coming from beneath my feet. I scan the rocks, searching for its source—and realize it's coming from the three standing stones on the edge of the shore, the ones Liz showed me. I hurry toward them, leaping across the gaps between the rocks with Mac shouting behind me to slow down. But I don't slow down. I am seized by the sudden conviction that here is the malicious spirit of the island—be it ghost or devil or still-alive Becky—and I want to confront it and tell it to go back to whatever hell it came from. *Haven't we all suffered sufficiently?*

I am moving so fast that I slip on the sloping rock and pitch forward. A hole opens up before me, a dark, gaping pit from which the voices of the damned call out for me—

We're coming for you, Barbara.

—but then Mac grabs my arm and wrenches me back. Below us the voices wail and water spits up, striking my face.

"It's just the sound the hole makes at high tide," he says. "There are underground caverns that extend deep into the island."

I imagine them reaching back to the Dead Pool, where Liz has joined Becky, and to Dead Man's Cove, where Crosby's body may have washed up by now. I imagine the dead crouching beneath the thin skin of rock and moss, waiting to rise up and drag us down with them. There's no way I'll be able to make the journey back to the house alone.

"I don't want to go back without any good news," I say, crawling away from the pit. "Let's go check on your boat."

I HAD ASSUMED that Mac's cabin was on the same side of the island as the Main House so I'm surprised when he sets off north across the shoreline.

"You've been coming out here every night?" I ask. "You could have stayed in the Main House with us."

"I like my privacy," he says gruffly, and then, in a softer tone, "I figured you and Reed wanted yours as well." Which makes me wonder if Reed had discouraged him from staying with us. I shiver and Mac peels off his flannel shirt and hands it to me and walks ahead quickly so I can't refuse it. I stop to put it on and am glad for its warmth. The temperature is dropping quickly, the sky lowering over our heads. Mac had been right about a storm coming.

I hurry to catch up with him. He's waiting on a rock ledge where a wide inlet cuts into the shoreline. A flock of terns is sailing in from the sea, skimming over the water. There are more birds in the inlet—geese, seagulls, wild ducks, even something that looks like a puffin.

"Wow, are there always so many birds here?" I ask.

"This is a layover for birds migrating down from Canada," he says, pointing north. The wind here feels like it's coming straight from an arctic tundra, like we're standing on the edge of the planet. "These are coming in to shelter from the storm. We'd better keep moving."

"Are we far?" I ask.

He points across the water. "It's on the other side at the mouth of the inlet." All I see are trees and rocks. And how are we supposed to get across the inlet?

He turns away from the shoreline and walks along a narrow shelf clinging to the rock wall. "Be careful," he says. "The footing is tricky."

The footing would be tricky for a mountain goat, I think, following close behind him. How did he do this in the dark after downing a six-pack of beer? Below us is a sheer drop down to the blue water. One wrong step and I will plunge down into the sea. How easy it would be for Mac to tell Reed, *She slipped, man, there was nothing I could do.* Just as Becky and Liz slipped into the Dead Pool. But still, I follow because going back alone is unthinkable.

Finally, we come to a spot where the rock falls away into open air and, far below, the rushing sea. Unperturbed Mac turns to the rock face and clambers up a narrow crevice. Then he twists and holds out his hand for me.

"The path continues through the woods here," he says as matter-of-factly as *turn left on Broadway.*

I take his hand and look into his eyes, where I see myself reflected against a backdrop of empty air and churning sea. If he lets go I will plunge straight down to my death—

As Liz did when the rope broke. A rope that had been in *his* backpack.

He must see the hesitation in my eyes. "I'm not going to let go," he says plainly, without defensiveness or injury, as if it's the most natural thing in the world for me to be afraid of him. As if he's used to not being trusted.

I'm not sure if that's reassuring or not but I grip his hand, step up into a shallow foothold, and hoist myself up. I feel the rock crumbling beneath my feet, hear the skitter of pebbles cascading down to the water below, and taste the coppery tang of fear in my mouth.

For a moment I am weightless, suspended between sky and sea like those seabirds, between life and death as I hovered for those three minutes and thirty seconds in the hospital. That empty place—like the air trapped in those glass floats fishermen use to string in their nets to keep them from submerging—is always waiting for me to return; but then Mac's hand pulls me out of the void. I crash into his chest and we both fall against a pine tree, shaking free a cascade of sweet-smelling pine needles. In a moment he finds his balance and steadies me on my feet, and we continue on our way.

The path is well-trodden, although not marked by buoys, and leads us along the shore of the inlet and then across stepping-stones over a shallow stream—the mouth of the inlet. Here the land levels into a meadow full of wildflowers and tall grasses, so pretty and peaceful I have to blink to make sure it's not a mirage.

When I open my eyes, the cabin appears as if it has sprung from the ground. It's made of the same speckled pink, green, and yellow quartz that lines the shore, and pine logs as dappled as a fawn, with green moss and lichen. A fairy-tale cottage, I think, walking toward it across the meadow.

"Wow," I say, "did you just build it this year?"

"Not exactly," he says, following me. He seems suddenly reluctant to enter his own house, as shy as one of those dappled fawns the cottage resembles. Maybe it makes him feel exposed. This pretty, charming place doesn't fit with the image he projects of himself: rough, careless, *unrooted*. There are wind chimes made of seashells and sea glass hanging from the pitched eave, a mosaic of stones laid out as a path, stone markers in the grass—

I stoop to look down at one of the stone markers. There's writing on it, worn and moss filled. I kneel and trace the blurred words with my fingertips and make out a name: *Bridget McCrory d. 1848.* I look up and scan the meadow and notice the stones grazing the tops of the swaying grass. One taller stone at the edge of the meadow is framed against the blue sea—a circle with a cross inside.

"I thought—" I begin, standing and seeing that the stones are everywhere, spreading to the tree line and beyond, all facing the sea like a flock of birds waiting out a storm, poised to take flight. I feel a flutter in my own chest, something fighting to get out. "I thought you said the ones who died of the fever were all washed out to sea."

"I said that some were washed out to sea. There were more. These are the ones who stayed."

I stare at the sea of graves. It's as if he's talking about a group of settlers who have chosen to make their home on the island. Then I look back at the cabin—at the moss on the roof, the wild roses and herbs growing amid the rocks, the stack of firewood beside a circular stone firepit, and a weathered Adirondack chair facing the sea as if tracking the progress of the storm clouds racing toward land. All as rooted to the place as the stone grave markers.

"How long," I ask, swallowing my fear, "have you been living here?"

CHAPTER TWENTY-SEVEN

A SHEET OF RAIN COMES DOWN, CUTTING SHORT HIS ANSWER AND obliterating the meadow. He grabs my hand and pulls me up the path and through the unlocked door. "I'm going to check on the boat. Start a fire if you can."

Then he's gone, leaving me to survey the fairy-tale cottage. What I see is neat and trim—like a ship's cabin—but also *settled*. A brass captain's clock, barometer, and thermometer are mounted by the front door alongside a row of pegs holding binoculars, rain gear, a fishing net. The first floor is one room with stairs leading up to a sleeping loft. A bookshelf is built into the side of the staircase, holding a small but carefully curated library: sea charts, folklore of the islands, birds of Maine, edible plants of the Northeast, and *Moby-Dick*, its spine creased and tattered from multiple readings.

Yeah, I've heard of it, he'd told Crosby. *Book about a big fish, right?*

I take the book off the shelf and open it. There's a name inscribed in blocky handwriting, which I realize is Mac's full name; I've never thought to ask. It's on the flyleaf of all the books, from *The Boy's King Arthur* to a dozen Stephen King paperbacks, something called *Haunted Maine,* and a collection of Irish folktales.

Between the bookcase and the woodstove is an ancient Morris chair, the twin of the one in the great room, with a ceramic mug and a copy of Thoreau's *The Maine Woods* splayed open on the armrest. Glass orbs, wrapped in fishing nets, and bits of sea glass and crystals hang in the windows above ledges lined with seashells and driftwood. The only decoration on the walls is a large framed nautical chart of the northern Maine coastline, a tiny red X marking Fever Island. The house is steeped in the silence of long solitude, parsed by the ticking of the old captain's clock.

Mac returns as I finish my self-guided tour of the cottage. He takes off his raincoat and goes straight to the woodstove to begin laying the fire, a chore I'd completely forgotten about.

"How's the boat?" I ask, wondering why he's bothering to light a fire.

"Seaworthy," he says, "but I don't want to take it around the headland in this rain. The current's treacherous in that part, and there are reefs below the surface we'll founder on if I can't see them."

"We have to get back—" I begin.

"We will," he says, "as soon as the rain lets up. I don't think it's going to last long. While we're waiting it out, though, we might as well dry out." He eyes my soaking clothes. "There are some clean sweats upstairs in a trunk if you want to get out of your wet clothes."

Is he trying to get rid of me again to stave off my questions? To show me he has nothing to hide by letting me up into his bedroom? Or just to keep me from getting pneumonia?

I decide on the last and take the stairs up to the loft. I'm expecting a mattress on a floor—college-boy digs—but instead there's an oak Mission bed frame and a bed covered with a faded patchwork quilt. A hobnail-glass oil lantern on the night table beside a well-worn copy of the *Odyssey*. The only other furniture is a large wooden trunk at the foot of the bed. I open it and find a pair of clean sweatpants and a University of Maine sweatshirt, which I change into quickly. They smell like cedar and lavender.

Downstairs Mac's got a fire going in the woodstove, the glow reflected in the polished wood and the glass orbs hanging in the rain-
fogged windows. He's stripped down to a T-shirt and changed into
dry jeans. A kettle is hissing on the top of the stove. It's all so cozy
that for a moment I almost forget the horrors that have happened—
Crosby drowning, the fire, Liz dying in the bog, the fact that I'm
stuck in this remote cabin with a man I don't entirely trust—

"How long have you lived here?" I ask a second time.

The kettle whistling cuts short his answer. "Could you get that?
There's some tea and crackers in the cabinet over there—" He points
to a wooden cabinet beside an old-fashioned soapstone sink. Inside
I find packets of PG Tips, oyster crackers, and a bottle of bourbon. I
put the tea in a brown glazed teapot and sink into the chair by the fire
while he pours hot water into it. When he sits down on the hassock I
repeat my earlier question.

He looks up at me—looks around the room—and then back at me.
"Since that summer," he says. "I never really left."

Although it's what I guessed I'm still stunned. "All alone?"

He smiles ruefully. "Yeah, it's not really a place to bring company. I
mean, I go to the mainland, obviously, but yeah, mostly on my own."

"Does Reed know?" I ask. "That you're . . ."

"Squatting on his property?" The resentment has crept back into
his voice and I'm aware of how alone we are here, isolated in this
strange man's *lair*. What has ten years of living on his own in such a
lonely spot turned him into?

"I didn't mean—"

"Yeah, you did, but it's okay." He pours the steeped tea into two
chipped willowware teacups and adds a spill of bourbon into each.
"He knew I had a little camp here that summer—this was originally
a fishing hut—that he and I used to get away from his family. After
his parents died and Becky vanished, he and Liz got out of here

quickly. I don't think he really thought about whether I was still using this place or not. He just wanted to get away from the island and forget about everything that had happened. I didn't blame him—and I didn't want to remind him about the place, but I also thought it was a shame to let it all rot, so I kept an eye on things. I stayed with my mother at my uncle's house for a bit but I got tired of watching her drink herself to death. When Reed asked me to keep an eye on the Main House, I figured I could do that more easily if I was here."

"He said he sent your mother checks," I say.

"Yeah, he did. She mostly used them to buy booze and lottery tickets."

"Couldn't you . . . I don't know . . . have Reed send you the money and manage it, use it to"—I point to the logo on the sweatshirt I'm wearing—"finish college? I mean, you're obviously smart and like to read." I gesture toward his bookcase.

He snorts, takes a long swallow of bourbon straight from the bottle. "Big surprise! The island Caliban can read. One year at State showed me how little a difference that made to people like you. I was always going to be the fisherman's son, the local yokel college girls slept with over the summer and then dumped when they went back to school in the fall, the handyman the vacationers paid to clean up after their parties."

"So basically, you decided to stay here and stew in your own resentment," I say, pouring another shot of bourbon into my teacup.

"I understand you didn't hurry to get a job after graduating," he says.

"I wrote a *book*," I say defensively.

"Because you had Reed to pay the bills," he says, taking a long drink straight from the bottle.

"I guess we both had Reed taking care of us," I say, tapping the rim of my teacup against his. "Here's to Reed. I'm sure he was grateful to have you here managing the island."

He looks at me suspiciously, not sure if I'm being sarcastic. I'm not entirely sure myself.

"I think he always knew he'd come back. The island ties a knot in your heart that binds you to it." He waves the bourbon bottle toward the windows. They're dark and opaque with raindrops that bead on the glass and glow in the firelight like air bubbles. It feels like we're in a bathyscaphe at the bottom of the ocean. "I did try to leave a couple of times, but the world out there never felt as *real*."

I feel a chill at his words, as if they've somehow erased the outside world—who knows, after all, what has happened to it since we left it?—and we are the last survivors in this tiny escape pod floating in outer space. Then I notice something else. That phrase about the island tying a knot in your heart sounds familiar. It's what Liadan said to Nathaniel in Sea Witch Cottage. I look around for my daypack and see it hanging from one of the hooks by the door. I go grab it and open it, relieved the journal is still there.

"How far have you gotten in it?" he asks.

"To the part where they lose the boat," I say, thinking of what a strange coincidence it is that I'd gotten to that part just before Crosby drowned. "I haven't exactly had a chance to read any more since then. Have you read it?"

"Becky read it to us that summer." He holds his hand out for the book. I hesitate to give it to him but then I realize how absurd that is. I'm alone in this isolated cabin with this strange angry man. The least of my worries should be what he'll do with an old book. I pass it to him, and he cradles it as if it's a newborn kitten, picking delicately through the thin, brittle pages.

"Things go poorly for them after they lose the boat," he says, as if catching me up on last week's episode of a television series. "Sit down," he says. "There's something in here that I think you should hear before we go back to the house."

CHAPTER TWENTY-EIGHT

I insisted on remaining in the cove to see if any of the passengers might wash up onshore but after a few hours Mother Brigitte, along with Liadan, convinced me it was foolish to continue risking my own health.

"The poor souls are gone," she said grimly. "We cannot afford to lose you, too."

Dunstan McCree pledged that he and his men would continue to patrol the shore and Dead Man's Cove, where the currents often brought the refuse of the sea, but he had little hope of recovering more than the dead or the shattered remains of the boat.

Our only boat.

"Surely the Board of Health will send help when they don't receive your regular reports," Mother Brigitte conjectured when we gathered together in my study, where we could talk without fear of the patients or sisters hearing us and becoming alarmed at our situation. Liadan made her rose hip tea, to which I added a dollop of brandy.

"Yes," I agreed with an assurance I did not feel. The truth was that the Board of Health had been lax in their replies to me lately, sometimes not replying at all. Perhaps because they were overwhelmed by the number of fever ships passing up the St. Lawrence River this season. Officials and doctors alike had been diverted to the Grosse Ile quarantine station near Quebec. My own pleas for supplies and additional help fell on deaf ears. How long would it take for anyone to notice if they didn't get my report? Was anyone even reading them anymore?

Mother Brigitte looked at me as if she could read my lack of faith, but all she said was, "In the meantime we must take a thorough inventory and begin a rationing system."

"Certainly," McCree said, turning from the window. "You and your sisters should take charge of the medical supplies. My men and I will see to the stocks of food. I believe we also have some boatbuilders amongst their number. I will have them commence building a new boat as soon as the storm has passed."

"Will they have the necessary materials to build a boat?" I asked. "I have some experience myself with the craft."

"There's a stand of black locusts on the north side of the island that my men tell me is excellent for shipbuilding," he said. Then he bowed his head to us and left, leaving a damp spot by the window and a trail of wet footprints in the carpet.

"I applaud McCree's faith in his men and the island's bounty," Mother Brigitte remarked dryly. I had seen her eyebrows rise when McCree called the hunters "my men." "But I hope we will not have to wait until they are able to lumber, mill, and plane the wood for a boat before we receive a shipment from the mainland." She took another sip of her tea. "At least you have provided us with this delicious brew from your foraging, Liadan."

Liadan startled at the sound of her name. She had been staring at the footprints on the floor left by McCree. Now she looked up, her eyes wide and frightened. I feared that the loss of the boat and the drowning of its passengers had reminded her of her own brush with death in the sea and that she had become momentarily unhinged from reality. But then she shook herself and answered, "Thank you, Mother Brigitte. I will go out to gather more rose hips as soon as the storm has passed."

She looked at me as she finished, and I guessed her intent: she didn't want to be alone in the woods. "I'll go with you," I said, wondering what it was she was afraid of.

Our plans for the morning were dashed when the day dawned as wet and stormy as the night we had passed. The wind rattled the windowpanes and thrashed trees against the house, sending one limb crashing through the window in the long ward, terrifying the patients and the young Gray Sisters. When I went to inspect the damage, I found Liadan kneeling amongst the wreckage, paused in the act of sweeping glass into a dustpan. She seemed distracted as she had the night before, and I saw that she had scratched her name into the wall. She looked embarrassed when she saw me notice.

"It was just a fancy," she said, "to leave a mark of myself. . . . Do you ever feel as if you are . . . unseen?"

"Well," I said, attempting a jovial tone to rouse her out of her morbid fancies, "I have felt unheard lately as my pleas to the Board of Health have fallen on deaf ears."

She nodded. "And now you can't reach them at all." Then she touched the cuff of my shirtsleeve. "Have you ever wondered if they have been receiving them? It's one of McCree's men who has been taking them, isn't it?"

The notion that my reports could have been going astray was alarming, not least of all because it showed the state of mind the poor girl had fallen prey to. Nor was she the only one who showed herself susceptible to gloomy suspicions. I heard the Gray Sisters whispering amongst themselves of a bogeyman they believed to be prowling the wards and stealing away the souls of the sick and dying.

"It's the work of the devil," I heard Mairi whisper to one. "I've seen the mark of his cloven hoof upon the floor."

I chided the nuns for wasting time while patients required their assistance. But the whispering spread like wildfire through the wards, as infectious as the fever, and was taken up by the patients. The devil, they said, walked the wards at night stealing the breath out of the mouths of the dying. I spied Mairi one day sitting by the fire, doing some needlework. I stopped to observe her work, as I would often do when my sisters were working on some embroidery, and saw that she was stitching a pattern of daisies into the collar of her habit. I was surprised that decoration was allowed on a nun's habit and, thinking it might have some religious significance, asked her what the pattern was.

"It's a devil catcher," she said, turning bright red. "If a demon flies into your room at night it will get caught inside the pattern and leave you alone."

"And why would a demon bother someone as faultless as you?" I asked.

She looked at me as if I were the simple one. "Mr. McCree says the devil has an appetite for the innocent and that I must take care not to fall prey to his tricks."

Distressed that Dunstan McCree would put such ideas into a child's head, I went to see Mother Brigitte, who said such superstitions were not uncommon in times of plague, that people sought an explanation for the horrors of sickness, famine, and death, and that rather than turn their faces to the light of God they cast their eyes to the darkness of Satan. Which remarks made me fear Mother Brigitte is not immune from the contagion of despair that has settled over all of us while the storm rages.

At last, the third day dawned clear and since none of my patients demanded immediate attention, I suggested to Liadan we make our foraging expedition. I thought it would do her good to get out of the oppressive atmosphere of the fever ward and move in the sunshine and fresh air. In the last few days she had grown thin and haggard, the dark circles under her eyes deepening, her cheeks paling, her usually steady hands trembling. As we set out, she did not engage in her usual banter, but silently stopped to gather some rose hips and dig up some strange-looking roots, so distractedly that she cut her thumb on her digging tool.

"Let me see to that," I said, kneeling beside her and wrapping her wounded thumb with my handkerchief, "and perhaps you will tell me what is bothering you."

"Now you've ruined one of your good handkerchiefs," she chided, "and who knows when we'll get supplies again."

"Oh dear," I replied jocularly, "whatever will we do? A shortage of handkerchiefs is even more concerning than our diminishing store of carbolic acid and sugar."

She burst into a startled laugh—and then into tears. I waited patiently for the outbreak to pass as if waiting out a summer shower while I picked rose hips from the bush to add to her canvas sack. "Do tell me what is troubling you, Liadan," I said when the "shower" had passed.

"Surely we are all troubled," she answered while gathering some of the blossoms from the bush, "by the loss of our one boat and the lives of the passengers gone with it, not to mention the rise of sickness amongst our patients."

"Yes," I agreed, "but I think I know you well enough that such

challenges would not daunt you. There is something else and I
fear it may have to do with the superstitions running through the
wards—all this talk of a devil—"

She looked up sharply at that and then scanned the woods
with anxious eyes. "Best not to speak of such things," she said,
getting to her feet and taking the sack from me. "Or belittle the
beliefs of others."

She turned and made her way into the woods, picking her way
along the path. I followed, hampered by the branches fallen from
the storm that she navigated more nimbly. Finally, I caught up
with her when a thornbush snagged her skirt.

"I did not mean to offend you," I said, disentangling her. "I
didn't think you were susceptible to such fancies—"

"And you think you know me so well?" she asked sharply.
"How do you know what I believe, Dr. Harper? Or what I've
seen—whole families perishing of hunger, the roads full
of walking skeletons, bodies left to rot where they dropped,
hundreds crying out for water and food on the steps of the
churches and hospitals. Homes reduced to rubble and children
separated from their mothers—"

She faltered to a stop, her cheeks as red as the blossoms we
had gathered, her eyes burning so hot I feared she might truly
have been taken by the fever. Her hand fell on her stomach as if
she was in pain.

"Children?" I asked. "You said your mother and sisters had
died when you left. Did you . . . had you . . . I do not want to pry."

"Perhaps you do not want to know," she replied.

I felt the heat in my own cheeks then, conscious that she was
right. I was afraid, although I did not know of what. I glanced
into the woods surrounding us and felt it, the presence of
something undeniably evil watching us—

Wanting to do us harm.

She must have seen the fear in my eyes, but instead of causing her fear it seemed to give her hope. "You feel it, too," she said, and then, without waiting for my response, she vanished into the woods.

When I reached the rocky shore, I saw Liadan standing beside three tall stones on the water's edge.

"They say this is where the witch was buried," she said, tracing a pattern on the face of the center stone. "That she was lowered headfirst until she was wedged into the rocks, her hands tied behind her back so she couldn't move. Then they left her to die. They left her at the neap tide, when the water wouldn't have drowned her until the spring tide." She turned to me, her eyes brimming as the tide at full moon. "They wanted her to suffer longer so she would repent her sins."

"It's just a story—" I began, but she silenced me with a look.

"When a girl was in a long labor in the workhouse the nuns would say that she was paying for her sin. They would give her nothing to ease her pain or speed her delivery because the longer she suffered the less time she would burn in hell."

"Did you . . ." I began, wanting to ask her if she had been one of the girls to give birth, but she was already going on about the witch.

She looked down into the gap between the boulders, from which a sound had begun to rise—a low keening moan as of someone in pain. "I think this girl would have cursed her torturers. See this mark?" She touched the stone and again began tracing a pattern like a daisy. It looked like the pattern Mairi had been stitching onto her habit.

"Mairi called these 'devil catchers,'" I said, feeling dizzy as

I followed her finger tracing the pattern. "Do you think the settlers who condemned that poor girl carved it? Were they trying to catch the devil inside her?"

"Perhaps," she said, frowning. "Or perhaps her suffering a quarter turn of the moon was not enough for them and they wanted her to suffer here forever or—" She turned to me, her eyes flashing. "Maybe the mark was made by the witch's ghost as it broke free of the stone and was meant to trap her torturers and any who tarry on this island." She flashed me a hectic smile and, lifting her skirts, leapt across the chasm as if daring it to hold her. I began to follow her, but looked back and saw newer carvings on the stones on either side of the center stone, carvings that looked like the pattern the men had tattooed on themselves. I wondered if they had been made recently by those men. I wondered, too, whether the symbol was protection against the devil—or a way of summoning him.

I followed Liadan around an inlet, along a narrow path that clung to the stone cliff, and into the woods again. Finally we reached a saltwater meadow where a crude lean-to stood by the water's edge beside a campfire and a stack of fresh-cut wood. Liadan led me through the meadow and past granite boulders inscribed with names. This was where McCree's men were burying the dead. When we reached the shoreline, she sat on a boulder and motioned for me to sit beside her. The stone was warm from the sun and worn smooth. Liadan leaned back and closed her eyes, tilting her face up to the sun. As she spoke, her hands moved deftly, plucking long grasses and weaving them as if weaving her own tale, which I have transcribed here endeavoring to hew as closely as possible to her words.

"When I told you my story before I was not completely honest with you. It's true that I was sent to the workhouse, but I didn't tell you that when I got there I was with child. The landlord's son . . . he . . . well, I will not make excuses. I suppose, as the nuns were fond of telling us, I must have put myself in his way, or somehow shown my willingness, or failed in my prayers to God to stop him, but I am not sure how God would have stopped a rich man from taking what he wanted.

"I gave birth to my babe in the workhouse, and he would have been sent out to fostering until he would have been old enough to be taken back to the orphanage. Most of the babies sent out died and, as the nuns said, it would be a mercy rather than live with the taint of being a bastard. My sister, bless her, came and took him, and I hoped that I might soon be released and reclaim him.

"I was let go sooner than I might have been because the workhouses had become overcrowded and could not afford to feed us. I walked to the estate on roads thronged with the starving and the desperate, men and women and children with no flesh on their bones and madness in their eyes, heading toward the port to try their luck on the ships. I didn't know yet that my mother and sisters were amongst them. When I found the rubble their house had become I went, as you already know, to the landlord's house to ask where they'd been sent, but I did not tell you that the housekeeper told me that my babe had gone to the devil as all bastards did. She pointed to the ground where there was a mark in the mud of a cloven hoof. 'Follow that,' she told me, 'if you want to follow him into hell.'

"I suppose I must have been half-mad, because I did as she said. I followed the devil's footprints out into the lane, onto the road, and all the way to New Ross. As I walked I heard the whispers of the starving telling tales of the devil. He was on the road stealing souls at night with the last breaths of the dying; he lured the desperate into the bogs and made them do unspeakable things to one another; he was in the landlords chasing their tenants from their homes and in the agents selling false dreams of escape. There was one agent, spoken of in particular as a man possessed, who lured the unwary onto the ships of the damned, ships that sailed straight into the maws of hell. I feared that my babe had gotten onto one of those ships, but I knew that if he had I would follow him straight into hell itself.

"I went to all the shipping offices in New Ross and asked to see the logs of all the ships that had left for America and Canada, but I could not find my mother's or sisters' names on any of them. I heard then from an old man who had been on the estate that my mother and sisters had died on the road and that another family had taken my boy with them aboard a ship to Boston. The agent who booked their passage, he said, was the one spoken of as the devil's man, but I would not find him because he was wanted by the authorities for taking the money entrusted to him by the landlords for securing their tenants' passage and shipping them out on the cheapest vessels and keeping the difference for himself. I knew then that the only one who could tell me what had become of my child was this devil—so I followed his tracks onto the *Stella Maris* and hid aboard."

"Did you really think," I said as gently as I could, "that you were following the devil?"

Liadan turned and looked at me, her blue-green eyes glimmering like a glimpse of the sea between the feathery pines. "I understand why you, a man of science, would doubt my story, Dr. Harper. And I had begun to as well. But then the other night . . . Well, I thought that might have been an illusion as well, but . . ."

She got up and knelt in the grass at the edge of the meadow, putting aside the doll she had fashioned out of the grasses. She pushed aside a clump of ferns. There in the soil I saw an impression as of an animal's cloven hoof, a deer, perhaps. But then I traced the prints' trail between the gravestones. Two by two the prints marched, clearly left by a creature standing on two legs.

A stag on two legs.

A devil.

"I thought I followed the devil to this island," Liadan said, her voice low and troubled. "But now I think it has always been here."

CHAPTER TWENTY-NINE

MAC LAYS DOWN THE BOOK AND LEANS FORWARD TO ADD ANOTHER LOG to the fire. The flare of heat does little to dissipate the chill I feel deep in my bones.

A stag on two legs.

A devil.

The antlered figure I've imagined seeing in the woods flickers through my head, and I instinctively glance at the windows, but their fogged surfaces reflect back only my own frightened face. The rain had stopped while Mac was reading, as if to let the island listen better to his words.

A stag on two legs.

A devil.

There's nothing but sea and mist beyond the windowpanes. Nothing for miles and miles. We're alone here on this island with—

"Why did you think I needed to hear that? What does it mean? You don't think—"

"That there's a devil on this island?" he asks, looking up from the fire. With its glow on his face, he looks quite demonic himself.

"Of course not. That poor girl—Liadan—she must have been half mad after what she'd gone through. It would make anyone—" I break off, picturing the antlered figure I've imagined flitting through the woods.

"See devils?" Mac finishes for me. "Yes, you're right. See enough bad things in this world—the nasty shit people do to each other—and you *do* start seeing the devil's hand in everything. That's what I thought that summer. Mr. Harper—*Tibs*—was a raging asshole, isolated in his study, drinking all day. Even when you tried to stay out of his way you knew he was there, like some monster in the basement, only he was in that tower of his . . . *watching*. Everyone—every *thing*—on the island was infected with the madness. Becky with her games that got crazier as she realized she was losing Reed, Liz going out of her mind because her own father was calling her a freak, Reed twisting himself in knots to keep the peace."

"And you?" I ask.

"I was angry all the time just watching all these fucking rich people who had everything and all they could do was make each other miserable."

The anger in his voice crackles, too big for the tiny cabin, this snug bolt-hole he's carved out of enemy territory. "And what did your anger make you—" I almost say *do,* but at the last moment I'm afraid of confronting him. "What did it make you see?"

His eyes spark in the firelight. "Nothing before the séance. I thought it was all a game. Sure, sometimes, when I looked into the woods . . ." He averts his eyes.

"The antlered man?" I ask, my voice coming out hoarse.

He stares at me. "Reed said it was just a deer—or an optical illusion caused by the effect of branches crossing one another. Becky said it was the demon of the island that was brought here on the fever ships and that we raised it with our hatred, anger, and betrayal. Reed said that after I left she started saying it was stalking her and she could prove it because she found its footprints. That's when Reed asked me to come back to the island to help find Becky and take her to the mainland. I already told you how that went. She ran into the

Dead Pool as if the devil were chasing her and then—" He blanches. "After she died I found the footprints in the woods along the path she was running on as if the devil *had* chased her into the pit."

I think for a moment and then say, "She could have left those. It wouldn't have been that hard."

"No, it wouldn't," he agrees, getting up and rummaging around in a cabinet. He comes back holding a heavy piece of corroded iron in his hand. It's formed like a horseshoe with a V-shaped base linking the two ends. "I found this in Dead Man's Cove. This kind of horse-shoe is called a heart bar shoe. It matches the footprints we found that summer and the ones described in Nathaniel Harper's journal."

"So someone—Becky, for instance—could have made the foot-prints with this."

"Yeah, but then why was she so afraid of them that she ran into the Dead Pool?"

"Did you see any new tracks after Becky died?" I ask.

"No," he says, "and I haven't seen any for all the years I've been here . . . until . . ."

"Until when?"

"Until this summer. I've seen them again."

"Are you sure they weren't from back then?"

He shakes his head. "I saw these in the sand at low tide . . . so, no, they had to have been made this summer."

"So, you think someone else could be making them?" I ask.

"Yeah," he says, "the only other explanation is that you all brought the devil with you when you came to the island."

MAC GOES TO get the boat ready, leaving me alone to change back into my slightly drier clothes, an unpracticed gesture of privacy from a man who has lived as a hermit for years. As I splash some water on my face and under my arms, I look around the tidy cabin with its books and tea tins and collections of shells and driftwood and sea glass. I can see why it would be appealing to hunker down in a place like this. Even after the virus loosened its hold on us last time it was hard to go back out into the world, to trust the hug of a friend or share the air with a stranger. I couldn't blame Mac for wanting to hide away in this pretty spot where the late afternoon sun catches the sea glass in the window and turns each shard into a shimmering dragonfly—one of the pieces of glass even seems to have veins like a dragonfly wing—

I cross to the window to get a closer look, but then Mac is at the door, backpack in hand, asking if I'm ready to go. "Yes," I say and then, pointing at what I now realize is a glass oval locket hanging in the window, I ask, "Where did you get this?"

He frowns. "It washed up in Dead Man's Cove, where I found the other things."

"Do you remember when?"

"At the end of that summer," he says, coming closer. "I was into picking up that stuff then. And I remember this locket because of the wing preserved in between the glass. It reminded me—and I know this is going to sound stupid—of those pieces of amber that have insects in them from a million years ago. Obviously this one isn't that old and it probably came from a souvenir shop down the coast. Still . . . " He touches the glass oval locket and sets it spinning in the sunlight, which catches a tiny blue flower sealed in the glass. "It made me think about stopping time, capturing a moment and holding on to it. Like I could hold on to the time before that last summer forever."

"There have been moments since then," I said, "worth hanging on to."

"Yeah," he agrees, staring at the locket as if trying to remember one, "but not many." Then he looks back at me. "What is it?" he asks. "Do you recognize it?"

I shake my head. "I thought I did for a moment, but . . . it's like you said, it looks like the kind they sell in souvenir shops in beach towns everywhere."

He looks at me doubtfully, then turns away. "I'll be out at the boat when you're ready."

I wait until he walks out the door and then I remove the glass oval locket—the kind they sell in souvenir shops in beach towns everywhere—and put it in my pocket.

CHAPTER THIRTY

THE BRIEF GLIMMER OF SUN HAS BEEN SWALLOWED UP BY OVERHANG- ing fog by the time we row out of the inlet. There's just enough light to turn the fog a strange yellowish green. It's hard not to think of the columns of fog that ring the island as the ghosts of the drowned as Mac rows us around the steep rocky northeast headland. This is a part of the island I haven't seen since the day we arrived and Mac pointed to the cliff where the Gray Lady was supposed to appear. When I gaze up at it now through shifting layers of fog it looks as if the cliff might topple over into the water and swamp our frag- ile craft. There's so little difference between the color of the water and the hue of the sky that we might already have slipped between worlds and be traveling to a kingdom beneath the waves. Caught be- tween sea and sky, then and now, we're like a dragonfly wing pressed between two pieces of glass.

It's sad they only get to live one summer, Ada had said that summer on the Vineyard that we whiled away by the dragonfly pond.

I guess it depends on the summer, I had answered.

And so, at the end of the summer, which had been the best one of my life, I bought two glass lockets from a souvenir shop and placed inside each of them a dragonfly wing and one of the tiny blue flowers that grew by the pond and gave one to Ada so, I told her on the ferry going back, we would always have that summer. She hugged me so tight we almost fell over the railing. She wore hers every day of senior year. She was wearing it the day she left our dorm to take the bus to the city.

The next time I saw her, more than a year later, she wasn't. I asked her about it, and she said she'd put it in her locker at the hospital where she was volunteering, and someone must have stolen it. I'd felt silly for bringing it up, for caring about some sentimental trinket from our frivolous past of daiquiri parties and Frisbee tournaments. The locket was a little tacky, I saw then. I put mine away.

So how had Ada's locket, lost ten years ago in New York City, made it five hundred miles up the coast to find itself in Dead Man's Cove? What current could have carried it that far? Had it been drawn back the way the souls of those who had once lived on the island were pulled back?

But Ada had never been on the island before this summer.

Or had she?

I look back at the island, floating in the fog, trying to grasp an idea as elusive as the island itself, which seems to be receding—

"Hey!" I call to Mac. "Why are we so far away from the dock?"

Mac doesn't turn around. "We need to get to the mainland before dark," he says. "We need to go now."

"You said you'd take me back to the house first! I have to check on Reed."

"Reed will be fine. It's more important we bring back help from the mainland."

"Go back now!" I shout. "I have to make sure. There's something I've just realized."

"What?" he asks, still rowing away from the island.

There's no time to explain, even if I could. I stand up, determined to swim for the dock.

"Whoa! What are you doing? Sit back down!"

"Only if you'll take me back now," I say, bracing my legs against the rocking of the boat.

"Okay, okay." He turns the boat around. I nearly fall overboard at the motion and collapse hard into the hull. "I'll come with you."

"No," I say, "you should continue on to the mainland while I check on Reed and Niko . . ."

"And Ada," he says, squinting at me.

"Yes, Ada," I say, looking away. "Of course, Ada's fine—she didn't get burned . . ."

"Or drown when the boat capsized," he adds. "That locket hanging in my window . . . you looked like you recognized it, like it meant something to you."

"A hundred like them in beach town souvenir shops," I say.

"With dragonfly wings and little blue flowers?" he asks. "You recognized it, didn't you? Is it yours?"

"No!" I say too quickly. "I mean, I had one like it and another that I gave to Ada. But it can't be hers. She wasn't here that summer." I meet his eyes across the boat. We're almost at the dock. "Was she?"

"Not that I knew of," Mac says. He cranes his neck around to judge the distance and reaches out to grab the iron cleat at the end of the dock. I'm already up and jumping onto the dock. "But she could have been here when I was gone. And if she was . . ."

"There will be an explanation," I say, pushing the boat away.

"I should come with you," he says, maneuvering the boat back toward the dock.

"No! You need to get to the mainland. Get help. I'll be okay. And besides"—he's clutching the edge of the dock with his hands—"if you leave the boat there's no guarantee it will be here when we get back."

He looks up and meets my eyes. He doesn't say anything but I can see he gets my point. "All right," he says at last. "I'll be back as soon as I can. Be careful and"—he reaches into his backpack and removes a small bundle wrapped in a flannel shirt—"take this. You might need it."

I can feel the heavy metal through the soft cloth and know immediately what it is. I don't refuse it. "Okay," I say. "I'll be careful. You too. Get back as soon as you can."

AS I WALK uphill from the dock the house appears out of the fog. I remember thinking on our first day that it looked unwelcoming—a fortress erected against the world to protect its own. Now I wonder if it's ever possible to wall ourselves off from danger, whether the worse danger is the virus or the people who want what we have.

The rocking chairs are lined up on the front porch as if waiting for us to take our places for evening cocktails. I feel a pang thinking of Liz and Crosby and all the moments of camaraderie we shared as a group. Even when we were bickering I hadn't felt like I belonged anywhere as much since the days I spent in college with Reed and Ada, the three of us adventuring together. Had that camaraderie been an illusion? I have to find out.

I open the front door and enter the great room, dim in the fading daylight. As on the first day I feel as if I've come in just after the party ended, the echoes of voices lingering in the salt air, scattered cushions still holding the impressions of warm bodies, the faces of the departed looking out from the photographs—

Which have been pasted all over the back wall in a giant collage. Niko has cut up the old family photographs and arranged them with her own work on the wall, mingling her eerie rockscapes and fog studies with pictures of young Reed and Liz, blond cousins, women in clamdiggers and Jackie Kennedy scarves, strong-jawed Harper men going all the way back to Nathaniel Reed Harper. Liadan is in the center, her eyes dyed red with some kind of marker or paint.

"It started with them."

I jump at the voice and wheel around. It's Niko, but identifying her is no relief. Her eyes are as red as the painted ones in the photographs and her hands and face are smeared red, as if she has sewn this Frankenstein's monster together with bleeding body parts.

"Niko," I say, "your hands—what happened to the bandages Liz put on? You're bleeding."

Niko holds up her hands and grins. "Nah, it's just some of Liz's paint she left here. She won't mind . . . is she back?" Niko's eyes skitter around the room as if Liz might be hiding under a sofa. There's something wrong with her eyes besides the red; her pupils are huge.

"Niko," I say, ignoring the question about Liz. "Did Ada give you more of those pain pills? Where *is* Ada?"

Niko shrugs. "I dunno . . . I took a couple . . ." She gestures toward the pile of discarded photo scraps on the floor. Lying beside a can of paint fixative and the cap for an X-Acto knife is the orange pill bottle. I lean down and pick it up and notice several more pills are missing from it.

"Did you take this from Ada?"

She shrugs again, now standing inches from the photo collage, her nose almost touching the red demon eyes.

"What did you mean, it started with them?"

She shrugs. "The fever patients brought the devil from the Old World. That's why all those fever patients went crazy. That's why the Harpers are so fucked up, spending every summer here. They stayed here too long the last time and the devil got into Mr. Tibster and then when they killed him, it got into Becky and then—" She cocks her head as if listening to an inner voice. "Liz said it went to rest in the Dead Pool. Waiting." Niko turns away from the collage. "Where did you say Liz was?"

"She . . ." I falter. How can I possibly tell this drug-crazed Niko that her girlfriend has drowned in the Dead Pool? "She went with

Mac in the boat to get help from the mainland," I say with as much certainty as I can.

"She wouldn't leave without me," Niko says flatly.

"She's coming back. Mac needed her on the boat and . . ." I scramble for some reasonable explanation for Liz having to go with Mac on the boat but I've already lost Niko.

"It was you, wasn't it?" she says.

"What?"

"You were the one here that summer. Liz said the things that happened—the devil's footprints and the missing things—only made sense if there was someone else on the island. Becky couldn't have done it all. Liz said that after the séance Becky started acting scared, like the game had gotten out of her control, and then *something* killed Becky. It was you, wasn't it? You wanted to get rid of Becky so you could have Reed to yourself."

"That's crazy," I say, "I was in my college dorm hundreds of miles from here."

"Not so far by bus."

It was true there was a bus that went north from our college town. One that went south to New York City and one that went north to Boston and Maine. "I was sick," I say. "I got sick a few days after—" A few days after Ada left to take the bus to New York City.

"So you and Reed said. Of course, he would have covered for you."

I laugh. "Do you think Reed made up my three weeks in the hospital on a respirator or the damage to my lungs?" I bring my hands to my chest.

"I don't know," Niko says, her eyes burning with the same crazed fervor as the painted eyes in the collage. "Let's find out."

I see the flash of orange plastic in her hands a second before she leaps. It's just enough time to swing my backpack off my shoulder to catch the impact of the X-Acto blade. She grabs the pack in her hand

and pulls it toward her, upsetting my balance so that I fall forward and knock my head against Niko's forehead. We crash to the floor, the backpack between us, the hard shape of Mac's handgun digging into my ribs. The orange X-Acto blade skitters across the floor. Niko lunges for it, and I reach into the pack and pull out the gun. The metal feels so cold it burns. Niko's eyes latch on to the gun, then she grabs the can of paint fixative and aims it at my eyes. I'm blinded, my hand on the trigger, squeezing—

Do it, a voice says inside my head, *kill her!*

But then I hear retreating footsteps and through the blur of my ruined vision I see Niko running. I stumble after her to the back door and watch her vanish into the woods, the orange X-Acto knife in one hand, the orange pill bottle in the other.

CHAPTER THIRTY-ONE

I GO BACK INSIDE TO THE KITCHEN TO RINSE MY EYES, BUT NOTHING HAP-
pens when I turn on the tap. The electricity and water are still not
back on. I find water in the electric kettle and flush my eyes with it.
They still burn, and I feel like I'm staring at the world through a layer
of wax paper, but at least I can see.

And *hear*.

What I hear is silence. All the commotion of my tussle with Niko
and no one came running to help. Where's Reed? Where's Ada?

I pick up the gun from the counter and put it back in my bag, then
sling the pack over my shoulder, unzipped so I can reach inside for
the gun if I need it, and start up the stairs. I pause to listen between
each crackling step but all I hear is the stir of a breeze through the
curtains and the tick of old clocks. The last of the Harpers, those
spared from Niko's X-Acto blade, look back at me from their glass
frames as if I am the intruder creeping down the corridor.

It was you, wasn't it? Niko had accused. *You were the one here that
summer.*

I *had* thought about going to the island. Reed was posting pictures
of ocean sunsets and lobster bakes while Ada and I were living on
ramen noodles in our cinder-block dorm room. *We could just take the
bus up there,* I said one day, only half jokingly. *We could rent a boat
and row it out to the island. Surprise Reed.*

Yeah, Ada had said, *I'm sure Reed's parents would love that.*

Reed's always talking about all the places there are to hide on the island, I'd replied.

But when I contemplated trespassing on Harper land, of being the uninvited guest, I knew I didn't have the nerve to do it.

But Ada would.

When I get to the bedroom, the door is closed. Reaching for the knob I cannot shake the feeling that I am the intruder here, that this isn't a room I've shared with Reed—*my husband*—all summer. It will be locked, my way barred, as it would have been if I'd stolen onto the island ten years ago.

The knob turns in my hand and the door opens. The minute I see Reed—inert, eyes closed, deathly pale—I rush to the bed, sure I'm too late. All the time I worried about trespassing I should have been rushing to his side to save him. When I touch his face, I'm relieved to find his skin warm. He's alive! But then I realize that he's not just warm; he's hot. He's burning up with fever. His eyes flutter open, bloodshot and unfocused.

"Lu . . ." His voice sounds as if it's traveling across a scorched desert to reach me.

"I'm here," I say, scanning the night table for water. There's an empty pill bottle. Why has Ada left him alone? I help him sit up and drink from the canteen Mac filled at the cabin. He takes a few sips, his eyes clearing at the taste of the cold well water.

"Where's Mac?" he asks.

"He went to the mainland to get help."

"Liz?"

He's looking right at me; I can't lie to him. "She fell into the Dead Pool and drowned. I'm so sorry, Reed. We tried to save her but the rope broke . . ." My own voice breaks at the memory.

"It's this fucking island," Reed says, his words slurring together.

"It destroys everything. It took Becky last time . . . and Ada . . . it made Ada—"

"What about Ada? Was Ada here last time?" Even through the feverish delirium I see the flicker of guilt in his eyes. "It's true, isn't it? But why? And why didn't you tell me?"

"She told me you wouldn't come," he says, his eyes darting away from mine and locking on something behind me. I turn and find Ada standing inches from my back with a hypodermic needle in her hand. Before I can stop her, she leans down and jabs it into Reed's arm.

"That was true," she says, as Reed's eyes flutter. "You were too afraid to come here—or anywhere."

"What did you just give him?" I demand, shaking Reed as his eyelids sink shut.

"Just a sedative," she says, smiling. "I've got antibiotics, too." She pats a canvas satchel hanging from her shoulder. "But I thought he needed to calm down. You were getting him needlessly excited with all your questions." She lays her hand on Reed's forehead and checks his pulse. "I'm afraid his burns have gotten infected. Did you say Mac went to the mainland for help?"

She's acting so caringly—straightening Reed's blankets, refilling his water glass—that all my suspicions unravel. What do I think she has done? Even if she was here ten years ago, this is Ada, my best friend. She will be able to explain. I fish in my pocket and take out the dragonfly locket, not as an accusation of betrayal but as a reminder of our friendship, and hold it up.

"Oh," she says, sitting down on the opposite side of the bed so that Reed is between us, "I wondered where that went."

"Mac found it in Dead Man's Cove ten years ago. You were *here*—you came here instead of going to the city, didn't you?"

She nods, digging in her satchel for something. I tense, my hand reaching into my backpack for the gun, but she only brings out a handful of medical supplies: foil packets and tubes, gauze rolls and glass ampoules. She unwraps Reed's bandages as she speaks. "You gave me the idea, you know, with your little fantasy of going to the island. When I got to the bus station, I actually bought a ticket to the city but then I saw that the bus to Maine was coming in first. I sat there, scrolling through Reed's Instagram feed of all those beautiful sunsets and beautiful people and thought about going back to the city to my parents' crappy apartment that I'd have to share with half a dozen smelly interns when I wasn't standing on line at CTown to buy toilet paper, and I thought—" She winces, but it's at the sight of Reed's hands, which are red and oozing. She pours hydrogen peroxide over them, which makes him stir and murmur but he remains unconscious—*how much sedative did she give him?*—as she continues to apply ointment and tell me her story.

"I thought, why not go see this famous island Reed was always going on about? I didn't expect his family to welcome me, but I figured I could camp out in one of his Hardy Boys hideouts—Skullduggery Cove or Lonesome Lighthouse—and I might even get a glimpse of the famous Becky." She looks up and smiles. "I actually thought of giving him a good talking-to about how he'd been leading you on for four years and wasn't it time he dumped Becky and finally declared his love for you. So, you see, I was doing it for you."

"So why didn't you tell me?" I ask. "You could have texted me."

"Well . . ." She frowns as she begins to wrap Reed's hand in clean gauze. "We had just had that big fight and I was angry at you for taking the Lexas' side instead of mine and for being such a wuss—not just because you wouldn't come to the city with me but because you'd let Reed get away with stringing you along for years without ever standing up for yourself. I thought I'd show you what could be accomplished by taking a risk, by being brave, and that you'd see I'd been right all along. I'd send you a selfie from the island and Reed would tell you to get the hell up here and we'd spend the rest of the summer swimming and eating lobster, like you and I did on the Vineyard." She reaches across the bed and takes the dragonfly locket from my hand, smiling fondly. "So, you see, I was doing it for *us,* for you and me."

"Okay," I say, picturing Ada sitting at the bus stop scrolling through her phone, her expression a mixture of desire and loathing. I can see her going up to the counter and exchanging her ticket and smiling the same secret smile she had on her face when she scrolled through the pictures of the Lexas' party and knew she'd gotten them into trouble. But there's something wrong with the picture.

"So, what happened?" I ask. "I don't think I ever got that text telling me to 'get the hell up here.'"

"Well," she says, taping off one end of the gauze and moving on to the other hand, "first of all, it was a whole lot longer a ride than I expected. Man, who knew how fucking big Maine is? And how many rest stops full of pasty-faced tourists in L.L.Bean sweaters buying moose and lobster tchotchkes—even in the middle of a fucking pandemic—I'd have to get through. By the time I got to Jonesport I smelled like three-day-old fish and burnt coffee. And lo and behold, there was nothing in Jonesport—no hotel or campground or *anything.* When I texted Reed with a picture of me under the 'Welcome to Jonesport' sign he didn't answer. It was raining so I sat under the awning of a closed Dairy Queen for half the night, shivering. He texted me at three A.M. and told me he'd row across first thing in the morning and that I could wait in the boathouse on his family's dock. I mean, I'd been expecting to camp out but not in a rusty shed that smelled like fish."

I could point out how foolhardy it had been to expect anything, but she doesn't need me to tell her that. I'm still trying to get my head around the idea that she had done what I had only daydreamed about. It makes me feel jealous. "So, Reed came for you in the morning?"

"Yes, rowing out of the fog like a Viking—two Vikings! He had Mac with him, but he let him off at a different pier and then waited until he was gone to come get me. Like he was ashamed of me. When he picked me up, he explained that Mac had gotten cagey about a stupid séance and wanted to leave the island. I told him that *you'd* been too scared to come up with me, and he was really disappointed."

"But that wasn't true! I didn't know you were going to the island!"

She looks up and gives me one of her *gotcha* smiles. "You mean you were only too scared to go to New York City with me? You would have been fine going to Maine?"

"I, I," I splutter. Her *gotcha* smile settles into a grimace. "I thought as much, which was pretty much what I figured out as I froze my ass off in that stinky shed all night. Why should I be your ambassador to the country of Reed Harper? Was I Cyrano fucking de Bergerac? So, I told Reed that you were too scared to leave our dorm room, and he confided that he was sick of people living in fear, and he told me about what a jackass his father was being and that he was tired of the games Liz and Becky were playing. By the time we got to the island he'd come up with a great idea to teach everyone a lesson—"

She stops as Reed stirs and murmurs in his sleep.

"That's right, Reed *darling*," she says, stroking his forehead, "don't pretend it wasn't your idea or that you didn't help me hide out in that fishing shack in the middle of those creepy graves—did Mac take you there, Lu? That's why you've been gone so long, huh? I don't know how he stands living in that boneyard. I thought I'd go crazy. Everyone else had by then, the Great Becky most of all. Reed told me to stay away from her because she'd gone feral living at the lighthouse cottage, communing with the spirit of Liadan and all that pagan shit, believing that Liadan had brought the 'stag on two legs' to the island."

"You've read it," I say, recognizing the phrase from Nathaniel's journal.

"Oh yeah, Reed got it away from Becky and gave it to me. That's where I got the idea for faking the devil's footprints and drawing Celtic knots on the trees and leaving little straw dolls for her. The journal is like a gaslighting how-to! Look how eagerly she took the bait! As easily as you did—all I had to do was put the journal back in the study."

"What do you mean, put it back?"

"I held on to it all these years thinking it might come in handy. Reed came down to the Cove House the second night we were here to ask me if I had it, not because he wanted to give it to you, but because he wanted to make sure *I* didn't give it to you. I told him I didn't have it, but after he left, I changed my mind and decided I would give it to him. I followed him to Dead Man's Cove and . . . well . . . you remember what happened that night."

I can feel my face burning. "You were *there*?" I ask, appalled. "*Watching*?"

"Well, I didn't *think* you and Reed were going to get it on alfresco, certainly not from what Reed had led me to believe about your marriage."

"What he *led you to believe*?" I repeat, appalled that he would talk about such a private subject with *anyone* else, let alone my best friend.

"Well, let's just say I got the impression that you were not *intimate* anymore," she says.

"Did he *say* that?" I demand.

"Well, not in so many words, but I could *tell*. I saw, though, that he had misled me and that he might need a little coaxing to come back to me. And I had the means right there in my hands—the journal that had driven Becky crazy. The idea came to me then that if Reed could see you as he'd come to see Becky then he'd understand that I was the right one for him all along. I just had to encourage you to read the journal so you would go as nuts as Becky had. And boy, did you ever take the bait! I even found the horseshoe right where I'd left it so could make footprints like I did last time. Man, you should have seen Becky's and Liz's faces when they saw those hoofprints. First Liz accused Becky of leaving them . . . Where is Liz, by the way?"

"She fell into the Dead Pool," I say, deliberately stating the fact blandly. "Apparently the buoys had been moved and someone cut Mac's rope."

"That's too bad," Ada says, looking down a second too late to hide the twitch of a smirk on her lips. I hug the backpack to my side and inch my hand inside. Only moments ago, I hadn't been able to believe that Ada could wish me harm but that moment has passed while listening to her cool recital of how she came to the island ten years ago and plotted with Reed to gaslight his girlfriend and family. Most chilling of all, I realize, is that it all sounds *familiar*. It sounds like the revenge plots she would hatch late at night against the Lexas of Levittown or the *skank* who spilled beer on her or the boy who wouldn't lend her his notes in Bio 101. I just never thought that *I* would be the object of one of her schemes. And maybe I'm still not.

"It could have been me," I say. "If I had been walking in front of Liz I could have followed those buoys into the Dead Pool."

She lifts her head up, a pained look on her face. "I'm glad it wasn't, Lu. I'm glad we've gotten to have this talk and that you can see how well I'm taking care of Reed." She strokes his forehead with such tenderness that I think I must be wrong—Ada can't mean either of us harm—and then she leans down and kisses him on the lips. When she lifts her head, she's smiling. "You don't have to worry about him. He's always been a little slow to realize what he wants. He told me that summer that he regretted wasting so much time because he was afraid of hurting Becky's feelings and that he wouldn't make the same mistake with you."

"You mean," I say, trying to unsee that kiss and the way she's stroking his forehead, "that he would tell me how he felt when he got back to me?"

"No," she says curtly, her hand curling into a fist over her heart, "I mean he wouldn't worry about hurting your feelings. He was going to tell you how he felt about *me,* that he loved *me,* and that he was going to be with *me* from then on." With each *me* she pounds her fist on her chest.

"But . . . I don't understand. You never seemed to even *like* Reed very much. And you were always telling me he liked *me.*"

Ada gives me a pitying look. "Please, that's just something girls say to each other. 'He likes you, he's so into you'—" She pitches her voice in a mocking falsetto that sets my teeth on edge. "I was just trying to find out if you liked him, and you always assured me you didn't feel that way about him so I figured Reed was fair game. And he *did* like me that summer when I showed up to the island. But then his parents got sick and died, which made him feel guilty because he thought I'd given him the virus—"

"*You* brought the virus to the island," I say, "not Hannah, not Becky."

"I *guess,*" she says, shrugging, "but I didn't have symptoms, so it wasn't my fault. Anyhow, when you wouldn't answer his texts, he figured something was wrong so he went to check on you. He said he was going to explain to you about him and me, that we were going to be together, but when you almost *died,* he stupidly changed his mind. Out of pity and guilt. So, you see, he only chose you because he pitied you."

The words sting not least of all because she's flung them at me knowing how much they'll hurt. "That's not true," I say, "Reed loved me, he wanted to be with me."

"Oh really? Didn't you tell me during our 'gals' weekend' that you guys were having problems? That you were afraid you didn't make him happy enough? Let's face it, Lu, you've never really been happy together. That's what he told me when I met him in the city in March."

"March? You mean—"

"When he was staying for that conference, the one you couldn't be bothered to go to. That's when we got back together. Really, Lu, it's like you were handing him to me on a silver platter. Haven't you noticed any changes in him since then?"

I remember that when he came home from the conference he had seemed edgy and that his OCD had gotten worse. But then we started hearing about this new virus, and I figured that was why. "So, it was just that one time," I begin.

She laughs. "Not exactly. Where do you think he was the night before you left for the island, when he told you he was buying those tests on the black market? Did you really think that took all night? And why do you think he didn't want to invite me to the island? He was afraid you'd catch on to what was between us. I could have told him that you were too self-absorbed to notice, even with him almost giving the game away when he found out I was pregnant."

"It's not . . . it's not . . . ?" I stutter, reeling at each revelation as if I've been hit over and over again by a wave. This last one, though, may drown me.

"Reed's?" she asks, laying her hand on her belly. She laughs. "It's not anyone's. I only made up the preggers story to get Cros to agree to come." She smiles and strokes Reed's forehead, and then frowns. She looks down at her watch. "It's time for his next antibiotics shot."

She unwraps a hypodermic needle and inserts it into one of the glass ampoules.

I stare at her, and she pats her stomach. "A little extra weight from all the fucking baking. Plus baggy clothes. Really, people believe what they want to."

"If you could lie about that," I say, gasping for breath as if I'm trying to grab on to a lifesaver, "you could lie about anything. I don't believe any of it. Reed wouldn't . . . he couldn't . . ."

"Cheat on you? Why not? After all, he cheated on me." She holds the needle up, pushing the plunger until a tiny bead of liquid shivers on the needle's point, shimmering like the venom in her voice. I notice that her thumb is covering up the writing on the vial, as if she doesn't want me to see what's on it. She could be about to give Reed a lethal dose of morphine, for all I know, as punishment for abandoning her ten years ago. An hour ago, I wouldn't have believed she was capable of such a thing, but each revelation has peeled away a layer of who I thought Ada was, revealing a total stranger.

I stand up and reach across the bed to stay her hand. "Don't," I say. "I want to see what that is before you give it to Reed."

"Oh, actually, it's not for him," she says, grabbing my wrist with one hand and jabbing the needle into my arm. "This one's for you."

CHAPTER THIRTY-TWO

I SNATCH MY HAND BACK, CLUTCHING MY ARM AS IF I COULD STOP THE numbness spreading up to my shoulder. I should instead be reaching for the gun in my backpack but Ada has beat me to it, drawing a gun from her own satchel.

"Don't worry, Lu, this isn't going to hurt. You should be feeling quite nice in a few minutes. Remember when we took those Vicodins from Lexie's stash and sat up on the roof looking at the moon? It will be just like that."

She's speaking so calmly that I can almost believe we're back in college planning a fun night out, except there's that gun. "What are you going to do with me when I pass out?" I ask.

She purses her lips. "Don't worry about that, Lu. Sit down"—she waves the gun to a chair—"before you fall down."

I stumble past the chair to the door. I can't pass out here; I have to get away—

I hear the click of metal—the gun's safety being thumbed off—and turn back to see that Ada is aiming the gun at me. "Getting shot will hurt more, but I'll do it. I'll say it was self-defense, that you'd gone nuts reading that journal this summer and had started getting violent, ranting about devils and ghosts. Be a good girl and sit down."

I can feel the drug creeping through my veins, pulling me down like a riptide, as if I have fallen into the Dead Pool . . . then I notice that Reed's eyes are open. He's staring at me, his lips moving—

Run, he mouths silently as he reaches for Ada's hand.

The word releases me from the spell of Ada's voice, and I dart out the door. The wood jamb explodes behind me in a spray of splinters, Ada's shot gone wide because of Reed's interference. But he's too weak to hold her back for long. I stumble down the hall, careening into the walls, wiping smiling Harper faces from the wall in a shower of glass. The staircase plunges under my feet, shooting me out into the great room, where Niko's collage greets me with the red eyes of a devil.

Where do you think you're going?

The devil has a point. I have a gun. I should stay and defend myself—but I'd have to kill Ada before I lose consciousness and I don't know if I can do that—

Can't do it or won't do it?

I don't have time to debate these finer points. I hear Ada on the stairs. I know now that she has no compunction about shooting me. I run out the back door, across the clearing, dodging Mr. Tibster, who's leaning drunkenly in my way, and into the dark woods. I have to hide somewhere Ada won't find me before I pass out, which means I can't stay on the buoy path.

I head into the unmarked woods lit now by the newly risen moon, my feet sinking into the moss. *Shit, she'll be able to track my footprints.* If only I could swing from the branches. I look up through shafts of moonlight at the intertwining pine boughs. I could climb into them but then I'd fall when the drug takes over. Just the motion of looking up makes me dizzy. The woods spin around like a carousel ride, twig blurring into twig, branch meeting branch like hand clasping hand—*Reed grabbing Ada's hand*—

He didn't want her to kill me. Whatever else he's done—

I trip over a root and land in a clump of ferns. I look through the fronds and see a figure in the spinning greenery—*the stag on two legs.* Or Ada, prowling through the woods, gun in hand, stalking me. I press myself flat into the moss, praying the ferns will hide me. I'll wait until she passes by and then run back to the house . . . no, I'll pass out before I can make it there. I have to hide someplace she can't find me until the drug wears off. I get to my feet but stay crouched, out of view, and stumble on, my vision so blurry I have to feel my way through the woods by pressing my hands on rough bark. Branches scratch my face. *Stupid, coward,* they call me, *blind.* How did I not know all these years that Ada wanted Reed? How did I not know she was here that summer?

And Reed? Was what she said true? Did he want her, too? Had he only stayed with me out of pity—*poor sick Lucy*—and guilt that he'd let the virus onto the island by bringing Ada here?

Reed's problem is he's used to being liked; he can't stand being the bad guy.

My face is wet with tears and sap and blood. The trees are so thick here I can barely make my way through them. I've burrowed myself into the heart of the island, the place where all the veins tangle together into a bloody knot, like the Celtic knot on Reed's bracelet or the ones carved into the standing stones. . . . The whole island is a knot connecting all of us—Liadan and Nathaniel Harper, the Gray Nuns, the fevered dead, Reed's parents, Becky. *The island ties a knot in your heart that binds you to it.* I can feel them all here at the center, crowding around me, tugging at me, pulling me down—

My foot slips on something wet and slick. Then I'm sliding down a steep slope—into the Dead Pool? Or into the arms of the dead?

WHEN I OPEN my eyes, I'm surrounded by ghostly white figures silhouetted against a white hovering globe. I'm in the hospital and the masked nurses and doctors are laboring to bring me back to life. *It's* *no use,* I think now as I did then, *I'm already dead.* My back is broken, my lungs filled with sand, my heart crushed. This time Reed isn't coming for me. I blink away tears and the white globe resolves into the full moon, the white-garbed figures into a stand of birch saplings. I am lying flat on my back in a gully filled with ferns and birch trees that hid me while Ada's drug wore off and night fell.

At the memory of Ada jabbing me with the needle it all comes flooding back—Ada was here that summer. She and Reed—

I flinch away from the image of them together, but if it wasn't true, then why has Reed never told me she was here? And if he lied about that, how much more has he lied about? I do remember he was acting strangely when he came home from the conference. I thought he was mad at me for not going but was it because he had been with Ada? Had they really been seeing each other since then?

Did you really think it took all night to get those tests?

How did Ada know he was out all night unless she was with him?

I remember the look on his face the next morning, like he'd made some terrible deal with the devil. I thought it was just because he'd had to spend a lot of money or engage with unsavory characters, or because he felt guilty that he was able to buy resources that other people couldn't afford. I could have asked him. We could have talked about it. But I didn't ask him because, deep down, I knew something was going on. Our marriage hadn't been the same for a while.

And apparently, things were worse than I realized. He betrayed me with my *best friend,* Ada.

If your best friend slept with your husband, who would you be madder at? Ada had posed in one of our late-night discussions.

Wow, I'd replied, *I don't think I could choose.*

I could, Ada had said with certainty, *the best friend, of course. I wouldn't expect loyalty from a man, but if a woman betrayed me, I'd never forgive her.*

Somewhere along the line I'd let Ada down—maybe when I took Lexie's side instead of hers, or when I wouldn't go with her to the city, or when I left with Reed instead of waiting for her to come back— and failed to live up to her girlfriend code. Somehow that had made it okay for her to sleep with Reed. And now it made it okay for her to kill me. Even now she must be prowling the woods hunting for me. I'd been lucky that I fell in this gully. I look around at the bed of ferns that are hiding me. But I can't stay here. I have to get someplace where I can watch for Mac's return. I have to warn him about Ada and save Reed . . . if she hasn't already killed him.

I make myself put aside my jealousy to remember how she stroked his forehead and kissed him, looking for proof that she loves him. Because if she really loves him she won't kill him. But what I saw on her face was the same look she'd get scrolling through her social media— a mixture of desire and envy. She *wanted* Reed. She wanted to possess him. Most of all, I suspect, she doesn't want *me* to have him.

But he'd stopped her from shooting me. Would she kill him for that? Or would she wait until she killed me? I couldn't know what Ada would do; I could only decide what I should do—go back and get him or stay here in hiding until Mac comes back with the boat. *Why should you try to save him?* a voice whispers in my ear. *He's been un- faithful to you, he's lied to you, you're not even sure if you still love him.*

I don't even know whose voice it is—mine? Ada's? Maybe it be- longs to the island, to the devil buried in its cold stone heart. *Save yourself,* it whispers, *that's what he would do—*

But that's not true. Reed came back for me ten years ago. And he stayed. Maybe Ada is telling the truth, and he only came back to tell me goodbye, but then he stayed. He chose me, not Ada. Because he felt sorry for me? I won't ever know unless I ask him.

That is, if my back isn't broken and I can get myself out of here.

I start by wriggling my fingers and am gratified to feel the ooze of mud beneath my hands, but when I try to roll over the muscles in my back spasm. I've pulled something in my lower back and my hips ache as I push myself up. Feeling around, I find my backpack and check to see if the gun is still inside—it is, along with Nathaniel Harper's journal.

There's your book! Ada had said that first week, and then she'd had the perfect vehicle to keep me busy following in Becky's footsteps, down the path of obsession and madness. She had me seeing devils in the woods. *It was just a trick,* I tell myself as I use the birch saplings to climb out of the gully. Shining in the moonlight, they look like women dancing around the bonfire—*the bone fire*—just a trick. And just a trick that branches crossing branches creates a mirage of antlers.

A quote comes to mind—something someone had on a poster in our dorm—I think it was from Gandhi. *The only devils in the world are those running around in our own hearts.*

It's not, I think as I crawl out of the gully, a reassuring thought.

WHEN I COME out of the gully, I notice that the moon is lower in the sky. It's setting, I realize, which means I don't have many hours of night left. At least, though, it points the way west to the Main House. I can hope that Ada is out in the woods looking for me and not guarding Reed. I take out the gun and hold it in one hand as I follow the path of moonlight through the woods. Crouching, I place each foot down as softly as I can, straining to catch each rustle and twig crack. The woods are eerily still, as if transfixed by the light of the moon. When a shadow passes over me my heart races, but it's only an owl, gliding on silent wings, hunting smaller prey than me.

The moonlit path skirts the edge of the cliff and passes a rocky fissure that must lead to the Gray Lady Cliff. Past there the path goes down to the rocky cove below the dock. Dead Man's Cove, where Reed and I made love while Ada watched and hatched her plan to drive me crazy so she could have Reed for herself. It makes me feel sick to think of it, to imagine her jealousy and hatred honed by the sight of Reed and me together.

From here it's a short walk to the house, but I'll be exposed in the moonlight. Ada might be waiting for me. Should I just hide here until first light and hope that Mac arrives? Let Mac go first into the house?

But that leaves Reed longer at her mercy. So, I make my way up the lawn, clinging to the tree line in the shadows of the pines. The house seems to be waiting for me, the windows opaque with moonlight like cataract-clouded eyes. The rocking chairs stir at my footsteps on the stairs and the wind chimes ripple an alarm. As I creep into the great room, Niko's collage looks back at me with the eyes of Harpers dead and gone. *Who invited you?* they seem to ask.

I'll be out of your hair as soon as I get Reed, I answer silently. The stairs shriek at my every step. If Ada is waiting for me it would be the work of a moment to shoot me now, but with each unmolested step I take, the surer I am that she's not here. The house feels empty; the suck and pull of curtains at the open window at the end of the hall sounds like the last gasps of a patient on life support. Crunching over the glass in the hallway I feel like I am invading a tomb long buried in the sands of the desert—a place cursed and empty. I half expect to find Reed's mummified corpse waiting for me on the bed.

Instead, I find a note on the pillow. I take it to the east-facing windows and read it in the gray light of dawn.

Sorry, Lu, Reed and I had to bounce. We're waiting in the place where Nathaniel and Liadan planned to meet (have you gotten that far in the journal?). Hoping things end better for us than for them. We'll wait as long as we can! xo Ada

CHAPTER THIRTY-THREE

IT'S JUST LIKE ADA TO PLANT A CLUE TO LEAD ME TO A MEETING PLACE. *I'm studying under the eyes of T. J. Eckleburg* meant she was in the library stacks where *The Great Gatsby* was shelved. *Meet me in hell* meant the secret space under the stage in the theater. Always the game required that I'd been paying attention to her most recent enthusiasms. Now it requires me to sit down and finish reading Nathaniel Harper's journal, which, in itself, could be a trap, a way of becalming me while she does away with Reed or lays in wait to kill Mac when he comes ashore. I take Nathaniel Harper's journal from my pack and flip to the last pages.

That's cheating, I hear Ada tsking as she did when I tried to skip to the end of *Tristram Shandy* before class. *Besides, it won't work. You can't understand the end without seeing what led up to it.*

She's right, I have to conclude when I try to skim the last pages of Nathaniel Harper's scrawl for a quick answer to Ada's puzzle. The handwriting looks as if he was scratching in the dark with a piece of broken glass. I'll have to sit down and read it—but not here. I need a room with a good lock and a view.

I hurry down the hall to the study and lock the door behind me, then run to the windows, scanning the front lawn, the dock, the edges of the woods, and the clearing in back. All is quiet and placid, the only sign of disaster the still-smoking ruin of the barn. When I

turn to go back to the desk I recall Dunstan McCree turning from
the window and tracking mud across the floor as Liadan looked
down . . . and saw the devil's footprints.

"It's McCree," I said. "That's what frightened you the night in
the tower when you looked at the floor. You saw his footprints.
There's something in the heels of his shoes."

"Yes," she said, "I suppose that explains the mark. He's the
agent who sent all those starving men and women on the coffin
ships—one so bad it sunk before it cleared the harbor—"

"Mairi told me about that. Her mother and brother were
aboard. And she's been ranting about the devil—"

Liadan's eyes widened. "If Mairi confronts McCree with his
crime she may be in danger . . ."

"We must return and make sure she is all right," I said
urgently.

We hurried back on a path Liadan knew that cut through a
grove of birch trees and skirted the edge of the rocky incline
leading up to the steep cliff that towered over the north side of
the island. As we came to the cove below it, Liadan stopped at
a rock marking the path that went up to the cliff and traced the
knot pattern carved into the stone with her fingertips as she
spoke.

"There's a cave up there," she told me. "I think pirates must
have used it as a lookout—and to drink, judging from the
empty ale bottles. You can see to the mainland. We could build
a bonfire there to hail the mainland—and it would make a good
hiding place."

I agreed that was a good idea once we knew that Mairi was
safe. As we approached the hospital we heard a shriek coming
from behind the house. We ran toward it and found one of the

Gray Nuns screaming and pointing at a pyre that had been built in the middle of the garden—just where the bone fire had burned on the night of the solstice. A figure lay on the smoldering ashes, limp and smoking. I pushed my way through the crowd, angry that they all stood doing nothing to help whoever lay there, but when I reached the pyre I saw why. It was not a flesh and blood body but one made of straw and cloth. A scarecrow dressed in the habit of a gray nun burned in effigy. Most horribly, where the thing's face should have been was a stag's antlered skull.

"This is but an ugly joke—" I began, but then I felt Liadan's hand on my arm.

"Look at the habit," she hissed, "the embroidery—"

I looked closer at the habit and saw it was decorated with the daisy pattern Mairi had embroidered on hers. If this thing was dressed in Mairi's habit, what had become of Mairi herself?

"Does anyone know where Mairi is?" I demanded, looking around the faces surrounding the pyre until I found Mother Brigitte. She was looking at me oddly.

"Don't you know?" she said, staring at me and Liadan. "She left to follow you this morning."

"We didn't see her," I told Mother Brigitte and then, scanning the faces again and noting that none of McCree's men or McCree himself was present, I demanded, "Do we know where the men are?"

"Where they ever are," Mother Brigitte answered, "roaming the woods."

"Could one of them—" I began, but I was cut short by a voice that seemed to emanate from a long shadow cast across the carnage.

"My men were securing food for us. This looks like the work of some kind of devil worship."

I turned to face Dunstan McCree. He was standing with his
back to the sun, his face cast in shadow, his men arrayed behind
him. Had he always been so tall, I wondered, recalling the
cringing man I'd first encountered on the *Stella Maris,* or had he
somehow grown in stature during our time here on the island?
I dismissed the idea as ridiculous—a product of shock—and
addressed him. "Why do you say that?" I asked.

"The smell of it," he answered with a repulsed sniff, which
Mother Brigitte echoed by a sharp intake of breath. He reached
down into the pile of still-smoldering straw, as if his hand were
insensible to heat, into the bodice of the scarecrow. Beside me,
Liadan hissed, as if he were defiling an actual body, and I felt
with her that the gesture was somehow obscene, the more so
when he pulled out something red and knotted. For a horrible
moment I thought that he held a beating heart—I remembered
what Liadan had said about the island tying a knot in your heart
and thought, This is it, a knot tied of veins and bloody sinew.

"Mandrake," McCree said, and I saw that what he held in his
hand was a twisted root. "A plant used by witches. I can smell
it on her, too." His eyes went straight to the bag hanging from
Liadan's shoulder.

Liadan clutched her bag closer to her body and looked to me.

"What are you suggesting? Liadan and I left before dawn
to gather rose hips for tea—as you requested of her, Mother
Brigitte." I turned to Mother Brigitte to find her kneeling beside
the burnt effigy. I could make out the smell now, the same
bittersweet reek that had risen from the roots that Liadan had
dug up in the woods. "Liadan has been with me all morning,
while this . . . vulgar trick has clearly been played recently, given
that it's still smoking."

"Are you sure she was with you?" McCree asked in a low insinuating voice.

At first I thought he was accusing me of lying, which was insulting enough, but then I caught the drift of muttered remarks being passed amongst the men—*shade, double, fetch*—none of which was very clear to me, but then I heard *fairy* and finally, like the toll of a bell, *witch*.

"That is absurd," I said, turning to Liadan to reassure her. Already, though, McCree's men had forced themselves between her and me. One grabbed hold of her sack and dumped out the contents. Amongst the herbs and rose hips and roots was the straw figurine Liadan had made while we sat talking in the cemetery. Look, I thought to say, that proves how long we've been gone! But one of the men snatched it up and cried, "Poppet!"

"Oh, for heaven's sake," I said, "are you such superstitious fools? This isn't the seventeenth century."

When I met Dunstan McCree's eyes I saw that I had struck the wrong tone. To me he said, "Even in these godless times, some of us have not quite lost the faith of our forebears." To his men he said, "Take her to the tower room and lock her inside until we can decide how to ascertain her guilt or innocence."

I demanded who had put him in charge, to which he replied: "The men who provide our food and answer to me, Doctor. But don't worry, there are ways to test a witch."

I saw Liadan's eyes widen with fear and knew I could not let this happen to her. I launched myself at the men holding her with such fury that they lost their grip on her. "Run!" I cried, and then in a lower voice, which I hoped only she would hear, "Find Mairi and hide."

She gave me one glance that told me she understood and then

she was gone—so quickly that if I believed in such things I would have thought she had vanished by witchcraft. I watched to be sure she made it to the woods but something heavy came down on my head and sealed my vision with a black pall. The last thing I thought was that I was back in the sea with Liadan, drifting to the bottom of the ocean.

I came to in the tower room, whole in body although somewhat battered and with a knot on my skull the size of a goose egg. The door, I soon discovered, was locked. When I went to the window I saw that I must have been unconscious for several hours because it was nearly dark and, more importantly, I saw a ship on the horizon. I felt inside my pockets and was relieved to find my spyglass and journal. I took out my spyglass and trained it on the horizon. An English ship, I saw from the flag, and flying the black flag of contagion. Its name, I saw, was the *Regina Maris*. A spark of hope alit in my heart at the similarity of the name to the ship that brought Liadan. Surely they would send an envoy to the island—but that hope was soon extinguished at the thought that they would be met with Dunstan McCree and his men. While I did not believe that McCree was a devil, I saw that he was a desperate man who would do anything to avoid the prosecution of the law. Who knew what he and his men were capable of? He had gathered these ruthless men to him and bound them in a cult of superstitious fealty that defied all sense and morals. First they had seemed to worship Liadan and now they had turned against her. What would they do to Liadan if they caught her? What had they done to poor Mairi?

So caught up in feverish speculation was I that when I heard a key at the lock I grabbed my spyglass and prepared myself to bludgeon whoever came through the door—even when I saw that it was a woman in a gray cloak my thought was that McCree had corrupted the Gray Nuns to do his bidding and I went to seize the woman—then her hood fell away and I saw it was Liadan.

"Be still," she whispered, "I've drugged your guard but another might be coming. You'll have to hide. McCree has convinced his men that we are in league with the devil because he fears Mairi and I will expose the crimes he committed in Ireland."

"He would be harmless enough if he hadn't gathered to him this band of followers—"

"None of them are harmless," she said. "They tried to kill Mairi. I found them at the Witch Stone, about to sacrifice her. I distracted them long enough for her to run away. She's hiding in the woods, along with some of the Gray Nuns who have fled there as well . . . but I don't know how long they will be safe."

As she began to sob, I took her in my arms. I could feel the vibration of her pulse thrumming through her slight frame, as if she were a violin string strung too tight. "We will save them," I said, holding her tightly to still her trembling. "But we must get off this island and bring back help. We'll go to that cave on the cliff and build a signal fire—"

"It will be too late if Dunstan's men see the boat first. They'll swim for it and swamp it. I will go to the cliff and light the fire. You must run straight down to the dock and swim for the boat as soon as you see it. Then make the boat go around the headland and come into Dead Man's Cove. If the men try to follow you they won't be able to swim around the headland. I will make my way down from the cliff and be waiting for you in the cove. When we get back to the ship, we can arrange to send another to rescue Mairi and the rest."

I wasn't happy with her plan, but I could see that she was set on it. I made her take my spyglass to watch for the boat and promise to come straight down to Dead Man's Cove as soon as she saw that the boat was coming.

She looked up at me, eyes full and trusting, and nodded. She had stopped trembling. It was only as she stepped away that I realized she had somehow passed her affliction on to me. I was shaking from head to foot and have been shaking since she left.

I have spent the time waiting for Liadan's beacon from the cliff penning this last entry. I cannot take this journal with me without losing it to the sea. I cannot take anything with me, I fear, only my love and determination to save Liadan. Perhaps I will come back for this someday. If not, I leave it here as a record of what happened.

The journal ended there with no clue to what went wrong with Nathaniel and Liadan's plan but at least I know where he and Liadan had pledged to meet: Dead Man's Cove. That's where Ada has gone with Reed. All I have to do is follow them there—

Where it will be easy to shoot me as I approach. I look out the window, half expecting to see the nineteenth-century *Regina Maris* anchored in the bay and its lifeboat rowing toward the dock. What I see is fog. A thick fog has rolled in while I've been here reading, obliterating the lawn, dock, and the sea beyond. The island has been sealed off. Will Mac be able to get through? It feels as likely that the sailors of the *Regina Maris* will come rowing out of the fog and Dunstan McCree's men will rise out of the water to swamp their boat, or that Ada is waiting for me, hidden behind the rocks that shelter Dead Man's Cove, to shoot me.

But what choice do I have?

I put on a raincoat and slip Mac's gun into the pocket. I leave Nathaniel's journal behind, as he did. It has nothing left to tell me.

I have less faith that I'll be coming back for it than he did. At least not in this life.

WALKING DOWN THROUGH the fog is like swimming through a cloud. The only way I know which direction to go is by following the sound of water lapping against the dock. I'm so drenched in mist that I might walk into the water without knowing it.

As I get closer, I can make out dark shapes drifting toward me. They seem to be floating in the air, but that's only because the water is the same color as the fog, and the shapes are floating on the water, coming in with the tide.

Tidewalkers, I remember Mac called the debris that floated to shore during high tide as I climb over the rocks to reach Dead Man's Cove. It's not a reassuring memory as the waves slap against the rocks, snapping at my heels. The tide is so high that when I climb down on the other side cold water laps over my ankles. How could I have thought I wouldn't know when I reached the ocean? The water is so cold it snatches the warmth from my body like a hand pulling me under.

Something cold and wet *does* wrap around my ankle. I kick it away, picturing the hands of drowned sailors, and feel something spongy connect with the toe of my shoe—

Rotten wood, I tell myself as I look down at a tidewalker that happens to have the look of a man's body, down to an arm flung out—

An arm with the latest Smart Watch attached to its wrist. This tidewalker is a man—or at least what's left of Crosby.

CHAPTER THIRTY-FOUR

I PULL CROSBY'S BODY AS FAR UP THE BEACH AS I CAN, TRYING TO SPARE his face from the ravages of the rocks and shells. Not that there's much left to protect after the salt water and crabs have done their work. There's also a large swollen bump on his forehead that could have been caused by being tumbled on the rocks, but then, it wouldn't have swelled if he had already been dead. It must have happened when he went overboard. He could have hit his head on the side of the boat—or someone hit him over the head.

I take off my flannel overshirt and cover his face with it, hoping it will keep the seagulls that are circling overhead from doing more damage. *I've never met a man so vain about his looks,* Ada confided to me during our gals' weekend, *he takes an hour to trim his goatee.* She'd often mocked him for his vanity, but I had thought that was just her way. Sometimes I suspected that she was disappointed with him. Crosby wasn't exactly the soul mate she had dreamed about in college.

I want to be like Cathy in Wuthering Heights, *so in love with Heathcliff she is Heathcliff.*

That doesn't work out so great for either of them, I pointed out.

Yeah, but she loves him so much she haunts him after she dies. Don't you want to love someone so much they won't leave you alone even after death?

I don't believe Ada will want Crosby to haunt her, I think, as I scan the narrow beach for her and Reed. I already suspect, though, that they're not here. The tide is so high that there's barely any beach at all. I recall that Liadan said the only way to reach Dead Man's Cove at high tide would be from the open sea or the cliff path. I scan the shore for the cliff path, but it's impossible to find since the rocks are the same color as the fog. I reach out to touch one and feel carvings. I trace the pattern, my finger following a now familiar series of loops that double back on themselves. A Celtic knot. I could be standing here forever, trapped following the pattern, just as I'm trapped on this island, but when I pull back my hand I see blood. I wonder for a moment if it could be the red paint on Niko's hands, but the smell is unmistakably of blood and the print is too big to be Niko's. Is it Reed's blood, left as Ada forced him up the path? There's only one way to find out.

My feet crunch on pebbles and broken shells as I begin the climb. I can barely see a foot or two in front of my face and so I grope from one rock to the next, finding more of the carved knots marked with blood. I make out hand marks, the prints so close together they must be bound. I picture Reed drugged, prodded on by gunpoint, lurching—

Leaving a blood trail for me to follow.

How could Ada do this to him if she really loved him? What kind of love is that?

I remember that she dated a boy for a few months sophomore year. He was a senior, a film major, whose father was a big Hollywood producer. Ada scoffed at his money and his privilege, at how easy everything would be for him. When he broke up with her she hatched an elaborate revenge plot in which we would break into his frat house and plant child pornography on his computer to get him kicked out of school.

Yeah, but his computer's probably password protected, I'd said, playing along with what I assumed was just an idle revenge fantasy. She was just venting; she'd never follow through with her scheme.

Oh, I have his password, she'd said. *Idiot let me watch him put it in dozens of times.*

That had alarmed me a little so I added, *And besides, we'd have to download child pornography.*

Yeah, she'd conceded, *I'll have to come up with a better plan.*

A few weeks later I'd heard that the boy had been kicked out because he submitted a plagiarized paper. *What an idiot,* I'd said, *didn't he know it would get flagged on Turnitin?*

Yeah, Ada had replied with one of her secret smiles, *not the brightest bulb in the pack.*

Only later had I wondered if she had submitted the plagiarized paper under his name. It was a long way, though, from getting an ex-boyfriend expelled to killing one.

I hold on to that thought as I continue to climb, fighting back the fear that each step will lead me to Reed's lifeless body. The fog thins suddenly, like a curtain snatched away, revealing a rocky plateau and a shallow cave facing the sea. Someone's lying at the mouth of the cave, propped against the rock wall, legs splayed out limply, bloody hands bound with rope. I rush forward and find Reed, as I feared, pale and lifeless. I kneel by his side and shake him, crying out his name.

"Really?" a voice says from behind me. "You're still running to his side after he betrayed you?"

I look up and find Ada, sitting on a rock cross-legged, the gun dangling loosely between her knees. Beneath my hand I feel Reed stir. He's not dead. "I don't care about that," I say. "If you and he wanted to be together you could have told me. I didn't *own* him."

"Oh, so you would have wished us good luck and still wanted us all to share an apartment in the city?"

"Maybe," I say, thinking back to the pictures I'd invented of our lives together. It feels like watching one of the magic lantern shows Reed put on for us, one made up of sepia-toned portraits from an antique age. The world I'd pictured us inhabiting—crowded city streets and bars and movie theaters and kissing and hugging and jostling shoulder to shoulder—had ceased to exist before any of us set foot off the campus. Maybe it had all been a mirage. "I think I would have been willing to try it. I loved you, Ada. I loved both of you. I think, most of all, I loved the three of us together."

Something passes over her face, as if the mist has cleared and I'm seeing her for the first time. She looks naked and exposed, caught wanting something badly, but then she flinches and waves her hand, her face hardening. "Too late. Reed, it turned out, loved only you. I wasn't good enough. He went back to you and tossed me aside, but he felt oh-so-bad about it." She simpers, affecting the patrician drawl she liked to use to represent Reed even though Reed never talked like that unless he was imitating his father. "Even after we got together at his conference, he wouldn't stop whining about how you couldn't know. 'You won't tell Lucy, will you? It would kill her.'" She smiles a wide demented grin and gets up. "So why aren't you dead yet, Lu? Why hasn't it killed you?" She tilts her head and steps closer, forcing me to inch back toward the edge of the cliff. "I think it *does* kill you. I think when you found out your husband was leaving you, you went crazy and tried to kill us both and then threw yourself from the cliff." She recites the events as if they have already happened—as if she's directing a play. This, then, is why she drew me here. She wants to force me over the cliff and then pretend that I killed myself.

"You don't want to kill me, Ada. What will be left for you? Do you think Reed will be okay with you killing me? That you'll live happily ever after together?"

She looks down at Reed, who is stirring, eyes fluttering, trying to fight through the drugs into consciousness. I think to use the moment of distraction to disarm her, but the instant I step forward the crunch of gravel under my feet alerts her and she looks up and aims the gun at me.

"We could have," she says, "if he had seen that you were the same as Becky. You should have seen her at the end when I chased her through the woods with my deer mask on. She looked like she'd come face-to-face with the devil. She practically *dove* into the Dead Pool to get away."

I stare at her speechless, remembering Mac telling me that Becky had looked like she'd seen a monster.

"I didn't realize, though, that Reed would blame himself for Becky's death and go running back to you. *This time* I thought I'd just let him see how unhinged you were. He was already questioning your marriage. When I saw him in March and told him all the doubts *you* had he didn't seem surprised—"

"You *told* him I had doubts about our marriage?" I repeat, aghast. "But that's not what I said—"

"Isn't it? You told me on our 'gals' weekend' that you thought he would have been happier with Becky. You knew he wasn't happy with you, so why shouldn't I tell him that you weren't happy either? I thought he deserved to know. He admitted that the two of you had been growing apart. I thought he would realize that he and I were more suited to each other."

I swallow back the hurt and shock that she had repeated to Reed—and twisted—the things I'd said to her in confidence. No wonder he had come back from the conference acting strangely. I shake my head. "What about Crosby?" I ask. "What was he supposed to do when you and Reed got together?"

"*Pft*," she puffs dismissively. "Crosby would have signed us up for some mindful-uncoupling workshop and sulked off the island. But then he got his back up about Reed and demanded I leave the island with him. What a bully! I only meant to keep us from leaving by sinking the boat but then he had to go and get himself drowned."

"You knew he couldn't swim," I say, recalling the swollen lump on Crosby's corpse.

The sharp snap in her eyes reminds me that I shouldn't be angering her. "I thought Mac would rescue him but he thrashed around so much Mac couldn't help him. So, you see, that wasn't my fault."

I know that I should accept her self-justification—my only way out of here is to convince her I'm not a threat to her—but I can't help myself. I want to know what happened. "Crosby's body washed up in Dead Man's Cove," I say. "It looks like someone hit him over the head."

She looks unsettled for a moment and glances into the fog as if she expects his bloated form to trudge up from the cove to exact his revenge, but then she turns back to me and shrugs. "He was flailing about, trying to hang on to me. You remember what we learned in lifesaving class—if a drowning victim tries to take you down with him you have to stop him."

"I believe the instructor said you should swim away, not hit them over the head."

"Well, then, the instructor was a fucking idiot. If someone tries to drag you down, you stop them."

"Is that why you burnt down the barn?" I ask. "Because Liz and Niko were 'dragging you down'?"

"Honestly, I was just tired of the two of them—Niko with her artistic pretensions and Liz always nagging Reed about how she'd been cheated out of her inheritance when most of us don't have a fraction of that kind of money. Most of us have to work jobs we hate and make do with our puny salaries."

"I didn't know you hated your job," I say, noting out of the corner of my eye that Reed's eyes are open. "I thought you liked being a nurse."

"I was going to be an actress!" she cries, the raw emotion catching me off guard. She'd spoken of drowning Crosby and setting the barn on fire with far less fervor. "But then the stupid pandemic came along and killed the theater and the funding for my scholarship vanished and my supposed best friend ran off and married my boyfriend."

"It upended all our lives," I begin.

"*You* ended up married to a rich man and getting to live your dream of being a writer. Plenty of people got rich when their property values in the suburbs and stock portfolios went up. My parents *died* and my dreams were crushed."

"Reed's parents died," I remind her.

"He *hated* them. Just like he hated Becky. I did him a favor bringing the virus to the island."

"I didn't want them to *die*," croaks Reed. He has struggled to his feet, clinging to the rock face using his bound hands for balance.

Ada snorts. "Poor Reed. You can't stand to look like the bad guy. You didn't have the nerve to get rid of Becky so you used me to do it. You brought me here. You hid me and came up with the plan to drive Becky crazy with that journal and that game. You wanted her to burn down the house and then kill herself. You wanted your parents to die of the virus so you could be free *and* still get to think of yourself as the good guy. I gave that to you and then you abandoned *me*." She strikes the hand holding the gun to her chest when she says *me*. Then she smiles slyly. "But I always knew you wanted to come back to me. And you did."

Reed looks up at me, his face rent by so much pain that I know it is true. "It was only that one time," he says. "She told me you said you weren't happy with me . . . she said I should let you go and that if

I didn't tell you about what had happened on the island, she would. I was afraid that if you knew everything, I would lose you—"

A shriek comes out of Ada that sounds inhuman—like the rock has split open and disgorged a vengeful fury. "No!" she screams. "That's not how it was. You wanted *me*! When you asked me to come here I knew you wanted me to free you from *her*"—she points at me—"just like I freed you from your parents and Becky."

Reed shakes his head. "That's not what I wanted," he says. "And I never wanted you—" He turns to me. "I've always wanted Lucy."

"You betrayed *me*," she says, striking the gun to her chest again. "You lied to—"

As she strikes her chest a third time, I hear that fury's shriek again but this time it's not coming from Ada. It's coming out of the fog—a flurry of gray that looks as if the fog itself has curdled into flesh and gained a horrible voice, a shriek that lances the back of my neck like an ice pick. Ada's eyes widen with horror and she steps back, batting at the air with the gun, her back turned as Reed pushes off the rock wall and rushes toward her. Ada, distracted by the seagull—that's all it is, I see now, not the banshee I had imagined at first—has no time to aim the gun at him. She is forced past me, arms flailing, toward the edge of the cliff. I reach for her hand, but her fingertips only graze mine as she flies out into the empty air.

Followed by Reed.

I grab the flapping tail of his shirt. It slows him just enough that he skids to a stop, feet teetering on the edge of the cliff as he tries to pivot away from the air beyond, his eyes locking on mine as the rock beneath his feet crumbles. I fall to my knees and grab his bound hands. I can feel the ground loosening beneath me, pulling me down to the cove below, where I can see Ada's body broken on the rocks, the surf crashing over her, right beside Crosby. I must not have dragged him far enough above the high-water mark because as I watch a wave breaks over his body, carrying it to Ada and lifting his arms as if he means to embrace her. And then, as the wave retreats, it drags them both out to sea. They are surrounded by other shapes rising out of the fog and moving in the water—driftwood, no doubt, that's come in with the tide and is now going out, but for a moment the shapes look like dead bodies and as they surround Ada and Crosby; it looks as if all the drowned dead of the island have come to welcome them into their company. Reed's hands are slipping out of mine. I lurch forward, half my body suspended above the abyss, Reed's eyes locked on mine.

"You have to let go," he says.

It's what he said when I was too afraid to climb up onto the tower of Main Hall. *You have to let go of your fear. I've got you.*

"Okay," I tell him, meaning I can let go of the fear I've always had that he didn't love me. I can forgive him for what happened between him and Ada. But when I feel his fingers loosening in my grip, I realize he means something else.

No, I begin to tell him, *that's not what I meant,* but he's already slipped away from me. He's already gone on without me.

CHAPTER THIRTY-FIVE

WHEN REED FALLS, I SHUT MY EYES. I DON'T WANT TO SEE HIM BREAK ON the rocks below. But then I force them open. *What if he's alive?* I tell myself. *What if he somehow survived and is suffering—*

But when I open my eyes I see nothing. The fog has completely swallowed up the cove. It is as if Reed has fallen into a void.

Maybe we're all in that void now. Maybe I came to the island ten years ago and we all died here and the life I believed myself to be leading was a mirage—an after-death hallucination while all along I've been *here* on this island of death.

A deep bass note punctuates this thought like a trumpet heralding the end of the world. It sounds two more times. *Woe, woe, woe.* A death knell for Reed that reverberates in my chest so hard I wonder I don't break apart.

Then I realize that the sound is a foghorn. A boat is coming into the cove, Mac returning. *Too late!* I want to scream. Let him find Ada and Crosby and Reed—

But then I remember how much Mac cared for Reed, and I can't let him find him without telling him that Reed died saving me.

I force myself up, the blood rushing to my head as I get to my feet. The fog is so thick I can't tell where the edge of the cliff is anymore. I think it's in front of me so I turn around and take one cautious step, arms out, and then another until my hands hit rock. I grope my way across the rock face, shuffling my feet, until my hands hit something smooth and cylindrical wedged into a crevice in the rock. It feels like a flashlight only I can't find the switch. I stick it in my pocket anyway.

I fumble my way down the path, following the carvings on the rocks. The tide has erased the cove. I have the feeling when I step into the water that I am stepping off the face of the earth. That the dead are waiting below the surface to reach up and grab my ankle to drag me down—

A hand does grab me but it comes from behind me, seizing me by the shoulder and turning me around. "Lucy! You're alive."

It's Mac, in a yellow rain slicker, his face and hair dripping with water. *Am I?* I almost ask. *Are you?* He looks half drowned.

"Reed—" I cry, the name a hoarse caw.

"I know," Mac says, wiping the water off his face. "We found him floating in the cove."

"He died saving me," I sob. "From Ada. You were right; it was her all along."

I begin blubbering the whole story between sobs as Mac puts his arm around me and steers me out of the water and across the rocks to the dock. When we get there, the fog has thinned, and I see a boat tied to the end of it and a husky fisherman in yellow oilskin lifting a long heavy object wrapped in a tarp into the boat.

"Is that—?"

"Reed. We'll take him back to the mainland with us." He raises his voice as we approach the dock. "Did you find anyone else, Sol? Lucy here says there were two more bodies floating in the cove."

"Nay-ope," he says, shaking his head. "Tide will have took 'em." He looks up and sees me. "But don't you worry; she'll bring 'em back in the end."

I shudder, wondering what end he could mean. I look back toward the woods, as if expecting to find Ada and Crosby standing under the pines, two new ghosts consigned to an eternity on this godforsaken island. As I watch, a figure detaches itself from the pines and heads toward us. Prickly with branches, the color of wet bark, it might be a tree come to life. It takes me a moment to realize it's Niko. She's soaked and barefoot, her wet jeans and T-shirt covered with greenish mud and pond scum, twigs sticking out of her hair like antlers. Her eyes are as wide and startled as a deer's.

"Niko!" I cry. "What happened to you? Where have you been?"

"I've been to the center of the island," she says matter-of-factly, "and met the stag-king." She looks down at Reed's tarp-covered body lying in the boat. "Liz is gone, too," she adds—a statement not a question. "He's eaten his fill for now." Then she steps into the boat and crouches down in the prow. She reaches into the front pocket of her too-tight jeans and extracts a crumpled pack of cigarettes. She draws out one bent but miraculously dry and intact cigarette and lights it with her lighter. I turn to Mac and Sol, who are both staring at Niko.

"We'd best be heading back before the tide turns," Sol says, kneeling to untie the line from the dock, "and washes up anything else."

AS WE MOTOR out of the harbor I face backward, watching the island recede. The fog is lifting as if the curtain is coming up for one last encore, revealing the boulders that ring the island. I remember that they reminded me of the monolithic gods of Easter Island when we arrived.

"I suppose you all thought you'd hunker down out here," Sol says, shaking his head, his voice thick with the disdain of the seasoned Maine native for foolish flatlanders from away. "Never ends well," he concludes, spitting over the side of the boat. "Yah can't cheat death."

I shiver, reaching to button my flannel shirt and then I remember that I took it off to drape over Crosby's face. I shove my hands in my pockets instead and feel the cylinder I found in the cave. I take it out and see that it's not a flashlight; it's a slim brass spyglass, green with corrosion and inscribed with the initials *NRH*. I gasp. This must be the one Nathaniel gave to Liadan to watch for the boat from the *Regina Maris*. I twist the brass cylinder and pull to extend the telescope to its full length—and several sheets of paper fall out. They're caught in the wind and nearly fly overboard but I grab them, the brittle papers crackling in my grasp. I open my hands cautiously, as if I've caught a live dragonfly, and see that the pages are covered with crabbed and spidery handwriting. Familiar handwriting. It's the same handwriting I found on the wall of the great room. Liadan. She must have sat up on that cliff with the spyglass Nathaniel gave her, waiting for him to come back. And then, perhaps when she knew he wasn't coming back, she wrote this last testament.

I'm not sure what the date is, only that it's been a few days now since Nathaniel Harper left this island. Mother Brigitte says that soon the seas will be impassable, and we will perish here if he does not send a boat for us. And so, I come up here each day to watch the sea. I imagine that Nathaniel is doing all he can to send a boat for us, but I do not think he will be on it. What he saw that last day frightened him too much.

He had done as I had asked him to. As soon as the lifeboat from the *Regina Maris* appeared, he ran from the house to the dock and dived straight into the water. I saw him swimming for the boat, his body cleaving the water like a shark. McCree's men dove in after him, but they could not keep pace.

I watched through the spyglass as Nathaniel boarded the boat and I saw him shouting at the rowers to make for Dead Man's Cove instead of the dock. For a moment I wasn't sure he would convince them but then I saw the boat turn toward the cove. The men tried to swim after them, but there is a treacherous current just beyond the rocks there and they were unprepared for it. I saw the first man's head slip beneath the water just as I heard a step behind me. I turned and found Dunstan McCree there.

"Liadan," he said, smiling, "I've been wanting to have a few minutes alone with you."

His words turned my blood cold, but I forced myself to smile back and answer, "As have I." Then I looked down at the ground, which was printed with the cloven footprints. "You had the estate blacksmith make a special shoe to fix your gait," I said.

"It did so much more than that."

I smiled again. "You think it is a charm to give you power, but your only power was your belief you were no longer bound by the rules of man and God. You took the money from the landlords, paid as little as you could for the cheapest ships, and pocketed the rest. You did not care what happened to the men and women you sent on those ships."

"They were starving already," he replied. "What did it matter if they had a few more or less mouthfuls of grain or a few more feet belowdeck? Most of them were bound to die before they set foot aboard those ships."

"And my son?" I asked. "What became of him?"

"If he was strong, he survived. I hear the people who took him landed safely in Boston."

"Tell me the name of the people in Boston," I said, stepping closer.

He seemed startled that I was the one to approach him, but he stood his ground. "Little good it will do you, but if it will give you some peace in your final moments . . ."

He said the name and then he braced his shoulders in that way men do when they are preparing to use their strength against you.

But I had made my preparations, too. With knife and switch I
have carved and woven my spells into the stone, bark, and mud
of this island. Round and round I've gone, marking rock and tree
and mossy ground. The frame was here already; I could feel it the
moment I stepped ashore. This place has always been used for
this, which is why they buried the witch here, but as she died, she
wove a spell around her to wreak vengeance on her torturers and
any who set foot on the island. I only had to darn a few holes into
the spell's threadbare fabric to reinforce the binding. Only a few
moments ago I sealed the last mark in my blood and drew tight
the noose. As Dunstan McCree stepped toward me he stepped
into my snare. The thing I had summoned flew out of the dark
mouth of the cave—all claw and horn, feather and screech—the
demon at the heart of the island sealed here by spell and talisman.
At least, that's what Dunstan saw in his last moments. Others
may have seen a poor, angry girl in a gray nun's habit pushing the
man who killed her family to his death on the rocks below.

I don't know what Nathaniel Harper saw but when I looked
seaward, he was staring up at the cliff with horror on his face.
The wind that had come with the thing I summoned was blowing
the little boat away and the sailors were struggling to right it and
drag him down into the hull. Would he have tried to swim for the
shore? Perhaps. But he let them restrain him as they rowed away.
I don't blame him. Once you've seen what lies at the heart of this
island it is only natural to flee.

I know he'll come back someday. But I'll be gone by then.

I saw an approaching ship on the horizon today. They will
send a boat to take the nuns and surviving patients to shore and
what's left of the sailors (the ones who didn't drown have been
quite docile since they lost their leader), and I will go with them.
Mother Brigitte and the Gray Nuns will take Mairi with them to

Quebec, but I will make my way to Boston to find my son. I've come this far; I feel sure I'll find him.

I won't come back here in this life, but I feel as if I am leaving behind a piece of myself, a tether that will someday draw me back.

For now, I hail the boat and leave this message as I might leave word for the child I lost. Go forward. Don't look back, even when you can hear the angel of death beating its wings at your back.

I look up from the letter, which is falling apart in my hands. Just before the wind takes it, I see a name written on the bottom . . . a name that I've seen recently . . .

"Mac," I say, turning to him. He's right behind me, feet braced against the rocking boat. "What's Mac short for?"

He snorts at the unexpectedness of the question, but answers. "MacArdle," he says, looking down at me, his green eyes like a glimpse of the sea. "It's an old family name from back when the MacArdles were lace-curtain Irish in Boston. Why?"

I shake my head and turn back—

—to the island guarded by its ring of stones. They are not, I see now, guardians to keep us out, but sentinels to keep something in. Something dark and cold that lives in the heart of the island. Waiting. The stones vanish now, one by one, behind a scrim of fog, the stage curtain pulled at the end of the play, and I turn away from it to face forward into the mist.

ACKNOWLEDGMENTS

THANK YOU TO ROBIN RUE, FOR HANDHOLDING AND TRUTH-TELLING, AND to Beth Miller for keeping things together at Writers House. Thank you to Liz Stein for astute and thoughtful editing, and to everyone at William Morrow who make the books happen—Ariana Sinclair, Karen Richardson, Shelby Peak, Ryan Shepherd, Deanna Bailey, and Christina Joell.

Thank you to my early readers and listeners who keep me going during the long months of dreaming, plotting, and writing—Roberta Andersen, Gary Feinberg, Alisa Kwitney, Nancy Johnson, Scott Silverman, Lee Slonimsky, and Ethel Wesdorp.

I owe a special debt to Nathaniel Bellows for his invaluable consultation on all things Maine. Thanks for the vetch.

I could not have written this book without a generous invitation to Norton Island in the summer of 2019. Thank you to the Damn Few for putting up with my constant plans to do away with you and not doing away with me instead—Xavier Atkins, Andrew Blossom, Sherri Byrand, Jackie Clark, Morris Collins, Jennifer Hand, Melissa Larsen, Ryan Matthews, Dan Poppick, Alane Spinney, Christine Stroud, and Emily Tusynska.

Thank you most of all for the generosity of Stephen Dunn, founder and leader of the Eastern Frontier Educational Foundation, for creating a safe harbor in a perilous world, and to Rosemary Faver Dunn and her son Henry Dunn for sharing Steve with us, continuing the legacy, and graciously allowing me to dedicate this book to him.

About the author

About the book

Read on

Insights,
Interviews
& More . . .

Meet Carol Goodman

Franco Vogt

CAROL GOODMAN is the critically acclaimed author of twenty-three novels, including *The Widow's House*, winner of the 2018 Mary Higgins Clark Award; *The Night Visitors*, winner of the 2020 Mary Higgins Clark Award; and *The Seduction of Water*, which won the 2003 Hammett Prize. Her books have been translated into sixteen languages. She lives in the Hudson Valley with her family and teaches writing and literature at SUNY New Paltz and the New School. ∽

No Man Is an Island
(but Some Give Us One)

In the summer of 2019, I was fortunate enough to attend a writer's residency on Norton Island off the coast of Maine. I'd been duly cautioned by the Eastern Frontier Educational Foundation website that the island was rustic; the environment beautiful, extreme, and unadorned; and that the residency was an *outdoorsy experience* that might come as a shock to those visitors who had spent time at other residencies. Undeterred (but not wholly unworried) I drove eight hours to arrive at a rustic dock marked only by a sign that read: NORTON ISLAND LANDING: PASS AT YOUR OWN RISK. No one was there. I'd corresponded with the founder and director of the residency, Steve Dunn, and with artist and cook Alane Spinney and received the somewhat cryptic message, "We don't exactly have a favorable tide on Friday. Dead Low is at 3:00 P.M. so we're all shooting for a 5:00 P.M. meeting at the dock."

My overactive mystery-writer imagination was already concocting a book called *Dead Low*, or perhaps, *An Unfavorable Tide*.

By 5:00 P.M., I was joined at the dock by the writer Morris Collins and his wife, who both seemed equally unsure if the boat would arrive. Emily Tuszynska, poet, and her artist sister Jennifer Leah Hand arrived next, both friendly and ▶

3

No Man Is an Island (but Some Give Us One) *(continued)*

intrepid. Then, out of the fog, a smallish boat appeared. At the helm was a lanky gray-haired man wearing a sweatshirt, rain slicker, and baseball cap. He introduced himself as Steve Dunn, founder and director of Eastern Frontier and our host on Norton Island. Emily and Jennifer took one look at the water in the bottom of the boat and handed out garbage bags for us to wrap our luggage. Robert Lee, a local friend of Steve's, and his dog, Daisy, joined us to help pilot the boat back to the island. He advised us to load the luggage in the front and sit in the back to keep the ship level. I couldn't help but overhear Steve remark that the compass was broken. And then we were off into the fog, which Steve said was a sign of good luck for our arrival, and for me, at least, into the unknown.

I wondered if I was too old for this kind of adventure. I'd turned sixty that year and although I was and still am, thankfully, in good health, I wasn't entirely sure how I'd do walking from the plumbing-less cabins to the lodge in the dead of night or how my arthritic knees would handle squatting in the woods. Also, I wasn't certain what I was going to write. I'd begun and abandoned a few ideas in the last few months and found myself unusually—the metaphor was irresistible—*at sea*. As Norton Island appeared out of the fog, I could only imagine that this was what I should write about—this beautiful, rustic, *extreme* place, and also this sense of uncertainty about the future. I thought, at the time, it was just uncertainty about the next two weeks: how I would fare in this rustic environment; what I would write here; how I would get along with the other residents (most younger and fitter than I am); whether my knees would hold out.

The island was, indeed, a place of uncertainties and contrasts. Beautiful, as I discovered when the next day dawned clear and sunny. Remote and silent as I took off on a path armed only with a hand-drawn map and an injunction to "follow the buoys" that hung from the tall pines. A carpet of emerald moss concealed twisted roots and muddy bog. Focus too long on your footing and you could miss a buoy and find yourself in a trackless pine forest swarmed by gnats. The eastern end of the island was a rockscape of huge granite boulders, their wind- and sea-worn surfaces speckled in improbable Easter egg shades of green, yellow, and pink. In spite of the beauty, though, something terrible could still occur. You could slip and break an ankle. You could sink into the bog and never be seen again.

None of those things happened but after I circumnavigated the island each day, I would come back to the lodge to gleefully inform my fellow guests that I'd found another way to kill off a potential character. That's when I decided to write an Agatha Christie locked-room murder mystery à la *And Then There Were None* set on this beautiful, extreme place perched on the eastern frontier. The island was literally perfect material: pine, moss, granite, sea, and fog, a place that would handily reveal the fractures of any group that landed there. Inconveniently, the group *I* had landed with were, without exception, kind, lovely, and talented. Alane captured ferns and wildflowers in jewellike watercolors, Emily read to us an ode to a blanket that captured the cold dark nights, Jennifer carved leaf shapes out of the island's textures, Jackie Clark's oils summoned the turbulent sea that surrounded us, Melissa Larsen plotted and refined a story of obsession and violence.

Above all, Steve Dunn, our leader, created a refuge out of his enormous generosity and vision and piloted us through our days. He let us know when we had to be more careful about water usage and when we might have to leave off a supply run because of high winds. When our backup generator caught fire one rainy day, he came to the rescue. For a worrier like myself, the island taught me that although the future may be uncertain that's not a reason to stop taking chances. It taught me that if you surround yourself with good people and tackle the crises as they come, you will be all right. Besides, the island whispered, the crises that *do* come are likely not to be the ones you worried about anyway.

Which brings me to March 2020.

I'd like to say I spent the nine months after Norton Island happily writing my Agatha Christie mystery, but it foundered on the shoals as some novels do. The accident-prone characters I'd imagined on the trails of Norton Island had wandered off into the bog and fog. When I returned to my writing desk at home, they felt a bit . . . *lifeless*, as if I'd come back with a pack of ghosts. What I was left with was the island itself, more alive than any ▶

of the characters I'd peopled it with, a place that remained in my imagination as a beacon of calm—beautiful, extreme, and remote.

That's where I was in March 2020 when the pandemic hit. Like many, I was thrown off course, my life altered, my nights haunted with fears for myself, my family, my friends—and perhaps, most of all, for my students. When the college where I teach shut down in the middle of the semester, watching their faces and seeing them struggle in remote learning made me think about what their futures would look like. The future for all of us seemed suddenly more unknowable than ever, but most of all for young people on the brink of beginning their lives. How would this abrupt severing of their lives affect their futures? How would they look back on this time? What would the fallout be for them?

Somewhere in between fretting for the young people in my life and trying to buy toilet paper, I thought about the island. I'd brought home with me a handful of rounded stones the colors of the granite boulders that rang the eastern shore and looking at them brought an odd peace and a longing for that austere place— an extreme place for extreme times, an island surrounded by fog just as our lives seemed suddenly hemmed in by masks and precautions, the future unclear. I began to think that *this* was why my castaways had gone to the island: because of a pandemic.

After all, islands had been places of quarantine in the past. Like others during 2020 I was drawn to thinking about past pandemics and plagues and wondering how people had weathered them. I reread Camus's *The Plague*, Boccaccio's *Decameron*, and Katherine Anne Porter's "Pale Horse, Pale Rider." I thought about the Irish potato famine that had brought some of my ancestors to America in the mid-nineteenth century and learned that many of the immigrants fleeing the famine traveled on ships plagued by typhus and had to be quarantined when they arrived in Canada or the United States. One of those quarantine stations was an island off the northern coast of Maine. From there I began to imagine a history for my fictional island that included the ghosts of fever patients fleeing their own historic disaster . . . and hence was born the story of Nathaniel Harper, a doctor who comes to work on a quarantine island and discovers a mysterious Irish stowaway named Liadan.

Imagining my future castaways sheltering from a future pandemic was oddly comforting to me, maybe because it presumed there would be a future. It was my panacea and distraction, my sourdough and *Animal Crossing*. I didn't know if anyone would want to read a book set in a pandemic when this one ended—I didn't even know when or if this one would end—all I knew was that this was the book I had to write to get myself through it.

No one on my fictional Fever Island is the least bit like the Summer 2019 residents of Norton Island. Nor does my fictional island have a steward as skilled and kind as Steve Dunn. Things would have been better for my characters if it had. We'd all be better off with Steve Dunn, who died in February 2021, in our lives. He left behind a loving wife, a large extended family, countless friends, and the artists and writers he sheltered for over twenty years at Norton Island. While my fictional Fever Island is cursed, the real Norton Island is blessed with Steve Dunn's legacy, maintained and honored now by his wife, Rosemary Faver Dunn, and the Eastern Frontier Educational Foundation. May that legacy of generosity and vision be a beacon that guides us through the uncertain shoals of the future. ∾

Reading Group Guide

1. Reed decides to bring his friends and family to a remote island to shelter through a pandemic. If you had access to a remote island, would you retreat during a pandemic? If you had to quarantine in such isolation, who would you bring? In what ways do retreat and isolation present their own dangers?

2. Everyone on the island had suffered through a traumatic event during the 2020 pandemic. What are the long-term effects of this trauma and how are they represented throughout the novel? How have the characters been able to heal, or not heal?

3. Ada points out the inequities between how the rich and the non-rich weathered the 2020 pandemic. Do you agree that the pandemic impacted certain classes more than others? In what ways are these inequities demonstrated in the novel?

4. The island housed a quarantine hospital for fever ships fleeing Ireland in 1848. How much did you know about this history? What parallels can be drawn between the Irish potato famine and the 2020 pandemic?

5. Ada spends her nights in college scrolling through her phone observing her classmates' social media feeds. How does social media affect our psyches and emotional well-being? How do you think it influenced Ada? How do you feel this is heightened during a pandemic?

6. Ada says it's moving how people come together in bad times, while Liz maintains that people turn into monsters when challenged. Which point of view is proved true in the book?

7. Betrayal plays a large role in the novel. Do you think Ada is justified in her belief that she was betrayed by Lucy? By Reed? What would you do if you were in Ada's position? Lucy's?

8. There is a clear class divide between Reed's family and Mac's family, something that tested the men's relationship into their adulthood. How do you think this was addressed in the book? Speak to Mac's role as the outsider and how that influenced his relationships with the others on the island.

9. How did Nathaniel's story mirror Lucy's story? Ultimately, do you think Lucy reading Nathaniel's diary did more harm or good? ∾

An Excerpt from
The Stranger Behind You

Chapter One

JOAN

IT HAPPENED THE night the story went live. My editor, Simon Wallace, had rented out the restaurant across the street from *Manahatta*'s offices to celebrate—a lavish gesture even for Simon, who ran the magazine as if it were 1989.

"You've worked on it for three years—it's a damned fine story—you deserve to celebrate before the wolves circle." He'd given the last phrase in his husky vibrato with a wink as we stood outside the door to the restaurant. He'd warned me three years ago that if I went forward with the story I'd be letting myself in for a "holy shitstorm."

He'd delivered the warning during my interview for a job writing for the style section of *Manahatta*. I'd already interviewed with the Style editor, Sylvia Crosley, but apparently the "big boss" had to personally meet all potential new hires. The first question Simon Wallace asked when he looked at my résumé was "Why'd you leave the *Globe*?"

It's what I'd been afraid of. No one left an internship at the *Globe* voluntarily. It was the plum of journalism internships. I could have lied—made up a bullshit story about wanting to work at a different kind of publication—but instead I told the truth. "I saw Caspar Osgood put his arm around his assistant and then I saw her crying in the ladies' room. She told me she'd been sleeping with him for six months and she was afraid that if she complained to HR, she'd be fired. She had a black eye that she'd tried to hide with makeup. The next day she was gone and I found out she *had* been fired. I went to HR to ask what had happened to her and to tell them that I was worried she'd been sexually harassed. Then *I* was fired. No reason given because, of course, they don't have to with an intern."

Simon had been silent for a moment, and then said, "You sound angry."

The truth was I'd been fighting back tears, digging my nails so hard into my palms I had little crescent scars there for days after. "I suppose so. Caspar Osgood shouldn't be allowed to get away with treating women that way. No man should."

"It sounds like you're carrying a grudge," he had said.

"Maybe," I'd admitted, clenching my jaw to keep it from trembling. "But someone should expose him."

"Is that what you want to do? Expose Caspar Osgood, the darling of the conservative elite? He donates to the most powerful Republican causes and politicians and uses the *Globe* to crusade for reform. He's well connected and rich enough to pay for the best lawyers. A story like that would raise a holy shitstorm. It could break your career—or make it."

He'd said the last three words with a little upward lilt in his voice and a tug at the corner of his mouth. It felt like a lifeline being tossed to me just when I thought I was going under. "Yes," I'd responded, not realizing how *much* I wanted to expose Osgood until the word was out of my mouth. I'd spent the last three weeks weeping in my apartment, sure my career as a journalist was over before it had begun. "That's what I want to do. I'd like to write that story. But in the meantime, I'd really like this job writing for your Style section so I can pay my rent and not have to move back in with my mother and grandmother upstate."

That had made him laugh. "Why not both?" he'd asked. ▸

"How about we hire you to write style stories for Sylvia, and in the meantime you see what you can dig up on Osgood? If you think you've got a story in six months, pitch it to me properly and if I think it's got legs, I'll back you up. And by the way, there's nothing wrong with holding a grudge," he'd added, winking. "After paying the rent, it's the best motivator in the world."

Simon had been true to his word. He put me on staff, practically unheard-of at the e-zines I'd freelanced for since graduating from journalism school two years earlier. When I'd been working there for six months I went back to him with the names of two more women who said that Osgood had sexually assaulted them when they were working at the *Globe*.

"There does seem to be a pattern of behavior," he said. But he still seemed unsure and I thought I knew why. I'd learned since I began working for him that he'd gone to college with Caspar Osgood.

"I understand if you feel that you can't pursue the story because of your personal connection with Caspar Osgood."

He had bristled at that, as I had perhaps known he would, and said, "I would never compromise my journalistic objectivity. Keep working on the story but make sure you have contemporary corroborating evidence to back up every allegation."

We agreed that I'd stay in the Style section until the story was done, though. "It will be good cover for what you're working on and you'll need the distraction of shoes and gallery openings when you get deep into this." He'd been right about that. Writing about fashion and style might have seemed superfluous at times while I was listening to stories from victims of sexual assault, but "Put lemon in your water and drink at least sixty-four ounces a day" was a nice change from "He put his fingers in my mouth and told me to suck like a baby." Now, three years later, I was coming out with a groundbreaking exposé—a story that, as Simon had said, would either make or break my career—and my skin had never looked better.

"Aren't the wolves already circling?" I remarked to Simon as we stood in front of the restaurant. We'd both gotten cease-and-desist letters from Osgood's lawyers the day before. Simon had made a big production of lighting them on fire with the vintage cigar lighter some old reporter at the *Times* had given him when he started out.

"Oh, they're at the door, Joannie," he said, grinning. "All the people who have enabled Caspar Osgood all these years and overlooked the rumors and the gossip as they lined their pockets with his money are going to say you're an angry feminist who's attacking Osgood for his politics and who's bitter she's working for a two-bit rag instead of the great *Globe*. In fact"—he turned to me, his grin sobering to a wistful smile that melted the icy trepidation in the pit of my stomach—"it's not too late to back out. We posted the story to the staff's private online site half an hour ago, but it won't appear on the public site for"—he checked the vintage Patek Philippe watch on his wrist—"ten minutes, and the print edition won't hit the stands until tomorrow morning. I could tell Sammy to stop the presses. You could probably still get a job at the *Globe* if you played your cards right."

I snorted—then saw he was serious. "I'd rather work at this two-bit rag," I told him, my own voice turning hoarse.

He held my gaze another moment, as if testing my conviction. I felt the force of that gaze like a magnetic attraction—not, as I had realized over the last three years, a romantic or sexual attraction. It was his approval I wanted, the validation of his faith in me. I felt it now as he nodded. "Good," he said. "Let's give 'em hell."

He pushed open the door to the crowded restaurant, then took my hand and raised it over our heads as if I were a prizefighter who'd just gone fifteen rounds.

"Ladies and gentlemen of the press," he boomed, "I present the reporter who's just taken down Goliath. All hail to our own David. Hang on, kids, the ground's gonna shake when this giant goes down."

The ground did shake as my colleagues and friends pounded the floor with their feet and applauded. A dark-haired server handed me a glass of fizzing Champagne and someone thumped me on the back. Marisol from accounting shouted, "Let's take the fuckers down!" and everybody laughed and Simon gave my hand a squeeze that I felt all the way in my chest. Then he let go and I drifted untethered into the crowd. ▸

An Excerpt from *The Stranger Behind You* (continued)

Everybody was pushing forward to congratulate me, but they all parted for Sylvia Crosley. In a black Chanel dress, Louboutin heels, and her signature round glasses, Sylvia looked as cool and collected as always, but my stomach clenched in trepidation as she approached me. She'd been my boss for three years—and a good one. I'd learned more about how to write from being line-edited by her sharp blue pencil than I had in journalism school. I'd also learned how to go barefoot in pumps without getting blisters (spray-on deodorant), what to order at a business lunch that won't go to your waist or stick in your teeth (poached salmon on Bibb lettuce), and where to get this season's couture at half price (I can't reveal that last one; she made me sign an NDA). But I hadn't told her about the story that I'd quietly worked on for the last three years and I was afraid she was feeling betrayed.

I eyed the flute of Champagne balanced between her lacquered fingernails and wondered if I was about to get it in my face. Instead she lifted it to me. "You sly dog," she said. "All this time you were filing fluff for me you were busting balls with the big boys. Brava!"

"I learned from the best," I said.

She lifted her chin up and clinked her glass against mine. We each took a sip—a mere lip-wetting kiss for her and a long sizzling gulp for me. I hadn't realized how worried I'd been about how she would take my story. Sylvia Crosley wasn't only a style editor; she knew everybody in New York, from the wholesaler in the Flower District who could get her Casablanca lilies out of season to this season's chair of the Met Gala. She kept a little book with the names and phone numbers of everybody from the concierge at the Carlyle to the mayor. I didn't want her for an enemy; I was about to make enough of those.

She sidled in closer to me and whispered in my ear. "You might have told me what you were working on. There are some sources I could have directed you to."

"Simon thought we should keep it as confidential as possible until we were ready to go public with the story." What Simon really had said was *Sylvia's a doll but she trades information like currency; there's no way she'd keep a story like this to herself.* She held my gaze a moment, as if she could hear me thinking, and then gave me a tight nod. Then she smiled and touched my arm. "Truly, you did a remarkable job—tracking down all those interns, finding corroborating evidence from their friends and families—it's all very . . . *solid*."

"Simon insisted we have contemporary corroborating evidence for everything," I said.

"Of course he did," she said. "Any editor worth his salt would have done the same. I was just a little surprised he'd give you the go-ahead on a story about Cass Osgood. You know they went to college together."

"Yes," I said, bristling a little at the implication that I wouldn't have known this. Simon was right: Sylvia liked to be the one who knew everything.

Sylvia gave me a small, pained smile. "It could look as if Simon were seeking revenge. The rumor is that Cass got Simon fired from the *Times* back in the '90s and then there was that thing with the club three years ago."

"What thing?"

Sylvia smiled, clearly glad to be the one to enlighten me, and leaned in to whisper: "I nominated Simon for membership to the Hi-Line Club but he didn't get in. I found out that Caspar Osgood had blackballed him."

"Oh," I said, reassured. "Surely Simon wouldn't care about something as frivolous as membership to some club."

"Honey," Sylvia said, her voice dripping with condescension, "never underestimate the pettiness of men and their egos."

We were interrupted then by Sam, one of the interns who had worked with me on the story. I looked apologetically toward Sylvia, but she shooed me away with a wave of her Champagne flute and a benign smile. I tumbled into the crowd of young reporters and interns—all bubbling with my success, genuinely glad for me because I'd gone out of my way to be kind to them and at twenty-eight I wasn't *that* much older, so if it could happen to me, it could happen to them. Their happiness added to the glow from Sylvia's seal of approval.

"Look." Sam showed me her phone. "The article is live! There are already pictures on Twitter of Melissa Osgood receiving the news at that fundraiser of hers." ▸

"What?" I asked, the warm glow fading. "Do you mean her fundraiser for suicide awareness?"

"Yeah. Didn't you cover it last year?"

"Y-Yes, but . . ." I remembered spending the whole night of the fundraiser trying to avoid Melissa Osgood. A better reporter might have tried to get her on record saying something about her husband's reputation with women, but I'd been afraid of compromising the story. Or maybe I'd just been too mortified to shake the hand of the woman whose husband I was working to destroy. I should have remembered the date of the fundraiser, though—the summer solstice because it was her son's favorite day—

"Oh no," I said, remembering the history of the foundation. "I feel awful. The fundraiser is for suicide awareness because their son tried to kill himself. If we'd known—"

"Oh, Simon knew," Khaddija, Simon's assistant, said, looking around to make sure her boss wasn't within earshot. "He always had me keep tabs on the Osgoods. You know he used to be friends with them."

"Wow, some friends," Atticus, one of the graphic designers, said. "I've heard there's always been a rivalry between him and Caspar."

"Oooh," said Lauren, a style reporter, "I heard a rumor that Simon was in love with Melissa but she married Cass because he had the money. . . ."

The chatter around me became a cacophonous blur of he-saids and she-saids, exactly the kind of rumor-mongering I'd tried to avoid in my story. Why hadn't I remembered Melissa Osgood's fundraiser? Why hadn't Simon said anything about it?

The same server as before handed me another flute of Champagne and I drank it down too quickly. She seemed to be on my heels, as if someone had paid her to keep my drinks flowing. Looking around the room, I spotted Simon out on the restaurant's patio talking to Sylvia. He didn't look happy; neither did Sylvia. I imagined she was taking him to task for not telling her about the story beforehand. I couldn't blame her. I remembered suddenly that Sylvia had been at Melissa's fundraiser last year. *They* were friends too—

Which of course was why Simon *hadn't* told her.

Something didn't seem right. Was it true, I wondered, taking yet another flute of Champagne from the dark-haired server's tray, that he had a thing for Melissa Osgood? Was *that* why he had agreed so easily to me doing the story—because he wanted to hurt his rival? Surely it couldn't have been something so trivial as resentment at not getting into a club, but then there was the thing he'd said about a grudge being the best motivator in the world.

But what did that matter? I knew that Caspar Osgood was a sexual predator—I'd heard story after story and corroborated each of them with evidence from colleagues and friends whom the victim had told of the assault around the time it happened. As I'd said to Sylvia, I hadn't used anything I couldn't back up. I wanted to ask Simon if he'd known about the fundraiser. I wouldn't ask about the club thing; that was too ridiculous. He was still on the patio but now, instead of arguing with Sylvia, he was on the phone. As I was wondering if I should go out and talk to him, a petite brunette in a Theory suit approached me and announced, "You're part of the new vanguard. Have you thought of writing a book?"

Glad for the distraction, I laughed and asked, "What self-respecting journalist hasn't?"

"Do you have additional material that didn't make it into the story?" she asked.

I snorted. "Are you kidding? After three years of research? I've got enough on the cutting-room floor for *two* books," I bragged, realizing I was pretty drunk by then.

"Really?" Theory asked, lifting one heavy eyebrow (I could recommend an eyebrow threader on the Upper West Side for her). "More of the same? Or anything more . . . *combustible*?"

Even through my Champagne high I knew this was a loaded question, but Sylvia's story about the Hi-Line Club had sparked a memory and I found myself telling the brunette that there'd been one line of inquiry that Simon had pulled me back from because I couldn't find corroboration.

"Oh?" she asked.

"Yeah, something that happened in a private club with an ▶

underage girl . . ." I waved my empty flute and nearly collided
with Sylvia, who had her head down looking at her phone.
She looked up briefly, glanced at the woman I was speaking to,
curled her lip at the Theory suit (Sylvia thought the brand was
unimaginative), and hurried toward the front door with her
phone pressed to her ear.

"At a private club?" the woman repeated.

"Um . . . I can't really talk about that," I said, watching Sylvia
leave the restaurant. What had she and Simon been arguing
about?

"Well," Theory said, retrieving a card from her jacket pocket,
"if you're interested in doing a book let me know. I'm a literary
agent. I think I could get you a seven-figure advance."

And then she was gone and I wasn't sure if I'd heard her right.
Seven figures? That was, like, a million dollars. That was . . .
I could pay off my student loans, live in a building where the
stairwell didn't smell, afford the kind of clothes that wouldn't
curl Sylvia's lip . . . and then I was talking to someone's wife who
said she'd been groped by her uncle when she was five and the
dark-haired waitress was saying *she* had a story for me and she
was writing her name on a napkin and stuffing it in my pocket
and I saw Simon standing on the other side of the room looking
at me, and I started walking toward him, but somehow I ended up
tilting toward a banquette, and Atticus grabbed my arm saying,
"Whoa, Nellie! We'd better get you an Uber." And then I was in
a car, only whoever had called the Uber had gotten my address
wrong and the car dropped me off at the corner of East Tenth
and Avenue D, two blocks from my apartment.

Thank God for gentrification, I thought, stumbling down
streets that only a few decades ago would have been littered
with hypodermic needles but now were completely changed
as evidenced by the Lexus cruising the street, probably club
kids looking for some chic after-hours spot. My mother had
turned green when I told her where I was living. But she was
remembering the neighborhood from her own brief residency
in the city in the gritty '80s, before she scurried back home to
the safety of upstate New York. Now there were artisanal coffee

bars that offered six-dollar cold brews and boutiques that sold hand-sewn felt serapes that looked like something I'd worn in my kindergarten pageant and cost more than I made in a week. So what if my vestibule smelled like urine and the lightbulbs on floors three through five were burned out? I was living the dream! Small-town girl comes to the big city after J school, lives in a dive on ramen noodles and dreams for five years, and finally makes it big.

I was opening my apartment door when my phone rang. *Maybe it's Simon*, I thought, *with more news about the story.* I pulled my phone out of my purse, dropping my keys. As I bent over to pick them up I was shoved onto the floor. I tried to scream but a large hand covered my mouth pressing a damp cloth over my nose and mouth. A sickeningly sweet smell flooded my brain.

Chloroform.

My brain immediately went to a story Ariel had done a few years ago on a serial rapist who chloroformed his victims. She had researched its effects and learned it took five minutes to knock someone out, and too much could kill the victim.

I bit down hard on the hand and when it pulled away I tried to twist around to see my attacker—but he pulled something down over my head—a knitted cap that covered my eyes and nose and mouth. I couldn't breathe. The smell was overwhelming. I was getting dizzy. I heard metal jangling and then I was being pushed through my own door, into my own apartment, where this invisible attacker would do whatever he wanted.

I just want you to be safe, I could hear my mother pleading as I hit the floor.

Here it was, my mother's worst fear, the thing she lay awake nights worrying about. If I died it would break her heart.

No! I thought, pushing myself off the floor to fight, *I can't die like this.*

I must have taken my attacker by surprise. I got all the way to my knees and managed to grab a handful of his coat, but the fabric was slippery, like a raincoat, I thought, picturing my attacker dressed head to toe in blood-resistant nylon the better to bludgeon me in. *What to wear when attempting a murder,* ▶

ead on

An Excerpt from *The Stranger Behind You*
(*continued*)

I blearily imagined proposing as a story
as the slick fabric slid through my fingers.
Then I was tackled so hard that my head
slammed against the floor. I had just
time enough to think that my mother
had been right—the world really was a
dangerous place—and then I wasn't
thinking anything at all. ∾

Discover great authors,

exclusive offers, and more

at hc.com.